Dan Gooch grew up in North London in the 1970s and now lives in Gloucestershire. The years in between are a bit of a blur.

Solomon Grundy

Dan Gooch

An *Abacus* Book

First published in Great Britain in 1997 by Abacus

Copyright © 1997, Dan Gooch

The moral right of the author has been asserted.

A CIP catalogue record for this book
is available from the British Library.

ISBN 0 349 10910 9

Typeset in Ehrhardt by
Palimpsest Book Production Limited,
Polmont, Stirlingshire
Printed and bound in Great Britain by
Clays Ltd, St Ives plc.

Abacus
A Division of
Little, Brown and Company (UK)
Brettenham House
Lancaster Place
London WC2E 7EN

For Esther

Solomon Grundy
Born on a Monday
Christened on Tuesday
Married on Wednesday
Took Ill on Thursday
Worse on Friday
Died on Saturday
Buried on Sunday
That was the end
Of Solomon Grundy.

Foreplay

"How can you regard the time before your conception as anything other than a preparation for it? But it was not. People were thinking of other things entirely. You were conceived on a houseboat. At least, that's what your parents believe; that's what they told their friends. On the Norfolk Broads. 'The Norfolk Broads' are not a gaggle of buxom, mini-skirted women of easy virtue who congregate in and around Norwich. The name refers instead to the ever-shifting system of partially navigable inland waterways, marshes, bogs, ponds and sluggish rivers that is East Anglia's peculiar version of a coastline. They are a constant sneer at the conceit that air, earth and water constitute discrete elements. Citizens spend damp weeks on houseboats there to remind themselves why they live in cities.

You were conceived on such a houseboat. It was June, but an electrical storm blew in from the North Sea, and the tiny generator fused. One minute they – your father and mother-to-be – were watching a tatty 50s' film on the portable black-and-white, the next all was pitch black. Even the pumps were suddenly silent and the drumming of the rain on the roof and the howling of the wind across the marshes only intensified the stillness. Your father-to-be pulled back the small square curtain. The rain hissed on the water. The moon was full. Nothing else was visible but the trees caught in fractal silhouette against the skyline of the immense, flat landscape. Then came a crack of thunder, dying slowly into the night.

– I'm not going out in that, he announced. – Where's the torch?

– In the kitchen, said your mother-to-be.

– Bugger.

The houseboat was not the easiest of spaces in which to manoeuvre, even in daylight. Not only was the central gangway only negotiable side-on, but every inch of the walls and roof had been commandeered for the exhibition of pictures and the hanging of coats, mugs, cassettes, a guitar, even a dead geranium in a pot. Your father was not designed for such an environment. He was also, he found when he stood up, considerably more stoned than he had realised whilst seated. He stretched out an arm to brace himself, but a sudden lurch of the environment sent him crashing into the wall, precipitating a shower of cassettes and stale earth. The kitchen seemed suddenly impossibly distant.

– Let's go to bed, he surrendered.

The bedroom was at the rear, a low squat cabin accommodating a square piece of foam. There was just enough space between the foam and the cabin walls to lose keys and small change, and not quite enough space to insert a hand to recover them. Furnishings were otherwise restricted to the bare necessities. A small shelf, upon which your father-to-be had cracked his head several times, and with which he had finally lost his temper, was currently stashed, with its brackets, under the foam. Two rusty nails emerging viciously from the wall were the cabin designer's reluctant concession towards a wardrobe. There was also a light-cord, currently useless, and a small grimy porthole. They undressed awkwardly, one at a time, in the passage outside and dived, one after the other, under the covers. There they welded themselves pneumatically together in an effort to squeeze some warmth out of the night. For some reason, the very awkwardness of this embrace was erotic. The discomfort lent an air of fornication to the proceedings, and the proximity of the elements, too, was exciting. From time to time an electric flash illuminated the lovers in their tiny chamber, or a peal of thunder boomed through the atmosphere. They were naked and warm and miles away from anyone. She felt him pressing insistently at her belly. His tongue reached further into her mouth.

She broke free to whisper – I want you inside me.

These were his thoughts entirely.

– Where are they? he panted.

They were in her handbag, next to the torch, in the kitchen. Since the surroundings were not conducive to anything more imaginative, he clambered clumsily on top of her. She guided him in. It was fairly sedate, his one attempt at exertion causing the cabin to rock alarmingly from side to side, but gradually they found their rhythm. His thrusts became deeper and stronger. She felt herself melt and as she came she heard him roar. They roared together, in celebration of their isolation. When her last ripples were spent, he was still roaring and still inside her. She felt something warm and wet dripping on her stomach, and was reassured: he had managed it somehow after all, without her even noticing. He rolled off, gasping. As her breath returned, he began to roar again, and she realised that the trickle down her hip was not semen but blood. He had roared not in exultation but in agony. He had sliced open his elbow on one of the nails.

As suddenly as the lights had cut out they came back on, the pump coughed back into life and Ronald Reagan's voice intruded from the television next door. A vermilion stain was spreading across the duvet. With his semen swimming around inside her, she bandaged his arm. Thus were you conceived, in pain and in pleasure, as much by accident as by design, in blood and sweat and tears. Your father remembered it, retrospectively, as the most intense orgasm of his life. He felt, he said, as if a great cosmic Fury had shot through him instantaneously, like a spark. It was this, he said, which caused him to lose control and flail spastically, and thus to rip open his elbow. Your mother always maintained it was just a trick she had learned from a flatmate, who used it professionally. She pointed out that your father never said anything at the time, as she rinsed the wound with Dettol. He winced and cursed and worried about the sheets and tried to remember the date of his last tetanus shot. He never mentioned any great cosmic Furies then.

Your mother, on the other hand, knew, as she swabbed the wound, that an event had occurred that changed everything. At least, looking back, she remembered that she had known. She felt the warm ooze between her legs, and knew that in that sludge of proteins and nucleic acids a face was being assembled. A process had been triggered that could not now be un-triggered. It was beyond her control. She was far from overjoyed. Had she not spent the rest of the night trying to persuade your father that the gash in his arm was serious enough to warrant a trip to Accident and Emergency, and the next morning single-handedly manoeuvring the boat towards the nearest town, she might have found the time to be angry. When a blue line in a test tube confirmed your existence, or at least your forthcoming existence, she considered stopping the story before it had even started. It was not a good time to be pregnant. She had just started a new job, a proper job, with a pension and a union and her own telephone. She was not at all convinced that she wanted to spend the rest of her life with your father. They were good friends, but she had never seen him as permanent. She had never seen anything as permanent, except her parents. Neither of them had any money, and they were renting a poky flat in Pilsbury. But she had always known that one day she would have children. Now the music had stopped, and your father was left holding the parcel. Your father, meanwhile, said it was never a good time, that if you waited for the omens to be auspicious you would wait for ever, because the world was falling apart. He also said he would be profoundly depressed if the four stitches in his forearm had all been for nothing. She didn't take much persuading. She just wanted to hear him say these things. She rang her best friend Helen, a friend since primary school. Helen asked how she felt about it. She didn't really know. She felt sick in the mornings. Was she going to go ahead with it? She supposed she was, or she would have done something by now.

– Well in that case, concluded Helen. – Congratulations.

In the office, too, it was congratulations all round, and Tony sent out for a bottle of champagne (which of course she couldn't drink), but they were irritated all the same. She knew that she had become a non-person. She stopped drinking, gave up smoking, declined proffered joints, and turned down invitations. Her friends teased her, but she enjoyed her growing domesticity, her new life of slippers and Ovaltine. She didn't bother to ask if her job, or her life, would still be there at the end of it all.

She couldn't imagine the end of it all. Everything would be changed. It would be changed so much that she had no idea how it would be changed. She read the books, but she couldn't imagine it.

Born on a Monday

17.30

Now she lay on this clumpy bed in this neat, square room in the half darkness, the thick black tubes connecting her to a purring machine that rendered audible your protesting kicks and lurches. A faint orange glow around the blinds told her it must be dusk outside. The street-lamps were coming on. In the morning, when they were extinguished, she would be a mother. The last day of her childhood was ending, and all she could think was that it had been very long, but she had made it, and everything would be all right now. Your father was in the room somewhere, but she could not see him without lifting her head, and she could no more lift her head from its nest of cushions than she could get up and walk away. Her consciousness had seeped slowly away through the cracks opened up in her brain by pain and fatigue and pethidine. It now drifted aimlessly around her bloodstream on a tide of numbing hormones before finally washing up in the marrows of her long bones. Death came to tempt her. She weighed up the pros and cons, and decided that she did not wish to die just yet. She had some odds and ends to tidy up first, and people that she wished to see again. If she was going to die, she wanted to die in the autumn. Then she remembered she had not come here to die. She was going to have a baby.

– Paul, she called softly.

Your father was at her side instantly, and took her hand, asking if she was all right.

– I'm fine, she assured him. – I was in a dream. I don't know how long, seemed like hours.

– About ten minutes, he said, kissing her on the forehead. – Have you got everything you need?

She laughed. It seemed absurd that there could be anything she needed, when she had him, and you inside her. The contractions seemed to be slowing down, she said. Perhaps it wouldn't be tonight after all. The books always warned you against impatience. But she knew it would be tonight. She couldn't imagine a child born into the light. How strange, to explode like that into the bustle and commotion and energy, the traffic and Radio 1 and men digging up the road, and stadiums full of football supporters. Night was the time for babies, the small hours between midnight and the dawn, when the world was asleep and there were just the three of you, a solitary window burning yellow in the blackness. The small hours were the time for intimacy, for illicit love, for sex, for birth and for death. Nothing of any importance happened in the daylight: there were too many distractions, too many shouty salesmen and politicians and shock-jocks competing for your attention. Samantha, she knew, would be a night baby.

Your father wasn't keen on Samantha. But then with your father it wasn't a question of simply choosing a name for a baby. Nothing was that simple. A name stayed with you all your life. It had to meet all sorts of criteria: aesthetic, phonetic, ethnic. He didn't want to give you a Christian name at all, not even a Jewish one. It would be an offence against your freedom of conscience, he thought. He wanted a neutral name, but names all came with religious baggage. Had you been born five years earlier, he would have called you Ganja or Batik or Moon, or something, if your mother had let him. Nowadays, caught in a late-twenties identity crisis, he oscillated. Sometimes, in a fit of sentimentality or idealism he would have called you Ganja or Batik or Moon. Other times, the main criterion seemed to be that your name should sound plausible followed by 'M.P.' or 'Q.B.'. Sometimes, when he met women he fancied, he would use their names as an excuse to talk about them. That he was confusing 'Gail is a nice name' with 'Gail's got great tits' did not seem as evident to your father as it did to your mother. But then men are like that. They think they're talking about something, and really they're talking about something else entirely. There's no point in trying to contradict them, or to change their minds, because their minds will change anyway, because the things they hold as principles are in fact feelings. Thus your mother knew she could bring him round to Samantha after you were born. It was all right to vacillate until then: it was probably healthy. Worrying about names gave him a chance to worry about fatherhood without having to admit that he worried about it. Choosing a name would represent his final word on these subjects, and no word of your father's was ever final. But once you were there you would need a name, and Samantha would be your name. If it wasn't right, she would think again, but it *would* be right. Everything would be right. She knew it, and she was not wrong about these things.

23.08

Your father surveyed the panorama of snacks and nibbles framed in the window of the vending machine and was seized with indecision. He did not have a sweet tooth, and the world of confectionery was novel and perplexing to him. Even the *idea* of snacking he found vaguely disturbing, an activity akin to cross-dressing or aerobics that was, he supposed, fairly harmless and that could hardly be prohibited but an activity that nonetheless did not seem quite grown-up. A constant craving for sweet things had always struck him as a potent symbol of national decline until he had travelled abroad and discovered that, far from being a peculiarly British idiosyncrasy, this eating disorder was apparently diagnostic of industrial civilisation. Confronted by the glossy tack of a display that would have brought saliva to the glands of any ordinary citizen, he stood transfixed and troubled.

The waiting room was deserted, the overhead lights dimmed to the minimum required to negotiate the room without overturning the pointless magazines collected into piles on the long, low tables. Only the vending machines burned on into the night.

Suddenly he remembered why he had come and, thrusting pound coins into the slot, began pressing digits more or less at random until his credit was exhausted. A series of mechanical arms extended towards him, jerked open their steel claws and deposited packages in the scoop below. A four-pack of cheesy biscuits caught on its hook, but a swift kick brought it tumbling down to join its fellows. At the soft drink machine he repeated the performance. The machine was even designed to look like a can. As he reached into the hole to retrieve his drink it occurred to him that what he was doing had eerie parallels with the event he was about to attend. Big things producing little tiny copies of themselves, perfect in every detail. He thought, out of habit, how extraordinary, how marvellous and then he considered the vending machine and thought how humdrum, how mundane. But then producing a baby, an entirely new person who had never before walked the earth, wasn't really the same as producing a can of coke. Or was it? Bloody hell, he thought, imagine having me for your father.

Your mother's labour had been a disappointment to him so far. The books, the counsellors, the other fathers he had spoken to, had all promised a time of raw emotion, in which he would lose all consciousness of who he was, of where he was, of night and day even, and be overcome by primeval hormones and atavistic spirits. He had looked forward to this, as an antidote to a fairly unexciting period in his life. It seemed like many years since he had been overcome by raw emotion. In fact, looking back over his life, he did not seem to have been overcome by raw emotion since the age of about eight. He read about people driven to murder and suicide by the intensity of their passions and was mildly envious. He read that men were cut off from their emotions, but this did not seem plausible: it seemed unlikely that he could be in the throes of violent passions and yet not be aware of them. It seemed far more likely, all things considered, that he was unaware of his emotions because they were pretty unremarkable. There had not been much worth getting excited about after the age of eight.

Even the birth of his child had not proven particularly out
of the ordinary, so far. It had not even been very hectic. Your
mother had gone into labour three weeks early, in the middle of
the Easter Bank Holiday. They were in the garden, he wandering
around aimlessly waiting for things to grow, and she squatting
with a trowel planting what looked like rather scrawny weeds. At
least, that was what she was supposed to be doing. In a squatting
position and eight and a half months pregnant, she couldn't really
see *what* she was doing at her feet. It was March, and quite cold.
Suddenly she stood up, grimacing, put her hands on her hips and
with a rapid exhalation of breath folded at the waist. By the time
he had hurdled the picket fence to get to her she was standing
straight again, panting slightly, and laughing.

– Are you all right? he asked. – Is it starting?

To which she replied simply – Help!

They went inside and he made her a cup of raspberry tea.
After twenty minutes without repetition they went back outside,
but halfway through the door she stopped again, braced herself
against the door jamb and began breathing very deeply and
slowly. He had wanted to do something, but didn't want to break
her concentration, so he scampered upstairs to pack a nightie and
toothbrush, some nappies and a little suit that suddenly seemed
much too small, like a doll's clothes. He wondered whether
he shouldn't pack a larger one as well, and decided that he'd
better. The chest was full of baby clothes of various sizes. He
was paralysed by the choice. It suddenly seemed very important
that your first apparel should not be just any old thing, the first
thing that came to hand. He decided to take them all: then your
mother could choose.

They drove to the hospital, the car starting first time and the
traffic being very light. On the way they talked about names
again. Again. They seemed to talk of little else these days.
Twice during the journey the contractions came; he saw all
consciousness drain from her face, and then the strangulated
cry, and then the breathing. He wondered whether he should
stop, but he knew that by the time he had pulled over and undone
his seat belt it would all be over, so he drove on. He remembered
he was supposed to be encouraging her, reassuring her.

– That's it. That's good. Won't be long now. Slow and deep. That's it. You're doing so well. I love you so much Sue.

He managed to keep it going until the breathing subsided, when she turned to him and smiled.

– Thanks, she whispered.

A rite of passage was taking place within which his presence was simultaneously absolutely crucial and entirely superfluous. Nonetheless, he was glad to have done the right thing.

They drove on in silence. He wanted to hold her hand, but had to keep changing gear.

– What about Tricia? she asked suddenly.

– What about her? Who is she?

– No, as a name.

– You're delirious, he diagnosed. – It must be the hormones.

– What's wrong with Tricia? Patricia. Pat. Trish. Patty.

It seemed to comfort her to roll the names around. But Tricia was no good.

– I had a great aunt named Patricia, he lied. – She had a moustache.

– You never told me about her before.

– You never threatened to name my baby after her before.

– OK, not Patricia then. I wasn't really serious. It's just a nice word to say. Trish, trish, trish, she trished.

– You *are* delirious.

– What about Helen?

– Sorry.

She sighed.

– We can't write off Helen purely on the basis that you once had a crush on Helen Ferguson.

– I don't want to be the kind of father who gets a hard-on every time he hears his daughter's name.

Your mother looked suddenly miserable. His attempts at casual banter had backfired.

– Not very thoughtful of me, he apologised. – Sorry.

– I don't want to hear about your old flames, and your wild, free, single life, she said. – Not now. Let's talk about the baby.

– OK. Do boys' names.

– Connell. Paddy.

– That's just Patricia again.

There were plenty of spaces. He helped her from the car and into the lift, leaving the suitcase in the boot. They registered at the desk. A conscientious midwife must have phoned ahead, for the hospital was expecting them. Someone would be along in a minute, said the nurse, and motioned them towards the blue plastic chairs. They held hands, and read leaflets detailing the dangers facing babies once they left the safety of the womb and made an appearance in the world of juggernauts, boiling saucepans and paedophiles. Your mother had another contraction, and the nurse smiled patronisingly at your father as he supported his wife and self-consciously whispered encouragement and endearments into her ear. Another nurse came and showed them into a delivery room. Your father recognised the assortment of furniture and machinery from a previous visit with the birth class, a strange mixture of the high tech and the familiarly banal. The bed dominated the room, hinged at waist and neck and embellished with handles and levers that raised and lowered its various sections. Arranged like bridesmaids around its headboard were what looked like a hat-stand, a keyboard amplifier and one of those machines that produce tickets in pay-and-display car parks. Thanks to his preparatory visit, he knew that they were actually a something-scope and a something-ometer. The other furnishings were more familiar – a sink, chairs, an uninspiring black plastic beanbag. On the wall hung a torn print of sunflowers, and an Alpine meadow in springtime. He guessed that these little touches were designed to make the room feel less institutional, though you never found them anywhere but institutions. A grey light seeped into the room.

– Sorry, said the nurse. – It's always a bit gloomy in number six. You won't notice it once you get going.

The window looked out on to the half-empty hospital car park. This was divided by a line of exhaust-stunted shrubs from the car park beyond, which was attached to a superstore that seemed to be doing much better business. He watched an angry man trying to load a selection of timber and fencing into a boot and on to a roof rack that were clearly inadequate for the task. A woman was sarcastically urging him on, one child screaming in her arms, another sullen in a pushchair. Tempers were obviously frayed, and inter-personal violence seemed depressingly inevitable. He wondered if that would be he and your mother in three years, then felt ashamed of the thought. Surely they could do better than that?

– Can I get you anything? the nurse asked, pleasantly enough. He couldn't think of anything.

– No thanks, he replied.

– I was thinking more of your wife.

– No, I'm all right, I think, said Sue. – OOOOoooooooohhhhh.

He saw the consciousness drain from her face again, but this time he was able to hold her properly, as he had been taught in Birth Class, and to say the things that seemed to be called for. It wasn't as if he didn't mean them, it was just that it all felt so contrived, standing there murmuring

– You're doing wonderfully well, Sue. I love you. Slow and deep now.

while the clatterings and squeaks of the hospital routines filtered in through the half-open door and the nurse made a great show of fiddling with some metal trays and washing her hands again, as if to make out she hadn't noticed that a woman was giving birth three feet away. He had to remind himself over and over again that this time it was for real, that your mother wasn't pretending as she had done in the classes, that a life was at stake. Yours.

When the contraction had ebbed away and your mother was sitting on the edge of the bed, he realised the nurse had departed. She was soon replaced by the midwife, who introduced herself as Joyce and skimmed through the notes.

– Lovely. No problems there then. A bit sooner than you expected, eh?

He realised she was expecting an answer and grunted affirmatively.

– Babies have their own agendas, she informed the prospective parents.

– Have you got children? your mother asked.

Joyce held up four fingers.

– This is our first, your mother said.

Joyce smiled an inscrutable professional smile that could have meant anything, and began asking the same questions they had already answered several times in the last half-hour, as if they were merely pretending to be about to have a child and she were trying to catch them out. Further notes were made.

– Let's have a listen, Joyce suggested.

Husband and midwife made your mother comfortable on the bed, pinioned and buttressed between pillows, cushions and beanbags. Joyce smeared blue goo on her abdomen (your mother's abdomen, that is, not her own), fastened a belt around her smooth, spherical belly and fiddled with the equipment until the lights were flashing to her satisfaction.

– Let's see what that sounds like then, she said, turning a knob.

A rapid, muffled, subterranean heartbeat filled the room. Suddenly, for the first time, your father feared for you, so tiny and helpless in there, so ill-equipped to cope with the next few hours, and obliged to rely upon such clueless parents. Before, fear had been cerebral: what if? how would I cope if? But as the tiny, amplified heart throbbed in the room, it became immediate and visceral. In there, enclosed within taut membranes, little did you suspect that within the next few hours the membranes would tear, the vessels rip, the walls of your womb would buckle and expel you into a world where you could no longer rely on others. Surely it was better to leave you where you were, he thought, out of harm's way.

Your mother was transported again, but when he gripped her hand she smiled at him. The midwife explained the workings of the machine, and introduced various significant knobs and buttons. The machine had to be left on for half an hour, during which time your mother should move as little as possible.

– Do you want the blinds up or down? she asked.

– I think I'll try and get some sleep, your mother replied, and the blinds came down again.

– If the green light goes off you'll let me know then?

Your father said yes, he would, and off she went, promising to look in on them in half an hour. There seemed to be something of a rush on, now. Twice already they had been disturbed by midwives seeking a vacant room. The woman next door seemed to have stepped her groaning up a gear, or perhaps it was the silence and the stillness, and the hypnotic thudding of the heartbeat. He became conscious of his own heartbeat: it was much too fast.

– Are you all right? he asked.

– Nervous. I thought we had a few weeks yet. Do you think it'll be all right?

– I'm sure it'll be fine, he lied. – They wouldn't leave us alone here if there was anything to worry about.

– It's funny, she said, after a while. – All that agonising over home births and hospital births and water births and natural births and active births, and in the end it's completely out of our hands. I'm going to try and sleep.

Your father read the newspaper, in the half-light. The world seemed on the point of collapse again, as it did every time he read the papers. He wondered if it would collapse one day, as everybody said it must, or whether the purveyors of magazines simply had a vested interest in maintaining this atmosphere of panic. Then he too dozed off.

Joyce came back forty minutes later with another midwife, saying, – Let's have a look at how you're doing, shall we?

She appeared satisfied, and made some more notes before introducing Carmen, who would be taking over when Joyce went off-shift at two. Was it only two? They seemed to have been in that womb-like room for days already, while the world collapsed around them. Joyce put on a thin, translucent rubber glove and gave your mother an internal. Another midwife came and said Joyce was required in theatre urgently. Joyce departed, sucking her teeth and leaving Carmen to make her apologies and finish the internal.

– How am I doing? your mother whispered.

– You're doing fine, Carmen announced, peeling off the glove.

– How many fingers?

– Just the one. Mother Nature takes her time. But baby's fine. That's what matters.

The afternoon and evening passed in similar fashion. The blinds went up and down. Women – usually Carmen but occasionally others similarly attired, whom your father did not recognise – popped in to check the three of you were all right. The professional fingers were inserted, and your mother reassured that she was making good progress. Five fingers now. Periodically, your mother would gasp and her eyes glaze. Your father would support her as best he could, whispering

– That's goooooood. That's goooooooood. Won't be long now.

He had no idea how long it would be. Nothing seemed to be happening at all, as far as he could see. But the women seemed to have it all under control, and they smiled at him. Between contractions, your mother slept and your father passed back and forth between the chair and the window. As the afternoon wore on, the traffic gradually thinned in the superstore car park. From his vantage point on the hill above the town he watched the dusk settle, the lights come on, the gloom slowly thicken into night. It was interminable. For the first time in his life he had exhausted the Sunday papers. At ten precisely, Carmen was replaced by Jackie. Neither of them liked the look of Jackie. She was friendly enough, and seemed to know what she was doing, but her heart didn't seem in it somehow. It was as if she had other priorities. Jackie suggested that, as things appeared to have quietened down, your mother should try to get forty winks before the second stage. Your father was dispatched to stock up on provisions for this second stage, liquids and glucose. He needed no persuasion. He was by now desperate for a smoke.

Smoking was forbidden anywhere in the hospital, and he found a small, sad huddle of patients, visitors, doctors, porters and a nurse sheltering under a concrete canopy that afforded the only protection against a cold drizzle. The patients were in pyjamas and nighties, slippers and dressing gowns. After the piped heat of the delivery room, the night was bitter and fierce. Nobody spoke. Gradually they finished their cigarettes, ground them into the sand-tubs provided and drifted away, grumbling. Suddenly, only two of them were left, and conversation was unavoidable.

– Cold, isn't it? your father ventured.

The man nodded. Your father tried again.

– My wife's having a baby.

The man turned to look at him.

– My mother's just died. Good night.

The man ground his cigarette into the sand-tub, and went back inside. The night was black and wet and indifferent to the tiny new life that was about to be born into it. He went in search of the canteen. It was shut. A cleaner suggested the vending machines. He stared at the armful of snacks and drinks. They seemed proud of how little nourishment they contained. But there was nothing else. He retraced his steps, and arrived in the corridor of the delivery suite just in time to hear his wife's agonised wails, and to see Jackie dart suddenly from her desk. He broke into a trot.

Your mother was up on the bed, on all fours and roaring. Her swollen belly hung down underneath and her head seemed disproportionately small. He dropped the confectionery onto a chair, and put his arm over her back, which was damp and shiny with sweat. Jackie was holding your mother's arm and whispering something into her ear, and your mother was nodding violently. Slowly, the roaring subsided, and she rolled exhaustedly over on her back, where she lay panting. Jackie began collecting and reassembling the nest of cushions and beanbags that had scattered over the floor.

Your father told your mother that he loved her. Her eyes remained closed but she squeezed his hand. Her breathing was deep and rhythmic. She looked drained, but at the same time seemed to glow, and to radiate energy, as if she were possessed by a spirit. Jackie pressed a cold flannel to her forehead, and slowly she came round. The hospital seemed suddenly quiet and reverent. Finally she opened her eyes and smiled.

– Where the hell were you? she demanded, though more in relief than anger.

– You sent me to get some stuff, he reminded her.

– You were gone ages.

– Everything's closed.

– What does it feel like? asked Jackie.

– It changed suddenly. One minute I was trying to keep it in, and the next minute I just had to get it out.

Jackie told her to eat and drink, donned rubber gloves and commenced another investigation. She pronounced her fully dilated. Between them they made her comfortable with beanbags and cushions. Jackie said that it was OK to push now, when the contractions came. She reckoned they would have you by midnight, or soon afterwards anyway. Your father clasped your mother's hand.

– You're doing wonderfully, he told her, and kissed her on the forehead. He was surprised to find himself close to tears.

– Drink, she whispered.

He inserted the straw into her mouth and she sucked. Then suddenly she was writhing and roaring again.

– Deep breath and push, shouted Jackie. – Deep breath and push.

23.51

You were born just before midnight. At 11.51 Jackie took your mother's hand and placed it between her legs to feel your head. She shrieked with joy and began to weep, gripping your father's hand even tighter. Another midwife had been summoned.

– Look! said this new midwife. – Look at that hair.

Your father peered, but could make out nothing. Certainly there was hair there, but most of it was pubic, and all was now soaked in blood and mucus. It was just a mess of blood and hair and mucus as far as he could see.

– Is it supposed to look like that? he queried.

Jackie gave him a look to remind him that, modernity notwithstanding, he was still there on sufferance, that women had managed birth for millions of years without men, that his presence was at best superfluous when not actually hampering the proceedings. He bit his tongue. Then your mother was clenched again, the effort squeezing beads of sweat from every pore and forcing peripheral veins into relief along her arms.

– NNGGHGHGHGHG, she said.

He mopped her brow, and watched the bloody mess between her legs. There was no point saying anything. Your head appeared, slithering out from your mother in one easy motion. You were mauve. Your father gasped involuntarily. Your face was scrunched, your eyes apparently welded together. Your scalp was covered in fine black hair, smeared with vernix. You did not look at all pleased to be dragged out of your burrow. Your father was unable to breathe. He felt himself quaking.

– Big push now, whispered Jackie, and your mother tensed again.

– NNGHGHNGHNG.

Your head jerked alarmingly, twisted, shot forward, and a shoulder appeared.

– Oh God Oh God, shrieked your mother.

At the third push you slithered forth, were scooped up by Jackie and transferred to your mother's chest in a single flowing movement. Your mother was sobbing and panting, and tears rolled down her face. Your father could not bear to watch, or even to breathe.

– It's a boy, said the midwife. – And a whopper too.

Your father opened his eyes and beheld his son. You did not move beyond a wrinkling of the left nostril, a reflex twitching of the fingers. Your eyes remained clamped together.

– My baby! howled your mother.

He had not seen a baby naked before, not one so tiny. Always in his experience they were wrapped up for public display, in nappies and cardigans and woollen bootees. You were the length of his forearm, he guessed, if you straightened out. This you showed no inclination to do. Everything was there, already formed – eyebrows, nails, knees, lips, penis. The hair was a shock – somehow it made you look even more formed than he had expected. He had envisaged something shapeless, something mouldable, something hardly begun. But you were already finished, and perfect, more perfect than anything he had ever seen. His vision blurred, and he realised he was crying. He felt simultaneously omnipotent and terrified. Jackie positioned you on the breast, and you latched on instantly. He could see your cheeks sucking ferociously, your jaw bobbing as you swallowed. Your mother was beaming, radiant.

– We have to cut the cord now, Jackie announced.

He realised it was he who was being addressed. He knew it was expected of him; he could hardly say no. This was what they had found for men to do at births. Jackie placed a little clamp around the umbilical cord, which still throbbed and pulsed purple and blue, and tightened it. She handed him some scissors and showed him where to cut. For an act of such supreme symbolic significance, it was a fairly banal operation. Presumably that was why they got the men to do it, he thought – not only was it absolutely crucial, but it was difficult to see how you could screw it up. Your mother was quite oblivious, and you were sucking noisily away beneath your thin crocheted blanket. You appeared not to have noticed the severing of your link to the womb. He swallowed, and cut.

Christened on Tuesday

00.04

Now you were wailing inconsolably, clenching your tiny white fists in rage.

– I think he's finished that one, said your mother, gingerly turning you round.

Instantly you latched on to the other breast. The wailing shut off as abruptly as it had arrived.

– It'll get easier, promised Jackie, who was already beginning to assemble and pack away some terrifying surgical instruments that thankfully had proven surplus to your requirements.

– Sorry?

– I said it'll get easier, Jackie repeated, – the feeding. Next week it'll be turning it off that's your problem.

– It's not a problem, said your mother, puzzled. – He's just finished the first one.

Jackie smiled indulgently, and did not pursue it.

– We do have the placenta to come yet, she reminded them. – Perhaps your husband could hold him for a minute?

Your mother was clearly disappointed.

– A minute, Jackie promised.

Your father took the bundle nervously. As his hand slid behind your neck, your arms shot suddenly outwards, relaxing only when you were safely transferred. Your head rested limp but heavy against his forearm, and your eyes blinked open. Your first sight was of your father, his own eyes red and swollen, terrified of dropping you. He guessed your inscrutable stare had some meaning but could not decipher it. One moment it suggested resentment at being dragged into the world, the next simply bafflement. Don't be silly, he told himself, it can't even see you. It's only just been born.

– One more push, the midwife exhorted your mother, tugging cautiously on the cut end of the cord.

The placenta, when it slithered forth, was larger and bloodier than your father had expected, resembling an over-ripe liver. Your parents had talked before the birth of what they would do with it, what other couples did with it, other women. Some couples, apocryphally, dug a hole in the garden, into which it was deposited accompanied by blessings and chants. They planted a tree or a fruit bush over it and it was reported to have marvellous properties as a fertiliser. But your father could not contemplate symbolically tying the fate of his child to that of some fruit bush. Suppose it shrivelled up, or caught some slimy fungus? Or simply remained stunted, and failed to produce any fruit? He had been told that there was a market for placentae amongst the manufacturers of rejuvenating face creams and moisturisers but no one had approached them offering hard cash. Neither were they inclined to advertise it. Presumably it had to be fairly fresh too. He understood very little biochemistry, but enough to understand that, tempting though the analogy might be, smearing a placenta over your face was unlikely to counter the effects of ageing. If you wanted any serious results, you would have to have it surgically installed.

Anyway, they had come to no firm conclusions about the placenta, and suddenly there it was. He felt no more affection for it than he would have done for an unusual turd – a momentary curiosity, no more. Jackie flipped it into a kidney-shaped steel dish and carried on mopping up the blood.

Your father paid her no attention. He was petrified that if he took his eyes off his son for a second you would stop breathing. You hardly seemed to be breathing anyway – only when he stooped and held your mouth right up against his ear could he hear your breath, short and shallow, like a faint whisper. Your chest however rose and fell in a satisfactory manner. There was a person in there (who could doubt it?). A person who had not existed ten minutes ago was here in this room with them. Your father could not accept that this baby was the product of no more than the fusion of microscopic bags of chemicals. Not something as perfect as this. You had surely come from somewhere else pre-formed. He was sure of it. But where? Heaven seemed as likely a candidate as anywhere else. Heaven. You had come from heaven. Via your mother's snatch.

– We should get him dressed, Jackie said, then, seeing your mother's frown at the thought of further separation, added, – when he's done. And weighed too. And there are a few quick tests.

Your mother was not convinced.

– Don't worry, Jackie reassured her, – it's nothing. May I?

She took you from your father, flipped you over on your back and placed you in the scales.

– Twelve pounds nearly, she read off, once the flashing digits had settled. – Who's a big boy then? she cooed at you.

You smiled toothlessly at her. At least, the corners of your mouth turned upwards, and your lips parted to reveal two pink gums. It wasn't a real smile, she knew, just a serendipitous configuration of the muscles of the jaw. Nonetheless, she felt a brief stab of love and tenderness pass through her. You *were* a rather special baby, she thought, a particularly . . . she didn't know what. But not run of the mill. There was more going on in there than was usual. She tickled your stomach. You smiled again. There was no question this time. She winked at you, half expecting you to wink back. But you began to whimper.

Your mother was growing impatient now.

– Have you finished? she asked.

– Let's get some clothes on him, the midwife suggested.

She spread a nappy on the bottom of the bed and transferred your bundle on to it.

– You dress him, your mother told your father.

Your father found a babygro in the bag. It was the one your grandfather had given him, the one your father himself had been wrapped in on first entering the world.

– I should stick to a night-shirt for the time being, Jackie advised.

Irritated that his parenting skills had been called into question before his son was twenty minutes old, your father replaced the babygro and found a tiny shirt, tied at the back with a bow. It was the size of a large handkerchief.

– Hurry up, your mother urged, – or he'll get cold.

He slid your chubby forelimbs into the sleeves with ease, but could not work out how to fasten the bow.

– You have to pick him up, explained Jackie. – Look, like this.

She slipped you on to your front and tied the bow.

– Keep him well wrapped up, she counselled, enveloping you once again in the crocheted blanket and returning you to your mother. You belched ferociously, then fell asleep on your mother's chest under the blanket. You were still very tense, almost rigid. You belched again. Your mother burst out laughing. Your father grinned.

Jackie had by now almost finished cleaning up. Everything was disposable, it transpired. Your father wondered if this was for the sake of hygiene, or whether it simply helped minimise the time between deliveries, like McDonald's. Jackie was now writing up some notes in a file. From surprisingly close – through the wall – came a sudden bloodcurdling and protracted scream. He remembered that there were half a dozen women on this corridor in various stages of labour, and more who would be summoned during the night. Human life was irrepressible. Your mother was oblivious to anything beyond the adoration of her baby. Your father felt suddenly awkward.

– Busy tonight? he asked.

– Quiet tonight, the midwife replied, without looking up from her notes. – Always quiet on a Monday.

– What happens now?

– I'll leave you a few minutes together, and then I'm afraid we'll have to get you downstairs.

– Downstairs?

– Someone else will need the room I'm afraid.

– You said it was quiet on Mondays.

– Quieter, she corrected herself. – Anyway, it's Tuesday now.

– But . . . we've just had a baby . . .

For several months, your mother's condition had proved a useful bargaining chip in their negotiations with officialdom – transferring to better seats, barging to the front of queues, speeding along recalcitrant workmen. Few could resist the moral authority of a heavily-pregnant woman. Here in the delivery suite it did not quite have the same effect. He was grateful that she resisted the easy option of sarcasm.

– You'd be surprised, she said instead, – how quickly we can fill up. One extreme to the other in half an hour. One minute there you are filing your nails wondering if anybody's going to turn up, the next you're delivering triplets in corridors. It's policy anyway. Sorry.

Your father looked around the room. He had inadvertently come to think of it as *their* room. It had witnessed the most extraordinary event of his adult life. He wanted to remain here for ever. At least until the morning. But already the moment was gone. The world moved on. The Grundys were shunted one place further down the line and someone else moved up to take their place. It was inexorable. The routine chewed them up and spat them out.

– I'll leave you then, called Jackie, disappearing with the trolley. – Five minutes.

Your mother did not notice the midwife's departure. She was gazing into her new-born's eyes with such fascination that your father was reluctant to interrupt. He watched them for a minute, unnoticed. He thought 'I could slip away now quietly and they wouldn't notice me gone for hours.' He was tempted. He needed some time to compose himself. His heart still pounded, his shirt was wringing and his eyes damp with tears. He felt the need to release something, and threw open the window. It was black outside and very still, the soft cold rain moistening and refreshing his face. The moon was full and clouds drifted across it in a soft wind that rustled the branches of the poplars below the window.

– Paul, your mother was calling. – He'll catch a chill.

Horrified, he slid the window shut. It would be like that from now on, he realised. He would be obliged to put the baby first, always to remember his son. He suspected he would not be very good at it.

    – I'm sorry, he said. – I didn't think.

She arched her eyebrows, but she was not cross.

    – Never mind. Come and see our baby.

He joined her at the bedside. You stared ahead, expressionless.

    – Well done, lover, he said.

    – Well done you. You were great.

    – If you say so.

    – You made all the difference. Sorry for the things I said. Did I?

    – You did.

    – Everyone said I would. I didn't mean it, whatever it was. What did I say?

He put his finger across his lips.

    – Not in front of the children, he demurred.

    – No go on.

    – I can't remember. Honestly.

All that mattered was to preserve this moment as long as possible, this fragile bubble of joy and love. He had never known such elation, or such irritation at the knowledge that it would last only as long as Jackie decided to leave them. All he wanted was for nothing to change, and the knowledge that this was asking the impossible was painful.

    – I was sure he would be a girl, said your mother.

    – Are you disappointed? your father asked, kissing her forehead.

    – How could I be disappointed? Look at him.

They watched you. You watched them back. Would you ever get used to one another? your father wondered. Would you even like one another? The parents had the advantage there of course – it would be decades before you realised that things might have turned out otherwise. By the time you got to know your parents' limitations, it would be too late to change them.

    – They won't let us stay here, you know, he told your mother.

    – I know. Bastards.

– Our time is up. How are you feeling?

– Elated. Exhausted. Ecstatic.

He kissed her again.

– Me too.

– We should ring people, she suggested.

– Now?

– They'll want to know. I'd want to know.

– Can't we keep him to ourselves just a little longer?

Jackie appeared to tell them that they couldn't. Husband and midwife wheeled the bed containing mother and new-born out through the door, past the small, anxious party waiting for the room to be vacated, past the desk, along the corridor, through the swing doors into the lobby. You curled in your mother's arms, gazing in terror and awe at the crowd of strangers. Once more you clamped your gums around the nipple. This time, however, there was no guzzling, just a constant, gentle suction. Jackie pressed the button to summon the lift. The four of you waited in silence. The lift came, the doors sliding open to reveal a collection of people in pyjamas and dressing gowns, who flattened themselves against the side of the box to make room for the bed. One held the doors open for you. You descended a floor in silence, all eyes on the motionless bundle. The doors slid open again and they wheeled the bed back out into the lobby, back through the same swing doors, past an identical desk, into an equivalent room one floor lower. They pushed your mother into an empty cubicle containing only what looked like a washstand (which your father guessed was a cot) and a chair. Jackie drew the curtains around them.

– You can come back at half-seven, she whispered.

Your father was expected to leave now.

– I'll only be a minute, he whispered back.

– Be very quiet, she hissed, and withdrew behind the curtain.

Your mother looked up at him and smiled with such radiance that he felt it suffuse the whole room and the rest of their lives together in a cocoon of triumph.

– I have to go, he said, taking her hand.

– Come back soon, she said. – Do you want to hold him before you go?

She disengaged herself, and he received the proffered bundle. You seemed heavier than he remembered. You blinked, your mouth quivered and you sent forth a pathetic squeal of anguish.

– Whoops, grinned your father.

– He's hungry again, diagnosed your mother, stretching her arms. But the cry was answered by another, from some concealed corner of the ward. Jackie poked her head in.

– Come on then, she said.

Your father passed the bundle back to your mother. She took you and became oblivious to him again. He kissed the top of her head and withdrew.

00.44

Your mother stared at the tiny man gobbling on her nipple. It was absolutely crucial, the books all said, those first few hours. You had to bond. Your child's future mental health depended upon it. But how to? What did it involve? How would you know when you had achieved it? There the books were less helpful. It was yet another of those things that you couldn't describe, but you'd know it when you saw it. Don't worry about it, they counselled her, it will be fine. But if there was nothing you could do about it (except worry about it) then why mention it at all? It was just another thing to worry about, one more to add to the in-tray of futile angsts pending. This pile was already overflowing on to the floor. There was your father for a start. Would he stick around? Could he adjust to a life where mornings began in the middle of the night, and nights in the early evening? Strange nights too, back and forth from bedroom to bathroom with bowls of warm water and pooh, and even the occasional night out spent worrying what if? what if? and ringing the babysitter. Your mother had tried to assess your father's commitment by suggesting that he read this book, that book, come to her appointments, trying to gauge his reaction. He said he couldn't get the time off work. In the evenings, when her nagging left him with no option, he flicked listlessly through the books, frowning at the anatomical diagrams, and occasionally becoming quite distressed at the revelation of the myriad polysyllabic potential mishaps of parturition. When she tried talking about 'us' he tried to change the subject. It was always you, me and it. He used words like 'breadwinner' and 'security' that had not featured in his vocabulary previously. In some ways, she was glad he was taking it seriously, but at the same time she caught something accusatory about the way he said them. He told her she was imagining things. She was reassured for a while, until some unguarded sarcasm made her wonder once more if it wasn't some idea of responsibility and duty and doing the right thing that was keeping him. She didn't want him to stay because he felt obliged to, in the circumstances; it had to be because he wanted to. He told her he *did* want to, he wanted nothing more in the world than for them to become a family. It was what he had always wanted, he had said, at some point. But why had he never said so, then, until it was already a *fait accompli*?

But when she held you, and stroked your fine black hair, and kissed your little hand she felt suddenly indifferent as to whether your father stayed or left. Who cares? she thought, and was then horrified at her callousness. They weren't just a couple any more. You were a family now. Sue and Paul and Solomon. She started. Solomon. The name had just appeared fully-formed in her mind and affixed itself to the end of her sentence. It was so obviously the right name though. She would tell your father in the morning.

The curtain was whisked open.

– Everything all right? the nurse enquired.

You clenched and unclenched your tiny fist. Your eyes closed and she felt the suction on her nipple release. You were asleep.

– He's asleep, your mother whispered.

– Bet you could do with some yourself.

She had forgotten, until reminded, how exhausted she was. The woman took you, and placed you gently in the cot, tucking the blankets around you. But how could she sleep? Who would watch over you? What if you woke, and she were asleep, and you were suddenly all alone in the world?

– He'll be all right, promised the nurse. – He'll call you when he wants you.

She placed you on your back, tucked the covers over you, whispered

– Goodnight, sweetie

and withdrew.

You slept beside your mother. The warm, conditioned air entered your nostrils and trachea, bifurcated into your lungs, meandered through the myriad tiny vessels and chambers and gave off its tiny puff of goodness. For the first time, you were self-contained, your blood simply circulating within its orbit, and not shared with another. Now there was no limit to your world. You could stretch your arm to its full extent. The muscular walls that had confined you had ceased to limit your movements. Everything you knew was gone: where before had been only darkness there were now shapes and shades and bright lights. Where before had been only warm viscosity now came the rubberiness of flesh, the itchiness of woollen blankets, the abrasiveness of an unshaven cheek. Your mother's milk sloshed around in your mouth, warm and sweet. The smell of blood and amniotic fluid, and strange sensations from inside that were neither tastes nor smells – your stomach gurgling, your heart thumping, your bladder filling, your bowels opening. Gases rose in your interior and forced their way out in great farts and belches, meconium was expelled from your digestive system as surplus to requirements, your lungs rose and fell, filled and emptied, your fingers clenched and unclenched, blood pounded through your veins. You swallowed. You had been terrified for a while back there, compressed beyond endurance, battered by contractions and squeezed forth into the bright lights. But now all was calm again. Things seemed to have started to happen at last.

01.47

Your mother was being smothered. She had been left alone, by some irresponsible supervisor who should have known better, in charge of a roomful of toddlers; perhaps a hundred in all. The toddlers came up to her knees, and there were so many of them that she could not see the floor. They pulled on her skirt, all clamouring for attention, shouting

– Mememememe

until they began fighting, pulling each other's hair, scratching and biting. She tried to intervene, but the little bodies threaded in and out of her legs and there was nowhere to put her feet. Then one of them gave a mighty tug at her skirt and pulled her off-balance. She slipped and stumbled and the toddlers swarmed over her in triumph, like soldier ants or piranhas. She awoke in panic. A child was whimpering in her ear. The bed, the room were unfamiliar. Was this the dream continuing? She remembered. It was Solomon.

She turned to pick you up, and screamed.

– Aaaaaargh.

You were sitting up in the cot, whimpering, and rubbing your eyes on the back of your chubby hands. You looked about thirty pounds. You were not Solomon at all. You were a changeling. On hearing her scream, your whimpering spilled over into a fully-fledged bawl. A nurse appeared almost instantaneously.

– What is it? she asked, concerned.

But your mother had turned away and hidden her eyes and could only gesticulate towards the cot, from which you were now trying to climb. The nurse gasped, and shouted.

– Sister!

The Sister appeared, and was shown the changeling, still bawling, and now halfway out of the cot.

– Well, don't just stand there, she admonished her subordinate, – poor thing's terrified. Pick him up, woman.

The nurse did as she was told. It was only a baby after all. A bigger one than was familiar on the maternity ward, but a baby nonetheless. Upon being hoisted into the air, you wailed ever louder, kicking your feet and waving your fists, throwing your head back and screaming. Your shitty nappy burst open and slithered to the floor. You wanted your mother.

– He seems to want you, said the nurse. – Would you take him?

Your mother stretched out her arms to receive you. That was all you wanted, and you were instantly pacified, and snuggled into her chest. The sobbing died down. Gingerly, she stroked your hair. Your mouth clasped around her nipple and you drew in great gulps of nourishment. She did not feel able to resist, and the sensation was strangely comforting. The Sister and the nurse, meanwhile, were engaged in an intense, whispered conversation a few feet away. Suddenly your mother remembered what was missing.

– Where is my baby? she demanded. – Where is my baby?

Nurse and Sister broke off, and stared at her.

– Where is my baby? your mother repeated, more urgently this time, feeling a wave of nausea and panic break within her.

– This is your baby, Mrs Grundy, said the nurse.

– Don't play games with me, warned your mother.

– We're not playing games, Mrs Grundy, the Sister promised her. – Look at his armband.

– This is not funny.

– This is your baby, Mrs Grundy. Look at his wristband.

The band was cutting into the flesh on your wrist. It said 'Grundy. Boy. Twelve pounds' and was followed by your serial number.

You finished the first breast and surfaced for air, gasping. She saw your face. Of course it was you.

– Bloody hell! she exclaimed. – Did that really come out of my fanny an hour ago?

The nurse and Sister looked at each other for support.

– Er . . . yes, they said together, nervously.

Your mother was suddenly embarrassed by her irreverence.

– I'm sorry, she blushed. – It was just . . . for a terrible moment . . . I don't remember him being this big . . .

You dived back under the covers for second helpings.

– Or having all this hair, she continued, – or sitting up, or OW . . .

She winced.

– Or teeth, she concluded.

– He is a size, the Sister was obliged to acknowledge.

– Amazing, isn't it, how something so big can . . . I suppose you hear this all the time.

The attendants smiled.

– Are you all right now? asked the nurse.

– I think so, your mother replied. – It's been a very strange few hours. I'm a bit disorientated.

– We'll not be more than ten feet away.

– Thank you.

– Look, he's finished now, said the Sister. – Off to sleep again. Shall I take him off you?

But you were far from asleep. From under the covers your head appeared, grinning broadly. You looked your mother in the eye and put your hands out to feel her face.

– Hello, Solomon, she smiled, delighted.

– Low Somonom, you repeated.

She nearly dropped you. This wasn't right surely. You were sitting bolt upright upon her chest now, still staring into her face, still grinning, waiting for someone to say something else. Nurse and Sister, however, were equally transfixed. All three of them stared at you, open-mouthed.

– Somonom, you repeated, quite unaware of the sensation you were creating. You poked your mother in the eye, giggled, and set off crawling to the far end of the bed, where something had caught your eye.

– Something . . . something very strange is going on, your mother informed her attendants.

They nodded, sheepishly.

– If I didn't know that was my baby, I would swear someone had switched them while I was asleep. But it is my baby. I can see that. Only . . . he appears to have doubled in size, and he can sit, and even crawl a bit and he says 'Somonom'.

– Somonom, you demonstrated.

– Is that possible?

– It's certainly unusual, confessed the Sister.

– I don't know what to say . . . It's . . . it's marvellous, isn't it? Come here, Solomon.

She stretched out her arms. Having found nothing of any great interest at the end of the bed, you were happy enough to be swept up and hugged and kissed and fussed over.

– You *are* an extraordinary baby, she told you.

– Strawny, you confirmed.

She laughed. You laughed. With mother and infant entirely absorbed in each other, nurse and Sister slipped away. Only when out of earshot did they allow their panic to find expression.

02.01

Frank Parker was absorbed by the scene on Monitor Number Seven. One of the doctors had his trousers round his knees, the other had unbuttoned her blouse. The phone rang. Surely they would stop now? But they didn't seem to notice. He realised that it was his phone ringing, not theirs. He let it ring a few more times, just to let whoever was on the other end know he didn't just sit around in his dingy little room playing patience and waiting for the phone to ring (which was, of course, exactly how he did pass the time, when there was nothing worth watching on the monitors). On the sixth ring he picked it up and announced himself.

– Security.

– Who's that?

– Parker.

– Ah.

There was a pause. It was a woman's voice, not one he recognised.

– Is there a problem? he asked, one eye still on the screen.

– Rather a delicate one. Where are you?

He gave her directions. She would be there in five minutes, she said, and hung up. As he replaced the receiver it occurred to him that he had not even asked her name. Too many nights alone up here; he was losing his grip. He removed the videotape from the slot, labelled it and placed it carefully in the cardboard box with the others. He knew the collection was worth a considerable sum of money, if handled correctly. Not for the mass market – the picture quality was too poor, the angles were all wrong, the participants the wrong ages and shapes and sizes, the whole performance all too frequently spoiled by inappropriate giggling, or ridiculous accidents. Apart from that, he had no idea how he might get in touch with the mass market. He had the supply, and it seemed a fair assumption that the demand was out there somewhere, drooling – from the amount of it around, you would think that very few men ever did anything else beyond read, watch and listen to porn – but Frank Parker had no means of connecting their demand with his supply. Blackmail was a more realistic and potentially more lucrative avenue to explore. At some point, he would decide what to do with the evidence he had collected; for the moment he was just accumulating it, in a cardboard box.

He realised with a shock what a tip his office had become – empty cans and crisp packets, newspapers, half-drunk cups of coffee, fingernails, leaky biros. It was weeks since he had had a visitor. He swept it all into the wastepaper bin, and wiped the surfaces with a damp paper towel. No sooner was a degree of order restored than a knock at the door announced her arrival.

– Enter, he called, officiously.

She entered. A short, severe woman. He didn't recognise her. So many new staff. In the old days he had known them all. Nowadays you just couldn't keep track – agency staff, temporary stand-ins, locums, students. She stood in the doorway transfixed, her eyes on stalks. He had grown so accustomed to the performance on the monitors that he had forgotten them. He switched rapidly to another camera. Thankfully, it showed no more than an empty store cupboard.

– Hang on, she flapped, – put that back on, will you?

– I'm afraid it's against regulations, he extemporised.

She turned to look at him, incredulous.

– I know it's against regulations, she said. – But wasn't that Dr Shearsby? Oh, do put it back on.

– I mean, it's against regulations for unauthorised personnel
to view the . . . er . . .

– To view Dr Shearsby having it off?

– It's classified, he explained.

That was what people said in films.

– Classified?

– You shouldn't really be in here at all, he said, trying to sound
official. – I've no idea who you are even.

– I'm sure that was Dr Shearsby, she said, handing him her
security tag.

– I wouldn't know, he admitted.

The doctor's face was familiar, and the distinctive scar on her
bottom; he had no idea of her name.

– Can't you just put it up once more? Pleeeeeeease?

– What's the problem, Sister?

– Problem?

With a start she remembered why she had come.

– Ah yes. It's a bit tricky. That's why I've come in person.
You can't trust the phones.

She gave him a strange look.

– I must admit, Mr Parker, she continued, – I had no idea of
the lengths to which you security people went.

– That's because you have no idea of half the things that go
on in this hospital, he replied, irritated by her tone.

– Evidently. Tell me, where do these cameras cover?

– I can't tell you, he refused. – It's classified.

She sighed.

– At least not until you tell me the problem.

She composed herself.

– Sometime in the last hour and a half, she began, – someone
entered the maternity ward and removed a new-born baby.

Parker whistled.

– Exactly.

– You haven't just . . . mislaid it?

– No.

– How can you be so sure?

– Because, she continued, – and here is the truly extraordinary
part, whoever removed the baby left a toddler in its place.

He considered his reply. She watched him, waiting. He couldn't think of a suitable reply, and prevaricated.

– And?

She looked puzzled.

– And? he repeated.

– Well, we need to find the baby and swap them back.

– Without anyone knowing?

– I said it was a tricky one.

– This puts me in an awkward position, he said at last.

– Me too, she pointed out.

– Both of us, he acknowledged, chewing his pencil. – Somebody took a baby and left a different one in its place.

– Not another baby, a toddler.

– A toddler then. And the mother?

– She is convinced that the replica baby is her own. We have . . . we thought it best to let her think that. There's nothing to be gained from panic.

– Of course. You realise, though, that the most likely explanation is a cock-up.

She stared at him, incredulous.

– It does happen, he said.

– Mr Parker, if I had any reason to doubt that the roots of this crisis lay in cock-up, I would not be here now.

– If there's a cock-up, he said, – there might be an enquiry. You're not dragging me into no enquiry.

– You already are dragged into it, I would have thought.

He reflected on this.

– How's that then?

– You are employed to sit and watch those monitors.

She took his silence to indicate a reluctant acknowledgement of her point.

– You are paid to sit and watch those monitors for suspicious activities, instead of which you prefer to spend your time watching Dr Shearsby having it off in a broom cupboard somewhere.

He was ashamed. She made it sound perverted.

– Look, he said, – I just watch the monitors. I can't help what people do in front of them.

– Is there a monitor in maternity? she asked.

He consulted his schedules.
– Apparently not.
– Why not? she demanded.
– There's nothing worth nicking in maternity, I suppose.
Only babies.

She began to remonstrate, but there was no use. Her hopes of finding the baby quickly and quietly and making a surreptitious substitution were rapidly fading. There was nothing for it. It was time to activate the Procedures.

02.35

Left alone with you, your mother tried without success to reconcile reason, memory and current experience. She had no way of telling which was which. She had a picture in her mind, vivid and constant, of you as you had appeared from the womb, as the midwife had scooped you up from between her legs and laid you upon her breast. It had only been an hour ago, two at the most. She remembered the way your tiny body had nestled into the folds and curves and bulges of her breasts and belly, still felt your imprint upon her. But what was this picture? She had tried, before the birth, so often to imagine you. She had pored over a thousand photographs of new-borns at their mothers' breasts, had practised at ante-natal classes with rag dolls and then, in the last few weeks, with ersatz babies moulded in plastic but so realistic as to cause her to shudder when the demonstrator stuffed them clumsily into a plastic bag. What was this picture in her mind? You as you had been, you as she had once imagined you might be, or you as you ought to have been?

Her instincts, whatever instincts were, told her this image was a memory. Not a distant one either but fresh. How could it be otherwise? She had never felt so alive as at that moment, a few hours previously. If one instant from her life could be burnished upon her memory, surely it would be that one? The shock and the recognition combined; the tiny man whom no one had ever seen before, but for whom she had been waiting all her life; whose life she could snuff out just by walking away, but who commanded simply by his helplessness that she remain and minister, and to whose will she would submit her own without question, without regret. How could she forget those deep brown eyes of yours that pleaded and commanded simultaneously, those fists clenched in rage and bliss, those gums that gulped the nourishment from her like air into a tyre? Babies were so pneumatic. Presumably there were muscles in there somewhere but submerged under such layers of blubber that your limbs did not so much bend and stretch as crease and tuck, as if made of pastry. Such stumpy little arms and legs. When she looked at you, dozing in her arms now, she knew you were indeed part of her. You had your grandfather's protruding ears and your mother's own thin and elegant eyebrows. How could she fail to recognise someone who was already so much a reflection of herself, and the people she loved?

There was more of his mother than of his father in her baby, though. Or did people always say that? That girls looked like their fathers, and boys like their mothers? Presumably, those were the bits that stuck out, that struck one as distinctive – a man's nose on a girl's face, a woman's feet on a boy's legs. She couldn't see much of your father in you at all, awake, apart from your slightly vacant, trusting expression. Your father was not, it had to be said, possessed of very striking features. He was neat and pleasantly proportioned but hardly striking. In sleep, you reminded her of him, but this was perhaps because your father was the person she was most familiar with, asleep. Your nostrils flared and collapsed as you breathed, and your eyes were clamped shut. One arm draped casually over her own, the other was bunched up tight against your chest, your miniature fingers resting against your tiny lips. Your chest rose and fell. She ran her fingers gently through your hair and you stirred, your free arm rising to brush her away.

You were returning to consciousness again, your body wriggling, your free fist clenched. You began to chew on your dimpled knuckles, whimpering softly. Your eyes blinked. Slowly, hitching yourself up on your mother's night-dress, you roused yourself to a sitting position, smacking your lips and yawning. You did not look at all happy to be awake.

– Hello, darling, she whispered, conscious that the ward was still asleep.

You stared at her, frowning and squinting.

– You scared me, she told you. – I thought someone had taken you away.

You looked puzzled. Waking up was clearly occupying all your energy and attention.

– What were you dreaming of, little one? your mother cooed.

You buried deeper into her. From the other end of the ward came a piercing cry. You turned, alarmed and fascinated, but could see nothing beyond the orange plastic curtains that screened your cubicle from the others. The wailing continued for what seemed like an age, and was taken up by another infant. You listened, together, intrigued. Finally, you heard the rustle of bedclothes and a woman's voice, weary and embittered, groaned

– Fucking . . . not again.

A door was thrown open. You sat bolt upright, terrified. Rapid footfalls. Your head followed the footsteps as they paced up and down on the other side of the curtain. You shrank back into your mother.

– It's all right, she reassured you. – It's just the nurses. It's morning. It's the first morning of your life.

This seemed to comfort you a little, but you remained pressed against her, your knuckles white where you gripped her arm. You were amazed by the commotion around you, your eyes following sudden distinct noises that emerged from the general confusion of rustlings and creakings. Suddenly a head appeared between the curtains at the end of your bed. It was the Sister.

– Mrs Grundy.

She seemed disappointed that your mother had not disappeared, and nervous somehow, as if she were about to break some dreadful news.

– Is anything up? your mother asked.

– We're going to move you somewhere more private, the Sister explained.

– Why?

– We thought you'd prefer somewhere a bit more private.

– Look, is anything the matter? I'd much rather know.

– Somewhere a bit more private, the Sister repeated. – If that's all right with you.

– Well, I suppose so.

As soon as the words were out of her mouth the Sister and two porters were through the curtains pulling a large and cumbersome trolley. You watched, agog.

– Hold tight then, said one of the men, and they swung your mother, yourself, the mattress and the bedclothes on to the trolley in one practised movement.

– Let's go then, said the Sister.

She seemed keen to avoid meeting your mother's eyes, let alone your own. The curtains were thrown back and you set off. The ward was in darkness, each mother/child unit concealed behind an orange curtain. It was not morning at all. It was still the middle of the night. Your mother held you tight against her, and you were infected osmotically by her anxiety and confusion. You passed back through the double swing doors, past the long desk with the computer screens, along the deserted corridor and into a side room. The two men slipped mother and baby effortlessly off the trolley and on to the bed, then departed. Another nurse arrived with a cup of tea, closely followed by a woman in stripy dungarees. The Sister fussed over something. The nurse plumped up the cushions in the armchair. The woman in the stripy dungarees was examining her fingernails. You watched them, taking it all in but understanding no more than your mother. The woman in the stripy dungarees sat down suddenly on the edge of the bed. Your mother was by now on the verge of panic.

– What is it? she demanded. – What's happened?

– Bad news, I'm afraid, said the woman in the stripy dungarees.

You sensed the rising tension, and scanned your mother's face anxiously.

– What bad news? your mother wanted to know. – Is it Paul?

The woman in the stripy dungarees paused dramatically.

– I'm afraid so, she said.

– What's happened? Where is he?

The woman took your mother's free hand and held it, looking her straight in the eye and speaking slowly and calmly, as she had been taught to do.

– Mrs Grundy, I'm afraid we have to face the awful possibility that Paul has been abducted.

Your mother felt terror and bewilderment fighting for control, but caught sight of your apprehensive gaze and reminded herself that she must keep calm.

– Abducted?

– It looks like it.

– But why?

– Have some tea, suggested the nurse.

The woman in stripy dungarees shot her a disapproving glare.

– Why? your mother repeated. – Why would anyone want to abduct Paul?

– We don't know, the Sister confessed.

– What do they want – money? We haven't got any money.

She realised she was beginning to sound like a character in a lacklustre episode of *Eastenders*. But what else could you say? It was just so unexpected. She had worried about the birth. She had worried about you. She had never thought to worry about your father. What was this, some bizarre plea for attention? She dismissed the thought, angry with herself.

– It may be a woman who has herself just lost a baby, guessed the woman in the stripy dungarees, who was still holding your mother's hand – or a woman who can't have a baby . . .

– So she kidnapped Paul?

– I know it sounds bizarre, Mrs Grundy. But people do strange things in such situations. Dreadful things. They're not really responsible for their actions.

– Well who is responsible then?

The Sister shrugged. Your mother tried to put herself in the abductor's position. It was still impossible, incomprehensible. Why take your father, of all people? What did she want from him? If it was impregnation she wanted, she only had to ask. You could get laid on the NHS these days. Money? How much did she think Paul was worth? Or perhaps it was just revenge she wanted? Not a specific revenge, just a general revenge against life and fate and men? The thought made her shudder.

– We've got to find him, she pleaded, – before it's too late.

The Sister and the woman looked at each other.

– I'm Janice Black, the woman replied, unhooking your mother's hands from the straps of her dungarees. – I'm a social worker. If it's any comfort, she continued, – we've no reason to believe that Paul's in any danger. They almost always turn up safe and sound after a few days. I know it's a terrible shock, but do try and bear that in mind. It's more a question of sitting tight usually.

You had lost interest in the conversation taking place above your head, and turned your attention to the nurse, who was smiling and waving at you, and making funny faces. She had been instructed to win your confidence and had half succeeded, for though you hid behind your mother, you were peeping out from behind your hands and giggling.

– So what do we do then? asked your mother.

– The first thing to do, said Janice, – is to find your husband. Have you any idea where he might have got to? Where did he go when he left you?

Your mother tried to recall but nothing came to mind. She had hardly noticed him slip away, even, let alone asked where he was going.

– What does he look like? the social worker asked.

She described him as best she could, but it was not easy. Thirty, slight build, scruffy, brown hair a bit thin on top, about five ten. There were a thousand people in Pilsbury who looked like that.

– We'll see what we can do, Janice Black promised. – I should think the most likely thing is that he'll just turn up here, wouldn't you say?

– I don't know. If you say so, I suppose.

Your mother had no idea what to expect. It seemed like the kind of thing that happened to the social worker every day, but it had never happened to your mother before. There was a long pause. None of them knew what to say. You, meanwhile, were still smiling and peekabooing shyly at the nurse.

– When we do find your husband, the social worker said eventually, – do you want to tell him, or would you rather we did?

– Tell him what? asked your mother, mystified.

– Well, about what's happened. About Paul . . .

– But . . .

Enlightenment shone upon Sue Grundy. A shiver of relief flushed through her and she could not help laughing. You looked up and laughed too, your shoulders shaking in a rather grotesque caricature of your mother. The social worker stared at the pair of you, horrified. Your mother recollected herself.

– Oh hell, she exclaimed. – God, I'm sorry.

The social worker made no reply. It was her turn at bewilderment now.

– I know it's not funny your mother explained. – I'm sorry. It's just, you've got the wrong woman that's all. It's just a weird coincidence. You see, my husband's called Paul.

– Your husband?

– My husband, yes.

– It was your baby I was talking about, Mrs Grundy.

– Yes, I see that. It's dreadful though. I shouldn't have laughed. I was just so glad it wasn't me.

Your mother was ashamed. The fact that it was someone else's baby hardly made a laughing matter out of it. In fact it was worse, much worse. Husbands could more or less look after themselves – more or less, anyway, in a crisis. That was what they were good at, crises. It was when they came alive. It was in the long gaps between the crises that they needed watching. But to lose a baby, and only a few hours old. It was horrible. To know that your baby was somewhere out there in the big cold world and that its survival depended upon the goodwill of a lunatic. It was something you didn't expect to have to face for years. She drew you to her, though you resisted. You were enjoying your game too much.

– If there's anything I can do . . . your mother offered.

She knew it was a lame gesture, but she wanted to make amends. Janice Black bit her lip.

– It's me who should apologise really, she said at last. – You asked me if it was about Paul, and I just assumed Paul was your baby. I should have checked. Only there's no name on the card. It just says 'Grundy'.

Your mother grew worried again. Why wasn't this woman leaving now? There seemed to be something else. It wasn't over yet.

– Look, she demanded, – can't you just tell me what's wrong? Is something wrong? Have you lost a baby? Have you lost a husband? Have you got the right room? the right hospital? the right month? Is it my problem or someone else's?

The social worker took a long time to reply and when she did reply, chose her words carefully.

– This baby, Mrs Grundy, she informed your mother, – is not your baby.

Your mother was gobstruck. She stared open-mouthed and no words came.

– I'm so very sorry, Mrs Grundy.

– But . . . but he's got his name on. The wristband.

She held up your arm for the social worker to see. There was no band on it. It must have come off, or snapped. It had always been much too tight. Your mother grabbed you and held you to her breast, shielding you with her arms and inching backwards on the bed, away from this mad woman in stripy dungarees. What would they do now? There were three of them – social worker, Sister and nurse. She had heard about situations like this. Would the others – the men who had moved her bed?—burst through the door and pin her down whilst this Janice woman wrestled you away from her and spirited you away to some anonymous safe house? You had gone quite rigid, and your breathing was shallow. She thought you were trembling, then realised it was herself. Was that your heart pounding, or was it hers? She wrapped the covers tight around you, as another protective layer. Where the hell was your father? She wanted to scream, but was terrified of drawing attention to herself. If she screamed they would burst through the door and pin her down. They didn't want to make a scene, she realised. They didn't want any of the other mothers to know what they were doing.

– You're mad, she gasped.

– No, Mrs Grundy, replied the social worker, patiently.

– Mistaken then. You've made a mistake. You've got the wrong woman. The wrong ward.

– No, Mrs Grundy.

– But you were wrong before.

Janice Black took a deep breath.

– Mrs Grundy, a terrible thing has happened. We are all deeply, deeply sorry, but we must face facts.

– We?

It was just like the films. It was a conspiracy.

– Paul! she screamed. – Paul!

The door flew open.

– No! screamed your mother, – No! No!

She threw the covers over you, and lay in the darkness, waiting for the brutal hands, the sedative in her buttock, her baby dragged kicking and screaming from her. She held you so tight you were frightened you would burst. But nothing happened. A minute passed. She heard muffled voices, footsteps on the stone floor, the door closing. Another minute. The longest minute of her life. They were deciding on the angle of attack. They didn't want a scene on the maternity ward. Then she heard the social worker's voice, muffled through the covers.

– Mrs Grundy, please come out. We have to talk this through.

– No! your mother yelled defiantly.

– No! you added pathetically.

– Mrs Grundy, we have a problem.

– Go away!

– We have to talk about it.

– Leave me alone!

– Mrs Grundy, I can't leave you alone until I know that the child is safe.

– He's safer with me than he'll ever be with you.

Suddenly, the covers were thrown back. Your mother braced herself. She was not a big woman but she felt power and strength flow through her arms. She could kick, she could scratch, she could bite. She didn't care what they did to her. Maybe she couldn't stop them, but

– Mummmmeeeeee.

– You're hurting him, Mrs Grundy, Janice pointed out.

Horrified, your mother relaxed her hold. You rolled away, disentangled yourself from the covers and sat panting at the end of the bed. The social worker was still sitting where she had always sat. There was no one else in the room.

– We have to talk.

– He's my baby. You're not taking him from me.

– What's his name?

Your mother eyed her suspiciously.

– Why?

– What do you call him?

– Solomon.

– Mrs Grundy, take a look at Solomon.

Your mother did so.

– What do you see?

She saw her son sitting on the end of the bed, picking his nose and watching them both nervously.

– I won't let them take you away, she promised you.

You turned your back, swung your legs and lowered yourself to the floor. Here you stayed, clinging to the bedclothes, sucking your thumb and scowling.

– Mrs Grundy, this is not your baby. This is a small child. A toddler.

Your mother looked at her baby. It was hard to dispute what the social worker was saying.

– He's my baby, she said simply. – He'll always be my baby.

The social worker bit her lip, and fiddled with her dungaree strap.

– If this is not my baby, hissed your mother, – then where the fuck *is* my baby?

– That, admitted the social worker, – is the missing piece in all this. Whichever way we arrange the evidence there's one piece that doesn't fit.

– This is my child. This is my life. Not a fucking jigsaw puzzle.

– We're not really getting anywhere, are we? the social worker acknowledged.

– You're not going to take my baby, your mother confirmed.

– Mrs Grundy, he is not your baby. Whatever he is, he is not your baby. He is not a baby at all.

They glared at each other across a chasm of suspicion and misunderstanding. Janice Black needed time to reconsider.

– I'll come back later then, she said in the doorway.

– Don't hurry.

Janice Black opened her mouth to speak but decided against it. Then she was gone. End of Round One. Your mother seemed to have won at least a postponement. She had kept them at bay for the time being. But she was exhausted. Where was your father? Oh God, where was your father?

03.58

How did dead people feel about reincarnation? Were they clamouring to be released from wherever it was that they waited, to once more take human form and experience pain and pleasure, love and loss, sex and death? Or did they drag their heels, moaning at being made to get caught up once again in the demands of nappies and potties, of homework and examinations, of dentists and garage bills? What if there were no beginning and no end? If it did all go round in circles? Certainly, your father's mind was going round in circles. His wife slept, his child slept, the whole world slept, but he could not. Partly, this was because he was chronically uncomfortable on the sofa in the waiting room. The chairs were too narrow, the table too hard, the floor filthy. The bangs and clatters disturbed him. He found it hard to relax knowing that people were being born and dying all around him. Partly, too, it was the hormones still surging around his bloodstream, overloading his receptors. He needed to talk, but got only answerphones. So he tossed and turned, racked by waves of adrenaline and existential doubt, and stabbed periodically in the lower back by a broken spring. He had passed on his genetic baton (such as it was) to the next generation, and was left wondering what to do next. Eventually, he rolled off the couch, cracked his head painfully on the table and was no longer able to sustain even the illusion of sleep.

He seemed to have half existed in this half-darkness, half asleep, for days. The clock told him it had been four hours. Fed up with waiting, he went to the reception desk and asked to be allowed to see his baby. The nurse informed him tersely that visiting was allowed between the hours of 7.30 and midday and again between 2.00 and 8.30. Certainly not at four o'clock in the morning.

– But I'm the father, he protested.

The nurse arched her eyebrows.

– All these babies have fathers, she reminded him.

This had not occurred to your father before. He supposed it was true, at least in the technical sense.

– Where are they all then? he asked, mystified.

– At home in bed if they've any sense, she told him. – They'll be here during visiting hours no doubt. You'll have to get used to the routines, she warned him. – There are ten mothers and eleven babies in that ward and they deserve a little privacy. How would you feel if a strange man burst into your bedroom at four o'clock in the morning?

Your father was about to reply that if a strange man, or indeed any kind of man, were to burst into his bedroom his reaction would not be remotely influenced by whether it were four o'clock in the morning or Sunday lunch-time, but bit his tongue. She would not let him in before the appointed time, and it was pointless to try to force the issue. Even if he had his way they would take it out on Sue and the baby when he departed. He slumped down into one of the chairs lining the wall. The nurse eyed him malevolently. Reluctantly he rose and trooped once more back through the double

doors. No sign of any of the other fathers. This he found
suddenly worrying. Where had they all got to? Was there
a special fathers' waiting room somewhere, that no one had
told him about? Did everyone else know something he didn't,
as usual? He could not believe there were fathers who had
found better things to do than to be as close as possible to
their new-born sons and daughters, even if it were not possible
to see them until there was a window in the administrative
routine. Perhaps they had all experienced what he was now
experiencing, and accepted the futility of arriving at any time
other than that specified in the rule book. Perhaps this was
just another of those tiny, agonising disillusionments that everyone else had grown to accept long ago but which still caught
him unawares. The world was full of injustices nonetheless
outrageous for being perpetrated by bureaucrats rather than
by dictators, but the rest of the world seemed prepared to
shrug and carry on. He could never decide whether they were
sensible and realistic, or cowardly and timid, or simply too stupid
to realise.

All in all, it was a fraught and messy business, fatherhood. He
began to understand why some women preferred to go it alone.
If you believed the Tory papers, he and your mother were an
endangered species these days – both parents not only married,
but married to each other. On this subject too he swung from
self-righteousness to self-loathing, feeling sometimes that he
alone carried the banner of bread-winning masculinity forward
into the new generation, and sometimes that he alone stood
stuck in the mudflats of timidity and conformity, whilst the
rest of the world experimented with exciting and fulfilling
new lifestyles, sailing along the viaduct of the future whilst
he crouched with his finger in the dyke of the past. It wasn't
true, of course, either way. Whether it was pre-modern or
post-modern, it was still what most people did. The papers
made a fuss about people who did it other ways precisely
because they were a minority. A few people might get worked
up about the things that majorities did, but not many. Everyone
hated minorities.

Unable to sleep, he sat and watched the clock.

04.30

A knock on the door caused you to look up in expectation. You had already begun to find your immediate surroundings inadequate to your developmental needs. There was nothing to do. You had unpacked your mother's handbag and the holdall. The holdall contained nothing but tubes of cream and nappies and baby clothes which no longer fitted you. Your mother had explained the role and function of them all to you, but you hadn't understood, or been particularly interested. The handbag was more exciting; keys and cheque books and things. Shiny things, jangly things. Things she took away from you and said you weren't allowed to touch. Coins, you had learned, were of a satisfying solidity and heaviness when pressed between the tongue and the roof of the mouth, but tasted foul. After half an hour you had exhausted the possibilities of the handbag. You had then done a huge pooh in the middle of the floor. This wasn't the result of a conscious decision on your part, though. The pooh came easily and accidentally, slithering forth onto the cold floor and filling the room with its rich and exotic odour. It was bottle green. You wanted to examine it further but your mother called the nurse, and the nurse took it away, returning five minutes later with a pot. Your mother told you that if you wanted to do a pooh you should do it in the pot. So you did another, to please her, in the pot. This one was sludgey and bright orange. The nurse was pleased, and ruffled your hair, but your mother cried and said you were growing up too fast, and you wondered what you'd done to upset her. She still wouldn't get out of bed. Then came the knock. Your mother beckoned you over to her, and reluctantly you went. She lifted you up on the bed and pulled the covers up around both of you. You liked that. It was warm and cosy. Only when she was sure you were safe did she reply. A tired man appeared in the doorway. He had clearly been recently roused from a deep sleep. He was unshaven and his flies were open.

   – Mrs Grundy? he enquired.

   – Who are you?

Your mother was instantly suspicious.

– My name's Humphries, he introduced himself. – I'm the consultant.

– You're not taking him, your mother warned him. – Not out of my sight, not for a minute.

You scrambled out from the covers for a better look. You saw a short, chubby man in a white coat. His face was kind, but there were bags under his eyes. He didn't look at all happy.

– Can I come in? he asked.

– You're not taking him, your mother repeated.

– I have no intention of taking him, Humphries said wearily. – I've come for a chat, because I was told to. The Procedures have been activated, and I'm on the top of the list apparently. But I don't know any more about it than you do.

– You'd better come in then, she allowed him.

He thanked her, and made his way over to a chair.

– May I? he asked, indicating the case notes, which had already spread to a second volume.

– Everyone else has, your mother consented.

You watched as he read slowly, pursing his lips. Sometimes he flicked back a page to check some apparent contradiction. They weren't apparent contradictions, however; all were genuine. Mother and son waited patiently. Finally he closed the file, leant back in his chair and stared at the ceiling.

– Well? demanded your mother.

– A strange tale, indeed, he observed at last. – The Sister informs me – and it says here in your notes – that you gave birth last night to a twelve-pound boy. That's right?

Your mother nodded.

– At approximately half-past two you awoke to find your new-born baby gone . . .

– No! your mother cut in.

He paused again, with exaggerated patience. Or perhaps it was just fatigue.

– My questions first, yours at the end, he suggested. – How's that?

Your mother had no energy left to argue, and decided to give him the benefit of the doubt. Words seemed fairly harmless, anyway. It was violence you had to watch out for.

– You awoke, Humphries continued, – to find the baby which you had given birth to gone, and another baby in the cot beside you. A much bigger one.

– No, your mother disagreed. – The same baby, but . . . much bigger.

Humphries' brow furrowed.

– Well, whether it's a different child or the same child at different points in time seems rather an imponderable. Let's leave that for the philosophers. Or at least until I've had some coffee. May I continue?

She permitted.

– It would appear that in the time between the initial . . . discovery, and the time it has taken me to drive here, the child has been switched yet again.

Your mother could do no more than echo his words, while her brain worked furiously to make sense of them.

– Switched again?

– Well this lad – Solomon you call him?

Your mother nodded.

– This boy is three years old if he's a day. I would hazard a guess somewhere around four and a half.

Your mother nodded again. This man seemed no less mad than the rest of them, but his agenda did not seem to coalesce around the need for separation.

– So we are left with three possibilities, are we not?

Your mother shrugged. She was used to her own, familiar existence, and had no idea how to cope with its disappearance, and the arrival of a choice of three possibilities in its stead. Three sounded a reasonable number, though.

– Firstly, began Humphries, – that this whole thing is a joke or a hoax, or a dream, or an experimental novel or something.

– It's not, she promised. – It's not a hoax. I don't think it's a dream either.

He stared at her, licking his lips in thought.

– The second possibility is the one we were working on an hour ago. Or Sister Nuttall anyway. That somebody switched the babies. And now they've done it again.

– He's my baby, your mother said. – Aren't you, Solomon?

– Not a baby, you corrected her. – A big boy now.

– My big boy, then.

You scowled, and raised your eyes heavenward.

– The third possibility, Humphries continued, – is that your child is just growing. Growing at a phenomenal rate. Whhoooooosh.

You laughed.

– Again! you ordered.

– Whhooooooossshh, Humphries repeated the effect. – Straight up. No stopping. Which is pretty far-fetched. It has an air of fairy story about it, does it not?

Your mother's heart sank.

– But I think the third is the most likely. What do you think?

– I think you're right, said your mother.

– I think so too, said Humphries. – For the time being. I'm quite prepared to be proved wrong. If someone were to come through that door now and show me that it was all an optical illusion or something, I'd leap up and slap them on the back, and shake their hand.

– Me too, said your mother.

She was beginning to feel that she might have found an ally. Humphries turned his attention towards you.

– You're a bit of an oddity, Solomon Grundy, lad, he told you.

Your brow furrowed.

– What's an oddity? you asked.

– It means you're very special, darling, said your mother.

– Exactly, agreed Humphries. – Quite, quite remarkably special. Unique. One in a billion.

– I'm an oddity, you repeated, pleased with the sound of the word.

– What can we do? your mother asked the doctor.

She was not sure whether oddity constituted a diagnosis, or an acknowledgement of the impossibility of diagnosis. Either way, the prognosis remained obscure.

– Well, the first thing to do is to get the social workers off the case.

Your mother could have kissed him. For the first time in a desperate hour she allowed herself to hope that it might all turn out all right.

04.53

– Well? demanded the Sister.

Alan Humphries inspected his fingernails.

– It's a miracle, he declared at last.

– It's a disaster, the nurse disagreed.

– Miracle, disaster, shrugged Humphries. – Miracle, disaster, it's all the same.

The Sister sighed, exasperated beyond endurance. It was always like this when the consultants got involved. It never helped. They didn't know the first thing about it. Oh, they knew all about the drugs, the technology, the symptoms, the Latin names for it all, everything you could read in books, but in the end they were men and there was no place for them on the maternity wards. Birth, babies, gynae things were a mystery to them. It wasn't really their fault of course, but they never helped. In the end you almost felt sorry for them. But then what sort of man chose to devote his career to the study of women's privates anyway? She had always wondered that. What sort of man chose to spend his life prodding and poking women's bits? But she had made the decision. Something quite extraordinary was going on in the labour wards. There would almost certainly be an enquiry. Every action would be scrutinised retrospectively, every decision re-examined under the clear penetrating beam of hindsight, in an attempt to find someone to carry the can. It certainly wasn't going to be her. From now on everything went through the proper channels, by the book. The Procedures would be followed to the letter, and the procedures said 'Call the consultant at the top of the list', who happened, through a combination of sickness and Buggins's turn, to be Alan Humphries. It was not her fault, it was just bad luck. But why did he have to talk in these riddles?

– Miracles and disasters are not the same thing at all, she snapped back at him. – They are opposites.

– One man's miracle, aphorised Humphries, – is another man's disaster. One man's ceiling is another man's floor. One man's mistress is another man's wife. It's all relative.

– Nonsense.

– I should calm down a bit, he advised her. – You're all red in the face and hyperventilating. Relax.

– Relax? Relax?

– At least stop hyperventilating.

– Stop hyperventilating?

He took her by the elbow, but she shook herself free.

– A baby has been stolen from this hospital, she reminded him. – I do not feel that relaxation is the appropriate professional response.

– Nobody has been stolen, Sister Nuttall.

– Well, what then? Is he hiding under the bed? Perhaps he's gone down the shop for a pint of milk?

She was on the verge of tears. He knew that a single remark might tip her over the precipice, and was sorely tempted. He was restraining his impatience with great difficulty.

– Sister Nuttall, it was you who called me here, he reminded her.

– It was not my choice, she informed him, – I am obliged to do so by the Procedures.

– You called me here, he repeated, – you asked my opinion, and I have given it to you. If you wish to ignore my diagnosis, I wish you would have the decency not to drag me out of my bed to drive thirty miles though the night to deliver it. Is that unreasonable?

– I called you, she hissed, through gritted teeth, – because a baby has been stolen, and I thought you might want to find out from me, rather than the radio.

– No baby has been stolen, he sighed.

– We should at least inform the police.

– Why? he snapped, his patience finally exhausted. – No crime has been committed. Yet. No one has been hurt. Yet. Why inform the police?

– If *you* will not inform the police, she warned him, – then *I* will. I should have done so an hour ago.

– Sister Nuttall, I expressly forbid you to inform the police. Or anyone else, for that matter. Leave that family alone. He is growing up, that is all. It is not a crime. Who else have you informed? he asked, his suspicions suddenly raised.

– I have informed the General Council.

– What?

– It is in the Procedures.

Doctor Humphries buried his head in his hands.

07.28

Your father watched the clock move slowly towards the half-hour. Twenty-eight minutes past. Twenty-nine. At half-past seven precisely he appeared at reception, and the gatekeeper of the babies reluctantly nodded him through. He negotiated a route through trolleys that seemed placed there specifically to impede his progress. Your mother's cubicle was curtained off, but from within he heard the wail of his son. It was unmistakable, different from all the other babies, more vigorous, more highly developed. He pushed back the curtain. A woman, interrupted in the act of removing an engorged breast from her nightie looked up at him, surprised, and told him to piss off. He blushed, apologised and withdrew. He could have sworn that one was your mother's. He had made a mental note – left-hand side, against the far wall. He listened, trying to make out her voice amongst the babble of mothers chatting and cooing. Most of the cubicles were open at the front, and some at the sides too, the women comparing their offspring, swapping stories of labour and delivery, the primagravidae listening reverently to the advice of those on their fourth or fifth. It was an entirely female world, and he did not know where to begin. Only three cubicles remained closed off, and one he had already tried. He stood next to another and called timidly.

– Sue?

No reply. He tried again. There was no door to knock, no bell to push. He could not help but intrude.

– Sue?

– Who? came a tired voice from within.

– Sorry. I'm looking for my wife, and my baby.

– She's not in here, the voice said. – Only me in here. Me and the little one.

– Sorry.

He repeated his performance at the last cubicle, calling your mother's name each time a little louder and more anxious, until the woman in the next bed told him the cubicle was empty. The baby had died. It had been born with no face. He began to feel a growing panic. Then it occurred to him that he was in the wrong ward. There was another, identical ward next door. He went next door. Your mother wasn't there either. Perhaps he was on the wrong floor. Quelling his panic he asked at reception.

– What's her name? sighed the nurse.

– It's a boy, your father said.

The nurse's expression conveyed very well the less than flattering opinion she had formed of your father over the past few hours.

– The mother, she sighed.

– Grundy.

Her expression changed suddenly.

– You're Mr Grundy?

Your father's blood chilled. Something terrible had happened. You were in intensive care. Your mother had had a haemorrhage. You were dead. You had suffered terrible brain damage. You would never walk again.

– What's wrong? he barked.

– We've been looking all over for you, said the nurse. – Where were you?

– About two hundred yards away. Look is something wrong?

– We moved Mrs Grundy to a private room. And Solomon of course.

– Solomon? Who's Solomon?

– The baby. That's what your wife calls him, anyway.

– But they're all right?

– There's no cause for alarm.

Whether with or without cause, your father was by now thoroughly alarmed. Something had happened, and nobody seemed very keen on telling him what. He would sue. Heads would roll. He would . . .

– Doctor Humphries is in with them now, the nurse informed him. – You can talk it over with him if you like. Down the corridor, second on the left.

Your father knocked nervously on the door, and heard scrabbling around on the other side. Finally, the handle turned and the door swung open of its own accord. He peered in and around and it was not until he peered down that he realised that the door had in fact been opened by a child, a small boy, about waist high, who stared at him with a mixture of curiosity and suspicion. Your father was somewhat taken aback. Had he got the wrong room again? He double-checked the name on the board.

– Yes? you enquired.

– Hello, said your father, hesitantly.

– How are you? you asked.

This, you had learned, was a standard conversational gambit.

– I'm fine, replied your father, mystified.

He knew as he spoke that this was a lie. He was not fine at all.

– I've had quite a night, actually, he added.

– Me too, you said, wearily. – They want to take me into care.

– PAUL! came a scream from inside the room. – Thank God! At last! Where have you *been*?

Your father burst past his son, and ran to your mother, and held her tight. Both were in tears. You watched them, fascinated. For a while your father just held her, rocking back and forth, while she sobbed. All the while, however, he was conscious of you, still scrutinising them, your head tilted on one shoulder, your thumb in your mouth. You made your father uneasy. He relaxed his hold. Your mother sniffed and took a deep breath.

– What's happened, Sue? your father begged. – Where's the baby? Where have they taken him?

You shot past him on to the bed, forcibly inserted yourself between the pair of them and dived under your mother's encircling arm, drawing the covers over yourself. From this safe haven, you peered anxiously out at your father.

– Sue, who is this boy? For God's sake, what's going on?

– I don't know, Paul, your mother sobbed, – I don't know at all. It's just been horrible. Thank God you're here. You won't go away again, will you?

– Of course not, he promised her.

You stuck out your tongue. This was too much for your father.

– Look, he snarled, – I don't have time for this right now.

You froze, terrified. Your mother stared at her husband, aghast.

– Paul!

– I'm sorry, he snapped.

– Paul . . .

– I've said I'm sorry. It's been a long night.

– Paul, this is our son.

Now it was your father's turn to freeze. He saw it all instantly. Something terrible had happened to you. Your mother was delirious with grief, or anxiety.

– Sue, he pleaded, – just tell me what's happened.

– Nothing's happened, Paul. This is Solomon.

– Solomon?

You had now buried your head in your mother's lap, and showed no inclination to reveal yourself.

– Solomon. Do you like it? It just sort of . . . came to me. In a flash. We can change it if you like. He had to have a name. I thought that . . .

– It's not the name, your father interrupted.

He stared at her, bewildered. She smiled at him, sheepishly.

– Just tell me what's been going on, he suggested.

So she told him as much as she knew herself, which was as much as anyone knew, and comforted you and stroked your hair while she told your story, so that by the end your wailing had died down to a whimper. Your face, however, buried possessively in her lap as she stroked your hair. Your father listened incredulously. The story struck him as pure fantasy, the sort of fantasy with which a bereaved mother might comfort herself. The world seemed grey and cold and still. What would they do now? They had stood upon the threshold of a new life, and the door had slammed shut in their faces. It was different when adults died. They left you something behind – memories, photographs, letters, even children. They left you something to grieve. But when a baby died it left nothing behind, except a knowledge of what might have been. There was nothing, no one to grieve, just a hole. The loss wasn't the loss of a person, it was the loss of a potential person, a life that might've been lived, and now would never be lived. You were mourning the loss of your own hopes and expectations and fears, and in the end they were all illusions. There was no absence because there had never been a presence. You expected everything to change, and nothing changed. He did not know what he could say that would make it better.

At the same time, the fantasy was miraculously detailed. There was no doubting its consistency, either. When he pointed out apparent contradictions, she was able to resolve them. And if this boy wasn't his son, then where had this boy appeared from? You certainly resembled your mother enough to persuade anyone who saw you together that you were related. And you had obviously formed an intense and alarmingly exclusive attachment to his wife, which was evidently reciprocated. Anybody who saw you together would say 'mother and son'. No sooner had he begun to accept the possibility that your mother's fantasy might have some grounding in the truth, however, than the patent absurdity of it all struck him with renewed clarity. Whichever way he turned he was faced with a frightening situation. Either your mother was right, in which case his son was some sort of freak, or the baby was dead, and your mother had gone off her rocker. He hardly knew which was preferable.

– You don't believe me, do you? she accused.

– I don't know what to believe, he confessed.

– I hardly believe it myself. I keep thinking I'm going to wake up, but I still haven't, and now you're here, and you're included in it, so I don't suppose I ever will. But you haven't seen what I've seen.

– No, he acknowledged.

– And in the end, it doesn't really matter whether I'm mad, or it's all a dream, because when I look at him, I know he's my child. You can't fake that.

But your father was, not listening. He was pacing furiously up and down the room, trying to work it out. Whatever had happened, he had been cheated. His baby was gone, and in its place was someone new, someone he did not recognise, who did not recognise him. His child had gone for ever. He looked at you, and you seemed to know what he was thinking, for you stared him out and your father could not tell if your expression was one of fear or of fury or both. Suddenly he hated you, and wanted to strike you, simply for being so helpless, simply to teach you that there were no rules, that people did as they wished, that if good triumphed from time to time it was nothing more than the law of averages. But he did not strike you.

– Sue, he said, – listen, Sue . . .

She stared into his eyes, trusting him, waiting to hear what he had decided.

– Sue, this is not my son. My son is a baby.

She covered her face with her hands and her head sunk onto her chest. You watched, sucking your thumb in silence, taking it all in. Your mother had been expecting something like this. It was asking too much to expect your father to just accept the situation. She could hardly accept it herself, still had moments of panic when some part of her rebelled against the absurdity of it all, and sought to make sense of this strange child of hers in the banal and pedestrian terms with which a twentieth-century education had equipped her – administrative errors, conspiracies, a mix-up of the files, the wrong bracelet on the wrong wrist. And if she herself still grasped at the straws of explanation, she who had lived through it all, how could she expect your father to do otherwise? It would take time, at the very least, for your father to reconcile himself to something which could not happen and yet which clearly had happened. She must be patient with him, for your sake. Already she sensed an atmosphere of mistrust, even hostility between her husband and her child. They glared at each other as if demanding that the other justify his presence.

– He *is* a baby, she said, simply. – He's my baby, and yours too.

Your father turned away.

– Does it matter anyway? she pleaded. – He's here, he's got no one else. He needs us. Does it matter?

Your father read the notes. It was all in there, everything confirmed. The initial entries were routine – a description of the birth, weights, lengths, times, initials, so bland and matter of fact that he wondered whether he and whoever it was who had written the report had been present at the same event. There was as much space devoted to the emergence of the placenta as the appearance of a new life. After this description, the pen and the handwriting changed, and the text was dotted with question marks. As he turned the pages, the handwriting changed again, and the question marks were supplemented by exclamation marks. The tone too, altered: after the calm administrative jargon of the first entries the authors gradually lost confidence. Evidently, there was no procedural precedent for these reports. Finally, text was abandoned almost entirely in favour of question marks and exclamation marks, and the notes ended in disarray and panic. The word 'urgent' had been underlined three times. He found the graphs on which your height and weight were marked. You started high, but just scraped in at the top of the normal range. Where the normal range increased gradually over the coming year, rising slowly from left to right, your line rose almost vertically. You had gone completely outside the normal range about half an hour after your birth, and had disappeared off the top of the graph half an hour later.

As he read, your father surrendered gradually to helplessness. He was beginning to feel the effects of an uncomfortable, sleepless night, and the unpleasant tingling sensation produced from subsistence on coffee and chocolate. He longed for someone to arrive and take control of it all, to point out the obvious fact that they had all overlooked, that made sense of everything.

Meanwhile, you took advantage of his distraction to peer at the man who had temporarily usurped your mother's affections. You saw a slightly built man, unshaven, with little round glasses, slightly balding on top. The man had shouted at you, and you had every reason to feel hostile. You were used to shouting, people dashing around, frantic hissed exchanges, people bursting in suddenly and dashing off equally as suddenly. Your entire life to this point had been lived at this intensity. But no one had ever shouted at *you* before, putting his face so close up to yours that you could smell his cigarette breath and see the scum on his teeth. Neither had any of the previous visitors embraced your mother like that. With the others, you knew where you were; you were with your mother, they were visiting. They would stay a while and then leave. This new man seemed determined to stay for good. You had taken a profound dislike to your father. You wanted to lash out, to drive him away, but you were old enough to know that your tiny feet and fists, your childish arms and stubby legs, would be no match for this brute. You would have to find some other way to get rid of him. For the moment you must conceal your hostility. Until the time was right.

Finally, Humphries returned.

– Mr Grundy, I presume, he addressed your father.

Your father nodded.

– I'm Dr Humphries.

– The specialist?

– Paediatrician, yes.

Your father suggested they went for a walk around the gardens. It was the only place he was allowed to smoke. It was a bright morning, but cold. The world was returning from its long weekend. There weren't any grounds as such, your father discovered, merely islands of scuffed grass and withered shrubs and the occasional tree planted in random tubs round the various car parks. They found a bench, and your father lit a cigarette.

– Is this a joke? asked Humphries suddenly, turning to fix your father with a hard stare.

Your father was incredulous.

– I thought . . . he stammered, – I thought you were the one who was . . . who knew . . . who was supposed to understand it all . . .

Humphries sighed and shook his head.

– May I ask a frank question?

– Go ahead.

– Is your wife the sort of woman who might think it amusing to do something like this?

– My wife, replied your father, – is bearing the brunt of all this. She does not play jokes at her own expense.

– May I ask another?

– She isn't mad either, if that's what you're thinking.

– Not at all, not at all. But birth is an extraordinary time – physically exhausting, emotionally draining, spiritually overwhelming. Channels are opened between this world and others. It is possible to lose your grip on reality. What is reality, after all? It is less . . . concrete than you think.

– It's certainly a lot less concrete today than it was yesterday, your father acknowledged.

They lapsed into silence again, pursuing their own thoughts.

– What are you going to do? your father asked.

– Me? I don't really see what *I* can do, confessed the specialist. – What would you like me to do?

Your father was stumped.

– Can't you at least say what's gone wrong?

– Has anything gone wrong?

– Everyone else seems to think so.

Humphries composed his thoughts.

– There are four pertinent facts, he began, – each of which is plainly visible to the naked eye. Firstly, the child I saw just now is about six years old. Secondly, he is quite obviously the offspring of the woman who claims to be his mother, who you claim is your wife. Thirdly, there doesn't seem to be anything remotely wrong with him. I could do some tests, if you like?

– What will that achieve?

– It passes the time, said Humphries. – Some people like tests.

– What's the fourth fact?

– Well, before we get to the fourth fact, I'd like to stress exactly how commonplace the first three facts are. There are no end of six-year-olds in the world. Most of them live with their mothers, and a fair few, despite what you might read in the papers, with their fathers. Most are fine and healthy, more or less by definition. The fact we have to account for is that this particular six-year-old was born last night. Is that right?

– What's going on? your father pleaded.

– Well, it's fairly obvious, Humphries declared. – The boy is just growing up much too fast. It's quite miraculous. I've never seen or heard of anything like it. But there's no denying it. I have come across considerable numbers of sick children in my time. Many of them have recovered whilst in my care. Some I may even have cured. I have read a lot of books, even written a few. I know the meaning of words which others struggle merely to pronounce. Every now and then, though, one comes across something that isn't in any of the books. Then what do you do, eh?

He examined the back of his hands.

– Do you know what I would do? he asked. – In your situation?

Your father had no idea. The world had begun to offer up possibilities previously undreamt of. Humphries took him by the arm, and leaned forward conspiratorially.

– This is strictly off the record mind.

– Of course.

– I would get back in that room, pack up your things, take your wife and the boy and clear off while you still can.

Your father was dumbfounded.

– I mean it, warned the doctor. – Go somewhere they can't track you down. I'm afraid that if you don't extricate yourself and your family from this situation pretty sharpish, you will find yourself in deeper than you knew existed. Do you take my meaning?

Your father nodded. He, too, was coming to a decision.

08.24

– I have called this meeting, the secretary resumed, – in accordance with regulation fifty-three, paragraph four.

– What on earth is that? asked Brian Hawkins, mystified.

– Abduction of an infant from the premises.

The assembly instantly stopped fidgeting, and gave her their full attention.

– A serious matter then, Hawkins observed.

– Oh, do let the girl finish, snapped Dame Barbara Hershkovitz. – Some of us have proper jobs to get to.

The secretary glared at Dame Barbara. She did not appreciate being referred to as a girl. She cleared her throat and continued.

– It would appear that a new-born baby, by the name of Grundy, was abducted sometime during the early hours of this morning.

The Council was stunned.

– Where from? asked Brian Hawkins, eventually.

– From the hospital, said the secretary.

– Yes, but from where in the hospital?

– From the maternity ward, presumably, Khan saved her the trouble of answering.

Hawkins was relieved. Not his department at all. Percy Burns whistled through his teeth.

– Have you informed the police? he asked.

– They are with the mother even now. And a social worker.

– Grundy? queried Hawkins, – what sort of a name is that? Is it Turkish or something?

No one answered.

– I think, said Dame Barbara Hershkovitz. – We'd better wait for Sir John.

08.51

Your mother wanted desperately to sleep, and knew that she had to sleep if she were to have any chance of fighting off the doctors and the social workers who swarmed round her child like wasps round a rotting plum. They had the advantage over her: they worked in shifts; first one then the other. Where one approach failed they could withdraw, take stock, regroup, try another. But she had the advantage of being prepared, more or less obliged, to fight to the death. For them, it was only a job. They were bound by procedures and regulations. She was not. If they assumed she would just roll over and let them do as they wished, they would be forced to rethink. She had certainly sent that social worker away to lick her wounds.

Rubbing your eyes, you pushed yourself away from your mother and sat up.

– Do you want your bottle? she asked you.

You nodded.

– Here you go, darling.

She removed the top of the bottle, filled it with juice from the jug, refastened the top and handed it back to you. You took a long, deep draught and she watched. There was no denying it – you were a baby no longer, not even a toddler, but a child, with your own wishes and feelings and opinions, which were as yet one and the same. You had a phenomenal appetite. You drank in sleep as if your continued life depended upon its sustenance. Everything about you was somehow desperate. As you drank, you watched her from the corner of your eye. Why? Were you worried she might slip away while you were otherwise occupied? Or simply curious to see what she might do next? She knew you were observing, taking it all in, working it all out, but what were you thinking? You said nothing.

She waited for your father, without much confidence that he would return with any solutions. What could she reasonably expect from him? He hadn't carried you inside him for nine whole months, hadn't felt you daily draw nourishment from his body as she had. No wonder he was disoriented, confused, unsure of where to turn. Who should he believe? The experts, who handled thousands of babies a day, or his wife, who was quite new to all this? But she had to know, one way or the other. Either he was with her or he wasn't. He had to decide, to make a leap of faith, now, one way or the other. If he couldn't make that leap of faith, that commitment, then she wanted to know now. You had not got off to a very promising start, father and son. You didn't seem to like each other very much, seemed wary of each other, frightened even. That was something your father would have to work on, and he would have to start soon. Better no father at all than a father who ummed and erred about it, a father who couldn't make up his mind if he was a joint parent or simply a vague relation of some sort. She would confront him with it when he returned: choose now, one way or the other. There were human beings involved – children even. It was better to make the wrong choice than no choice at all. Where human beings were concerned there weren't right choices and wrong choices anyway. You made the choice, then you made it work. If you didn't make the choice, it could never work. It was too important to straddle. It wasted everybody's time, and that was the worst thing you could do to people, because, in the end, it was all they had. If your father could not make that leap of faith, it would be better if he cleared off altogether.

Then suddenly he was back. She could tell by the look on his face that there was no need to turn the screws: he had come to some form of resolution already. You looked up from your drink but gave no sign of affection, or even recognition.

– We're leaving, your father announced. – I'll pack your things. Here – he threw her a dressing gown – put this on.

It landed on the bed. She stared at it, blankly. The idea of movement, of getting up from the bed, was quite beyond her.

– Are you coming or aren't you? he wanted to know.

– Of course, I'm coming, it's just . . .

– Well, come on then. We're going home.

You stopped sucking on your bottle, and peered at your father suspiciously. Your mother swung her legs over the bed. Your father had already crammed everything that was not screwed to the wall into a carrier bag.

– What did Humphries say then? your mother asked.

– He said scram, your father filled her in. – I'll explain on the way. Come on, Solomon.

He was in the doorway now, his hand on the knob. You returned to your drink.

– What if they stop us? your mother asked.

– How? How can they stop us?

She had no idea how the authorities could stop them leaving. She presumed, however, that there would be some regulation that would allow them to do so. But they would not know until they found out.

– Come on, darling, she called to you.

You remained, however, bottle up, immobile and impassive on the bed, scrutinising them from the corner of your eye.

– You'll have to carry him, Paul.

Your father approached, his arms outstretched. You scampered to the far end of the bed, where you pressed yourself against the headboard and stared at him. There was a look in your eye – your father could not make out whether it was defiance or simply terror.

– It's all right, mate, he tried to reassure you, – we're going home. Out of here. You'll like it.

– He doesn't know where home is, Paul. All he knows is here.

– C'mon, mate.

He went decisively to lift you. You sank your teeth into his arm.

– Aaaaaarrrghhhh.

Your father withdrew, clutching his damaged limb.

– You better take him, Sue, he winced.

Your mother approached now, forcing herself to smile. You backed even further into the headboard.

– Not going, you hissed. – Not with him.

A terrible presentiment of doom welled up inside her.

– We can't just drag him out, your mother said, – if he doesn't want to come.

Your father groaned and approached once again.

– Look, Solomon, he growled, menacingly, – we're going home, and it's going to be nice and you're coming with us.

– NO! NO! NO!

You gripped the bedstead.

– You're coming with us because we love you, all right? your father shouted into your face. – They don't love you. We love you. Daddy loves you and Mummy loves you. NOW GET OFF THAT FUCKING BED.

Your mother grabbed his shoulder.

– That's not going to help, is it? she chided him. – He's frightened of you. You can't force people into not being afraid.

For a terrible moment, your mother thought he was going to hit someone. Then he sat down on the bed and buried his face in his hands. No one seemed to appreciate the urgency of the situation. They didn't have time to reason with a day-old baby. How could you reason with a day-old baby?

– Well, you think of something then, he ordered his wife.

– Come on, Solomon, she said. – Let's see if we can find some . . . some . . . surprises.

– What sort of surprises?

You stared at her, dubious.

– They're nice surprises, she promised.

– OK, you said.

You slithered down from the bed.

– Daddy will carry you.

– No! you yelled, emphatically. – I'll walk.

– OK, said your father, relieved. – Fine, OK, whatever. You walk. Let's go.

Your father opened the door and peered up and down the corridor. A nurse sat at the desk. Otherwise, all was deserted. He had already reached the swing doors by the time he realised his family was no longer with him. You had been distracted by something. Your mother was urging you on, without success, and gesticulating frantically at her husband. The nurse looked up from her novel.

– Come on, er, Ryan, urged your mother. – You can bring the magazine with you.

– I'm not Ryan, you reminded her. – I'm Solomon. What's that called?

You were pointing at a picture.

– It's, er, I don't know. Some sort of medical thingy. They stick it up you. Come on, darling.

– Don't be silly, you laughed.

– Come on come on come on come on, Paul hissed.

The nurse watched.

– He won't come, said your mother.

– Stick it up you, you crowed, delighted. – Stick it up Mummy! Stick it up Daddy!

– Right.

Your father strode back down the corridor, grabbed you and yanked you into the air.

– Put me down, put me down, put me down, you yelled.

– It's for your own good, your father told you.

The nurse half rose from her chair. Your father turned towards her.

– You shut up and sit down, he told her, with such menace in his voice that she did.

You were far from persuaded that being hoisted into the air was for your own good. Your father carried you, kicking and scratching, towards the double doors. He was amazed at your ferocity, at your weight and strength. Your mother watched nervously.

– Put me down! Put me down! you wailed miserably.

The doors swung open and the social worker in the striped dungarees and a uniformed policewoman blocked your father's path.

– Excuse me, said the social worker, – but where do you think you're going?

– None of your business, snapped your father, trying to force his way past them.

The doorway, however, was too narrow, and your squirming and struggling did not help.

– I think you'd better put the boy down, sir, suggested the policewoman. – He doesn't seem to want to go with you.

Janice Black caught sight of your mother, who was watching her presentiments fall neatly into place.

– Mrs Grundy, she called. – Who is this man? Do you know him?

– He's my husband, your mother replied weakly.

She hardly recognised him any more.

– You can't just walk out like this, you know, said the social worker, more placatory.

– Can't we, snapped your father. – Who says? Who's going to stop us? You? Who the fuck are *you*? Aaaaarrrrrrggggghhhh.

You had taken advantage of your father's momentary distraction, and finally managed to position your teeth close enough to his ear to lock your jaws on to it.

– Put him down, eh? suggested the policewoman.

Your father dropped you awkwardly. You scampered back to your mother. She caught you, and lifted you up into the air. From this position you regarded the three adults in the doorway in triumph.

– Sod this, spat your father in disgust, and he had barged between the two professionals and was away down the stairs before they had time to decide whether or not to try to stop him.

– Paul! your mother screamed. – Paul! Come back!

– Daddy's gone, you told her, – and he's not coming back. I bit him.

Janice ushered you back into the little room.

10.36

Tony Bowles had graduated confident in the knowledge that newspapers consisted of news reports illustrated by pictures. Page after page of dense type, sixteen columns to the page, was simply too monotonous for the human brain. You had to make some concessions to human frailty and laziness. Three years on the Pilsbury *Evening Sentinel*, however, had convinced Tony Bowles that an entirely different process was at work. Despite their undoubted ingenuity, the design people could not realistically be expected to tessellate their motley selection of photographs and advertisements in such a way as to ensure that they filled all the available space. Text, being essentially fluid, could be used to fill in the gaps, as one might pour beaten eggs over lumps of vegetable to prepare a Spanish omelette. The public was led to believe that the journalists found the stories, the photographers took pictures to illustrate the stories, the design people laid it all out, and the advertising people filled in the spaces. That was how it was designed to look. In reality, the advertising people provided the copy, the layout people arranged the advertisements, the photographers filled the big spaces and the journalists poured over the beaten egg that set it all into a single omelette. The text existed simply because the newspaper-buying public felt cheated if their newspaper contained blank spaces. (Why they felt cheated, when most of them only bought the paper to find out what was on at the pictures anyway, he couldn't fathom, but his editor assured him it was so.)

All in all it was bloody hard to be Tony Bowles. It was hard to be a professional on a newspaper run by amateurs. It was hard to be an urban sophisticate on a newspaper read by rednecks. It was hard to be a man of words in a society that was barely literate. It was hard to be a black man in a town where eating curry was considered liberal. Most of all it was hard to be Tony Bowles because you had to work with Chalkie White. Was it just coincidence they had given him a photographer called Chalkie White? Or did someone somewhere think it was funny? It was hard not to be paranoid in a place like Pilsbury. Chalkie White thought it was funny. He sang 'Ebony and Ivory' as they drove to and from stories, and called Tony 'Smokey'. When Tony asked him, politely, not to, he said it was just a nickname, like 'Chalkie'. It didn't mean anything, it was just a name, there was no need to get touchy. It meant no harm.

– You people are so touchy, said Chalkie White.

Many times he had asked Brian if he could be assigned a different photographer.

– Best there is, Brian claimed, unconvincingly.

– He's an asshole, Tony pointed out. – And a racist.

– He doesn't mean any harm. That's just how he is. It's his generation.

– Yeah, yeah.

– My best reporter, my best photographer.

Chalkie White was apparently the best photographer in Pilsbury. The other ones must have left the lens cap on, or forgotten to put any film in the camera. Or perhaps they forgot to bring a camera at all.

This particular morning, Chalkie White was in characteristically high spirits and smelled characteristically of stale beer and urinals. Brian fidgeted with a pencil, which snapped suddenly.

– What have you got this morning then? Chalkie asked him.

– Right up your street this one, Tony, said Brian. – Human interest story. A baby.

Tony Bowles groaned audibly.

– Good oh, beamed Chalkie White, – I'll get me gear.

He departed, whistling.

– He's gone to buy a film, explained Tony Bowles.

– Do make an effort, Tony, Brian urged. – It's a small town, Pilsbury. One day, when you're rich and famous on the London broadsheets you'll be bloody glad you learnt your trade at the hands of old pros like Chalkie.

– What's this baby then? A special baby or just a baby baby?

– You're obviously not a parent, Tony.

– Just a baby baby then?

– Not at all. Would I send my top man to get the low-down on a just a baby baby?

– So what does this baby do? Play the piano? Read palms? Eat nails?

– It won't stop growing.

Tony Bowles was puzzled.

– Is there any reason why it should? I thought that was more or less all they did. That's why Chalkie likes taking their pictures. They don't move. He can't stand it when things move. He has to start all over again.

– It was born last night, Brian reported. – By dawn it was walking and talking. By now it'll be about four foot tall and still growing. Real Jack and the Beanstalk stuff.

– It doesn't play the piano though.

– I kid you not.

– A pity. And who, may I ask, is your source for this earth-shattering piece of claptrap?

– My sister-in-law. She works at the hospital. On the switch-board.

– Ttttsssssssss, hissed Tony Bowles.

– I know I know. I don't want to know. Just check it out, will you?

Chalkie White reappeared in the doorway with a holdall and an attaché case.

– We off then? Your car or mine?

Chalkie White drove towards the hospital. Tony Bowles, in the passenger seat, attempted to minimise the area of his freshly-cleaned suit in contact with the fabric of Chalkie's ancient Cavalier. It was a lose-lose situation. Either Tony's car ended up smelling of Chalkie, or Tony ended up smelling of Chalkie's car. This way was marginally preferable. Afterwards, he could go home, change his suit, have a shower, put on some after-shave and the smell of Chalkie's car would be so faint as to be unattributable in company. The technology that might rid his car of the smell of Chalkie had not yet been invented. He could have suggested they each take their own cars, but that sort of creative thinking was frowned upon in the big happy family that was the *Sentinel*. It got you a reputation for being too big for your boots. People like Chalkie White understood it to mean that you considered yourself too good to be seen with them. That this was an entirely accurate diagnosis of his motivations did not diminish Tony Bowles' irritation at this attitude. Anyway, Brian wouldn't pay expenses for both cars when they could have got away with just the one. The price to be endured was to sit in the passenger seat trying to find somewhere to place his shoes amongst the discarded chip wrappers, porn magazines and soft-drink cans that had accumulated on, in and under the dashboard. It might politely have been referred to as a bachelor's car, but Tony Bowles was a bachelor too, and his car wasn't like this: that was why he was loath to allow Chalkie White into it. Was Chalkie White a slob because he was a bachelor or was he a bachelor because he was a slob? He was a bachelor because he was Chalkie White. No woman in their right mind would get into this car with this man, even professionally.

Chalkie White was driving with one hand and filling his pipe with the other.

– Of course, he said, – they won't let us in just like that.

– Surely you can wangle us in?

Tony had never attended a function where Chalkie White did not know the security guard or the head waiter.

– Not this one, Chalkie admitted. – Not the hospital. They're very choosy at the hospital. You don't want to go making enemies at the hospital.

Tony Bowles was fascinated. There was a group of people whom even Chalkie White held in awe – nurses. You didn't want to get on the wrong side of the local nurses, especially if you were fifty something and smoked like a Rumanian power station.

– No strings to pull here then?

– It's like a bleeding nunnery. They don't even let the husbands in without blood tests and marriage certificates. And let's face it, no ones gonna need a blood test to see that you're not the father.

They had arrived at the car park. Chalkie leaned over, conspiratorially.

– The only men allowed in the maternity ward, he confided, as if revealing a great secret, – apart from the fathers, and them reluctantly, are the doctors. And the undertakers.

Tony Bowles was sceptical.

– Trust me, said Chalkie, – I know.

– Why are you telling me this?

– Put this on.

They had stopped. Chalkie White rummaged in the holdall on the back seat and produced two of the filthiest lab coats Tony Bowles had ever seen.

– It's filthy, observed Tony Bowles.

– Authentic, Chalkie corrected. – I'll be Doctor White, you can be . . . Doctor Smokey.

– This is mad.

– Trust me. Trust me.

– I don't trust you. Not an inch.

The lab coat smelled as if it had spent the last decade in a laundry basket full of rancid underwear and soiled sheets. It probably had. Tony Bowles inspected it with obvious disgust.

– It won't hurt you, said Chalkie.

– I'd like that in writing.

– Oh, come on.

– I have grave doubts about this.

– Spare us the fucking ethics, do. This is Pilsbury, mate.

– Chalkie, it's not a question of ethics. It's a question of hygiene.

– Are you coming or aren't you?

Reluctantly, the Voice of Pilsbury adopted his ridiculous disguise.

10.40

Within minutes of his dramatic arrival on the roof of Pilsbury General Hospital, Sir John Parker was taking command of the boardroom. The Council breathed an almost audible sigh of relief. The testimonies they had received from Sister Nuttall and Dr Humphries, far from illuminating the events of the past twelve hours, had plunged them into deeper obscurity. The security man Parker was no help at all and the Council were confused as to whether they were dealing with a serious crime or a medical freak, whether they were the victims of an elaborate hoax, or whether one or two of their staff were in need of an extended holiday and some form of expensive therapy.

– This had better be bloody important, Sir John warned them as he strode into the room, removing his coat as he went and tossing it on a chair.

– You won't be disappointed on the seriousness stakes, I assure you, Percy Burns assured him.

Sir John flung him a contemptuous glance and took his place at the head of the table. Strictly speaking there was no head of the table, it being a circular table, but wherever Sir John sat instantly became the head. No one spoke. The Council shuffled uneasily. They really had no more idea what was going on than he did, and did not want their heads bitten off for their ignorance. Sir John scanned the faces round the table.

– Professor Khan, you tell me. What's up?

– We don't rightly know, confessed Khan, nervously. – Sister Nuttall called us here because a baby had been stolen but Dr Humphries assured us this abduction has not in fact taken place.

– The baby has been found?

– No, cried Sister Nuttall. – The baby has not been found, and is not likely to be either whilst Dr Humphries continues to deny that it has been lost at all.

– If I find I've been dragged back here because someone's miscounted the babies again, warned Sir John, – heads will roll. Humphries, what's your story? From the top.

Wearily, Humphries recounted the events of the past few hours.

– Sister Nuttall paged me about three o'clock last night, saying somebody had taken a baby from maternity and substituted a toddler. By the time I got here the wretched Procedures had been put into operation and the social workers were crawling all over it. I went to see the mother and found her with a third child, about four years old. The question is whether these three children are in fact three different children, in which case something absolutely bizarre and quite sinister is going on, or whether they are three different manifestations of the same child. In which case something equally bizarre is going on.

Sir John tried to decipher the gibberish he had just been fed.

– About as weird as they come, observed Percy Burns.

– We'd better take a look, he decided at last.

11.03

There was nothing to do in this little room. The nurses brought you toys, but they were baby toys, and all very much the worse for wear. The little cars had had doors wrenched off, the dolls were missing eyes and arms and hair. The teddy bears leaked stuffing. You had grown out of these things, anyway, the things you did on floors – the bricks, the bears, the little cars. You had sunk into a deep lethargic despondency, and sat listlessly flicking through *Modern Parent*.

– You're not going to let us go, are you? your mother suspected.

– It would be better for you to stay here for the time being, Mrs Grundy, confirmed the social worker.

– Am I being *advised* to stay here or *obliged* to?

– We want to do what's best for the child, said the policewoman. – We can't stop you leaving if you're really determined.

– Right, said your mother. – Come on then, Solomon.

– Only the boy, the social worker continued, – he stays here until all this is sorted out.

– It's the law, said the policewoman.

– What's the law?

– We are, said the social worker.

The door was pushed open to reveal two very disreputable-looking doctors.

– Yes? asked the policewoman.

They hesitated in the doorway. The younger pushed the elder forward.

– I'm Doctor White, he introduced himself, – and this is Doctor Smokey.

There was an awkward pause.

– And?

– We've come to . . . ask some questions, and take some photographs and things.

– Photographs? queried the social worker, – what do you need photographs for?

– Special medical photographs, Dr White explained.

– Well, you'd better come in then, said the social worker.

They shuffled nervously into the room. You barely looked up. You were beginning to seriously regret not having gone with your father while you had the chance. The horizons of your world seemed hopelessly limited. Ever since you could remember you had been in this room. You were aware of another world, outside the window, a world full of buildings and people. Your mother told you it was called Pilsbury and it was where you lived. She told you that one day you would go back there. But you had never been there before. You couldn't go back to somewhere you'd never been. The only place you'd ever been was in this room with your mother. Other people came and went, so many you stopped noticing. At first, you had been interested – perhaps one of them would take you and your mother somewhere else, with new things to play with and new things to look at. But the only one who had tried to had frightened you, and you had bitten him.

– Smile! called Dr White.

You looked up, but did not smile. A light flashed and splodges of red and purple swum in front of your eyes.

– Cheer up! he exhorted.

The light flashed again. Dr White nudged his partner.

– Dr Smokey's got a few questions, and then we'll be off, he told the gathering.

Tony Bowles felt ridiculous. It was humiliating. But he was here now.

– So, er, how old is . . . he? he asked your mother.

She glanced up at the clock.

– About ten hours, she said wearily. – Look I've been through all this too many times today. Why don't you just read the notes?

– You don't mind?

– When you've spent the night with other people's rubber gloves up your fanny, sighed your mother, and the morning fighting off people who've come to take your child into care, privacy begins to seem very relative.

The social worker blushed. As he read, Tony Bowles' eyes

grew wider and wider. The child before his eyes really had been born last night. It was miraculous. It was the news event of the decade and it was right here under his nose, on his patch, in Pilsbury. Chalkie White was trying to persuade you to clamber up on to the bed with your mother, which you showed no inclination to do. Or at least to smile. He was pulling funny faces, but you failed to realise, his funny faces being no more or less grotesque than the one he had adopted as his own. You stared at him, saying nothing but conveying through your wordless gloom exactly how you felt. This, however, was not good enough for Tony Bowles. It was fine for a photo. You could be as inarticulate as you wanted in a photo, but Tony Bowles needed words. Only a few, it didn't matter what they were, but words.

– Can you put your feelings into words? he asked you.

– No, you replied. – Can you?

– Excuse me, asked the policewoman, – but what kind of a doctor are you exactly?

Tony Bowles thought fast.

– I'm a . . . psychiatrist, he told her.

– And your friend?

Tony looked over at Chalkie, who was busily snapping away from as many angles as possible in the hope that one would come out all right. His subject sat there morosely, barely tolerating him.

– He's a . . .

What sort of a doctor could Chalkie White possibly be? He was clambering up on to a chair now, in an attempt to find a new angle on the story.

– He's a . . .

Chalkie wobbled. The chair was obviously far from stable. He steadied himself against the wall.

– He's a . . .

– Yes?

– Whooops, said Chalkie White, grinning embarrassedly.

– He's a complete dickhead.

The door burst open and in marched the General Council of Pilsbury General Hospital, with Sir John Parkes at the head. There was barely room for them all, and they stood packed together two-deep down the sides of the bed, craning over each other's shoulders for a glimpse of the strange phenomenon. The phenomenon, however, was nowhere to be seen.

– Come in, come in, all of you, sang the phenomenon's mother, bitterly. – Make yourselves at home.

Eventually the fidgeting and shuffling ceased. Sir John introduced himself personally and the Council collectively. Your mother caught Humphries' eye. He was standing at the back, trying to make himself inconspicuous.

– I did warn you, he mouthed.

Perched precariously on one arm of the chair, Chalkie White had just found the perfect angle when the invasion blocked his view. He tried to get down, but there was nowhere to put his feet. He remained perched on the chair, his head several feet above all the others. He looked down on the tops of their heads. It was a lovely shot. He couldn't resist it.

– What on earth are you doing? Sir John bellowed, his eyes swimming in blues and purples.

– Leaving, Tony Bowles replied.

Sir John turned his attention to this unfamiliar doctor in a filthy lab coat.

– And who the blazes are you anyway?

– Hang on, said the policewoman. – I thought you looked familiar. You're from the paper, aren't you? That stupid column.

On another occasion, Tony Bowles might have stayed to defend the integrity of his column. Right now, he had a story to file. The biggest story he had ever filed. Perhaps the biggest story anyone had ever filed, anywhere. He didn't need these people any more. He was out of here. He was out of Pilsbury. Fleet Street beckoned.

– I'm Doctor Smokey, he said. – This is Doctor Dickhead. We were just leaving.

– Wait for me, called Doctor Dickhead.

– You're not going anywhere, matey, said the policewoman.

Chalkie White tried once again to descend on to terra firma, but the chair toppled over. He fell, together with his cameras, on to your mother, who doubled up in agony. Tony Bowles took advantage of the chaos to make his escape. Chalkie could fend for himself. But his arm was gripped. He wheeled round and stared into the face of Percy Burns.

– We meet again, said Percy Burns.

– I didn't mean it, pleaded Tony Bowles desperately. – It was nothing personal. It's just my job.

– And this, said Percy Burns, – is mine.

No one noticed you leaving. You prised your way out through the packed legs until you stumbled through the door into the open again. Smooth, high walls disappeared off into the distance, from whence were carried clatterings and snatches of conversation, and laughter. It was vaguely familiar. There was nobody around. Excitement and fear pushed you onwards and held you back. You wanted to explore, but a tightness at the back of your throat and a cold chill down your back warned you of danger. You decided to return to your mother for reassurance before proceeding any further, and turned back into the forest of legs. The forest however was no longer static. From the midst came a crash, and shouting. You burst into tears, but no arm descended from the sky to scoop you up and hold you tight, no comforting face appeared. Instead, the door slammed in your face. You were left alone in the passage. You felt your heart pounding, but were too terrified to scream. From further up the corridor came footsteps. Someone was coming. The social worker. Coming to take you away. Hide. There was nowhere to hide. Footsteps getting louder. Quick. In here.

The nurse wheeled the trolley down to the laundry. It seemed heavier than usual, but trolleys always seemed heavier at the end of a shift than at the beginning. She noticed a commotion – doctors and nurses running round in a blind panic, opening all the doors, checking the roofs and the lifts – but she was used to commotion. It made them feel important. Two policemen asked if she'd seen a small boy, and she pointed out as politely as she could that the hospital was full of small boys. She suggested they try the children's wards, where they would be certain to find several, and they hurried off.

It was the last trolley of the day, but no sooner had she deposited it in the laundry than she was called back up to the ward. There was an emergency. They had lost a small boy.

– How small? she asked

– No one knows, replied the Sister.

It was too ridiculous. She volunteered to search the laundry, but slipped out the fire door and caught the bus home.

11.15

When next you dared open your eyes, you were enveloped in a pile of laundry, your limbs twisted and knotted within the sheets and lab coats. There was a sweet, sickly smell and you felt patches of body fluid against your skin. Again, you burst into tears, but there was no one to hear you. Realising this, you kicked and struggled some more, and managed to poke your head through into the warm damp air of the basement laundry, which throbbed with the beat of the washers. One hand free, it was easy to disengage the other, until you could pull yourself clear. There was no one about. The room was dominated by eight enormous washing machines that rocked and spun alarmingly. Other than these, it contained only laundry, mountains of it. There were no windows, and the walls and floor were concrete, cold and damp to the touch. For the first time in your life you were alone. It was a strange and troubling sensation. No one was watching. No one even knew you were here at all. You had no idea where you were, or how you had got there. You knew only that you had no desire to remain there. You wanted your mother. Thankfully, the door was not locked, but led into a dark corridor with stone steps at either end. You had not seen steps before, but some instinct told you that up was the only way out. There was no alternative anyway. Thick silver pipes along the ceiling dripped water. Which way? You chose left. The pipes gurgled around you as you passed, and the air was full of the rumble of the machines. With the help of the handrail you climbed the steps. At the top, another choice – double doors? Or more stairs? You pushed the doors and they opened a crack. Now you were in another corridor, but one more familiar. It was wider, higher, cleaner, with chairs down one side.

– There he is!

Two burly men were striding towards you, pointing. You ducked back through the doors and scampered up another flight of stairs. The door crashed open below you, the footfalls were rapid on the stone steps; heavy breathing and muffled threats. Another landing. Through the double doors you found yourself in yet another corridor. Directly opposite, an open door revealed a room full of beds. No sound. Subdued lights. It seemed deserted. You heard the men right behind you and threw yourself under the nearest bed. There was scarcely room for you amongst a jumble of carrier bags and coats. From this vantage point, you saw two pairs of legs enter the room. The legs came together in a huddle.

– He's in here somewhere, growled a voice. – You take the door. I'll start at the far end.

The legs separated. You felt your heart pounding, your mouth dry, your limbs trembling. You tried to bury yourself deeper into the plastic bags, but they rattled and clinked as you clambered amongst them. The footsteps stopped ominously, and you froze solid again. After a while, they started up again, and from further up the ward came the sound of beds being wheeled away from walls, hopeless and muffled protests, cupboard doors opening and slamming shut, curtains being whisked back. Occasionally the legs came into view along the tunnel of your vision, and then disappeared again. The noises were building to a crescendo. The legs reappeared, almost next to you, so close that you could reach out and touch them. The cupboard next to your head was opened. You could see your face reflected in the shiny black boots. The bottles clinked. The knees bent. You closed your eyes, tightened yourself into a ball and felt a warm liquid running down your thighs.

– What in heaven's name is going on here?

You did not dare open your eyes.

– Well? demanded the voice again, insistent and outraged.

But it was not addressed to you. You realised that it came from somewhere else. It was a different voice, a woman's voice. You peeked out from behind your hands. The knees had straightened again.

– What have you done to my ward?

– We were looking for the boy, growled a voice directly above your head.

– You will replace every single bed that you have moved, the voice instructed. – You will pick up every last object that you have displaced. You will return this ward to a pristine state, and then you will leave and not return.

– We have orders to find the boy, came another voice.

– He ran in here, added the growl.

– You now have orders to the contrary, the voice pointed out. – These are my patients and I will not have them treated like articles of furniture.

You heard footfalls, the squeaking of bed wheels, the closing of cupboards, muttered apologies. The swish of curtains, but this time slower, accompanied by grumbles. For what seemed an eternity you waited, until the voice bellowed once more, and with finality.

– Now out! Out!

You saw the legs pass once again in front of the bed, heard the ward doors creak shut behind them. All was still. You were breathing again. A voice wheezed.

– You can come out now.

You collapsed sobbing into the bedclothes. An arm came around your shoulder, and a kind voice whispered into your ear.

– There, there. It's over now. All gone away. All gone.

But it was not your mother's voice at all. Neither was it your mother's arm – it was thinner, bony, dry and mottled. Gingerly, you lifted your gaze. The face that it met was unlike any you had ever seen before: pale and stretched taut over the skull beneath, the scalp naked but for a few tatty wisps of fine grey hair. The skin was blotched and peeling, lips grey, eyes sunken. But the face smiled and, knowing somehow that it meant you no harm, you stretched out a hand to touch it.

– Who are you? you asked

– I'm Gloria, she said. – Who are you?

You did not know how to answer, and frowned.

– What's your name? she asked again.

Still no response. She decided not to pursue the issue. You stared at the face, and Gloria smiled back. She offered you a Digestive. It tasted good. You washed it down with orange squash, and took another.

– Who are you hiding from? she asked.

You remembered, and drew closer to her.

– Men, you whispered.

– Climb up here and let's have a look at you.

You climbed up on the bed. Suddenly the bedclothes were racked by a fit of coughing. Startled, you scampered to the far end. Eventually the fit subsided, and she opened her eyes again. You watched, horrified and fascinated, until she had recovered, before demanding

– Where's Mummy?

She laughed.

– I'm sure I don't know, love, she said. – Is she somewhere in the hospital?

You gazed at her, perplexed. Where else could she be? You looked around. You were surrounded by a terrible silence, broken only by coughs and groans. The room contained two rows of beds. Every bed contained a body. Attached to each body by a rubber tube were bottles hanging from metal frames. Some bodies were connected to machines, upon which needles flickered and lights flashed. The beds were partitioned into cubicles by tall, pink curtains. Some of these were closed. You went across the aisle and pulled one back. Inside was a bed like all the others. The body in the bed, like all the other bodies, was almost motionless – only the chest rose and fell, rose and fell, and the fingers twitched and the machine hummed.

– Who are all these people? you asked, bewildered. – Why don't they speak? Why do they sleep with their eyes open?

Gloria sighed, and took your hand.

– They got nothing to say, love. Old and weak and fed through little tubes. Now stop asking questions for a minute and try to answer a few.

But the process foundered before it had even got off the

ground. With a little prompting you knew your name, but that was more or less all.

– How old are you? Do you know that?

You shrugged. The question was incomprehensible. You realised you weren't being much help, and told her all you knew about yourself.

– I was with my mummy but there was a . . . something happened. I hid.

You stared at her, hopefully, and now it was her turn at incomprehension.

– Where do you live, lovie?

– With my mummy.

– Yes, but where, lovie? In Bibbley? Pute? Moss Green? Berry? Hamble Hill?

The names went on. Though the words were unfamiliar to you, you liked the sounds so much that when Gloria's geographical imagination ran dry you clapped your hands and shouted – More! More!

But Gloria did not oblige. She could no longer avoid the conclusion that there was something seriously wrong, something vaguely eerie even, about you. She wondered if concealing your whereabouts from the authorities had been a mistake. It just went against her instincts to turn people in, especially children. When a small, near-naked boy hurtled into the ward and dived under the bed, closely followed by those strapping great bullies in uniform, her instincts told her to shut up, to say nothing, to play dead. (It was easy enough to play dead in this ward.) Children didn't run from those who mean them well – children didn't even run from those who meant them ill, more was the pity. Now here you were half-naked on the bed and unashamed, talking gobbledegook. You did not seem handicapped in any way: you were quick and lively and took things in. Perhaps you had lost your memory?

– When you last saw your mother, she asked, – where was it?

You could not answer.

– Tell me about the room. Was it like this one?

– No, you told her, – smaller. Only one bed.

– Who was there?

– Mummy. Doctor Dickhead. Other people, lots of people.

The memory caused you to shudder, and to check your surroundings again, but there was no movement beyond the deep rhythms of laboured breathing and the bleeping of machines. She noticed your anxiety.

– Who's Doctor Dickhead, lovie?

– He takes photographs

– What sort of photographs?

– Special medical photographs.

Why were you half-naked? Had appalling things been done to you by someone, somewhere? Had you been locked in a cupboard, or kept chained in a kennel somewhere and fed dog-food – she knew there were children like that – or had you been beaten and raped? Or drugged? She did not know what to do.

– What did it smell like, this room?

– Same as everywhere, you shrugged.

– What did it sound like?

– Crying. People crying all the time.

– Crying, what sort of crying?

– Crying crying.

– Show me.

You tried to remember. Suddenly you could hear it vividly.

– Waaaahhhhh!

The doors of the ward swung open, and you saw, for the first time, the owner of the bellow. You had time only to notice that she was arguing with the same two men before you were bundled off the bed and on to the floor. Instinctively, you shot back under. The bedframe rattled as Gloria coughed and retched above you.

– I have already had my ward thrown into confusion once this morning, the owner of the bellow was saying. – These patients are frail and very poorly, Mr Parker. I shall ask them if they have any idea of this boy's whereabouts, but I will not allow you to go charging in again like yetis to throw things around as if my ward were some sort of car-boot sale.

There was a pause, and then the voice came louder and more distinct.

– Now, has anybody seen a small boy about? How tall did you

say he was? . . . About so tall, in the last half-hour? Has he been
in here?

No sound but Gloria's retching. Coughs and groans and bleeps.
You waited, throat dry.

– For the last time . . . Thank you.

A huge hand dragged you from under the bed, and hoisted you
into the air. You bit it, but the arm held you tighter, squeezing all
the air from your lungs. You kicked and flailed, overcome with
anger and grief, but your struggles had only the effect of tilting
you until you were quite upside down. From this position you saw
a pale, thin arm extending from one of the beds. It was pointing
towards you. Gloria was doubled up on the bed, heaving. The
Sister was shouting for assistance. The blood rushed to your
head, and you passed out.

12.14

Your grandfather had arrived during your absence. He had been
alerted by a garbled message on his answerphone, and had driven
directly down from London, stopping only to purchase a bunch
of flowers and a magnum of champagne. He received from a
grateful hospital the task of attempting to calm your mother,
with the aid of mild sedatives. Your grandfather was a man for
whom confusion was constitutionally uncomfortable, and he had
not been remotely prepared for the scene that confronted him
on his arrival. The hospital was swarming with police, porters
and goodness-knows-who-else apparently engaged in a desperate
search for an escaped felon, or lunatic. He had finally located
his daughter and new-born grandson, only to learn that his
son-in-law had gone AWOL, his grandson had been temporarily
misplaced – misplaced! – and his daughter was hysterical. Despite
your grandfather's distaste for strong emotion, this seemed an
entirely reasonable attitude in the circumstances. Your mother,
meanwhile, had ranted about his grandson not being normal,
about social workers wanting to take him away, about tests. His

son-in-law had predictably been completely useless, and had now
disappeared. Your grandfather had no idea what was going on,
but he seemed to himself to be the only one in full command
of his faculties. Your mother babbled incoherently, the medical
staff just blushed. Nurses came to offer assistance but when your
mother saw them she flew at them, shouting.

– Where's my boy? What have you done to my boy?

Your grandfather and the policewoman had to separate them. He
advised them not to come back. His patience was just about to boil
over when Humphries carried in a sleeping boy, maybe nine years
old, wrapped in a blanket. Your mother let out a shout of joy and
grabbed you. You awoke, and cried, and your mother put you on
the breast. The sight was quite repulsive. He watched in horror.

Having emptied both breasts in a matter of minutes, you
surfaced.

– I'm still hungry, you announced.

– I'm not surprised, said Humphries.

– I'll get you something, said the policewoman, and left
the room.

You stared at the faces. Two were familiar. The other two
were strangers.

– Who are you? you asked them.

– I'm . . . John Bottoms, said your grandfather, nervously.

– Your grandfather, your mother explained. – Grandpa.

– Oh.

You went to slide from the bed, but your mother caught you.
You shrugged her off.

– Where have you been? she asked.

– With Gloria.

– Who?

– Gloria, Mum, you repeated. – You don't know her.

– Is she nice?

– She gave me a biscuit.

Your mother felt a stab of jealousy.

– Hello, Solomon, said Humphries.

– Hello. Where's my food?

– It's just coming, the doctor reassured you.

In your absence, your toys had been cleared away. You

walked over to the window. Everyone was waiting for you to say something, do something.

– When can I go out? you demanded. – Properly out. Out there.

Your mother blushed.

– Not yet, she said.

– When then?

– It's up to the authorities, said Humphries.

Your meal arrived, cold and congealed. You decided to postpone further interrogation until more immediate needs were satisfied.

– What, enquired your grandfather of Humphries, – is our next step?

– It's up to the authorities, I'm afraid, Humphries repeated. – It's out of my hands.

– This is all quite beyond me, your grandfather confessed. – Quite, quite baffling.

– None of us are any the less baffled than yourself, Humphries assured him.

– But . . . how long are they going to keep him here?

– I would guess indefinitely, said Humphries.

– Indefinitely?

– Until something happens.

– Like what?

– Mister Bottoms, I really have no more idea of what goes on on the General Council than you or anybody else. In my limited experience, their chief strategy is to prevaricate. I would imagine they will suggest some tests.

You, by now, had despatched your first course in half a dozen gobbled mouthfuls and were on to the desert. Your mother watched in tears. Always they were behind you, she and the doctors, struggling to make sense of what had happened an hour ago. By the time they caught up you had moved on again, in a new direction, unforeseen and unforeseeable. You moved in a world beyond her imagination, a world so far removed from the one she knew as to cause her to doubt the possibility of communication between the two. In twelve hours you had learned more than she could guess at. What could she say that would prepare you for a life that had never yet been lived? There was no point in pretending that your life would bear any resemblance to hers. Even the skeleton – weeks and months and years – was missing. All you had in common was birth at the beginning and death at the end. Presumably.

She wanted to cry out – 'Solomon, we wanted to do everything for you. We had such plans, plans that you will never know, but there was no time. You grew up so fast, and there were so many other things to do, things we had never expected, had made no provision for, that seemed more pressing. And now you are nearly a man, and I don't know you at all, and I know you have no reason to stay but please don't leave us just yet.'

But when she opened her mouth to speak, she realised it was futile. You were scooping up custard with your hand. Your grandfather took Humphries to one side.

– Look, he said, – I appreciate your . . . tact. But tell me the worst. I have a right to know. He's my grandson.

Humphries was puzzled.

– What on earth do you mean? he asked.

– He's terminal, isn't he?

– He's what?

– Terminal. He's going to die, isn't he?

Humphries considered.

– Well yes, I suppose so.

– I thought so. Thank you for being frank.

– Not at all, shrugged Humphries, bewildered.

Your grandfather took your mother by the hand.

– Sue, he said.

She looked up at him.

– What?

– Solomon is going to die.

She stared at him, blankly. He seemed to feel he had discovered something extraordinary.

– He must be baptised.

He had no idea how she would react. She burst out laughing.

12.26

Percy Burns brought the news of your recapture. It was the first good news of the day, but did little to lift the spirits of the General Council. Reluctantly, they had been obliged to let the idiots from the paper go. The news would have got out eventually – it had gone too far by now – and there was no point further alienating the press. The story was unlikely to reflect very creditably on the hospital anyway. If it looked as if they'd tried to cover it up, that would be truly damning. Incompetence in public officials the public could tolerate: they even found it vaguely endearing. Mendacity was quite beyond the pale. They had struck a deal with Doctors White and Smokey: the hospital would provide exclusive access and interviews. The press would turn not a *blind* eye, since this would be unethical, but a partially-sighted eye to some of the less impressive aspects of the hospital's management of the affair. This was the most the institution could reasonably hope to salvage of its reputation.

– The situation is quite out of hand, moaned Sir John.

It was true. There was no point denying it. In five minutes it would hit the lunch-time bulletins, and then all would be bedlam.

– We'd better hear what they have to say, suggested Percy Burns.

They listened on Frank Parker's tiny transistor radio. The local station was very excited. Unconfirmed reports, they said. Further updates as they became available, they promised. It was all very vague. A woman began declaiming the virtues of Hobson's cash-and-carry. Sir John turned it off. The journalists were obviously playing their own game of news management. The affair had taken on a life of its own.

It was Khan, eventually, who broke the silence.

– The key to the situation, he declared suddenly, – is normality. We must normalise. A strange and bizarre thing has happened. We must return it to the realm of normality. We must bring it back within the bounds of our normal experience. They stared at him.

– Does anybody have any better suggestions? asked Sir John. Nobody did.

– It's worth a try, said Khan.

Sir John agreed. Anything was worth a try.

12.32

Father Tew arrived on the ward as Gloria departed. Their paths crossed briefly and became entangled, in the swing doors.

– You're too late, said the consultant, icily, – she's dead.

Father Tew moved aside to allow the trolley past and managed to suppress his irritation. The medics *never* called him until it was too late. At first he had presumed this was because they were engaged in desperate, last-ditch efforts to save their patients' lives. By now he was convinced that it was nothing but pure atheistic spite. They resented the fact that the hospital employed him at all, some of them.

– Why didn't you call me earlier? he asked.

– Because I didn't see the point, the consultant retorted.

It was more than a question of different priorities. There was real malice involved.

– Religion can be a great solace to the dying, he replied, summoning up as much dignity as was available to a man of God in a temple of technology.

There were other reasons too, of course, but there was no point mentioning those. One had to talk Utilitarian to these medics. It could be English or Spanish or Chinese or Punjabi Utilitarian, but God forbid you should speak anything other than Utilitarian.

The consultant departed with the trolley. Such exchanges depressed Father Tew far more than death. Death was not such a big deal. For most of the patients, it was a merciful relief. He wandered back to the office, to check for messages. There was little else to do. There were no services today. No Christian services anyway. On Tuesdays and Thursdays, the chapel became a mosque. It was the hospital's concession

to the new multi-cultural Britain. The General Council had
reasoned that it would be a misuse of scarce resources to build
a mosque that no one would ever attend when they already had a
chapel that no one attended. Far from welcoming the concession,
both the Christian and the Muslim populations of Pilsbury had
been predictably incensed, and both groups boycotted it. On
Tuesdays and Thursdays it was boycotted by Muslims, the rest
of the week by Christians. Both mosque and chapel were thus
rendered redundant at a stroke, and the General Council were
now mumbling again about efficient use of scarce resources.
Father Tew wondered whether closing the chapel hadn't been
their intention all along. Was there such a thing as a conspiracy
of incompetence?

There was only the one message, but it cheered him up no
end. It was ages since he'd done a baptism. It would be a rare
treat to be celebrating the promise and potential of a new life
rather than trying to reconcile parents to its likely brevity. With
a spring in his step, he set off for the labour wards.

12.40

– Come, called Humphries.

The expression that passed across the priest's face as he opened
the door was one of disappointment.

– Sorry, he said.

The occupants of the room waited to hear why.

– I'm looking for fourteen bee, he explained.

– This is fourteen bee, said Humphries.

– Someone mentioned something about a baptism.

– That's right, said your grandfather.

– Don't stand in the doorway, urged your mother. – Let's get
it over with.

– Right.

He had expected a baby. The thought crossed his mind that
the medics were playing practical jokes now, teasing him.

– Who's this? you asked your mother, suspiciously.

– I'm Father Tew, said Father Tew.

You thought you had got rid of your father. It hadn't occurred to you that the hospital might find you another.

– You're not my father, you told him.

He laughed nervously.

– Good gracious no. At least, not that I'm aware of.

Your grandfather scowled. Father Tew kicked himself. Why had he said that? It had just popped out.

– It's just a name, said your mother. – 'Father Tew'. Like 'Doctor Humphries'.

– Or 'Dennis', said Father Tew.

You stared at him, bewildered.

– Who's Dennis?

– Dennis is a name, explained Father Tew. – What's *your* name? he asked you.

– Solomon.

– And how old are you, Solomon?

– People keep asking me that.

– Can I have a word? asked your grandfather.

He took the priest to one side, and they conversed *sotto voce* for five minutes, the priest throwing an occasional glance over his shoulder and frowning a great deal. Eventually, he emerged. He now looked distinctly uneasy.

– Is there a problem? asked Humphries.

The priest hesitated.

– I can't do it, he said, finally. – Not unless the lad wants it. It wouldn't be right. If he wants it, I'll do it gladly. But it must come from him.

– Is that a problem? asked Humphries. – Do you want to be baptised? he asked you.

– What's baptised? you asked.

– You see? said Father Tew. – It's not so simple.

– Just say you do, urged your grandfather.

– All right, you shrugged.

– You promise to live a Christian life, explained the priest.

– OK.

– And then you are received into the Anglican church.

– The Roman Catholic church, corrected your grandfather.

– Well that's another of the problems, sighed the priest. – I'm not really authorised to receive people into the Catholic church. Or to do barmitzvahs for that matter.

– Why not? you asked.

– Do you have all day? asked Father Tew, wearily.

– OK.

He did not know where to begin. You suggested the beginning. This activated some psychic reflex in Humphries.

– In the beginning, he intoned, – was the Word.

All eyes turned upon him, and he blushed.

– What Word was that? you asked.

He was stumped.

– You know, he confessed, – I really have no idea.

– God, Father Tew enlightened him, – the Word was God.

– What's God? you asked.

– God is a comforting fantasy, said your mother.

Priest and grandfather shot her a disapproving glare.

– Mrs Grundy, sighed Father Tew, – do you have any objection to your son being baptised?

– No, no, she sighed, – go ahead.

– What's God? you asked again, realising that your mother's answer was not the correct one.

– All that you see around you was created by God, explained your grandfather.

– The hospital.

– Well, indirectly, said Humphries. – The East Shirley Health Authority created the Hospital.

– And God created the East Shirley Health Authority?

– Well, no, Mrs Thatcher created the East Shirley Health Authority. In 1986 I think it was.

– But God created Mrs Thatcher, your grandfather explained.

You stared at him blankly. You were trying to understand, but they didn't make it easy for you. Father Tew tried a different tack.

– God is the ultimate authority, he said.

Your ears pricked up. This was news indeed.

– God is an authority?

– Not just an authority, said Father Tew, – *the* authority.

– So he's the one that's keeping me stuck in here . . .

Now it was the priest's turn to look blank. Humphries came
to his rescue.

– That's the General Council, I'm afraid.

You were now thoroughly confused.

– So how is God involved in all this? you asked.

No one knew what to say.

– Rather indirectly I'm afraid, admitted Humphries.

Your mother was about to add a further, and no doubt equally
secular, contribution. Sensing this, your grandfather moved to
cut her off. Where was all this delay getting them? The minutes
of your life were ticking away. No wonder the church was in
such a state.

– Never mind all this claptrap, he snapped, – tell him about
good and evil and sin and heaven and hell. The basics. Right and
wrong. Tell him about right and wrong. That's what it all boils
down to.

The priest eyed your grandfather sceptically. He did not
appreciate lessons in theology from the laity. Particularly the
Roman Catholic laity. The inter-denominational coalition was
beginning to fracture.

– There's a bit more to it than that, he informed your
grandfather tersely.

– What's right and wrong? you asked, keen to move the
debate on.

Father Tew groaned.

– It's rather complicated, he said.

– Rubbish, interrupted your grandfather. – There are things
you should do, and those are called the right things, and things
you shouldn't do, and those are known as the wrong things.
It's easy.

– Or not do, added Father Tew.

– Eh?

– There are sins of omission as well as of commission,
explained the priest.

Your grandfather thought this a pedantic point, but was forced
to give way.

– Fair enough. There are things you should do, or not do, and these are the right things. There are things you shouldn't do, or not do, and these are the wrong things. Is that clear?

– No, you admitted.

– For heaven's sake, growled your grandfather. – It's very simple. Do the right thing. Don't do the wrong thing. Isn't that right, Father?

– And believe in God, said Father Tew.

– Believe in God, yes, that too.

You were completely baffled.

– It means, believe what they tell you, said your mother.

Again, priest and grandfather shot her a disapproving glare. Her comments were distinctly unhelpful.

– Why shouldn't I believe what they tell me? you asked, puzzled.

– It's not simply a question of accepting what you're told, said Father Tew, – faith comes from within. You must have faith.

– Faith in who?

– Faith in people who know more about it than you do, said your grandfather, exasperated.

The priest wheeled on him, mustering his reserves of diplomacy.

– Mister Bottoms, he said, – I hope you won't think me rude, but I can't help but wonder if you're approaching this in the right spirit.

Your grandfather was taken aback, and temporarily lost for words.

– Might I enquire, continued the priest, – why you are so keen to have your grandson baptised?

– The child is going to die, snapped your grandfather, – I want to give him the gift of eternal life. That's all. Is that too much to ask?

– The gift of eternal life is not yours to give, Father Tew reminded him. – Or mine either. We are getting into rather deep theological waters here, Mister Bottoms, he said, – and I'm afraid I find myself rather out of my depth. Not waving but drowning as one might say. I don't really see that I can receive young Solomon into the Catholic church.

Your grandfather was crestfallen. All this for nothing. No
wonder the churches were empty, when they were so pernickety
about everything. You asked them for a simple thing, and
instead of just doing it they spent their time thinking of reasons
why they *couldn't* do it. He suspected the involvement of the
Unions.

– Is that your last word? he asked.

Father Tew nodded.

– I cannot baptise a child as a Catholic. I'm not sure how God
would feel about it, but I know that the Bishop would take a very
dim view.

Your grandfather slumped down on a chair, holding his head
in his hands.

– There's no reason why *you* can't though, the priest added.

Your grandfather looked up.

– Me? he queried

– I don't see why not.

Your grandfather rose to his feet again, his interest rekin-
dled.

– Don't you have to be a priest or something? asked Humphries.

– It's the performance that matters, not the performer.

– It is?

– Well that's Augustine's opinion.

– And he should know, said your mother.

– The moderns take a rather different view.

This did not surprise your grandfather at all.

– Screw the moderns, he decided. – What do I have to
do?

– It's more a question of what Solomon has to do, Father Tew
reminded him. – Does he renounce the Devil?

– We don't know, said Humphries. – That's what we're here
to establish.

– Why don't you ask him? suggested your mother.

– Well, do you? asked your grandfather.

– If you want me to, you said.

– We'll take that as a yes, your grandfather decided. –
Now what?

– Now you baptise him.

– What about the water? asked your grandfather. – Isn't there water involved?

– It's optional, sighed Father Tew.

– Right, said your grandfather.

He hesitated.

– Well, go on then, said your mother.

– Right. Er. I baptise you. In the name of the Father and of the Son and of the Holy Ghost. For ever and ever. World without end.

– Amen, added Humphries.

– Is that all right?

– Now the crossing.

Your grandfather made a vague gesture. Father Tew insisted he do at least that properly.

– Now what? you asked.

– That's it, said the priest.

– That's it?

– That's it.

Your grandfather grinned broadly, and popped the champagne. He was glad to have found some use for it anyway.

– But what does it all mean? you asked.

– You have been received into the Christian church, explained Father Tew. – Holy Communion on Mondays, Fridays and Sundays. Weddings and funerals by arrangement.

14.05

Your father, meanwhile, was draining his third Scotch. He ordered another. The lunch-time crowds had trickled back to their shops and offices, and the barman was washing glasses. He did not look pleased to be interrupted. An old man on a barstool sipped slowly at a half-pint and read the racing pages. Three others were playing dominoes for cigarettes. A pair of backpackers were studying a map, discussing their forthcoming adventures in a crisp and violent language your father could not identify. He felt the need for human company, but knew that he looked a shambles, and was likely to frighten anyone that he approached.

He watched the television above the bar. An army of turtles waddled up a beach, cumbersome helmets dragged through the fine sand to deposit a clutch of smooth, white eggs in the dunes. He saw the wriggling reptilian babies emerge sticky from the broken shells and repeat the journey in reverse, thousands of tiny helmets trundling inexorably over the moonlit dunes towards the breakers. Those who escaped being flipped over on their backs and pecked to death by wading birds were finally swallowed up in the surf. The parents and children never met, unless perhaps by chance in some current on the other side of the earth, where they would not recognise each other. There was no pleasure involved in this reptilian cycle of birth, death and copulation. The turtles survived purely because there were so many of them, and the oceans were so vast, that one or two were bound to slip through unnoticed. He wondered why they bothered, and presumed it could only be because they had no choice. Their genes forced them ever onwards – life would not be denied. Previous generations had imposed their will upon their distant descendants, and the descendants wearily obeyed. If, by chance, a turtle was born in whom this instinct towards multiplication was misformed or absent, a turtle whose instincts directed them not towards reproduction but towards reflection on the purpose of reproduction, say, or towards seeing how long she could stay underwater on one breath, then this instinct would die with the turtle. The turtles were condemned to multiply purely by the breeding success of their own ancestors. There was no escape for them. Multiplication, once set in motion, was unstoppable. But who had set it in motion? Or was the urge towards life implicit in the rocks and the sterile salty oceans, the mud, the sand, the air? It was irrepressible, like an infant's wail, like an erection, like grass forcing its way up through concrete.

At the present moment, the balance of his own inclinations tilted more towards sleep, the cessation of thought, hibernation, vegetation. Had he been one of those tiny helmets, he would, at that moment, have flipped over belly-up in the sand and simply awaited the releasing beak. Parenthood had taken him by surprise. The books, the articles, the classes had not prepared him for the intensity of it all. Snap decisions to be made, everybody looking to him for the answers, and no way of knowing if he had made the correct guess, no way of finding his way back to the main track if he took a wrong turning. Last night he had been half of a couple. He had lived with others all his life. It was easy – you had rows, you had resentments, but if they became too frequent or too boring, or if the compensations ceased to be adequate, you just left, and tried again with someone else until you found somebody you could put up with. He could not remember how it had all changed. Whether it had been the doors of youth and liberty creaking shut behind him, or the demands that were suddenly being made of him, the faces turning towards him when a decision was required. Or whether it was just the steaming concoction of his emotions, his hormones, his thoughts, whatever it was slopping around his veins with the coffee and nicotine, that had obliged him to seek out a tranquil place in order to restore some order to his metabolism.

Then there was the feeling that he had been duped – the one feeling that he hadn't been warned of – when he saw your mother with you, whom she had christened Solomon, and realised that the reason why everyone made such a big deal of fatherhood these days was simply because it was such an implausible state. Mothers and babies were the world. Fathers were optional extras, accessories. If some strange virus colonised the Y-chromosome and poisoned all the men, the world would carry on. It would not be a very exciting world perhaps, rather bland and predictable, but women would find some way to reproduce, and within a generation or two it would be difficult to believe that there had ever been men at all. They would appear in the encyclopaedias somewhere between dinosaurs and Romans. Future generations of little girls would try, in vain, to understand what it had been that men had done, how they had contributed. What use had they been? He had suddenly seen his role exposed as that of a footnote. The books had warned him of this feeling, of jealousy, of irrelevance and superfluity. They had said it was natural, that he would get over it. What they had not said was that it was natural because it was so manifestly, poignantly true, or that he would get over it only by stopping to think about it. Fathers deceived themselves. Mothers and babies held it all together. The men came and went, interchangeably, causing trouble and bringing presents to make up for it.

The question now was what to do with himself? Should he go back and apologise? It was hardly the time – your mother would have her mind on other things, the room would be full of medics and media people. You would probably not even recognise him. It was all too daunting. But if he did not make his peace with his family, there was nowhere else to go back to – not to the flat, which was her flat now, hers and yours. Not to work. He could hardly contact their mutual friends, and he had no friends in his own right. He had the clothes he was wearing and a credit card, perhaps a hundred pounds in the bank. He could go somewhere where no one would track him down – abroad even – and be just another man with something to hide. Or he could formalise the separation, pay the maintenance, find a flat, get another job, start again. Maybe you could come and visit weekends. They would have arguments, your father and your mother, accusations and resentments – you let him stay up too late, you let him smoke, you don't give him enough space. It was all horrible. He wondered what he might say to you. Wasn't it better to be shot of the whole thing? But then what could he do – pretend that none of this had ever happened? He couldn't face his own parents, much less his father-in-law. Not that he owed him anything. It was you who were owed. But maybe what he owed you was to keep away.

He turned his attention to the television. The tiny helmets he had watched clawing their way down towards the surf had become parents themselves now. You could tell they were the same turtles, because the scientists had painted fluorescent hieroglyphics on their shells. They returned to the beach on which they had hatched, and the credits rolled.

14.30

– Of course, Professor Khan was saying to your mother, – we are shooting in the dark here. We are obliged to make this up as we go along. Normally, we might look to precedents in the past to inform our decisions in the present. Although such knowledge cannot guarantee that we will not make mistakes, we can at least be sure that the mistakes we make will be novel. In Solomon's case, there are no precedents at all. I have searched the literature and drawn a blank. It does not help that the questions become irrelevant almost as soon as they are asked. On the other hand, since they are questions without obvious answers, the fact that each dilemma is rapidly superseded by another is the only thing that keeps the situation within the bounds of toleration.

He was a small, neat man with a goatee beard. A misunderstanding in Casualty had left him blind in one eye, as a consequence of which he tended to fix his gaze about a foot to the left of the object he was actually looking at, though everyone was too polite to inform him of the fact. He thus appeared to be directing his observations across your mother to the bedpost. This, combined with a certain languid detachment of delivery, led your mother to wonder whether he was actually addressing her or simply soliloquising, to an imaginary audience, or to posterity, or perhaps even to no one in particular. She heard what he said but did not bother to follow his arguments. He seemed to be persuaded that an elegant logical proof of the impossibility of your existence would satisfactorily resolve the situation. His meanderings, meanwhile, gave no indication of the conclusions he was likely to reach. The justifications offered by the caring professions for intervention rarely did bear any relation to the interventions suggested, she was finding. The fact that *something had to be done* was taken as justification for any course of action proposed, under what seemed to your mother an argument conducted in reverse – from the necessity of action to the resources at their disposal. It seemed to her that the resources at one's disposal rather determined the wisdom or otherwise of action. In your case these resources seemed entirely hypothetical.

Khan's argument was beginning to crystallise, as she had guessed it would, around the need for decisive action. Too much time had already been wasted, he said, beating around the bush. Your mother wanted to point out that most of this beating had been done by people whose major motivation had centred on the need for decisive action. The fact that they had been unable to come up with anything more constructive than more beating around the bush was not her fault, or yours either. Khan, however, had a head of rhetorical steam, and was not to be interrupted. You looked on, bewildered, aware that as usual the subject of the discussion was your future but nonplussed as to the role you were expected to play. The adults were sorting it out, and would let you know what they had decided when they had decided it. Finally, Khan came to a halt.

– What are you suggesting exactly? your mother asked.

– We think Solomon should receive some formal education.

Khan took advantage of your mother's inarticulate incredulity to press home the advantages of his plan.

– We know next to nothing about young Solomon, he continued, – except that he is growing at a rate which would seem to place him . . . physically at least, somewhere around twelve at the present moment. He is on the verge of puberty, what we might call pre-adolescent. By this calculation he has missed the equivalent of his entire primary education. On the other hand, we also know that he has the capacity to absorb information at a rate essentially proportional to his growth. There is thus good reason to suppose that the prognosis is not as bleak as might be imagined. Provided of course that he starts today.

– Today? echoed your mother weakly.

– Today, confirmed Khan. – Right now. He has lost a great deal of time. Education is like concrete, Mrs Grundy. The longer one leaves it, the harder it becomes.

Khan was also acutely conscious of the fact that your grandfather might return at any minute. This would almost certainly complicate matters. He was keen to get your mother's consent on the dotted line before your grandfather could start making trouble. Your mother, meanwhile, was left mouthing objections which would not form themselves into words. Khan sensed the possibility of victory by attrition if not by persuasion.

– There is nothing . . . unusual about our proposals, Mrs Grundy, he pointed out. – All children go to school. You will have to face the fact sooner or later, and there is no time to lose. Youth is fleeting.

You began to show an interest. This man seemed to be talking about getting you out of here.

Khan continued, – Although Solomon is manifestly a child with special needs, he said, – and whilst we have no experience of a . . . of needs such as Solomon's, we do have a general policy of normalisation . . .

– Normalisation? your mother cried, moved finally to eloquence. – You keep us under permanent observation because you can't think of anything else to do, and now you want to drag him away from his mother and fill his head with claptrap. How normal is that? Is that normal?

– It is quite normal, Khan assured her.

– Normal is home, exclaimed your mother, – normal is family and home and . . . She trailed off. She had quite forgotten what normal was. How did normal people live? Suddenly she was unsure.

– He can't stay in this room for ever, Khan reminded her. – He will become institutionalised. School will expand his horizons. He must learn to mix with other children.

– Just let us go home, your mother pleaded. – Leave us alone, and let us go home.

Khan was torn. He did not enjoy conflict – indeed, the incident in Casualty had fine-tuned his instinctive tendency to flinch from it. He decided to include you in the deliberations. It was ethical to do so, and also covered his own back. If, as your mother claimed, you refused to be separated from her, there was little the hospital could do about it. It became a matter for the education people, and the social workers.

– Let us ask Solomon, he suggested.

Your mother was horrified.

– Solomon is just a child, she cried.

You took predictable umbrage at this.

– I'm not a kid any more, Mum, you protested. – I know what I'm doing.

Your mother understood that once again she had managed to find exactly the sentence that would drive you from her. Khan turned his attentions to the sink.

– Do you want to go to school? he asked it.

The pair of you watched, troubled.

– Don't be shy, Solomon. Do you want to go to school?

You realised the question was addressed to you.

– Will it get me out of this room? you asked.

– Certainly it will.

– Promise?

Khan grinned, satisfied that the matter was sealed. Not only had his plan been carried off, but he had avoided an entanglement with your grandfather altogether.

– Promise. I can take you there right now.

– Solomon . . . wait . . .

Your mother wanted to argue – that you knew nothing, that you had been born yesterday – but you were gone. You had not even said goodbye. This room was too cramped and stifling, the world too alluring. All that glittered was not gold, but at least it glittered. She herself could barely raise a smile.

14.51

As you sped through the passages separating the maternity ward from the school room, you slipped your hand into Dr Khan's. The corridors had been cleared of all unauthorised personnel and those whose presence was unavoidable were under strict orders to take no notice of the passing phenomenon. Nonetheless, both of you had the distinct impression of being scrutinised by everyone you passed, of heads turning the moment you had hurried by, of hushed conversations following your passage. Thus Khan propelled his charge as speedily as possible towards your destination, maintaining a banal conversation, gripping your hand a little tighter at every junction and stairwell and quickening his pace whenever you passed an open doorway or a corridor promising interesting sights, sounds or smells. Your capacity to be drawn off at a tangent to the plans that were made for you had been noted in your file, and underlined in red. He need not have worried however. You had enough experience of the hospital to find its odours, conversations and routines of little interest. Only escape from the tedium of confinement interested you now. Several times Kahn wondered who was leading who, such was your excitement at the prospect of novelty. You had begun to find adults excruciatingly bland company – always discussing and agonising over what was to be done and never, as far as you could see, actually doing it. As for the staff, you were beginning to come to the conclusion that they were not sentient beings so much as animate scenery. You were intent, too, upon preparing yourself for your new destination and had plenty of questions, which you asked as you walked, seeming to digest the information supplied without any apparent intervening process of listening or comprehension.

– What is a school? was your first question.

– A school, Khan replied, – is a place where people go to learn that which they need to know in order to live in the modern world.

– Where is that? you asked.

– Where is what?

– The modern world.

– It is all around us. This is the modern world, said Khan, indicating a passage which might have been any other passage as far as you could see. What was so special about the modern world then? From down the hall came a shriek and the clattering of a trolley. A phone was buzzing.

– Will school teach me the difference, you asked, – between right and wrong?

– Hopefully.

– There is no guarantee then? you noticed.

– All will be revealed, he reassured you.

You were not reassured.

– It seems to me, you said, – as if it just goes round and round in circles.

– Spirals, corrected Khan. – Not circles but spirals. The difference is crucial. Think of it as an artichoke.

– An artichoke?

Khan realised from your blank expression that further explanation was required.

– An artichoke. It's a vegetable, with many layers of leaves. One removes each leaf, one dips it in mayonnaise and one scrapes the meat off with one's teeth. But there is very little meat on every leaf, and very many leaves. Eventually, just as one is beginning to suspect that the artichoke is more trouble than it is worth, one reaches the centre – the heart it is called – and one feels fully compensated for one's labours.

Again, you pondered.

– And what light does this vegetable shed on the difference between right and wrong?

– None, sighed the doctor. It's a metaphor.

– A metaphor?

– One reveals the nature of the abstract by reference to the concrete.

You frowned.

– I have little knowledge of concrete, you confessed sadly.

– It is for that very reason that you will benefit from school.

– They will teach me about concrete?

– Certainly.

– About artichokes?

– If you ask them. Shall we be getting on?

By now you had come to a complete standstill, finding that locomotion and cogitation were becoming tangled up with one another. You were not yet satisfied. Here at last was a man who seemed to have some answers. Why should your education not begin here and now?

– This question of right and wrong. I should like to get this straightened out right now, if possible, you said.

Khan slumped down on a convenient bench and lit a cigar. It was completely contrary to regulations but he felt that the circumstances justified the misdemeanour. He did not know where to begin.

– Have you never wondered, he asked you, – where you are coming from and where you are going to?

You were puzzled, not least because the question appeared to be addressed to a rubber plant.

– We are going to the school, I thought, you said.

– No, I mean, after that.

– We shall return to my mother.

– After everything. Who made you, Solomon? Where will you go when you die?

– To the theatre, I presume. (This was where Humphries said they had taken Gloria.)

– Have you never wondered about the purpose of it all? Why are we here? cried Khan in exasperation.

– We are here because we have stopped on our way to somewhere else, you replied. – It is the modern world. We are here to learn how to live in it.

– Exactly! cried Khan. – We are on our way to somewhere else. But where?

You wheeled round, suddenly suspicious, and fixed your mentor with a stare.

– You told me, you reminded him, – that we are on our way to the school.

Khan abandoned the expressive approach in favour of the revelatory. It seemed rather more straightforward, though he suspected the authorities would take a dim view.

– The difference between right and wrong, he said, – is revealed by God through His prophets.

Your face lit up. At last you felt you were getting somewhere.

– And these prophets are to be found in the schools?

– No, no, no. The prophets are dead. But the words and deeds of the prophets are written in books, and the books are to be found in the schools.

You tugged at his hand.

– Let us proceed immediately, you urged.

With a sigh of relief, Khan ground his cigar into the floor

and struggled to his feet. Around some corners and down some
stairs you arrived at a double door more or less identical to all
the others you had passed.

– This is called the children's ward, Khan explained.

– Why?

– Because it's a ward full of children.

– What are children?

– Children are . . . people like yourself, replied Khan without
much conviction.

The effect of his statement, however, was to send you into a
state of great excitement.

– You mean, you spluttered. – You mean there are others
like me?

Khan blushed. His sole motivation now was an overwhelming
desire to be free of this strange and disturbing child at the earliest
opportunity. Nonetheless, he found it awkward to lie to one so
trusting and naive.

– Well, not exactly like yourself, he confessed. – But similar
in many respects.

– In what respects?

– Weeelll . . . began Khan, thinking desperately, – of about
the same size and shape, and the same colour most of them.

– Yes, you mused, – I had noticed that. People seem to come
in several colours, but the range is limited. Why is that?

– All will be revealed, promised Khan, pushing the door open
with his foot, and propelling you through it.

This ward was much the same as the others you had come
across, except that, as Khan had predicted, the inhabitants of
the beds were smaller. He led you to a bed at the far end of the
ward, where a woman was bent over a girl. Both were studying
a file of some sort. You considered this an auspicious omen. You
had noticed that the chief distinction in the hospital, between
those who did and those who were done unto, was precisely
reflected in the division between those who wrote in files,
and those who were the subjects of their observations. You
had tried to decipher the inscriptions in your file, but found
them baffling. Others, however, presumably with access to some
secret code, found illumination in it. From a position of complete

ignorance, they suddenly became aware of what needed to be done. Clearly, the files were the key to many mysteries. Perhaps the files contained the words of the prophets, of whom Khan had spoken with such reverence. You were eager to get started. The woman rose and smiled.

– Excuse us, said the doctor, taking the woman by the arm and drawing her into a conspiratorial huddle, from which emanated whispers and the occasional glance.

You were left with the girl. She was slightly larger than you, of a slightly different shape but much the same colour, and was eating an apple. You racked your brains for something to say, but could think of nothing. The girl, for some reason, was very pleasant to look at. You smiled at her and she smiled back, and offered you a bite.

– All right? she grinned. – What brings you here?

– I have to come to learn about concrete, you replied. – And artichokes.

She burst out laughing. You felt your skin tingling in a hot flush, and your heartbeat swell. Apparently you had said something ridiculous. You bowed your head and covered your face with your hands. A great urge to run back to your mother rose within you, until you remembered that you did not know the way. You were trapped here in the modern world alone with this terrifying and fascinating creature.

Thankfully, the commotion refocused the attention of the professionals.

– Come on then, Solomon, said the woman, steering you away.

As you left, you snatched a last glance at the girl, who had stopped laughing. She winked at you. You did not know how to interpret this gesture, but felt somehow cheered by it.

The teacher carefully drew the curtains around an empty bed, which she then patted several times. You interpreted this as an invitation to sit on it. She sat on the chair, introduced herself as Miss Poot, and produced an enormous file, which you recognised. It seemed to follow you around. Now, at last, all would be revealed.

– They tell me you've never been to school, Solomon, she began.

– I have never been given the opportunity, you explained.

– Well, where shall we start?

You knew where you wanted to start.

– Who was that girl?

– Tess? That's Tess.

– And have you taught her the difference between right and wrong?

The teacher laughed.

– Well, it's not quite that simple.

You were crestfallen. Nothing was ever simple.

– She's had a . . . a difficult life, the teacher explained.

This was simply bewildering.

– What other kind of life might one have? you asked, incredulous. – Life is very hard, it seems to me. It is hard to know what to do. People are kind. Then people are cruel. Nothing is predictable except that one's file will follow one around. People are strange. My parents in particular. My mother.

You stopped, apparently overcome by the strangeness of it all.

– Have you not had a hard life then? you enquired.

– Er, no, I suppose not, she answered, somewhat flustered. – I mean, yes, at times, things have been difficult, we all have our cross to bear, but really, compared to other people, no, not too hard. Yet.

You clapped your hands in triumph.

– I thought as much, you exclaimed. – And this is because you know the difference between right and wrong.

– Well, perhaps. Perhaps I have just been fortunate.

You sank back, dejected, into the pillows. Just as the answers were beginning to add up, there came a rogue variable into the equation. You decided to begin again at the beginning. It was necessary to establish the credentials of this woman.

– Do you know the difference between right and wrong?

– Yes, she asserted. Then, less confidently, – I think so.

– Are you not entirely sure?

Suddenly the curtain was thrown back, and there, in a night-dress, stood the girl.

– Are we finished then? she asked the teacher.

– Oh, er yes, replied the teacher, – sorry, Tess, I'll be with you in a minute.

You had never seen such loveliness. Every part of her seemed perfect, from the auburn curls cascading down her shoulders to the small firm breasts outlined against her cotton T-shirt, to her small bare feet, her arms covered in fine hair, her lips full and red. She smelled of soap. You felt yourself by contrast painfully awkward – your arms and legs in particular seemed to have become distended, as if you had been stretched. You did not know what to do with your limbs, and shuffled on the bed, in an effort to conceal them.

– Aren't you gonna ask me in then? she demanded. – Or is this a private meeting?

– It is really, Tess, said your teacher.

– No, no, come in please, you interrupted eagerly, beckoning her in and making a space for her on the bed. As she sat, her night-dress rode up, revealing the inside of a smooth white thigh. Almost instantly she covered it up, but the sight caused an aching in your heart, for what you knew not.

– Such thighs, you murmured.

– Sorry?

From the look on Miss Poot's face, you gathered that you had said something inappropriate again, and declined to repeat it. The bed was narrow, and Tess drew closer, so that your legs touched. You found yourself breathing rapidly and sweating, but forced yourself to pay attention. Both of your companions were looking at you, slightly concerned.

– Are you all right, Solomon? asked the teacher, anxiously.

You hesitated before replying.

– Yes and no, you said finally. – My heart is beating, and my palms are sweating, but it is not an unpleasant sensation at all, quite the reverse.

Tess began to giggle. Miss Poot too had noticed the bulge in your dressing gown. It was a delicate situation.

– Perhaps you'd better leave us, Tess, she suggested.

– Aw, why? the girl protested. – I ain't done nothing except sit here.

– Tess, please.

It was more an order than a request this time.

– Aw, miss.

She tutted and grimaced, but swung her legs reluctantly over the side of the bed.

Your reverie broken, you realised suddenly what was going on.

– No! No! you wailed in anguish. – Don't go!

Halfway off the bed, Tess stopped and stared at the teacher.

– Well? she asked.

– Stay! you cried. – Don't go! You are delightful.

– Well?

Under pressure, and against her better judgement, Miss Poot caved in.

– All right, she conceded. – For a few more minutes. Now where were we?

– The difference between right and wrong, you reminded her. – Do you know the difference? you asked Tess.

– No, she said, unsure of whether to sulk or to gloat. – They make it up as they go along.

– Hmmmm, you ruminated. – Doctor Khan mentioned philosophy. What is philosophy?

– Grab it before some other bugger does, and don't let go, she said.

– That is philosophy?

Something, at last, was simple. She shrugged.

– It's my philosophy.

The teacher, worried that your introductory lesson was rapidly escalating into a crash–course, attempted to regain control.

– Philosophy, she announced, – seeks to answer the questions which cannot be answered by observation alone.

– Ah, you said. – The question as to the difference between right and wrong would certainly seem to fall into that category. It is certainly not a question which can be answered with reference to the behaviour of those around me.

Miss Poot decided to change tack.

– Why are you so interested in the problem, Solomon? she enquired.

– I have been imprisoned against my will. I was told that it was necessary, but I cannot help but feel that it was wrong. When I sought to explore the world beyond my tiny little ward I was pursued and brought back, and told that I had done wrong, to make my mother anxious. I still cannot see why. It is her affair if she is anxious, not mine. Nobody has been able to furnish me with a satisfactory answer. Indeed, the most plausible answer thus far is precisely that, that you do indeed make it all up as you go along.

– Right on! shrieked Tess, laughing.

Miss Poot hesitated. She was unsure whether your speech had been intended as insolent. She decided in the end that it was not. You were genuinely confused.

– Solomon, she said, – you are still a child. All will be revealed.

– I know I am a child, you retorted, becoming quite indignant, – I have been told so often enough. I am not likely to forget. And Tess, is she still a child?

– Yes.

Tess sighed and stuck out her tongue.

– Children seem to talk a great deal of sense, you said. – I find their company very pleasant. Not only are they clear in what they say, but they are lovely to look at. The others, on the other hand, will not give you a straight answer, and are awkward, ungainly creatures. Many of them are quite hideous. Children are . . . what are people called who are not children?

– Adults, sighed Miss Poot.

– Morons, hissed Tess.

The teacher turned on her.

– Tess! You are not helping! Please get out!

– No!

– Now!

– Piss off!

You watched, horrified. Miss Poot raised her arm and seemed about to hit the girl, who instinctively curled into a defensive ball. Then the adult checked herself, and through clenched teeth repeated her command.

– Out!

– NO! you cried together.

You felt suddenly such rage that you sprang from the bed and stood between them, your fists clenched.

– It is you who should leave, you cried. – You have taught me nothing, and now you abuse my friend.

– Tess, growled the teacher, ignoring you, – this is your last chance.

– Leave me alone.

Miss Poot darted forward to catch her arm, but you intervened.

– I shall call security, she warned.

– Do so, you hissed. – You shall not separate us.

Miss Poot turned on her heels, threw back the curtain and stormed off to find assistance. You turned to the quivering, frightened ball that was your friend.

– Is she gone? it asked at last.

– For the time being, you replied.

The ball unfurled, and the girl stood. She smiled at you, then suddenly took your head in both hands and kissed you full on the lips, long and hard. Terrified, you pushed her away.

– My God, you gasped, my God!

– What's wrong?

– Look at this!

From your dressing gown you produced an enormous erection, thick and red.

– Bloody hell! she laughed.

– It's about to explode! you shrieked. Then, violently, you doubled up on the bed.

Tess watched, fascinated and horrified. She wondered whether she should call someone, until her eye was caught instead by Miss Poot's abandoned handbag. Thus when the teacher returned with reinforcements, it was to find only a curtain fluttering in the breeze from an open window and you, moaning softly on the bed.

– Good grief, gasped Khan, – what has she done to him?

They carried you, still whimpering, back to your mother.

Your mother screamed, – What have you done to him? and ran and took you in her arms and smothered you with kisses, smoothing your hair, which had stood alarmingly on end, and whispering, – Oh, my darling, my little boy, my love.

– I think you'd better leave, growled your grandfather to the porters, with such authority that they did not question the legitimacy of the command until it was too late. John Bottoms, having polished off a magnum of champagne, had come to a firm resolution. It seemed to your grandfather that the stage of observation, hypothesis and experiment had yielded precious little in the way of knowledge that was not immediately visible to the naked eye. It was pointless to bemoan the fact that you were growing at a rate far beyond the realms of possibility, pointless to speculate as to the likely causes of your pathology, pointless to mull endlessly over putative remedies to ameliorate your condition. It was worse than pointless, it was negligent. You were growing up wild, beyond control, unable to function adequately in even the most ordinary social situation. That was what mattered, in the end, though it was a point the rest of the world seemed to have overlooked entirely. It was all very well, he said to himself (and to anyone else who would listen), to conjure up excuses; the world was full of convenient excuses. The bottom line (the Bottoms line) was that somebody needed to take Solomon Grundy in hand, to show you the ropes, to instil – for heaven's sake – a bit of discipline. Your mother – his own daughter – had gone completely to pieces. Your father had shown his true colours at the first sign that he might be called upon to do anything beyond pontificate, and simply disappeared.

None of this had particularly surprised your grandfather. This spinelessness, this tendency to crawl back under the duvet at the first indication that things might not work out entirely in the way one had envisaged, seemed a universal malaise of the generation bought up with comprehensive education. No wonder you were such a mess, when your parents belonged to a generation that saw parenthood not as the apex of human development but as the harbinger of imminent redundancy. A generation that constantly put off its growing up until tomorrow, that went off backpacking round the Third World in the hope that someone would have sorted out their lives for them by the time they got back. And now that generation had produced this boy, who could not *stop* growing up, who already knew the value of everything and the price of nothing. If you were not entirely to waste what already promised to be a terribly brief life running around in circles, the situation required a firm hand. It was fortunate, he reflected, that one was available. Thus John Bottoms had become possessed of a quiet determination to stamp his authority on the situation.

The decision that something had to be done, however, was simpler than the question of what exactly it should be, and it was upon this question that John Bottoms was now ruminating. An atmosphere of gloom pervaded the room and had been osmotically absorbed by all present.

– How long am I going to be stuck in here? you demanded. – I want to go out.

– You can't go out, your grandfather said. – It's not allowed.

– Who says?

– Look, growled your grandfather, – we'd all like to go out. We'd all like to go home and get some sleep, but we can't, and that's that.

You groaned theatrically, and slumped back into the chair.

– I can't stand being stuck in here with you lot, you announced.

You sat vacantly picking your nose. Your mother watched, torn between love and fear. She wanted to tell you to stop – it was her duty as a mother to challenge your bad habits – but she dared not. Already you were cast in the mould of a man. She had had no chance to teach you these things, and she was afraid that any attempt to make a belated start would produce only resentment. Already she saw the tell-tale signs of a nascent adolescence – your lower jaw filling out, your cheeks hollowing, your nostrils flared, the incessant slow drumming of your hand on the arm of the chair. She was afraid of you, not that you might argue or shout, but simply that you might walk away. They had very little to offer you, your family, beyond indefinite confinement in this ward, tempers simmering, despondency descending. She wondered if you blamed them, or her specifically, for this mess. You had no relationship any more.

Suddenly you leaped to your feet and yanked open the door. A policeman, who had been relying on it for support, stumbled backwards into the room but managed to remain on his feet.

– What? he asked, aggressive in his embarrassment.

You shut the door in his face and slumped back into the seat in a dejected heap. Your grandfather ostentatiously turned his back and stared out at the grey and gloomy skies.

– There's no reason why *you* can't go out, Dad, your mother said.

That this was true did not diminish your grandfather's irritation. All in all, he preferred impotence to superfluity, though neither came very easily to him.

– Do you not want me either? he sniffed.

– Not if you're going to lose your temper.

You turned around.

– I had hoped school might teach me the difference between right and wrong, you hissed. – But I have learnt something of far more importance. That adults would not tell you, even if they knew. They are not afraid of doing wrong, only of doing different.

You stared at them, triumphant and mocking.

– Solomon! wailed your mother. – What have they done to you?

– Nothing! you cried. – You have tried, all of you, but you have failed and I see through your lies. You shan't stop me. I am sick to death of this room. There is a world beyond this ward, I know there is. I see it from the windows, and you pretend it is an illusion. You will not let me find out for myself. You say you are afraid for me, but you are afraid of me, afraid of the things I might do which you never dared do. Afraid of what I might discover.

– This has gone far enough! bellowed your grandfather. – You will show some respect for your mother and myself.

– Earn it, you sneered.

John Bottoms fumed. His face was bright red and every muscle in his body taut with rage. So this was what they taught them in schools nowadays.

– You know nothing, he yelled.

– That is because I have been taught by you, you retorted.

– Learn some respect.

– Piss off, Grandad.

Your grandfather's hand caught you a glancing blow across the face. Fortunately, the old man retained sufficient self-control to open his fist just before impact, and to pull the punch. Nonetheless it was of sufficient force and came so unexpectedly as to knock you two paces backward against the wall. You felt something thin and warm trickle from your nose over your upper lip, and when you reached gingerly up to touch it your fingers came away scarlet. Suddenly a rage erupted within you and you charged, with fists flailing and a bloodcurdling yell. Your head collided with the old man's face, and you both toppled over, locked together, on to the beanbags. Instinctively, your hands closed around your grandfather's neck and you squeezed.

16.43

Dr Khan brought dark tidings to the General Council, which was now in permanent session. Several members were slumped on the table, snoring unashamedly amidst the debris of half-drunk coffee cups, foil trays spilling half-eaten curries, overflowing ashtrays, newspapers and mobile phones. They were roused, much to their annoyance, to hear Khan's pronouncement.

– The situation has taken a turn for the worse.

There were groans all round. An orderly was dispatched for fresh coffee and paracetamol, and the evening editions. Sir John Parkes remained inscrutable.

– What is the current situation? he asked. – Where is the boy?

– He has been moved to his own room, sir, in E block.

– Is it wise to separate him from his mother so young? asked Brian Hawkins. – You know the guidelines.

– I wrote the bloody guidelines, muttered Sir John.

– We considered it essential they be separated, continued Khan, unperturbed.

– Did he *ask* to be separated?

– Not at first. He was quite adamant, in fact, that he should remain with his grandfather until he had finished him off. We considered this was not in his best interests. Security had to pull him off. Then he swung some punches at them, and nearly bit one of their fingers off. Quite nasty. I've just put four stitches in it. He was quite berserk. In the end it took four of them to get him off, and another two to restrain his mother. His grandfather is in shock, and has some nasty bruising around the neck. We ended up giving him a shot, the boy that is, which calmed him down a bit. Should have put him out like a light according to the anaesthetist, but in the end it just slowed him down enough for us to manhandle him out of the room. Then the lad got very depressed, said he couldn't bear being locked up with these nutters any more.

A general nodding of heads indicated a degree of sympathy with your assessment of your family.

– How is he now? asked Percy Burns.

– Still rather depressed and lethargic, Khan replied. – He lies on his bed playing with himself, and pays no attention to anything you say to him. Says it is all lies and nonsense.

– The dope?

– Unlikely, said Khan. – I think he is thoroughly miserable.

– A suicide risk? queried Brian Hawkins.

– He is under surveillance, Khan reassured them.

– And the mother?

– Under sedation.

– Damn!

Sir John's fist crashed down on the table.

– What a shambles! What a bloody cock-up!

He turned on the accumulated experience and wisdom of the General Council, and asked, – What are we to do? We can no more keep him here than we can allow him to leave.

Though phrased as a question, it was little more than an eruption of exasperation, and no one dared answer but Dame Barbara Hershkovitz.

– Why can't we just discharge him? she asked.

– We have no way of knowing what might happen to him, observed Sir John. – He must be kept under observation. We must be prepared for anything at any time. He is in our care,

and we are responsible. We must not forget that he is still a child.
He is still a child?

Khan assented, – He was when I left him.

Sir John continued, – His family seem quite incapable of
looking after him.

There was a long pause, during which the Council assumed
earnest expressions designed to give the impression of furious
cogitation.

– Is this a medical problem, really? asked Brian Hawkins,
finally.

In Hawkins' experience the most satisfactory resolution to a
problem invariably consisted of moving it sideways.

– Isn't this more a job for a psychiatrist, or a social worker?
he continued. – If the boy is a suicide risk, we are somewhat
out of our depth. Perhaps a psychiatric opinion might clarify our
options?

– It would certainly cover our backs, added Percy Burns.

Sir John considered his options.

– All right, he decided. – Let's see what the witch doctors
have to say.

17.35

You stared at the ceiling where the blades of a fan rotated slowly.
The blinds were drawn and the lights dimmed but you were
under no illusion of privacy. You had spent enough of your life in
institutions to know you were being watched. Objects that might
have had any value as weapons or instruments of self-injury were
conspicuous by their absence, and the room contained only your
bed and a cabinet, upon which had been arranged a plastic jug of
water and a polystyrene cup. In the corner, under a cloth, was
a plastic abdomen in garish pinks and purples. You were trying
to clear your head of whatever poison they had injected into it,
but to no avail. Every face you conjured up was accompanied by
a feeling so visceral as to preclude concentration. You thought

of your mother, and shame flooded through you, causing you to shiver, and to clench every muscle in an effort to make yourself invisible. You thought of your father and were overwhelmed by anger. Figures in uniforms passed through your drifting thoughts and you felt your mouth dry with fear, but your heart pound with resolution and courage. Finally, and most of all, you thought of the girl who had kissed you, and were overcome with longing, the bliss of her memory and the pain of her loss.

The forces which compelled you to remain in this institution appeared overwhelming. You had no doubt that the events of the last few hours would contribute a third volume to your already epic file, and your position seemed truly hopeless. The only window in the room looked down into a courtyard in which were stationed various upturned steel cylinders. Into these hospital staff periodically threw large black bags. The window was on the third storey, and the man who had dragged you out from under Gloria's bed stood guard on the door. Several people had been to see you, at suspiciously regular intervals – Dr Khan and some others you did not recognise – but you had lost your faith in the ability of conversation to achieve anything other than false hopes and misunderstandings. They asked you if you wanted anything, knowing full well that all you wanted was to be left alone. You ignored the men who came to see you, and in the end they drifted away.

Apart from the tumultuous rumblings of your mind, strange developments in your body were also a source of concern. Your head throbbed. Whether this was a consequence of the blow your grandfather had delivered or the needle they had stuck in your arm you did not know. Whichever it was, it was a highly disagreeable sensation, though it seemed gradually to be wearing off. Presumably more permanent was the fine hair which had sprouted all over your body. For the most part it was short and downy but in some parts – under your arms for example – it became quite luxuriant, whilst round your penis it was long, springy and wiry. It even grew on your face, around your mouth, and itched. Your hair had grown down to your shoulders, and somebody had tied it back in a pony-tail. There were compensations, however. You were now as tall and as strong as your adversaries on a one-to-one basis (not that your tussles with the authorities ever *were* on a one-to-one basis), and more than a match for your grandfather. And ejaculation was a most wonderful surprise, though your reserves seemed temporarily exhausted. But these pleasures were nothing compared to the pain of confinement. Would they ever let you go? You were beginning to become aware of the immensity of time which lay before you. You looked into the future and saw only the same four walls, the same endless corridors, the same faces, kindly but ultimately unconcerned, friendly and supportive right up to the point where the lines of regulation were drawn and not a centimetre beyond. You knew nothing else beyond this world, which Dr Khan called the modern world, except that there was a world beyond this one, which there was a well-organised and powerful conspiracy to prevent you exploring.

You made no response to the knocking. You had learnt enough to know that your requests not to be interrupted would be ignored. Sure enough, after a few seconds the door creaked open a crack, and a spectacled head appeared.

– Solomon? it ventured, nervously.

The door opened another foot.

– Solomon? the man repeated.

– Come in if you must, you sighed.

– Thanks.

The door was pushed right back to reveal a man in a suit.

– I'm Doctor Conway, said the man. – I just popped in to see how you were.

– Miserable, you grunted. – How are *you*?

This, you had learned, was the expected riposte.

– Can't complain, replied the doctor, cheerily.

You considered this. It seemed a fairly serious impediment to life in the modern world.

– You have my sympathy then, you told him. – I am glad to be allowed at least *that* luxury. If I couldn't complain, I would . . . You trailed off.

– You would what? Conway enquired.

– I don't know what I'd do, you admitted.

– You don't know.

– No.

The man smiled at you.

– Please don't smile, you requested.

– Don't smile?

– That's what I said. Why do you repeat everything I say? you cried, exasperated.

– Why do I repeat everything you say?

– Are you not even aware of it?

Conway apologised.

– What sort of doctor are you anyway? you asked, warily.

– I'm a psychiatrist. A doctor of the mind, the man explained.

– You must have your work cut out in the modern world, you observed.

– How so?

You stared at this man, unable to decide whether or not he was serious. You realised he was.

– How so? he repeated.

– I have been in the modern world nearly a whole day now, you told him. – And two things strike me over and over again. The first is that everyone I meet is some kind of therapist, and the second is that the entire race seems to be dying out – confined to their beds for the most part, and in need of pretty serious repairs.

– That is because you have only seen a hospital, Conway explained. – Everyone is sick in a hospital. As soon as they are well, they leave.

– Everyone except me, you pointed out.

– Perhaps you are not yet well, suggested Conway. – Perhaps you are troubled in the mind.

– Of course I am troubled in the mind, you snapped. – My life is miserable. There are so many questions, and the answers . . .

You stopped. An idea had occurred to you.

– If I am troubled in the mind, you began cautiously, – can you cure me?

– I can't guarantee it, admitted Conway, – but the chances are reasonable.

– And if I am cured, I can go?

Conway paused, wondering how to proceed. You waited, intently.

– Do you ever feel . . . suicidal? asked the doctor at last.

You shrugged.

– Suicide, Conway explained, – is the ending of one's own life.

This did not, however, produce any further illumination.

– Is that another kind of therapy then? you asked.

– No, no, no, said Conway hurriedly, wishing he had not broached the subject. – No, it's one of the symptoms which the therapies are designed to combat. The feeling that life is too painful, too humiliating perhaps, too sad to stomach, and that death is the only way out.

You pondered this information before coming to a conclusion.

– It is an interesting suggestion, you told him. – But I should hate to make a hasty decision . . .

– It was not a suggestion, interrupted Conway emphatically. – It was a question, a simple question. Just a question.

You stared at him, puzzled.

– It seems a perfectly reasonable solution to me. If that's how you feel about things . . .

– Yes, sighed Conway, – but that's the point. It's the feelings that are the problem. It's the ends which are pathological, not the means.

Conway realised he was not making himself clear.

– Let me give you an example, he suggested. – Now, I have a patient, a man who believes he is being bombarded by cosmic rays from a malevolent civilisation on a distant planet. His strategy to protect himself is to lock himself in a cupboard, which he has reinforced with lead. He sits in this cupboard all day and all night. Given his convictions, this course of action appears perfectly reasonable. He feels, moreover, that everyone else, who scoffs at his warnings and takes no precautions, is acting irrationally, not to say recklessly. My job is to persuade him, not that his cupboard is an inadequate defence against cosmic rays, which I could not do, but that the cosmic rays are all in his mind. They do not exist in the real world, only in his imaginary world.

Real worlds, imaginary worlds. There was so much to learn. It really *was* an artichoke.

– And what, you asked, – do you call someone whose ends are quite reasonable, but whose chosen means are entirely inadequate for the task?

– Stupid, said Conway. – Psychiatry has as yet found no way of improving their lot.

– Well perhaps you ought to try, you suggested.

– It is a subject that has received comparatively little attention, confessed the man of science, – but for good reasons.

– Oh?

– People would find the modern world considerably less tolerable if they were not so stupid, the doctor explained.

This seemed reasonable enough. You were warming to this man.

– And myself? you queried. – Am I sick in the mind, or merely stupid? Or perhaps both?

– That remains to be seen.

Dr Conway allowed a pause, whilst he considered his next approach.

– How do you feel about your life? he asked, at last.

You dismissed it with a shrug.

– But you must admit, it is somewhat unusual.

– It is?

This threw Conway completely. He stared at you, half in suspicion, half in incredulity. Was this a wind-up?

– You mean, he asked, – you mean nobody has told you?

– Told me what? you asked, bewildered and suddenly anxious.

– Oh dear, sighed Conway. – Oh dear, oh dear, oh dear, oh dear.

You were by now quite alarmed.

– Well, he began, – you have a condition . . . we don't have a name for it at the moment. It is . . . somewhat unique. Look, he said, – I don't know how to put this to you. It never occurred to me that you were unaware . . . the fact of the matter is that you are suffering from what we might call Accelerated Life Syndrome. You are growing at, I don't know, several hundred times, several thousand times the rate that is common amongst, well, amongst mammals. You are growing at a rate more reminiscent of . . . to be frank, there is nothing in the known world to which you might be adequately compared.

– I have no use for the known world, you snapped, – I do not live in the known world. Only a cure is of interest to me, if it will get me out of here.

– Yes, of course.

– Is there a cure?

– Well, there you have us stumped, I'm afraid.

– And is that why I am stuck here?

– I'm afraid so. You might be contagious or something.

– But what does it mean, Accelerated Life Syndrome?

– It means you cram as much life into a day as the rest of us manage in a decade. You have caused quite a stir in the world outside, you know.

The known world . . . the world outside . . . it was never-ending.

– I know nothing of the world outside, you confessed. – The modern world is the only one I know.

– Well, I dare say you will find out soon enough.

You seemed now to be approaching the heart of the matter. The Doctor's explanation, though quite fantastic, tied up a lot of loose ends. In fact, you sensed that in this new diagnosis lay the key to your entire experience. Here at last was someone whose explanations made sense of the world, who would tell you things about yourself which others would merely write in files. Again, you grabbed him by the arm.

– Tell me more, you urged.

– Steady on, steady on, tutted Conway, himself slightly alarmed by now. He was used to dealing with volatile patients but this particular scenario incorporated new levels of unpredictability. No matter how diverse, exotic and disturbed the backgrounds and experiences of his other patients, they shared at least a common time-scale, a consensual sensation of the normal rhythms of life. With you he was stepping into completely uncharted territory. But he had begun, and could hardly leave the matter half finished.

– How am I different? you were demanding to know. – How do other people live? How do they grow up?

Conway took a step backward, and perused his patient with an experienced, professional eye. You seemed now to be growing in front of his very eyes.

– Well, he concluded, – to reach the stage that you have reached, physiologically – nearly full adult size, reproductively mature – would take another child, well it varies but say . . . fifteen years?

The patient was rendered temporarily speechless. The doctor watched, prepared for any eventuality, mentally calculated the distance to the door, and scanned the room in vain for implements that could be used as weapons in an emergency. He had no idea how you would react. In fact, you burst out laughing, and fell back on the bed.

– Fifteen years?

Conway nodded.

– It is unimaginable, you declared. – So much time. Oceans and oceans of time.

Conway was relieved. You seemed to be taking it well, if only because you failed to understand it.

– How do I fill all those days? you asked.

Conway shrugged.

– It's your life, he said. – It's up to you.

You cast around for ideas, but none were forthcoming. You decided to raid the doctor's supply.

– What did *you* do for all those days?

– Much the same as you, shrugged the doctor. – I played. I learned about the world. I learned to walk, to talk, to think. I . . . er . . . I went to school. I had some adventures, got into some fights. Much the same as you.

– Is that all?

Conway was being forced on to the defensive, a position to which he was not accustomed.

– Yes, he confessed. – I was happy, mostly. I had bad days, of course.

– Entire days?

– Whole days, yes.

Conway realised that information was being supplied in the wrong direction. The patient asked so many questions, there was scarcely a moment for him to insert his own.

– So much time, you mused, – and so little to do.

– The world is larger and more complex than you think, Conway replied. – There is no shortage of work to be done. And it all speeds up, you'll find, as it goes on.

You fitted this new piece of the jigsaw into your experience.

– What exactly is work? you asked at last. – What do people do?

Conway shrugged. – All sorts of things, he said. – Drive taxis. Make things. Grow food.

– It doesn't grow of its own accord then? you extrapolated.

– Well, it does, Conway corrected, – but it doesn't grow fast enough or big enough. We need to help it along a bit – plant the seeds and fertilise the soil, clear the weeds, water the crops, feed the livestock and so on.

– And these things make the food grow faster?

– Faster and bigger and free of disease.

– Perhaps something similar might account for my own condition? you wondered aloud.

– An environmental pathogen? An excess of fertiliser in the bloodstream? Something like that? It's possible, Conway conceded.

– If everything grows, you continued, – then surely all things would remain the same size, relatively speaking? My experience, however, suggests that some other mechanism is at work. My mother, for example, and my grandfather, have always seemed to me to be slowly shrinking. Whether the world is shrinking or I am growing I cannot say. How could one tell?

Conway finally gave up.

– Oh, Solomon, he sighed, – it is all very complex. You are expecting me to teach you in half an hour what it has taken me forty-odd years to work out.

– Is *that* what one does with time then?

– I suppose so, yes. With one's youth. One learns. One observes. One imitates. One makes mistakes. Gradually, it becomes clearer. It takes time.

– Well, I have plenty of that, you laughed.

– Yes, replied Conway, without much conviction.

You noticed this.

– I can offer no advice, he explained. – The prognosis for your condition is quite, quite unknown. Ordinarily, when people reach your stage of development, the long bones set and they stop.

– Stop?

– Physically, they stop, more or less. In other ways – intellectually, spiritually, emotionally – one can carry on for as long as one likes, but physically one has reached one's limits.

– That is reassuring, you said.

– Whether similar limits will apply in *your* case . . .

You both waited for the other to say something. It seemed the interview was coming to an end. Conway stood up to leave.

– If there's anything I can do for you, he offered, holding out his hand.

You thought hard.

– Well, there is one thing, you decided. – This growth on my face . . .

– For that, Conway smiled, – we do have a therapy. I shall send up some shaving things.

The doctor left you in a happier state than he had found you, and went to make his report to the General Council.

18.41

A knock at the door aroused you from a vivid daydream. You had been dreaming of Tess. You were pursuing her through the corridors of the hospital, or perhaps she was pursuing you, it was not clear. She would disappear around a corner and you would find yourself at an unanticipated junction, unsure of which way to turn. Then she would appear behind you, laughing, and dart down another passage. The hospital was deserted and your voices echoed around the labyrinth. You came to the bottom of a disused stairwell littered with empty cardboard boxes, and so thick with dust that you could make out her footprints. You pursued her upwards and, bursting through a door, were suddenly on the roof. The world stretched before you – an alpine valley, pasture spotted with daisies, cattle grazing, bells clanging, a little wooden house with a pointed roof. A brilliant blue sky, domed distant white peaks. But Tess had vanished. Suddenly, she was there, in her dressing gown, in the door of the little wooden house, calling you, giggling, stepping back inside. You raced across the grass, clambered up on the platform and pushed open the door. It creaked on its hinges. Inside, all was dark, but deliciously cool and sweet-smelling. The air was thick with anticipation. She was on the bed. You gulped.

– I've brought some shaving things and a change of clothes, came a voice through the door.

You groaned in disbelief. Had she really interrupted your dream just to tell you this?

You covered yourself up again, as Khan had instructed you.

– I'm coming in, said the voice, and the door was pushed open to reveal another nurse. You felt vaguely that you recognised this one, but then they all looked and behaved much the same.

– You have interrupted a very lovely dream, you reproached her.

– Well, it won't be the last time, she retorted, equally rudely.
– That's the way it is with dreams. Dreams are a sign of rude awakenings to follow.

– Is that so? you asked, interested.

You had not had the opportunity to broach the topic of dreams before, and were wary of doing so, for you suspected intuitively that they would not be approved of. Although you were no further towards understanding the difference between right and wrong you were beginning to develop an instinct as to the sort of things which were likely to provoke displeasure. You were surprised, and a little relieved, to find that it was apparently acceptable to own up to having dreams.

– The nicer the dream the harder it is to wake up, the nurse informed you. – That's why you're better off without them. Why spend your time blowing bubbles for someone to come along and pop?

– It was you who popped my bubble, you pointed out.

– If it wasn't me it would have been someone else.

– But it might have lasted five minutes longer, and that might have been enough.

– It's never enough, she told you. – All good things come to an end, and always too soon.

– That is certainly my experience, you agreed.

– You need will-power, she told you. – When you find yourself beginning to dream, you must pinch yourself or take a cold shower. No good ever came of dreaming. Not in the modern world anyway.

– It passes the time, you said.

– It wastes the time, more like.

– But there is so much time. There is nothing but time. Surely wasting a little is not a problem.

– The problem is finding enough time, she chided. – It's all right for you, at your age, waited on hand and foot by people with much better things to do. You'll see.

You examined the shaving equipment: a towel, a bowl of hot water, a can of foam, a hand mirror and a plastic razor.

– This will remove the hair from my face? you asked, sceptical.

– It certainly will.

– How?

She showed you how to wash your face, to squirt the foam onto your fingertips and to spread it around your jowls. You studied yourself in the mirror.

– This is even worse, you complained. – The hair has not been removed at all, merely concealed beneath this foam, in a rather obvious manner. Sometimes I wonder if the authorities are not just an enormous fraud. They promise therapies, but their therapies merely substitute one problem for another. When you say you are sick of the hospital, they move you to another part of it. When you say you are miserable, they suggest you commit suicide. When you dream of something better than their miserable hospital, they suggest you take a cold shower.

– The foam doesn't remove the hair, Jackie said.

– I can see that.

– The razor removes the hair.

You were dubious.

– Won't it just grow back again?

– Not for a while, she reassured you.

You were not satisfied, however.

– Beards grow, she said. – You can't stop them. All you can do is hack away at them every morning. Try and keep them under control. Like life.

You sighed.

– You'll have to show me how, you told her.

– Hold still then. Like this.

She took the razor and removed a neat stripe of foam from your cheek, then handed back the blade. You put your fingers to the smooth skin and were impressed.

– You try, she said. – Watch yourself in the mirror.

With a deft and bold stroke, you removed another stripe of foam. Attached to it was a wafer-thin sliver of your face.

– Aaaaargh!! you hollered.

In the mirror, you watched, horrified, as the blood seeped into the remaining foam, turning it a bright pink. Blood dripped onto the sheet. You clutched your face and rubbed stinging foam into the wound.

– Aaargh!

Staggering out of bed you upset the basin of hot water. Foam got into your eyes. You crashed blindly about the room, screaming.

– Oh *do* stop fussing, Jackie commanded, in a voice which demanded obedience.

You froze and stood whimpering.

– I'm leaking, you gasped. – I am punctured.

– Put it under the cold tap.

Since you did not move, she took you by the arm and led you to the sink, where she splashed cold water on your face. You winced, but the shock had the effect not only of staunching the flow but of calming the patient. You submitted to her attentions. Finally the water ran clear but for a thin pink streak, and you stood panting, flecked with pink foam, your night-shirt drenched. The nurse dabbed at the wound with cotton wool until the blood congealed. You regarded each other, and found yourselves smiling.

– I'll shave you, she suggested. – You tell me about yourself. What you've been up to. I delivered you, you know.

– Perhaps it would have been better if you hadn't, you sighed.

She sat you down and covered your face with foam again. You told her the story of your brief and uneventful life, pausing only when the shaving procedure demanded facial immobility. When your face was smooth to your rather fastidious satisfaction, she shook out your pony-tail and washed and cut your hair, which had become thick and shapeless. Ragged clumps cascaded onto the floor. You watched with amusement, but did not cease your narrative. You found her very easy to talk to. She listened, and butted in only for the sake of clarification. The creamy mousse that covered your face, the caress of the blade, the hypnotic snip, snip, snipping of the scissors, the nurse's experienced fingers manipulating your scalp, massaging, soaping, rinsing and drying, searching out tangles and slicing through them, all combined to lull you into a sense of tranquil contentment and goodwill. Thus you found yourself at last able to recite your history dispassionately, and to reflect upon it. For you, it was third hand – you had lived the life, thought about it and were now able to begin editing it for effect, passing rapidly over the parts which you felt might reflect badly upon yourself, exaggerating the abuses to which you had been exposed, and generally organising the events into a coherent narrative. The theme of this narrative was 'injustice'. You were both encouraged and slightly perturbed by your listener's indignation at your treatment. It was not as if you yourself were not angry, but you found your anger difficult to sustain amidst the tumbling locks and the soothing snips. Jackie, however, was growing more furious with every petty tyranny recounted, and controlling herself sufficiently to finish the task in hand only by a supreme effort. Finally, attacking a particularly dense clump of tangles in a state of barely-suppressed rage she contrived to stab you with the point of the scissors.

– Aaaargh, you cried and shot forward. The pain, however, was brief. Placing your hand on the offending cut, you found blood upon it.

– Another puncture, you observed.

She apologised, with tears in her eyes half of pity, half of rage.

– It just makes me so angry, she fumed.

– Well, perhaps you shouldn't do it, you replied.

You admired your new look in the mirror. It was a vast improvement.

– You do it very well, though, you added.

– I don't mean cutting hair. I mean the whole thing – losing you, and wrenching you away from your mother and your family, the whole thing.

You wondered whether you should remind her that you had been as keen to get away from your family as the authorities had been to separate you, but decided not to. You were rather enjoying the image she had formed of you.

– It's shocking, she went on.

You nodded.

– I know it's ridiculous, she confessed, – but I never realised. I never realised what a mess they made of those beautiful little babies I produce. It's a wonder you're not more screwed up than you already are.

You weren't sure how to take the last sentiment, but it sounded vaguely sympathetic.

– It is very touching of you to get worked up on my behalf, you announced pompously. – But I have explored every conceivable avenue. I have done all that was required of me. The authorities have done nothing but continually move the goal-posts. The current problem, according to Doctor Conway, is both simple and bewildering. I cannot leave the hospital until I am cured, and I cannot be cured because I am not ill. The problem is not so much medical as . . . well, I don't know *what* it is.

She considered this, and resumed the task at hand.

– Where would you go? she asked eventually.

You were stunned. The question had not occurred to you. Your fantasies always ended at the doors of the hospital. Beyond was *terra incognita* – your fantasies could proceed no further. You could hardly admit your ignorance, however.

– It would depend on what I found when I got there, you declared, unconvincingly. – Where my destiny led me.

She frowned, and arched her eyebrows.

– All right, you confessed. – I hadn't really thought about it very much.

She pursed her lips in silent scepticism.

– All right. I hadn't thought about it all. For me, it is *not to be here* which is the important thing. Where I shall be when I am not here is hardly the point. It can hardly be worse than where I am now. I shall think about it when I get there.

– By which time, it will be too late to decide where you want to go, she pointed out. – Because you will already be there.

You dismissed her concerns.

– I am escaping, you reminded her. – One does not escape *to*, one escapes *from*.

Nonetheless, you were rattled. Conway had let slip that the world outside was very large. It suddenly occurred to you that it might even extend beyond the horizon. It might take several hours to cross, with ample opportunity to take a wrong turning. Perhaps it would indeed be prudent to have some idea of the landmarks by which you might orientate yourself, and the location of some convenient bolt-holes, in case the authorities came looking for you. You had, as yet, no friends in the world outside. Confronted with the practicalities, escape seemed rather daunting. Nothing was ever simple.

– All right, you said. You tell me. Where would I go?

She shrugged.

– Well, I don't know. Do you have any friends?

– I have no idea where she is.

– Relatives?

– Of course, you said, perplexed.

– Could you stay with them?

– They are the very people I am running from. My mother, my grandfather. They are all here, in this hospital somewhere. Apart from my father . . .

She raised her eyebrows in enquiry.

– Definitely not, you said.

– You must have aunts and uncles and things?

– If they share any qualities with the relatives I have already encountered, I would not wish to find out, you said, wearily. –

I am heartily sick of my family. They think they know what's best for me, but in the end they are more in the dark than I am. If I never saw them again, I would not consider it a loss. They have been little use to me.

– Oh, Solomon! she cried. – But they are your parents. I'm sure they care really. You must learn to make allowances for people.

– Why? you asked, imperiously.

She shrugged, having no answer. It was her feeling entirely.

– People mean well, she replied, unconvincingly.

– Do they?

– Sometimes.

– Perhaps.

Again she frowned, and shook her head.

– Why do you argue? you asked. – You know it's true.

– Yes, she admitted. – Yes it's true. But it's better not to think about it. Life is intolerable if you don't make allowances. You'll see.

Jackie O'Dowd had by now decided that she must get you out of the hospital. Between your family, the media, the politicians and the administration you were in deadlock. There was no way of knowing how long you would be made to stay in this little room, while the seconds of your life ticked away, or where they would send you if they did choose to move you on. They were playing for time, all of them, hoping that someone else would do something decisive. You, meanwhile, were growing disturbed, your moods swinging from elation to despair. You were a prisoner against your will. No one cared what happened to you, so long as it didn't happen in their ward, or on their shift. They had their deadlines to meet, their theories to test, their reputations to promote, their jobs to protect. Your parents had abused and then abandoned you. You were alone, and miserable, and not yet one-day old. Her heart pounded with the injustice of it all.

Apart from which, she rather fancied you. You too had standards, and had been sufficiently shielded from the world to retain some faith in them. She had never met anyone like you, and a nagging voice told her that she never would again. The opportunity had arrived, at last, to take decisive action.

She found her mouth speaking the words before the decision was fully-formed in her mind.

– You could stay with me, she proposed, suddenly shy. What if the Phenomenon had plans of its own? She had no need to worry.

You jumped off the bed and gave her a big hug. – Could I? you cried, and suddenly you were a child again. – Could I really?

She was astonished to see tears in your eyes.

You stopped, and the gloom returned. – It does not help me get out of here, though.

19.06

– The boy is not mentally ill, Conway informed the gathering. – In fact, given the circumstances of his upbringing, he is coping remarkably well. He is of above average intelligence, I would say, if the concept has any relevance. He does not understand what is happening to him, what is expected of him, or why his actions seem to cause offence. Fundamentally, he is incapable of empathy. Or it may be that empathy is not a realistic option for one whose experience of the world departs so radically from our own. He is no more able to put yourself in my position than I am to put myself in his.

– Is he suicidal? asked Brian Hawkins.

– Not in my opinion, no. He is rather gloomy. As any of us would be, in his position.

– Yes, yes, all right, spare us the editorial, snapped Sir John. – What would the psychiatric profession recommend in such a case?

– The boy is not mentally ill. He is chronically institutionalised. He is not, as yet, suicidal. I cannot guarantee that he will not become so. Besides, it is cruel. He must be released.

– Nothing would give me greater pleasure, declared Sir John. – Unfortunately, our hands are tied somewhat. Many considerations enter the equation.

Sir John took him by the arm and led him to the window. The crowd had swelled and thickened with the arrival of news' teams, vendors of snacks and drinks, and interested passers-by. The atmosphere was that of a spontaneous street fair. Conway surveyed the milling multitudes with unease. Someone thrust a pair of field-glasses into his hand, and he was able to decipher the writing on the vehicles, the banners proclaiming the coming of the millennium and the resurrection of the dead, dozens of figures talking excitedly into microphones, cameramen and sound men, men with booms and clapperboards and reels of cable.

– I say, exclaimed Percy Burns. – Isn't that Paxman?

Conway was obliged to reconsider, but only momentarily.

– Couldn't we sneak him out the back somehow?

– Damn and blast! bellowed Sir John, dislodging a precarious accumulation of cups, newspapers and ashtrays. The rest of the Council cowered, and sought to make themselves inconspicuous. Sir John's temper was legendary.

– There is nothing, he hissed through clenched teeth, – nothing I would like better than to get rid of this problem. For several hours I have thought of little else. This boy, through no fault of his own, has brought a large hospital with a catchment area of a quarter of a million people to a complete standstill. The potential for a tragedy multiplies by the minute. Do you not think that if I could get the boy out of here I would have done so hours ago?

– Why don't you? asked Conway timidly, still uncomprehending.

– Who could I give him to? The police? Social services? The men in white coats? Endless agencies there are, who would gladly take him off our hands, and I would be on the telephone right now if I were not convinced that they would not make an even greater hash of it than we have managed. You are not convinced?

Conway confessed that he was not, and Sir John spelled it out.

– There are three good reasons why that boy, child, man, whatever he is, cannot leave this hospital. Firstly, because I cannot guarantee his safety. Secondly, his family is a complete shambles. The father has buggered off to heaven knows where, the mother is a wreck – we've had to put her on tranquillisers –

and the grandfather, well the grandfather is one of the reasons why I cannot guarantee the boy's safety. Is that enough?

The room was silent, expectant. Sir John realised his slip too late.

– The third reason, he confessed, – is that the Minister is flying in to see him this evening. He has taken a personal interest.

The news sent a ripple of excitement around the room. The General Council began to straighten its ties and smooth its skirt.

– When is he due? asked Khan.

– Sometime this evening. His office would be no more precise than that. It's a security thing.

Regaining his composure, Sir John held the attention of all present.

– You see the position we are in. It is all very unfortunate. The Minister is anticipating a fairly sedate photo opportunity with the baby who has tugged the heartstrings of the nation. Instead of which, he is going to find a rather surly and depressed young man, whose reports as to the care and attention he has received in this hospital are likely to tend towards the uncomplimentary. This young man, moreover, is of such a volatile temperament that we cannot rule out some appalling scene, the details of which are best left to the imagination. It is a huge cock-up. This young man may be a miracle of nature but he is an embarrassment to science, to medicine in general and to this hospital in particular.

– I don't really see what more we could have done, someone protested from the rear.

– That is hardly the point. The public enjoys seeing heads roll. All heads roll in much the same way. The music has stopped, and we appear to be left without a viable chair.

A silence fell over the assembly.

– Any suggestions? Sir John enquired.

– Tell him the child is unwell, Hawkins suggested. – That it may be contagious. That he needs emergency surgery.

– That hardly reflects very creditably upon our ministrations, remarked Sir John.

– Illness can hardly be blamed upon the physician, protested Dame Barbara.

– Nonsense. Illness is entirely the fault of the physician. Illness is what we are here to prevent. Anyway, we would end up with the Minister in some ghastly anti-contagion suit with a silly mask. He is very determined. He has announced his intentions. He will not be pleased if he is made to back down.

– What if the boy refused to see him?

– That's more or less treason, isn't it?

– He will tell the Minister that he is being kept here illegally, and against his will, warned Conway. – You will have to let him go sometime.

Sir John groaned. – I am not, he said, – going to tell the Minister that the patient he has flown in specifically to be photographed with has thought of something better to do. He will look ridiculous.

The General Council was lost for words.

– I suggest, Sir John suggested finally, – we all cross our fingers, and pray to whatever God we feel we have most influence with. Unless anyone's got any other bright ideas . . .

22.40

You were all a-quiver. You sneaked a glance at your reflection and, though it was the hundredth time you had checked, were still thrilled by the transformation. Jackie finished at eleven, and had taught you how to read the time from the movements of the clock. The hour of waiting seemed unending. You paced the floor, checked your reflection again, and then the clock. You tried on the clothes she had brought you. They smelled of musty cupboards, and itched, and were already too small. You took them off again. You bit your fingernails. Ten minutes had passed. You lay back on the bed and tried to pick up your dream where you had left off, but to no avail. The moment had gone. Your heart beat faster, your fists clenched, your toes curled. You were damp under your armpits. You were comfortable neither in one position nor another. You washed your face with cold water and paced the room again, inspecting the pictures. Five minutes passed. You began to feel that you could not bear the tension any longer. Finally, a timid knocking.

– Come in, come in, you cried eagerly.

Conway pushed open the door. He was glad that he had bonded so well. He rather prided himself on his ability to win his patients' confidence. The patient, however, was obviously disappointed.

– Oh, you said disconsolately. – It's you.

Conway too was crestfallen.

– Why? Who were you expecting? he asked.

– I have so many visitors, you replied dismissively. – I never know who to expect.

– Really? queried Conway, displeased. – I gave instructions for no more visitors. I thought you had had enough. In fact, you told me so.

You made no reply. If Jackie returned now, all would be lost. You had to get rid of this man.

– I must say you're looking a lot better than when I saw you last, the doctor observed, lowering himself onto the end of your bed. – It's amazing the difference a wash and brush-up can make. Makes you feel like a new man, eh?

You smiled politely. When would he come to the point? You saw the minute hand click one notch closer to the hour. Conway noticed your preoccupation.

– Are you expecting anyone? he asked again, suddenly suspicious.

You were torn. Conway, you remembered, was quite sympathetic, and seemed able to supply some answers. It was obviously sensible to be as prepared for the world outside as possible. Perhaps you should take him into your confidence? Besides, you found it awkward to lie to him.

– Yes, you confirmed.

– Who?

At the same time, you were acutely conscious of Jackie's impending return, and the difficulties which Conway's presence would cause. You looked first at Conway, then at your feet, then at the clock and could think of nothing to say.

– Anyone, you said at last. – I am expecting anyone. There

is a knock at the door, and it could be anyone. That is my life here. I am at home to all comers.

You were quite pleased with this improvisation. You had avoided a direct lie, whilst managing entirely to mislead. You were beginning to get the hang of adult conversation.

– Well, that's all going to change, promised Conway. – I've had a word with the authorities and . . .

– I'm to leave? you interrupted, suddenly hopeful.

– Not exactly, no. You're to leave here though. Your mother is frantic without you. We've made an arrangement. Separate beds of course. With a screen down the middle. So that's some progress anyway.

– It is?

– Don't you want to see your mother again?

– Not really.

– Oh. Oh dear.

Conway's crest fell another couple of notches. He had suggested that you might prove less volatile if reunited with your mother. Your mother, meanwhile, was causing an enormous fuss, and would not be placated until her child was returned to her. It had not occurred to the General Council that you might have views on the matter yourself. Conway was at a loss as to how to proceed.

– I must say, he remarked, – you seem extremely preoccupied. Has something happened? Can I help?

– Not at all, you replied. – I am . . . I am rather tired as it happens. It has been a long day.

– Ah, said Conway. – I should apologise. It is late. I'll leave you to it.

He got up to leave, and then remembered the purpose of his visit. It would be highly embarrassing to return to the Council with the news that you had rejected his offer. He sat down again at the foot of the bed and sought words. Having been silently rejoicing at the speed with which you had dispatched this hindrance, you were distraught. The clock ticked on another minute. Conway had found a new approach.

– You know, Solomon, he began. – It's not unusual for . . . when . . . children . . . people . . . reach . . . the stage of development

you seem to be going through now, which we call adolescence
. . . it's not unusual for their relationships with their parents to
become a little strained. It's quite normal.

You said nothing until it was clear that the doctor would not
continue without a response.

– I'm glad to know that I am normal, you replied, tersely. –
In that respect, if no other.

– It's part of growing up, Conway continued. – One must
become one's own person.

– If you say so.

– On the other hand, one cannot simply reject one's parents.
Otherwise one is doomed to make the same mistakes as they
made. Time after time, generation after generation. There is no
progress. Do you see what I'm getting at?

– No, you answered.

– I think you should make your peace with your mother,
Conway counselled.

You were taken aback.

– I do not see what concern it is of yours, you retorted. – She
is not *your* mother.

– She is my patient.

– I thought *I* was your patient.

– A man has many patients, replied Conway, – but only one
mother.

You stared at him. This was the kind of gibberish that passed
for wisdom in the modern world. Conway was no different from
all the others. He pretended sympathy, but he had his own
agenda. He pretended knowledge, but his knowledge consisted
of aphorisms and generalisations without substance. He pretended
authority but he could not alter the situation, only rearrange its
constituents, and that only with the grudging consent of higher
authorities. He pretended friendship, but only because it was the
professional manner with which he felt most at ease, and because
it stroked his vanity to believe himself the object of reciprocated
affection.

Conway, for his part, was also realising that the easy rapport
he had earlier struck up with you was fast crumbling, to be
replaced by hostility and suspicion. Every approach he tried was

skilfully blocked. You were innocent still, and ignorant, but your bristles were up and you had become aware of your naiveté, and sought to conceal it beneath facetiousness and sarcasm. You were beginning to learn to negotiate, to give yourself away crumb by crumb, to withhold yourself. If you were not yet Conway's equal, you were gaining fast, and a force to be reckoned with. This made the doctor uncomfortable. His confidence in his ability to dictate the course of events, even the flow of the conversation, had been brought into question. But he was being relied upon to effect your reconciliation with your mother. The reputation of the hospital, not to mention his credibility with the Council, depended upon it.

– Why do you not want to see your mother? he asked.

– It is a phase I am going through, you replied, exasperated. – It is quite normal. You told me so yourself.

– Just because it is normal does not mean it is satisfactory, countered the doctor. – Normality is not a peak to be scaled. It is more in the nature of a base camp.

– It is all very well for you to say that, you cried. – You who can leave here any time, come and go as you please and fill your days with whatever takes your fancy because you are normal. You think it a thing of no consequence. Me, I would settle for normality any day.

There was an icy silence. Conway wondered if he had, perhaps, been a trifle tactless.

– I'm sorry, he said, at last. – I too have had a long day.

– Hmmm, you snorted, beginning to suspect that you had somehow achieved some sort of victory. Conway was humbled. Perhaps one last push would get rid of him altogether.

– I am very tired, you announced, yawning ostentatiously. – I will see my mother in the morning, if that is what is required of me. I cannot understand why you attempt to persuade me to do so of my own free will, when we both know that what has been decreed by the authorities must eventually come to pass, whether we like it or not. But for tonight I am exhausted, and wish only to sleep. It is nothing personal, you reassured him.

Conway realised that further efforts would only serve to antagonise.

– Of course, he said. – I . . . I didn't mean to offend you. I'm glad we're still friends. He extended his hand.

– What are you doing? you asked, bewildered.

Conway opened his mouth to explain, then thought better of it.

– Good night, Solomon, he said.

– Good night.

At last he rose to go. The clock showed two minutes to the hour. You turned over in the bed and closed your eyes, relieved. It had been a close shave. You heard the door creak open, and then – your heart sank – footsteps, not dying away but approaching. Through the half-open door, you heard voices in the corridor outside.

– I've brought . . . I've come to collect the stuff.

That was Jackie's voice.

– What stuff?

That was Conway's.

– The shaving stuff.

The door was shut, and the voices muffled.

– It can wait until morning, said Conway. – He is sleeping. He does not wish to be disturbed.

– I think I should get them, she pressed.

– Why? Surely it can wait?

– Razor blades.

You heard Conway's laugh.

– Nonsense. Why is everyone obsessed with suicide? The boy is no more suicidal than you or I.

– Just to be sure.

Conway's voice suddenly had an edge to it.

– He has asked for no more visitors. He is asleep. I will take the responsibility.

– It won't take a minute.

You detected a note of desperation in her voice now.

– Why on earth is it so important all of a sudden?

– I'd feel awful if anything happened.

– The matter is closed. Goodnight. He is not to be disturbed without my express permission, Conway ordered. – Or Sir John's. Except, of course, in dire emergencies.

You heard a third voice, the man Parker, but it was unintelligible. Then Conway again.

– Well dire emergencies . . . fire, earthquake, epileptic seizure, nuclear meltdown, that sort of thing. I leave it to your professional judgement.

More grunting, then Conway's voice, quite angry suddenly.

– Why are you still here? You're not going to see him. What do you think this is? A bloody peep-show?

Not knowing what else to do, you screamed.

22.59

High up on the roof, a fierce wind whipped the hair, trousers, skirts and lapels of the General Council. The night was black and starless. They scanned the skies, not entirely sure from which direction, or at what precise hour, their visitor was expected.

– Where the bloody hell is he? snapped Dame Barbara Hershkovitz

– More to the point, where's Conway? asked Khan. – He's not answering his bleeper.

– Bugger bugger bugger bugger, hissed Sir John Parkes through gritted teeth. He was acutely aware that at that very moment a plane was touching down in Tel Aviv with an empty seat reserved in his name.

– Are we sure he's coming? asked Dame Barbara. – We've been up here ages. Shouldn't we check?

– His office said he was on his way.

Down below, the media multitudes appeared to be packing up for the night.

– Do you think they sleep in those vans, then? Khan wondered aloud.

– I suppose so.

– It almost makes you feel sorry for them.

– Almost.

– Bugger bugger bugger bugger bugger, chanted Sir John, clapping his hands and stamping his feet in an attempt to restore his circulation. This sudden burst of activity was a mistake. Instantly, a powerful spotlight was illuminated, and tracked jerkily across the outside walls until it picked out the figures on the roof, blinding them in its glare.

– What the bloody hell is that? gasped Sir John.

– It's a spotlight, explained Khan, unnecessarily.

The unexpected sighting of figures on the roof caused a sudden stir on the ground below. Tiny figures could be seen scuttling around with lengths of cable, lights went on in vans, the crowd began to reassemble. There was a sudden hiss, as of a tap being opened, and a voice, shockingly near, but crackly and distorted.

– Hello, up there, it called.

– Good heavens, hissed Brian Hawkins, – the man's got a megaphone. Shall we reply?

– Certainly not, ordered Sir John.

– Hello, up there, came the voice again.

Down below, a small riot appeared to have broken out.

– Hello, up there, came the voice again. Any news?

– They won't go away until we give them something, sighed Khan.

– Bugger bugger bugger bugger, Sir John intoned, a mantra to quell his growing conviction that the world was falling apart, and that he had managed to wangle himself a pivotal role in its collapse.

– Try Conway again, he ordered.

Conway's bleeper was tried again. The voice came once again booming up from the courtyard.

– Hello, up there . . . any news of the boy?

Suddenly a window in the opposite wall shot open, and a head appeared.

– If you don't shut your fuckin' racket, it bellowed, – there's three of us here'll come down and shut it for you.

From inside the hospital came a muffled cheer. The window slammed shut, and for a moment all was silent, silent enough to make out the distant rumble of a helicopter, approaching from the east.

– Thank heavens, said Sir John. – Let's get this over with.

23.00

– What is it? demanded Conway, terrified.

What was it? Why had you screamed? It had been an impulse.

– A terrible dream, you stammered. – Terrible. About . . . about . . . my mother!

Conway's eyes lit up. It seemed to have worked. Jackie too was looking very worried. You had fooled them all.

– It's all right, Conway said. – You're with friends.

– Who's he?

You pointed at the guard. Conway dismissed him, and closed the door behind him. Jackie remained.

– Since I'm here . . . she began.

– Oh, go on then, said Conway, – but be quick.

He seated himself once more at the foot of the bed, and took your hand.

– Now tell me about your dream, he coaxed.

You had no idea how to proceed. You sat, staring blankly into his eyes. Jackie was taking as long as she possibly could, but you knew this pretext could not be sustained indefinitely. You waited for further inspiration, but none came.

– It's all right, Conway repeated. – You're safe here. She'll be gone in a minute. Tell me about your dream.

– It was about my mother.

– Yes.

Jackie dropped a bowl of water. Conway reeled round, furious.

– Do watch what you're doing, he snapped.

– I'm ever so sorry, she whispered. – I'll clear it up.

– Just get out, he barked.

Jackie hesitated.

– Now!

– Hang on, you protested. – You can't just leave the floor like that, all covered in suds.

Conway sighed. – All right, he said. – There are some paper towels in that dispenser. Mop it up and then get out.

– I'm ever so sorry, Jackie said, pulling at the towels so violently that the dispenser came away from the wall.

You had had time to improvise a new plan.

– I'm all right now, you informed Conway. – Thank you all the same. You can leave us now.

– Eh?

– I think I'll be all right now.

– Us, did you say?

– Sorry?

– You said 'us'?

Conway looked first at you, then at the nurse, and the mist fell from his eyes.

– Have you two met before? he asked.

– Yes, said Jackie.

– No, you answered, simultaneously.

Conway folded his arms.

– All right, he said. – What on earth is going on?

All was lost. Instinctively, you grabbed the nearest weapon to hand and sprang at Conway with a bloodcurdling scream, dealing him what would probably have been a mortal blow to the head had your chosen implement been a billiard cue or pickaxe handle. The pillow, however, did not have quite the same effect, and indeed your surprise attack would have made no impression on him whatsoever were it not so sudden and unexpected that Conway, no less instinctively, darted backwards, lost his balance on the soapy floor, fell crashing into the wall and cracked his head on the sink. He lay there, amongst the sodden paper towels, motionless. Jackie was stunned.

– What did you do? she gasped.

– I don't know, you admitted. – I think I scared him.

– You certainly scared me.

– Is he all right?

Cautiously, you approached Conway's crumpled body. Jackie cradled his head. A thin trickle of blood dribbled from his nose, but there was no sign of any other injury. His breathing was steady and his pulse strong.

– He's out cold, she pronounced.

– What do we do? you asked.

– Take off his shoes.

23.02

The rumble grew to a hum, and suddenly to a terrifying roar. The General Council ran for cover behind the control tower, and crouched there, buffeted by the wind as the helicopter hovered overhead and descended slowly onto the roof. As it touched down, three figures emerged from it, and scurried towards the tower. Reluctantly, Sir John emerged from his hiding place and staggered into the wind towards them. It was impossible to make out who was who, with the blades whirring and the lights flashing, the din and the blast. One of them shouted something.

– Sorry? he shouted back, but the reply was no more audible.

He shook each by the hand, but decided to postpone further introductions for more congenial surroundings. Finally, the steel doors swept shut behind them and they had escaped into the warmth and peace of the lift. Sir John felt the blood returning to his limbs. The Minister seemed in rather better spirits than his hosts, and apologised for keeping them all up so late, which was answered with a collective grunt in which the words 'not at all' and 'great honour' featured prominently.

– This, announced the Minister, – is Mr Stein.

He indicated a tall, bearded man, who was fiddling with some very elaborate-looking photographic equipment but broke off to smile and nod greetings.

– Mr Stein is my photographer. This – he turned to a stubby, red-faced man with a bald head – is Mr Raskutsov. Mr Raskutsov is the Tizian ambassador.

The assembly murmured welcomes, but were unsure of the etiquette of such occasions. The ambassador bowed, and they bowed in return, insofar as was possible in a lift.

– Mr Raskutsov was doing me the honour of dining with me, continued the Minister. – But when he heard of the nature of my visit, he . . . er . . . he decided he had to see such things for himself.

– In Tizi, the ambassador concurred, – we do not have such things.

The lift opened and ejected its occupants into the boardroom.

– I'm afraid we haven't had time to arrange much, Sir John apologised, gesturing limply at the sandwiches and cold meats procured at short notice from the all-night garage down the road.

– Hospital food, observed the Minister. – I could do with a stiff drink myself. Any chance?

Rather reluctantly, Sir John produced from the wall-safe a particularly fine malt, and poured everyone a half-inch, which was as far as the bottle would stretch.

– To Solomon Grundy, then! exclaimed the Minister, raising his glass.

The assembly followed suit. Introductions were performed, and hands pumped enthusiastically. The photographer assembled his apparatus.

– Shall we get going, then? he asked, once the formalities were completed. – I'm just thinking of the first editions.

23.08

Within five minutes, Conway had been stripped to his underwear. It was surprisingly easy, his body limp and unresisting. Jackie was obviously used to this sort of thing, and the garments came off effortlessly. You were impressed.

– Basic training, she explained.

Together, you dragged him on to the bed and arranged the covers over him. He looked very peaceful. Getting you into his clothes took a little longer for you were quite unused to dressing. You put both legs into one trouser and were temporarily paralysed, then forgot the socks. Jackie decided that the absence of socks would attract attention. The shoes would not fit at all until Jackie put them on the right feet. Conway's spectacles made the room swim in a blur, but the disguise was incomplete without them. Jackie wondered, yet again, what she was getting into, but was too far in now for second thoughts. Finally you were ready. Conway had not moved, and did not look likely to.

– What about these? you asked, indicating your old clothes.

– Better bring those, she said. – You never know.

You stuffed them into a carrier bag. Jackie gave you some final instructions.

– Don't say anything, she hissed.

She opened the door slowly. The guard was still there, sitting on a chair. He moved to let you past.

– Everything all right then? he enquired.

– He is not to be disturbed, Jackie instructed. – He is sleeping. Let him sleep. He is to see no one.

You nodded at appropriate moments, but kept your face averted. The guard grunted acknowledgement. Jackie moved off. You followed.

23.22

The General Council trooped off, revived by the whisky, to see Solomon Grundy. The Minister, however, hung behind, and motioned Sir John to do the same.

– I'd like to have something intelligent to say about this, he confided, when they were out of earshot of the others. – Can you help me out? It's not really my field, babies. I was always more on the transport side.

Sir John racked his brains, but came up with nothing.

– I was thinking along the lines of, well, you know, 'miracle of modern science', 'great breakthrough for medicine', 'another first for Britain', that sort of thing.

– It's none of our doing, shrugged Sir John. – I'm afraid Mother Nature must take the credit for this one. Or the blame.

– The blame? enquired the Minister.

– Credit or blame, whatever.

The Minister's voice dropped even lower.

– Is there something wrong? he asked, worried.

– The boy is growing up, Sir, replied Sir John. – All babies do so. It is part of the human condition. This boy is growing rather faster than is usual. Rather faster than was believed possible, until today. It is undoubtedly awe-inspiring, but whether it is cause for triumph or despair is an open question at the moment. That's all I meant.

The Minister frowned, and called to his photographer, who joined them at the rear. Sir John motioned the rest of the Council to keep moving.

– We have an ambivalence, the Minister informed his photographer. – This . . . er . . . situation could be read many ways. It is open to interpretation. Is it a tragedy or is it . . . the opposite of a tragedy?

– A comedy? suggested the photographer.

– It is certainly not a comedy, said Sir John, icily.

– Does it matter? asked Stein.

– You tell me, replied the Minister. – You're the photographer. What's our angle?

– It's a story, shrugged Stein. – Human interest. Babies. Death's door. Hanging by a thread. That's the whole point – could go either way.

Sir John realised, with heavy heart, that it was now or never. The Minister had to be warned.

– Could I have a word? he whispered.

The photographer rejoined the main party. The Minister was beginning to look uneasy.

– The thing is . . . began Sir John.

There was a sudden crash. The Tizian ambassador had collided with a trolley. He was picking himself up from the floor, brushing himself down. They fussed around him.

– Sorry, so sorry, the ambassador mumbled, then inexplicably burst out laughing.

– I couldn't get rid of him, sighed the Minister. – He insisted on coming. Now tell me, Doctor . . .

– Parkes.

– Tell me, Doctor. Is there something I should be aware of? My office told me there was a baby, a quite extraordinary baby, who would not stop growing. The newspapers also seemed convinced. Am I misinformed? I do not mind being misinformed, provided everybody else is equally misinformed. But I'd like to know now, before it goes any further. Am I misinformed?

– No, no, Sir John reassured him. – No, your information is correct. Was correct, at any rate.

– The situation has changed?

– No, the situation is much the same.

– There is something you are not telling me.

– This morning, we had a baby who would not stop growing, Sir John sighed. – But a baby that won't stop growing doesn't stay a baby very long.

– I see.

– It soon becomes a child.

– It stands to reason, the Minister agreed.

– And then it becomes . . . not a child any more.

– It becomes an adult?

– Eventually.

– I see.

There was a pause.

– And how is he? Our patient, who is a child and an adult and a triumph and a disaster all rolled into one?

Sir John considered his response.

– Volatile, he said at last.

The Minister digested the information.

– We must proceed with caution then.

The party were by now approaching your cell. As they turned the corner, Sir John was aghast to see, right in their path, a nurse and doctor locked in passionate embrace, apparently oblivious to the oncoming dignitaries. The Minister, however, either had not noticed or was sufficiently discreet to avoid noticing. Sir John had little choice but to brazen it out.

– I still need a quote, said the Minister, as they rejoined the main party. – Something pithy.

– Something pithy.

– Something pithy.

Sir John racked his brains.

23.30

The corridor seemed endless, and the journey to take for ever. You turned a corner, and both breathed a sigh of relief. Then suddenly a stairwell spilled a crowd of figures, headed straight for you. In an instant, she had taken you in her arms and was kissing you, locking you in an embrace so intense you feared you would suffocate. Your spectacles misted over completely, but you heard the voices as they passed, caught the word 'pithy'. Not until their voices had trailed away round the corner did she release you.

– Sorry, she said. – I couldn't think what else to do.

– Not at all. It was wonderful.

The lift was still open, and you stepped in. You were keen to repeat the experience, but she pushed you away, saying, – Not yet. Wait.

She laughed at your eagerness. You too laughed, and felt some of the tension drain away as the lift doors closed behind you. At the next floor, a woman in a dressing gown joined you, and you completed the descent in silence. The lift opened into a foyer, practically deserted and only half lit. A cleaner was dragging a polishing machine across a tiled floor. You stepped out, and the lift continued down into the basement.

23.31

Sir John desperately cast around for something pithy.

– Tempus fugit, he said.

The Minister looked up, surprised.

– You what?

– Tempus fugit, Sir John repeated.

– A touch pretentious for the tabloids, the Minister decided.
– Not even true in my experience anyway. A week is a long
time in politics and all that. An afternoon is a long time in
Stoke-on-Trent. But the summer recess is gone in a flash. It's
all relative. Anyway, it's too depressing. We need something a
bit more . . . hackneyed.

– His life is in our hands? suggested Sir John, as they arrived
at the door behind which lay the object of their deliberations.
The guard stood to attention. The Tizian ambassador belched.
All awaited the command of the Minister.

– Yes, he mused, – yes, I like that. Mr Stein!

The photographer produced a notebook, and licked his finger.

– Take this down. Quote. His future is uncertain, but what is
certain is that he will receive the best medical care that money
can buy. His life is in their hands. Your hands. My hands. Our
hands. Whose hands is he in?

– Our hands, Stein confirmed.

– Unquote. Read that back.

Stein did so.

– How's that? asked the Minister.

– A bit clinical, Stein observed.

– This *is* a hospital, the Minister pointed out.

– What about love? Stein asked. – Childhood? Family?
Emote a bit.

– Hmmm. Right. Insert. Dum de dum. The people of this
nation have taken him to their hearts, as a symbol of . . .
of what?

The assembly stared blankly. Nobody came up with anything.

– Of all that we hold dear. How's that?

There was a smattering of polite applause.

– Now, concluded the Minister, let us see what he has to say for himself.

23.35

– These doors, whispered Jackie, lead to the car park. – That desk – she indicated the sole light beaming and a woman sitting beneath it – is reception. The car park is full of journalists. Can you manage that?

You had not understood a single word, but nodded. Behind Conway's glasses you were still unable to make out anything but vague blurs of light and shade.

– Good.

You walked past reception and were astonished to find the door sliding back of its own accord. On the steps outside hunched a dozen figures, who sprang to life at your approach.

– Any news? called one.

– No news, said Jackie.

– How's the boy? from another.

– Not my department.

– Say something sexy, from a third.

– Something sexy, said Jackie, and they laughed.

– Good night, gentlemen. Sleep well.

But at the threshold, you stopped. Jackie was several paces beyond you when she realised you were not with her.

– Come on, she hissed, anxiously.

You did not move, but remained in the doorway, shivering. A figure with a microphone was approaching. She turned, took you by the arm and re-entered the building. The receptionist looked up. Jackie smiled and noticed two security guards playing cards on a sofa in the subdued half-light. The receptionist smiled back. The security guards looked up, then continued with their game. She led you to a seat half-concealed behind a huge rubber plant.

– Why did you stop? she asked.

– I was waiting for the lights, you explained.

– The lights?

– It was all dark.

– It's night–time.

– Night–time?

She realised suddenly what she was up against. Not only were you completely ignorant of the ways of the world, you were quite lost in the dark. You had never been outside even. You came from a world in which the temperature was regulated, every corner illuminated continuously, the air chemically purified, all noise muffled.

– Were you scared? she asked, taking your hand.

– Not scared, you replied. – I just couldn't see where I was going.

Perhaps it was already too late then. Perhaps you had adapted completely to the artificial atmospheres of the hospital. You had, after all, spent your entire childhood within its walls. Perhaps your eyes would never adapt to the dark.

– I was not prepared, you admitted. – I thought I could imagine what the world would be like, but it was less familiar than I expected. Colder and darker.

Jackie was aware that you were being watched.

– My car is at the far end of the car park, she whispered. – About a minute's walk. Do you think you can make it?

– If you stay with me, you said. – Hold my hand. I don't know where I'm going.

– All right.

23.38

– They can't have got far, said the guard.

– When did they leave? barked Sir John.

– Just before you got here.

– I say, said Brian Hawkins, – you don't suppose . . .

– Well, they must still be in the hospital then.

– With Conway's bleeper.

– Find that boy, snarled the Minister. – Find that boy, or heads will roll.

23.39

You took a deep breath, rose and, under the watchful eyes of the security guards, made your way to the door.

– We'll walk straight through, and keep on walking, Jackie ordered. – Take my arm.

You leaned against her. The doors swept open, and the cold washed over you. She walked through, and you stumbled after her. After ten yards, you could see nothing.

– Three steps down, she whispered.

Then you were on the flat again, and moving at speed. The darkness was thinning, blurred silhouettes forming and dissolving within it. There was a sudden flash of light, and blobs of brilliant colour swam in front of your eyes. You stopped. Her voice hissed in your ear.

– Wait here.

– Don't leave me, you pleaded.

– I have to unlock the car. Trust me.

You had no option. Her hand slipped from yours and you heard her footsteps, a rattle, a creak, a door slamming.

Then her voice again, from close by.

– Get in.

– BEEP BEEP BEEP BEEP.

Involuntarily, you screamed. You felt yourself on the verge of panic. What was that noise? It seemed to be coming from inside you, almost. You felt two arms pushing you down. Your head caught something sharp, but you landed in a chair. You gripped your carrier bag. A door slammed against your face.

– BEEP BEEP BEEP BEEP.

It was even louder now, piercing and maniacal. You heard

footsteps crunching towards you, then a door slam, and you felt
Jackie beside you.

– Sorry. Sorry if I was rough. Let's get out of here.

– BEEP BEEP BEEP BEEP.

The noise filled the air. You heard a click, a rumble, another
click, a tremendous roar. You struggled, but found yourself
pinned down by a strap across your chest.

– Let me out! you screamed.

– Shut up! she screamed back.

– BEEP BEEP BEEP BEEP.

You were thrown backwards. A screech and a jolt. You were
flung forward, and jerked back by the strap.

– BEEP BEEP BEEP BEEP.

– Will you turn that bloody thing off!

The footsteps were approaching rapidly now.

– BEEP BEEP BEEP BEEP.

You felt her weight heavy across your chest, a blast of icy air
across your face, a slam, and the noise was gone. The car sped
off into the night.

Married on Wednesday

00.03

∞

You had never seen people before. Not real people. In the cold, moonlit streets of Pilsbury, you found them: singing, dancing, fighting and snogging, laughing and crying and eating kebabs, whatever they could find to prolong the night another half-hour. Solitary drinkers stumbled home to ring the Samaritans. Arm-locked couples leaned grimly into the wind, giggling at private intimacies. Ragged clumps of baggy, hooded youths littered the pavement outside Kebabylon. You watched and marvelled. Jackie drove, head craned forward. She was habituated to the marvels of late-night Pilsbury, and quite unaware of your rapture. Her eyes followed only the traffic ahead. A few flakes of snow tumbled out of the night.

– Where are we going? you asked, as much to re-establish contact as because the answer was likely to clarify anything.

– I don't know, she admitted, biting her nails at a red light. – Away.

– Ha! you snorted, – I only brought you along because I didn't know where I was going.

– You didn't bring me, she corrected, – *I* brought *you*.

– But it was my idea.

She turned to face you.

– There's an idea behind all this? she doubted.

– Urge then. My urge.

– Well, it's very good of you to allow me to participate in your urge, she said.

– It's a pleasure.

Sarcasm was lost on you.

– We can go anywhere in the world, she said.

– Pute? you suggested.

Choice unbounded might have daunted anyone more familiar with the options, but Pute was the only place you had heard of.

– That's the first place they'll look for us. We have to get far away.

– Well, I am in your hands then, you abdicated. – Tell me when we get there.

Soon you were leaving Pilsbury behind, golf courses and country clubs giving way to open fields. The street-lamps stopped abruptly, leaving only the cone of white light thrown by the headlamps against the hedges and dry-stone walls. A wave of delight crashed over you, and you whooped and shrieked with the implausibility of it all.

– Faster! you yelled, slapping the dashboard. – Faster!

– If I go any faster, she said, – we'll come off the road.

As if to prove her point, a lorry rumbled past. The Mini wobbled alarmingly. You grabbed at her in terror.

– You're strangling me. I can't see.

As the car steadied itself, you released her and exhaled in relief. She laughed breathlessly, for she was excited too, her heart pounding against her ribcage and her hands clammy on the wheel. A little knot of determination had crystallised in her stomach.

– We're fugitives, she said, and instantly wished she hadn't.

– Eh?

– Runaways, she synonymised.

– Oh.

You sat in silence now, mesmerised by the tail-lights of the car in front. When it turned off, the Mini was the only car on the road. You sped through dormant hamlets, thrown briefly into relief by your headlights before plunging once more into anonymity as you departed. You seemed to be the only people alive.

– What's that? you wanted to know, pointing ahead. – That big blue thing.

– That's the moon, she said. – A full moon.

– I want to touch it, you announced. – It looks so smooth and cool.

– You can't, she said. – It's too far away. Millions of light-years away.

– Let's go there then, you suggested.

– It's too far away, she said. – And it has no atmosphere.

– One day, you promised, – we'll go there.

You were not the first man who had promised Jackie O'Dowd this. You were undoubtedly the first who'd said it with any sincerity. She felt a little thrill somewhere between terror and pleasure ripple down her vertebral column and go to ground in her perineum. Goosebumps rose on her thighs.

– You shouldn't make promises you can't keep, she reproached you.

– But I mean it, you protested.

– It's not the same at all. It's not whether you mean it that matters, it's whether you can deliver.

She drove on through the night.

– If we can't go to the moon, you said, – where can we go? Where do other people go, other runaways?

She admitted her ignorance.

– It depends where they're running from, I suppose. In the opposite direction to wherever they're coming from.

– But not to the moon.

– Not to the moon.

– Does anybody go the moon?

– It's not so simple, she said. – You have to have a suit and things.

– What do people do when they get there?

– I don't know. Same as anywhere else. They take some photos and come home and show them to the rest of us.

– It feels like we're the only runaways in the whole world, you said.

– Oh no, she said. – Not at all. Nearly everybody, sometime or another.

– Then we are all running away from each other, you calculated.

The world outside was a constant revelation.

– I guess so, she said, absent-mindedly. – Well here we are.
The motorway.

To your left the road sloped slowly downwards and round a
bend, from whence emanated an ominous rumble. You stared at
her, uncomprehending.

– Right or left? she translated.

– I don't know where we're heading even. I'm following you.

– We're not heading anywhere. We have to go one way or the
other, that's all. Now choose.

– What's west?

– The sea. Eventually.

– And east?

– East is London. I've a sister in Peckham. We could stay
there, she suggested.

London, the sea. It meant nothing to you.

– Decide, she ordered.

– I don't care where I go, you said, – so long as you
come too.

She leaned over and kissed you on the cheek.

East? West? West? East?

– East, you decided. – Go East.

The motorway was no less empty than the country lanes that
formed its veins. It soon became apparent that such traffic as
there was was in the opposite carriageway. You were none too
pleased to find yourself *still* heading in the opposite direction
to everybody else. You had had enough of running in a parallel
groove to the rest of humanity. It was time to join the flow. You
pointed this out to your driver.

– We're not going the opposite way to everyone else, she
sighed. – It's not even an option. Not in a car. You *have* to
go where everybody else is going.

You were not convinced, but did not pursue it. You were in
her hands, and obliged to bow to her superior experience. You
were in no position to argue, either, being entirely dependent
on her continued goodwill. Nonetheless, you were beginning to

suspect that Jackie's account of the world was no less partial than anyone else's. There was no alternative – if you wanted to know, you were going to have to find these things out for yourself. Once again, you pressed your nose to the glass.

01.36

– We're going to have to stop, Jackie announced.

You roused yourself from the trance into which you had fallen.

– OK, you said.

She pulled off on to the slip road and made her way through the empty car park to the fuel pumps. The service station was deserted but for a figure reading a book in an illuminated window. The fuel pumps were an island of sickly yellow light in a hostile black night.

– We might be on the news, she remembered.

At the turn of a knob, bland music throbbed dully around the car. Then three short pips and a longer one, and a little jingle.

– Pip . . . pip . . . pip . . . piiiiiiiiiiip. Bumbley – Buuuuummmm.

A mellifluous voice announced the imminence of the news, and Jackie went to fill the tank. You were the main item. An apocryphal account of the events leading up to the disappearance of the Phenomenon was followed by a press conference given by Sir John. A well-organised conspiracy was at the root of it, the great man diagnosed, aided and abetted by accomplices amongst the hospital staff. A reporter (who sounded very much like Dr Smokey) speculated on the nature of the conspiracy. You watched Jackie approach the little booth. The man put down his book and some sort of transaction took place. She came back towards you, flapping her arms against her sides to ward off the cold. Snow was falling again. She clambered back into the driving seat, accompanied by an icy gust of wind.

– Well?

– Lies and nonsense, you reported.

She did not seem particularly surprised.

– Are they after us? she asked.

– They are convinced I have been kidnapped.

– They're obsessed, she said.

But you were ignorant of the drama that had surrounded the first few hours of your life.

– There was a conspiracy to abduct me, you continued. – Aided and abetted by you. Sir John Parkes says you're a cult.

– Did he say that?

She was shocked. There was no need for that sort of language, surely?

– What do you want to do? she asked

But you were strictly a passenger.

– I'm relying on you, you reminded her. – That's why I brought you.

Not for the first time, Jackie wondered how long she could keep this up. You were absolutely draining. No good would come of this escapade, she told herself. Your eye would be caught by something or someone new and off you would go. You would shed no more tears over Jackie O'Dowd than you had for your parents, your home town, your roots. She should stop the car now, and push you out. That she had no intention of booting you out was due largely to her irrational hope that the situation would resolve itself long before the need arose for such drastic remedies. She would stick around as long as you needed her, she decided, provided it was not for long. Then you would slip out of her life as quickly and efficiently as you had slipped in, and her regret would be nine tenths relief.

– We've got two choices, she calculated. – Either we carry on, or we stop.

She realised as she spoke that this meant, 'we either stop now or later'. Eventually, you had to stop.

– Here?

You looked around, at the pumps, the snow dancing in the headlights, the man hunched over his book in the kiosk, the dark trees. It looked suspiciously like the modern world.

– In the motel, she specified.

She deciphered your surroundings for you. The low squat

building directly opposite was the motel. To its right, daubed with garish neon come-ons offering warmth, light and refreshment to the weary traveller, the service station. A row of stunted conifers shielded the motorway beyond.

– And what's this white stuff? you asked.
– Snow, she said. – It falls from the sky from time to time.
– It's nice, you said, – I like it.
– Good.

You agreed to give the motel a try. Your legs had grown an extra two inches during the journey. You were becoming uncomfortably cramped and on for anything that would get you out of the car.

– First, she said, – we need an alibi. They might have heard the news.
– I see.

Your expression belied your claims to comprehension. Her heart sank. But wherever you stopped it would be the same. It would have to be faced sooner or later.

– We'll be man and wife, she suggested.
– I'll be the man, you baggsed.
– That's the way I saw it, she confirmed.

You were relieved to have been given the easy part. You could hardly be expected to pretend to be someone other than you were, when you had no idea how such people looked or talked or behaved. You had very little idea of who you were, after all, even before you started chopping and changing.

– What is a wife, exactly? you needed to know.
– A wife, she explained, – is a woman who's married.
– Married?
– A woman and a man . . . go to the priest and ask him to marry them. They're sort of joined together. Not literally. Sort of spiritually. They take the same name. Sometimes. The woman then becomes a wife.
– But the man remains a man?
– He becomes a husband.
– And I am to act as if I were your husband?
– Exactly.
– How does a husband behave?

Jackie recalled the husbands of friends.

– He sort of tags along behind looking irritated, and pays for things, she said. – Look as if your mind was elsewhere. Try and make it seem like you'd rather be somewhere else.

The role was fortunately, she reflected, not so far from the one you presented to the world as a matter of habit anyway.

– And wives? How do they behave?

– Don't you worry about that.

– I can't pay for things, you warned her.

– It's not a problem, she assured you.

You would either muddle through or not. She cared less and less. The reception desk was abandoned. Jackie pinged a bell. A minute passed. Another. From a half-opened door came the sound of gunfire and tyres screeching. She rang again, more insistently. Eventually a girl appeared, smoothing down her skirt and blinking. She had clearly been summoned from a deep sleep and fixed you with a professional smile that barely concealed her irritation. She dissolved the screen save and apprised the computer of your requirements. The computer said you could have any room you liked. There was no one else in the building.

– Name? demanded the receptionist.

– Solomon, you informed her.

Jackie glared at you.

– Both of us, you clarified. – We are man and wife.

– Mr and Mrs Solomon, the girl typed.

– No, no, no.

The girl sighed, looked first at Jackie then at you, and pursed her lips impertinently.

– Name? she asked again, wearily.

– Mr and Mrs Hopeless, said Jackie.

Having ascertained the spelling, the girl rolled her eyes heavenwards and typed it in. Jackie filled in a form, and peeled off some notes from a fat roll, for she had been to the hospital cashpoint in preparation. The girl took the form, perused it, and indicated by illuminating the passageway that the formalities were completed. You followed your wife down the corridor. A series of identical doors were embedded into the wall at regular intervals. Jackie inserted a key into one and it swung open. You followed her in, sniffing the air. Apart from the pink fluffy carpet, the flowers in the vase and the fact that the bed was twice as wide, it bore a disturbing resemblance to the institution from which you had recently absconded. Even the Alpine meadow on the wall was vaguely familiar. Jackie noticed your unease.

– What's wrong? she asked.

– The world outside, you observed, – is very reminiscent of the modern world. Is that all there is to it? More of the same?

– What did you expect?

– I don't know, you confessed, – not this. Something . . . a bit more imaginative.

She shook her head wearily and sank down on the bed. You were impossible to satisfy.

– We'll stay here until the morning, she said. – There'll be more traffic in the morning. We'll be less conspicuous. It's only for the night.

You were far from comforted by this news.

– What do we do until then?

– Sleep, she suggested.

– Sleep?

You were incredulous. There seemed little point in having escaped from the modern world at all. The world outside was no different – just pinker and fluffier, and the staff were even ruder.

– Sleep, she confirmed. – Everybody has to sleep. Even me.

– Not me, you pointed out.

You were in a different orbit entirely.

– We are not going anywhere, she put her foot down, – before the morning.

The room was suddenly in darkness.

– What are you doing?

– I'm getting undressed.

She removed her shoes, her stockings, her belt, her dress. You could see nothing, but the rustlings, the pops, the creaks and thumps in the darkness were intriguing. The room was filling with her odour, an odour of sweat and soap and fear. It was very exciting. You felt her slip beneath the covers next to you, and stretched out your hand to feel the bump in the duvet that was her shape. But as soon as her cheek met the soft pillow she was asleep. You sat there in the darkness for a few minutes, growing progressively more restless. You prodded her, poked her, then poked her again until she could ignore the assault no longer, and sat up, blinking.

– What? she snapped. – What?

– I'm bored. I can't sleep.

– For heaven's sake, Solomon, I'm your wife, not your mother. You're a grown man, now. Not a toddler any more. You'll have to start taking care of yourself. I'm exhausted.

There was a long pause.

– I'm sorry, you said at last, – I'm sorry if your life is difficult right now. My life is difficult all the time.

She sighed.

– All right, she said, – all right, all right, all right.

The lights came back on. She scanned the room for possible amusements.

– Try the TV, she suggested.

So for an hour or so, you watched TV. Jackie snored beside you, curled into an S-shape, her arm draped across your chest. Television offered a crash-course in the sort of lifestyle you might expect to live when you got to London. Your chances of surviving even an hour out there were fairly slim without the acquisition of a vast array of gadgets. The most important single item was clearly a firearm – indeed it was something of a miracle that you had got as far as the Milestone Service Station without one – but a firearm was merely the first item on a shopping list that ran to several pages. Toothpaste, chocolates, canned drinks, furniture, perfume, jewellery, credit cards – none could be done without. You had no idea where you might lay your hands on such things. Presumably Jackie would know. It was all bewildering, but very exciting as well. There seemed unlimited opportunities for sex – indeed, it appeared almost compulsory in the metropolis – and for driving cars into each other at high speed. All in all, life in London seemed to be scored vivace and fortissimo, climaxing frequently in gunfire and explosions, collapsing buildings, multiple pile-ups, earthquakes and mushroom clouds. This was the kind of world in which you felt at home, and the kind of pace you felt comfortable with. You wished to proceed towards it without further delay. Your palms itched for action.

After a while, however, you began to lose the thread. Londoners shot at each other, and drove around at high speed. In between they sat around in cars drinking coffee and eating doughnuts. But there seemed no obvious motive for these activities, and what had seemed tremendously exciting to the noviciate was getting fairly predictable by its thirtieth repetition. You surfed the channels, but uncovered nothing more interesting than more of the same, and found yourself falling into a coma. You pressed a button, and the screen imploded into a tiny dot. You turned it on again, and then off again. Off and on. Now all was still and dark. You rose wearily from the bed, kicked off your shoes, and began to unbutton your shirt, scattering your clothes around you, until you climbed under the duvet, naked. Inside, the Jackie-smell was overpoweringly salty, and the heat from her body intoxicating. You gulped, and your member stood once more to attention. She fidgeted in her sleep.

– Solomon? she enquired, drowsily.

Who else was it likely to be? You reached out your hand in the darkness and touched bare flesh. She gave a little shiver. You ran your finger along her arm. She wriggled, and smacked her lips in her sleep. You moved closer and pressed your lips between her shoulder-blades.

– Mmmmmmm, she moaned.

Your skin tingled and your heart began to pound, a muffled thudding intense in the darkness. You had no idea what was about to happen but some sixth sense told you it was going to be good. You felt her move against you, and she turned to face you. Her lips closed upon yours. The hot kiss lasted for delicious hours. It was the wettest, most reckless sensation you had ever known. The tip of her tongue met the tip of yours. You were spellbound. She draped a leg over your thigh and hitched herself up. You felt her breasts swell against your chest, the nipples hard and insistent. She laid a hot hand upon your stomach. You grabbed her buttocks. She shivered and gave a little cry. You turned on one side, slipped a thigh between hers and squeezed the mound

between her legs. Again, she moaned. Her tongue was deep in
your mouth now, her hand massaging your stomach. You groaned
deliriously, and began to thrash as her hand descended. From that
point on, all was a surge of overwhelming, inexorable, irresistible
necessity.

03.10

The Minister was furious. He had no wish to discover how,
at an hour's notice, the newspapers would fill the large white
space reserved for the first stunning pictures of the Phenomenon.
Having planned on a discreet photo opportunity, the chance to
associate himself in the public mind with the little chap who
had played *Eine Kleine Nachtmusik* upon the heartstrings of the
nation, he had quite needlessly managed to inculpate himself in
a farcical catalogue of mismanagement and lackadaisical security.
He would be a laughing stock. Mr Stein had been dispatched to
see if he could find any way out of the mess, but the Minister
was not optimistic. The assembly scrutinised his expressions,
his gestures, his every word with fanatical interest for any
revelation that might be betrayed therein. But the Minister was
an experienced politician and refused to be scruted.
  – Yes, Tony, he was saying. – No, Tony. No. No no no.
  Tony Bowles scribbled frantically in his notebook. The hospital had struck a deal with Doctors White and Smokey: in return
for exclusive access and interviews the *Sentinel* would turn not
a *blind* eye, since this would be unethical, but a partially-sighted
eye to some of the less impressive aspects of the hospital's management of the affair. This was the most the institution could reasonably hope to salvage of its reputation. The Minister retracted
his aerial and paused, pursing his lips and scratching his nose.
Hawkins' fingers drummed nervously on the table. Dame Barbara
Hershkovitz cleared her throat unsuccessfully several times.
  – That was the PM, the Minister informed them, unnecessarily. – He wants a resignation.

– Singular? queried Hawkins.

– Singular, the Minister confirmed, – it's a scapegoat he's after, not another Waco. One name will do. The question is, whose?

A silence fell upon the assembly. This was indeed the question, but not one with which anybody wished to be identified as an answer.

– In my experience of such matters . . . began Sir John at last.

All eyes turned towards him.

– My *very limited* experience of such matters, he emphasised, – there are three ways of approaching this. One is to draw up a list of everybody involved, and cross out names one by one until only one remains. The second is a variation on the first, except that one eliminates names by getting everyone to put two fists into a circle reciting a rhyme about potatoes. The first contains rather more science, the second rather more justice.

– The PM is not interested in science, observed the Minister, – let alone justice. He wants a result.

– The first it is then, deduced Percy Burns.

– Hang on, interrupted Tony Bowles, – what about the third way?

– One asks for volunteers, explained Sir John.

There were no volunteers. They drew up the list of everybody involved. After much crossing out, readdition and recrossing out it contained the following names:

> Professor Khan
> Sister Nuttall
> Doctor Humphries
> Mr Parker
> Sir John Parkes
> The Minister

– But not, Khan was keen to establish, – necessarily in that order.

The assembly conceded the point. Sir John had been adamant the original shortlist be as long as possible, thus minimising his own exposure. Tony Bowles, however, had pointed out that, although scapegoating was inevitably a fairly arbitrary procedure, it did have to be demonstrable that the scapegoat had at least been involved in the scandal in some way, however marginal. Simply having been in the same building while it happened was not enough; the public would see through it as a cheap shot. Dame Barbara Hershkovitz, Percy Burns and Brian Hawkins trenchantly supported this point of view. The public weren't stupid, they reminded him. But the Minister pointed out that the public was *very* stupid, and unable to see a table through the bottom of a beer glass for the most part. The Ambassador said he had no idea whether the British public were gullible, but the Tizian public certainly were. This was not the legacy of Communism, it was genetic. He also pointed out, however, that the chief criterion by which one might judge the utility of a shortlist, apart from that it be a list of some sort, was that it should be reasonably short.

Having lost the first round, Sir John came out fighting for the second.

– The second criterion, he suggested, – is that the scapegoat not be too high up.

Khan exploded with indignation at this, but Sir John was backed up by the Minister.

– It gives a bad impression, the Minister explained.

Tony Bowles observed that in his experience of scandal, which although entirely confined to Pilsbury was extensive, it was indeed noticeable that senior management, though claiming huge personal bonuses when things went right, were rarely found to be to blame when things went wrong. The Tizian ambassador confirmed that, in his experience, this was the British way. At the end of the second round of elimination, the list thus contained four names:

Professor Khan
Sister Nuttall
Doctor Humphries
Mr Parker

– What about the Reverend Green? asked Chalkie White. – Doesn't he come into it somewhere?

– Why don't we try the second method? suggested Khan, desperately, – the one with the potatoes?

But the Minister felt that the current method was yielding encouraging progress.

– The third criterion, he suggested, – is that the scapegoat not be in possession of compromising information.

This left two:

Sister Nuttall

Mr Parker

Once it had been established that the scapegoat was not to be selected from amongst those present, the mood of the gathering relaxed appreciably. They stared at the piece of paper containing the two names.

– Both of them? suggested Khan

– The PM specified one, the Minister pointed out.

– Perhaps, said Sir John, – we have gone as far as we can with this method. Perhaps we should move on to the second.

Since neither of the prospective scapegoats were present, a coin was produced.

– Heads for Sister Nuttall, the Minister allocated, – tails for Mister Parker. Now this must be completely honest and above board. Mr Raskutsov, perhaps you would do us the honour?

– What honour? asked the Ambassador, warily.

Sir John explained the procedure. The Ambassador tossed the coin high in the air. Being a novice in the art, however, (and still slightly tipsy) he failed entirely to synchronise the closure of his fist in the air with the downward descent of the coin. He grinned sheepishly. The coin rolled under the table and disappeared down a crack in the floorboards.

– I'll do it, offered Tony Bowles.

He tossed, caught and flipped the coin on his wrist.

– Well, come on, urged Brian Hawkins, – don't keep us in suspense.

08.46

You came to some time later in a state of bliss and lay there in the early morning, your face split by a wide and mischievous grin. Suddenly, it all made sense. You had discovered what it was that people did for the thousands of hours between birth and death. It was marvellous. Extraordinary. Miraculous. No wonder people kept so quiet about it. They wanted it all for themselves. You toyed idly with yourself until you stood once more erect. It was time for a further consummation. Jackie had turned on her side, presenting her back. You pulled her towards you, but she resisted. It was only then that you realised she was sobbing.

– Jackie?

You stretched out a hand and felt her cheek. It was damp.

– Jackie, what is it?

For a few brief moments it had all been clear. Now, once again, the fog had descended. She took your hand and squeezed it.

– It's nothing, she sniffed, – don't worry.

The light revealed disarray, carnage. As your eyes grew accustomed to the morning, you became aware of the chipped vase, the strewn flowers, the damp patch on the duvet, clothes scattered around the room. You rolled over onto something hard in the bed. A shoe. You flung it into a corner. You rose and straightened the Alpine meadow, then collapsed on the bed and lay there on your back, your head cradled in your hands, staring at the ceiling.

– What a mess, Jackie observed.

It was not clear to what exactly she was referring. She nestled into your body and pulled the bedclothes around her.

– Why were you crying? you asked, mystified.

– You wouldn't understand.

– Try me.

– No, she refused.

So you sat there in silence, your limbs entwined, your hearts synchronised but your minds far apart. A sadness was growing inside you, a terrible restless melancholy.

– It's just . . .

But she trailed off, and it was several minutes before she tried again.

– I promised myself not to get involved again, she said, – ever. Not unless it was going to be for ever. You see?

You did not see at all.

– Didn't you enjoy it?

She had certainly sounded like she was enjoying it.

– It's not that. It's just . . . well what's the point? Where's it all heading? Another flash in the pan. It doesn't matter.

– Of course it matters, you said, – if it matters to you.

You placed your hand between her legs.

– Let's get married, you proposed. – Properly. Really and truly.

– Solomon, she sighed, – slow down. Slow down, do.

You snorted derisively.

– I like being married, you said, – I feel it's like what I was put on the earth to do.

But Jackie was having none of it.

– Last night, she reminded you, – I was a midwife in Pilsbury. I feel like all the familiar landmarks have disappeared. It's all a bit breathtaking. Everything you do is a whirlwind.

– Please?

Before she could say it you did.

– I know, I know, it's not that simple.

Things looked straightforward, but they never were. You couldn't escape the suspicion, though, that things might indeed *be* straightforward if only people weren't so determined they should be otherwise.

– It's not just a spur of the moment thing, she said. – Not just for a day. For ever. A promise. Can you keep a promise like that?

– How do I know until I try?

– It's not a promise to try, she said. – Anyone can promise to try.

– What do I have to promise?

– Not to sleep with anybody else, for a start.

– OK.

One at a time seemed ample.

– What else?

Jackie tried to remember. There had been a time in her life when she had attended weddings on a weekly basis.

– To love, honour and obey. In sickness and in health, she said, – for better, for worse. For richer, for poorer. Till death do us part.

– OK.

You had nothing else to do, anyway. Where she went you went. She had the car.

– And you have to have your parents' permission, she continued.

This was an unexpected obstacle.

– Who makes these rules up? you huffed, exasperated. – Why do people make life so awkward?

– Let's leave it, shall we? she suggested.

But there had to be some way out of this impasse.

– Can't we just pretend to be married? Like last night?

– You can pretend to receptionists, she said, – but not to God.

– God?

God seemed to crop up all over the place, and to hold the key to many mysteries.

– Look, let's leave it, eh? she sighed. – I wish I'd never mentioned it.

But you had the bit between your teeth now.

– We should get married right now, if that's what you want. If that's what'll make you happy.

– I never said that. Anyway we can't, she cried, finally exasperated. – We need a . . .

– A what?

– A priest for a start. And a ring. And a dress. And flowers and things.

You began to reassemble the demolished bouquet. She did not know whether to kiss you or strangle you.

– You're in too much of a hurry, she reproached you.

– Is that such a bad thing?

– It can be taken to extremes.

– So what do we do now then?

– I don't know about you, she said, – but I'm going to lie here in bed and drink my tea.

You stuffed the flowers back into the chipped vase. It was clear you were getting nowhere.

– I'm starving, you said, – I'm going out.

– Solomon! she called.

You were halfway down the corridor, but returned.

– What?

– Put some clothes on, eh?

09.03

Beyond the automatic doors, a whiteness had descended upon the world, and was still descending. Flakes of whiteness tumbled from a blue-grey sky. The world was changed beyond recognition. Was it safe? Cautiously, you stepped upon it. It crunched under your shoe, and you were startled to find the imprint of your foot left there. You made your way gingerly over to the main building, and were relieved to find that the shopping centre had resisted its advances. Your stomach rumbled. You scanned the boutique shelves, but were disappointed to find no nourishment, just shelf after shelf of cuddly toys. Tapes and CDs. Fudge. At last you found something that looked like food: a display of shrink-wrapped pasties and sausage rolls.

– What are those? you asked the shop girl.

– Pasties, she informed you, warily.

– Oh.

You had tried pasties before, and not found them very edible. You picked up 'Fish Breeder' and were troubled by the fish, the filters and pumps and miniature sunken galleons.

– And what are these? you asked.

– Magazines. Do you want them?
– Can you eat them?
– No?
– Can you fuck them?
– No.
– They're no use to me then.

You thought this rather witty. The girl, however, was less than amused.

– Well, put them back on the shelf then, she said.

Reluctantly, you did so. Your appetite was being overwhelmed by a more urgent need. You clutched the front of your trousers.

– I need to piss, you informed her.
– So?
– I thought you might have a potty?

She stared at you.
– A what?
– A potty.

It was a simple enough request.
– The gentleman's toilet, she said, – is directly opposite.
– In there? you queried.
– In there, she confirmed.

She set off to call the supervisor, but had barely taken three paces when you reappeared in the doorway.
– Aren't you coming with me?
– It's not allowed, she pointed out. – Men only in there.
– Right.

Nervously, you entered. A series of gleaming metal bowls was mounted along one wall. Facing them, a row of cubicles. Not a potty in sight. You pushed at the first cubicle, but it was bolted from the inside and would not budge. There was a powerful odour of faeces. The door of the second cubicle swung open to reveal a large porcelain potty. With some considerable relief you perched yourself upon it and enjoyed your evacuation. For several minutes you sat there, picking your nose and listening to the footsteps echoing around the facilities, until a prickling of the hairs on the back of your neck warned you that you were not alone. You were being watched. Then you noticed the hole. It was perhaps an inch in diameter, and had been bored in the wall at about eye-level. Craning forward, you peered into it. Another eyeball was already there. It was a familiar eyeball, too, though you could not instantly place it. It withdrew hurriedly. The toilet in the next cubicle flushed loudly, and the bolt was pulled back. This was unfathomable. Yanking up your trousers, you met your neighbour in the doorway. Father Tew reddened, and pushed past you to the sink, where he began furiously to wash his hands. He seemed not to have recognised you. You tapped him on the shoulder, and he wheeled round and stared into your face. He scowled, then turned his back and began fiddling with the towel dispenser.

– Do I know you? he asked. – Have we met before?

– At the hospital, you reminded him, – yesterday afternoon.

Again he frowned. Then his eyes opened wide and his jaw dropped.

– You're . . . you're . . .

– Solomon, you prompted

– You've . . . you've grown, he observed.

You offered your hand. This, you had learned, was the correct procedure in such circumstances. He looked at it, sceptically, and at the trousers around your ankles.

– Well, it's good to meet you again, Solomon, but I must be getting . . .

But the light of inspiration gleamed in your eye.

– Do you know what has brought us together in this place? you interrupted.

Father Tew gritted his teeth.

– The need to defecate, he said, – is a universal human need. One from which the clergy are not immune.

– No! you exclaimed, – it was fate. You are the very person I was hoping to bump into.

You were the very last person Father Tew had been hoping to bump into. In fact, had he realised that such an encounter might be even a remote possibility he would have held it in for another twenty miles. But he bit his lip.

– Marry me! you cried.

Father Tew doubled up against the sink and went quite red in the face. You became alarmed. He gasped and gesticulated but it was not clear whether his response was in the affirmative or not. A whistled ditty announced the imminent arrival of a third party. Father Tew regained control of his respiration, though not of his composure. The whistler came into view – an enormous, pneumatic man with sideburns. Every inch of his blubbery arms was festooned with tattoos in lurid blues and greens – birds and dolphins for the most part. He was bald on top, and what remained of his hair had been gathered behind in a pony tail. His whistling ceased abruptly upon the discovery that the chamber was already occupied. His grunt might have been greeting, or might have been threat. He made his way over to one of the basins. The whistling started again, and a cloud of steam rose from the urinal. Father Tew took advantage of your distraction to make another effort to extricate himself from what was fast becoming a very awkward situation. You had no intention, however, of letting him slip away.

– Marry me! you repeated.

The whistling stopped. The Priest looked panic-stricken. He glanced at the man's back, then at you, then at the door. After an awful pause the whistling took up again. When Father Tew found words to speak, his voice emerged somewhere between a whisper and a squeak.

– I cannot possibly marry you, he said, – it's out of the question.

– Why? you demanded.

He cupped his hands over his mouth and whispered in your ear – I am a man of the cloth. I am sworn to celibacy.

The whistling had stopped again. Father Tew's face turned crimson, and his breathing was short and shallow.

– Besides, he continued hurriedly, – I have no intention of marrying you. I met you briefly this afternoon, and now again in this toilet. I have no intention of marrying you.

You were cast down.

– In that case, you said, – I fear our love affair is over.

– Our love affair? the Priest spluttered.

– Over, you confirmed.

Father Tew made a strange gurgling sound and staggered back.

– You are insane, he accused. – Insane.

The third party turned slowly round. His trousers were soaked. He glared at Father Tew with such hostility that the Priest instinctively took a step backwards against the wall.

– Sick, the man said, and spat into the urinal.

– Who's sick? asked Father Tew.

– Get out of my way.

He barged past the pair of you and disappeared.

– Wait! called Father Tew, desperately.

But the man was gone. Father Tew barged past you and followed the man out through the exit. Your chances of making your peace with Jackie were rapidly fading. You pulled up your trousers, rushed after him, and collided with him in the doorway.

– Hide me, he hissed.

– But . . .

– Don't ask any questions. Just do it. Please.

You peered out on to the concourse. The man and the shop girl were talking to a security guard. They pointed in your direction. There was no way past them.

– Out the window, you suggested.

Exactly three minutes later you burst through the door of your motel room. Jackie had returned to dormancy.

– What happened? she yawned.

– I met Father Tew, you said, – it was fate.

The subject of your conversation collapsed wheezing, and lay groaning on the floor. Between you, you hoisted him to his feet and bent him double at the waist. One at each arm, you repeated the operation until his breathing was regular again. He fell back on the bed. Jackie fetched him a glass of water, and at last his eyeballs settled once again in the middle of his eyes.

– Are they gone? he asked nervously, – are we safe?

He darted to the window, and gingerly lifted the curtain.

– Are you all right now? you asked.

Father Tew glared at you.

– No, I am not, he hissed. – I am not remotely all right. I'm not even aware where I am.

– You're in a motel room, Jackie reminded him.

He turned his attentions to her, and a shock of recognition flashed across his face.

– Good grief! he exclaimed, – it's you. What on earth are you doing with this buffoon?

– I could ask you the same question, she pointed out.

Father Tew produced a handkerchief and began to dab at his forehead. Jackie handed him his teeth, and he replaced them.

– It was all a misunderstanding, he said, – a terrible misunderstanding.

– It was fate, you corrected. – Father Tew is going to marry us.

Jackie's jaw dropped.

– He is?

Father Tew took you by the arm.

– Hang on a minute. Us, was it you said? You and her?

You stared at him in bewilderment.

– Well, who else?

– Can we do that? asked Jackie.

Father Tew considered his options. His sole desire at that moment was to escape as quickly and as discreetly as possible from this cursed service station.

– Is that what you want? he asked.

Jackie didn't seem to have many alternatives either. Her future was inextricably entangled with yours. She could hardly back out of it now, go back to her day job and the quiet desperation of her former life. The embers of her bridges were already scattered to the four winds.

– I suppose so, she said.

There was no contest really. You were no worse than anyone else who'd asked, and you were here and you were now. And she *was* vaguely fond of you.

– I do, she said, decisively. – I will. Whatever.

You clapped your hands in triumph. It *was* straightforward after all. All you needed to make things straightforward was to let them be so.

09.27

Father Tew had no idea whether the ceremony he was about to perform would have any status in English common law, or in the eyes of the Church. He guessed that the Bishop would take a dim view – that seemed to be the Bishop's habitual myopic perspective – but would take an even dimmer view of an indecency trial. He was not so worried about God. God was fairly broad-minded about that sort of thing, in Father Tew's experience. So long as you meant well, that was what mattered to God. After all, you could hardly be held responsible for the mess people made of your good intentions. Father Tew's own intention, meanwhile, was to drive off into the anonymity of the motorway as rapidly as possible.

– Where do I stand? asked the receptionist, whom pecuniary considerations had persuaded to be co-opted as a witness.

– Wherever you like, replied Father Tew, – over by the shower there perhaps?

– We are gathered together in this ... place, he began rapidly, – to join together this woman and this man in holy matrimony ...

Jackie squeezed your hand. The girl from reception looked bored, and examined her fingernails. Father Tew had to ask her to refrain from humming. By the middle of the second sentence he had lost you completely. It sounded impressive though. The speech went on for ages, until it became clear from Father Tew's cadences that he was building to a climax.

– Speak now, Father Tew commanded, – or forever hold his peace.

He paused dramatically.

– You're doing it again, he chided the receptionist. – It ruins the atmosphere.

– Sorry, she said. – I can't help it.

The next stage was more interactive, and required the repetition of various lugubrious phrases by yourself and then by Jackie.

– Do you have the ring? Father Tew enquired.

You stared at him, uncomprehending.

– The ring? he repeated.

You had not come prepared for this. Neither your bride nor the witness could assist.

– Here, said Father Tew, removing one from his finger. – Use this.

He was anxious to be gone, and prepared to sacrifice a ring in the cause. It would not, however, go over Jackie's knuckle. You tried to force it, but she cried out.

– Never mind, said Father Tew, – it's not essential. It's largely symbolic.

– It fits mine, you pointed out.

– Well, you wear it then, the Priest advised.

So you did.

– I pronounce you – he paused briefly – man and boy. I mean man and wife.

– Is that it? asked the girl.

– That's it, confirmed the Priest.

He lifted the net curtains and peered cautiously out.

– The coast is clear, he said.

– Perhaps I shall see you again, you speculated.

– Tew hissed something under his breath as he made his second escape of the morning. The girl, however, showed no inclination to leave, until Jackie produced another twenty-pound note. Your wife hurried your witness out the door, and pushed it shut behind her.

– Are we spouses? you asked, – or are we spice?

Either way, there seemed only one ritual appropriate to celebrate the transformation. You took your new wife in your arms and toppled her backwards on to the bed. To your amazement, however, she wriggled out from underneath.

– Not now, she postponed you.

– But we're married.

– We've got a long day ahead of us, she said. – It may have escaped your notice but while one half of this partnership is out arranging little rites of passage for us, the other half is stuck in here trying to work out how the hell we're going to get through the next twenty-four hours.

This was exasperating now.

– Well, what do you want me to do then?

– I don't know, she said, – just be more sympathetic I guess.

– I'm trying, you said. – You don't make it easy sometimes.

– Well, try harder, she suggested.

– I'm trying as hard as I can.

– Well, it's not good enough!

At which point she clenched her fists, gritted her teeth and shook her head from side to side.

– Wrrrwrwrwrrwwr, she growled, and stormed out of the room.

She returned a minute later, contrite and composed.

– I'm sorry, she said, – it's been quite a night.

– Has it?

– For me it has been. By my standards. Maybe not by yours. I'm going to take a shower, and do my make-up. Then we'd best get going.

You watched her undress, but had no desire for her any more. She struck you suddenly as very old and very tired. You had done what she wanted, but it hadn't made her happy. All she wanted was to shower. What had you ever seen in her? Availability, that was all. She was available. You felt suddenly spiteful.

Jackie too was having second thoughts. You were certainly a singularity, she was realising – singularly selfish, singularly rude, singularly egotistical. Singularly unattractive, in fact. A little boy in the body of a man. The world was full of little boys in the bodies of men, but the little boys were usually aged eight or nine. The singularity she'd landed up with was barely out of nappies. You now seemed determined to provoke a reaction. You were annoyed with something and were trying to manipulate things in such a way that you could be annoyed with her instead. But she had no intention of rising to your bait.

– Solomon, she said, – I don't want to argue. Not on my wedding day.

She disappeared into the shower.

– What about me? you called after her, – what am I supposed to do?

– Find something to amuse yourself, she called. – Play with yourself or something.

– It's not the same, you sulked.

– Not for you, maybe.

She stuck her head round the curtain

– Did you get any breakfast? she asked.

You were reminded of your aborted shopping expedition, and of the emptiness of your belly. Anything was better than sitting around in this wretched room. It was like being back at the hospital. You sifted through your wife's clothes until you found her purse. You had no idea quite how commercial transactions worked, but enough experience to understand that money was an essential ingredient of them. Your wife's purse was fat with notes. You peeled one off and replaced the roll. One note suddenly didn't seem very much, with so many indispensable items to purchase. You replaced the note, and took the roll instead.

09.43

Tess Scoop slid herself slowly backwards – legs first, dangling in the air, then bum, until she was hanging from the window-ledge by one hand, the other clasping the box of drugs. Then she closed her eyes and let herself fall onto the roof of a convenient van. This kind of manoeuvre she had practised many times, in flight from her mother's initially, then from her Gran's, then from Don and Eve's, then from various other foster parents', and finally from the Larches, Pilsbury's infamous children's home. At the back of her mind, which was as close to consciousness as she ordinarily allowed her thoughts to venture, she realised that these Papillon-style abscondings were quite unnecessarily melodramatic. There was nothing to prevent her leaving by the main doors through reception. But it was no fun to walk out the door when you knew no one was even going to try and stop you. Even if you stood in the doorway taunting them they would cower in their offices and hide behind their desks and hope someone else would deal with it. This way, hanging from her fingertips from the window-ledge, allowed her to preserve the illusion that someone in the outside world cared whether she lived or died.

– Oi!

She had not envisaged the van being occupied. Now the door flew open and a man tumbled out, half a sandwich in one hand and a fag in the other.

– What the bloody hell you doing on my van? he demanded. – Off!

He shook the sandwich at her.

– Gissa hand then, she suggested.

The man dropped her off at Marble Arch in mid-morning. She had a friend to stay with, she lied. He didn't believe her.

– You look after yourself, he admonished.

– You sound like my mother. (He didn't sound remotely like her mother, but she had heard other children say it, and she knew it was a thing you said.)

Behind him, the traffic honked and hooted. He leaned out the window and threw them a V-sign. She laughed. He drove off. She wandered round, trying to keep warm. The sky froze over and began to weep snowflakes that made the pavements wet and slippery. She spent some of her earnings on a Big Mac and a Coke and made it last the best part of an hour. She met Leon, and they walked the three miles back to Leon's yard. Leon kicked over the embers of the fire and poked Martin with his boot.

Martin grunted, – Fuck off, Leon, but would not be roused any further. He smelled of glue. Leon led her to another car and unrolled a filthy sleeping bag on the back seat.

– I sleep here, he informed her, unnecessarily.

He climbed into the sleeping bag. She stood there, shivering, delirious with cold and fatigue, trying to work out what sort of place he had brought her to. She understood that she was in some sort of graveyard of machines, a place where they brought useless things in order that anything valuable might be ripped out before they were finally discarded. It was vaguely sinister. She was aware of purple clouds scudding over the rooftops of the metropolis and of the steam from her open mouth, and of a thin dog scavenging pointlessly.

Leon interrupted her thoughts. – Are you getting in or ain't you? he wanted to know.

She forced herself in next to him. It was ridiculously cramped. When she faced him, they stared into each other's eyes. Both found this disturbingly intimate. So she turned her back on him and felt his fingers fiddling with her button, and then two hands on her hips, inching her jeans down. Then he fell asleep, snoring into her hair.

10.02

As you pushed past, the girl caught your elbow.

– Are you going to London? she asked.

How could she have guessed that?

– You take me? please?

– Er . . .

Yet again a trip to the outside world had taken an unpredictable turn. You looked her up and down. She was tall and blonde, dressed in a suede jacket. She had a large sack. She arched her eyebrows in a combination of enquiry and invitation.

– Please?

You were torn. Some instinct told you that no such invitation could be extended without Jackie's say-so. A closely related instinct told you your wife would not be enthusiastic. But you yourself had no objection to this rather lovely creature tagging along. It would be fun. You might even get to have sex with her. Procrastination seemed the only way out of the impasse.

– You must have a car though, you pointed out.

– A car?

– Or how did you get here?

She clenched her fist and stuck her thumb in the air.

– I hitch-hike, she said.

– I Solomon, you said, repeating the gesture.

She giggled.

– No, no. I hitch-hike, to get here. But now this snow. Brrrrr. Too cold.

She beat her arms around her shoulders in illustration and did in fact dislodge a quantity of snow from her hair. There was no escaping it. She was ravishing.

– I'll have to ask my wife.

She shrugged. – OK.

You turned to go, and then remembered the purpose of your visit.

– And I've got some things to get first. We've just escaped from the hospital and we're not going to get very far without a gun.

– I have a gun, she said.

– You do?

She reached into her jacket and produced a small revolver.

– Is very useful, she said, – in the modern world.

That appeared to settle it.

The snow was falling faster now, dancing and whirling around yourself, Ingrid and her rucksack as the three of you made your way back to the motel. It was treacherous underfoot, too. You slipped, and Ingrid helped you to your feet. Eventually you regained the motel, where you stamped and shook the snow from your clothes. As you passed, the girl behind the desk gave you the kind of glare she reserved for the discreetly kinky, of which she saw a few in her line of work, but you failed to notice.

Jackie was brushing her hair.

– Hi, she said.

Then she caught sight of Ingrid in the doorway, smiling and looking ravishing.

– Who's this? she wanted to know.

– She's coming with us to London, you informed your bride.

– WHAT?

– My wife, you explained to your new acquaintance. – We're just married.

Jackie stared at the girl who had captivated her husband. Ingrid smiled back, and performed a cute little wave.

– This is your . . . honeymoon? she asked. – Congratulations!

Jackie was lost for words.

– Come on, you said. – Let's go.

Jackie had known it would be like this. You would find

someone else, and that would be it. She just hadn't expected
it to be so fast. You'd only been gone a quarter of an hour, after
all. It wasn't the losing of her husband she minded so much – in
some ways she was glad to pass the baton on to someone else. It
was the humiliation of it all – this gormless girl standing there
grinning at her, in this Travelodge.

– Go on then, she hissed at you, – clear off.

You stared at her, puzzled.

– I said clear off, she repeated. – Get out and take . . .

– Ingrid, Ingrid prompted.

– Take Dancing Queen with you.

– We need you, you pointed out, – to drive the car.

Now it was Jackie's turn at amazement.

– You don't expect me to drive the pair of you to London?

– Well, I certainly can't.

– Nor me, Ingrid chipped in.

– Jackie, you pleaded, – what's the matter?

– Get out!

She threw a pillow at you.

– Get out!

– Look, said Ingrid, dropping the cute broken English, – I'll
get another lift. Thanks anyway.

– Get out! screamed Jackie.

Ingrid heaved her rucksack onto her shoulders and departed.
You stared at your wife in astonishment. She was crimson, and
shaking with rage.

– I thought she would be useful, you said, – she had a gun.

– A gun? What use is a gun?

– In case . . . I don't know, you confessed. – It seemed like a
good idea.

– Aaaaarrrrrrghhhhh, she screamed.

It was a cry of sheer exasperation.

– You're so irritable, you said. – Moody and unpredictable.
Is that what marriage does to people?

– I don't know about people, she said, – it's what marriage to
you does to *me*.

– I have a good mind to just walk out of here and leave you.

– Go on then.

– What sort of a marriage is this any how? We haven't had sex for hours. It's worse than the hospital.

– Go on then, she repeated.

– You're worse than my mother.

Jackie had had enough of this by now. She wanted her old life back, its certainties and predictabilities. She had had enough of singularities. You could never tell what they were going to do next.

– Get out!

A cup smashed against the wall near your head.

– We must un-marry, you said, – immediately.

– Out! Out! Out!

Another cup glanced off the elbow you had raised to shield your face.

– All right. I'm going.

A plate smashed against the door as you slammed it behind you.

– My wife and I are no longer married, you informed the receptionist as you passed.

– All breakages will be charged, she warned.

10.23

You stepped out into the snow. It was bitterly cold. You wondered suddenly if you hadn't made rather a rash decision. You knew no one in the world outside, after all. You had no idea what to expect, how to behave, where to go even. And the world changed from one minute to the next. Where had all this whiteness come from? Then you caught sight of a distant figure struggling with her sack against the snow.

– Hey! you called, – Ingrid!

But she didn't hear. You ran towards her. She was the closest you had to a friend now. By the time you reached her she was standing by the side of the road, jumping up and down.

– Hi, she said.

She sounded as if she'd been expecting you.

– I've left my wife, you explained.

She laughed, ravishingly.

For ten minutes you stood there shivering. A dozen cars passed. None even slowed. The cold moved slowly up your calves towards your groin. You had lost all feeling in your thumb.

– Don't you have a coat? Ingrid asked.

– N-n-n-n-n-no, you shivered.

– You could have mine, she offered.

– Well, that's very kind . . .

– Only I need it myself.

– It's all right, you lied. – I'll manage.

But it wasn't all right. You weren't dressed for this. Your teeth were chattering, Dampness seeped through your clothes. After a further ten minutes you had had enough. You would make your peace with Jackie. Swallow your pride. Anything. You would suffer any humiliation. Just to be in the warm again, to thaw your thumb and restore some circulation in your legs.

– Hey! cried Ingrid, – come on.

A car had stopped fifty yards up the road. She ran towards it with her rucksack. She really was lovely. Again you were torn. The car was nearer than the services. You followed. Several times you stumbled, staggered and fell, then dragged yourself to your feet again. The vehicle seemed vaguely familiar, though camouflaged beneath a jacket of white. As you drew level a carrier bag was thrown from the window, then the car roared off so quickly that you toppled forward into the sludge. Prostrate in the road you watched the Mini shrink into the white distance, where it joined the motorway.

– Get up! Get UP!

Ingrid was tugging at your arm. Now a juggernaut was bearing down upon you, snorting and steaming, flashing its lights and honking. At the last moment, it veered to one side, spraying you with slush. With a great hissing of air-brakes, it stopped.

– Come on, urged Ingrid.

You picked yourself up, soaking wet and blue with cold, grabbed your bag and trudged through the blizzard towards the lorry. You saw Ingrid clamber on board. When you were level with the cab, she wound down the window.

– Only room for one, she said.

She blew you a kiss.

– Sorry.

The lorry honked. The brakes hissed and the juggernaut was gone. You realised you had lost a shoe. You sank down into a snowdrift and wept.

11.45

Coming out of the services, Parker nearly missed you completely. It was not difficult to do. In Conway's white coat you blended seamlessly into the winter wonderland like an Arctic hare. Neither, normally, did he stop for hitch-hikers. Today, however, he needed company. He needed to talk. He wanted to grab passers-by by the lapels and scream it into their faces, to daub it on flyovers in fluorescent letters a foot tall, to take out full-page advertisements in the *Sun*. Without some sort of release he feared he might combust, and he had been on the look out for likely victims. It was only when fifty yards up the road, however, that it occurred to him the tree-stump he had just passed was in fact human. He slammed on the brakes, a bad move in snow. The car came to rest with its offside wheels in the gravel. Parker looked in his rear-view mirror. You hadn't moved. Maybe you were a tree-stump after all. Your arm, jutting out grotesquely from your torso, certainly added to that impression. He honked. Still no movement. He clambered out of the car, put his cupped hands to his mouth and hollered.

– Do you want a lift or don't you?

You tried to shout back, but no sound emerged from your mouth. You tried to move your legs, but they had locked rigid. You were rooted to the spot. Your thumb was blue and numb, and swollen. But when you saw Parker shake his head and climb

back into the car, from the last dying embers of your life you
found the strength to shout.

– Wait! you called, – wait! please!

You even managed to wave. Then you heard the ignition, and
saw the exhaust, and understood that your last gasp had been
gasped in vain.

– Please . . .

You trailed off. It was getting bigger. It was reversing. It
pulled up next to you. The driver leaned over and pushed open
the passenger door. You threw your bag onto the back seat and
swung first one leg, then the other, through the door. Finally,
you collapsed onto the passenger seat, shivering.

– Door?

You sat, your teeth chattering, unable to reply. Your left arm
would not respond to your commands. Parker leaned over you,
and pulled the door shut.

– You must be out of your mind, he observed, lighting another
cigarette, – without a coat even.

But he cranked the heating up to full and set off. Gradually,
life flowed through your limbs again. Within ten minutes, it had
reached your wrists and ankles.

– You a doctor, are you?

You shook your head, dislodging a crown of half-melted snow
into the small pool forming at your feet.

– Good, he said, – I hate doctors.

You were glad to have given the correct response.

– Do you know why?

You shook your head. You couldn't care less. You didn't give
a damn about anything but heat. Slowly, slowly, your extremities
were defrosting. When your body had thawed out, perhaps
your mind would follow. Parker, however, was undeterred.
On the contrary, he was delighted to have found a receptive
audience, which in his book meant one that didn't answer back
or interrupt.

– Hypocrites and nymphomaniacs! he explained, – the lot
of them.

You nodded. It was plausible.

– Where are you heading? your driver enquired.

This seemed to demand an answer beyond a head movement. You essayed your voice, and were surprised to find some juice left in the battery.

– London.

– Me too, said Parker.

He had in his possession – he indicated the carrier bag on the back seat – incriminating materials of an audio-visual nature. The world should know, he said, what went on in the place he used to work in.

– You know where that was?

You confessed your ignorance. Why did he keep asking questions to which you could not possibly be expected to know the answer? Why did he insist on talking at all? Why couldn't he just shut up and let you concentrate on keeping warm? But you were under a sentence of obligation. At any moment, he could stop and pitch you back out into the cold.

– Pilsbury General Hospital, he revealed, – that's where.

You groaned audibly. You were not qualified to judge whether the public had a right to know what went on at Pilsbury General Hospital, but you doubted very much whether they'd have any great desire to know, once they did find out. Nonetheless, some instinct told you to keep your advice to yourself. This man held all the cards. Most things could be endured, provided they could be endured in comfort.

Parker was in full flow now. Sister Nuttall. She was the one responsible for all this. He'd been an innocent bystander until she implicated him. You listened, off and on, without any great interest. The men and women of whom he spoke were not familiar names to you. You were not surprised he had suffered at the hands of the hospital. It was the way in the modern world. Instead, you turned your attentions to your surroundings. You were on the elevated section of the Westway now, and through gaps in the barrier you caught glimpses of the city spread beneath you, its churches and its chimneys, its giant hoardings and its traffic. Its traffic most of all. There was no evidence of any people though. Presumably they were around somewhere.

– Solomon Grundy, your driver snarled with sudden vehemence, – Solomon fucking Grundy.

At the mention of your name you wheeled round. The self-preservation instinct you were beginning to cultivate warned you, however, that this was not the time to acknowledge your ownership of it.

– He's at the bottom of all this, Parker went on. – I tell you, if I had that bastard here in the car with me now, do you know what I'd do?

You shook your head.

– I'd wring his neck, and dump him in the nearest lay-by. I would too.

You understood from the way that his hands gripped the wheel that he was not joking.

– I'm not joking, he confirmed. – That boy has been nothing but trouble from the day he was born. Ask his father. Ask his mother. He bust up his family and he lost me my job.

– I'm ever so sorry, you gulped.

But he was not listening: he was in full flow.

– I mean, it's not natural, is it? Growing up like that. I mean, one minute you're a baby, the next minute you're a boy. Then before you know where you are, you're a man. It's not natural. No wonder. It's the end of the world, Parker prophesied, – the end of the world. You got an address? he asked suddenly.

You shook your head. He looked you up and down.

– What you going to do then? Sleep on the streets?

You shrugged. This was the sort of detail for which you'd been relying on Jackie. You were pretty lost without her.

– So where shall I drop you off?

You were travelling up a broad street, lined on both sides with shops. You had no great desire to remain in the car with this rather frightening man.

– This'll do, you told him.

It might as well be there as anywhere.

– You need to get out of them wet clothes, Parker observed. – You got a change?

– In the bag.

– You want a launderette really.

He indicated a shop window indistinguishable from all the others, and double parked outside.

– Good luck then, he wished you.

– How do I get out?

– Lift that knob and push the handle.

A small queue of traffic was rapidly collecting behind the stationary car. Someone hooted. The snow was falling all around you.

– You got everything?

The bag. You opened the rear door and extricated it.

– It wouldn't cost you anything to say thank you, Parker pointed out.

– Thank you.

The car honked again. Parker stuck two fingers out the window, and moved off.

You stood there, shivering, on the kerb. The world outside. Fat fryers, dog shit, after-shave, cigarette smoke, rotting vegetables, tandoori chicken, stale beer and cheap hash. A small dog yapped at your ankles and was dragged away with a curse. Vehicles trundled past – long red cars with two storeys, maybe forty windows in all, a different face in every one. You stood there, shivering, absorbing it through every pore. It was undeniable: life was faster here, wilder and more frantic. People scurried past, wrapped in scarves and hoods: men, women, children, short ones, tall ones, black ones, white ones, thin ones, fat ones, all heading somewhere important, and all grimly determined not to be distracted on their way. Wobbly women on heels clicking clacking. Hustle and bustle. Horns honking and brakes screaming. Deep, rich rhythms blared from an open window above one of the shops. Still the snow tumbled down around you: only here, in the city, it did not coat the world in white, it merely formed a soft grey slush on the road and pavement, that blurred the edges and made the colours run together.

Someone coughed behind you. Wheeling round startled, you were confronted by a short, bearded man. He grinned at you, and was missing several teeth. He was either very fat or wearing an implausible number of layers of clothing.

– Could you spare us a cup of tea? he enquired.

– I don't have one, you replied.

The man's expression changed. You seemed to have offended him, though this had not been your intention at all.

– It's not the sort of thing I carry around with me, you explained.

The man's expression was now distinctly belligerent.

– Are you taking the piss? he wanted to know.

– Not at all, you protested.

It was for just this sort of situation that a gun would have been so handy. How much simpler it would be to just pull it out and blow this man away, instead of having to explain everything to him, when you hardly understood it yourself. But you had no gun.

– I'm from the hospital, you explained.

The man pondered this, rubbing his beard with a grimy hand.

– Do you have any money? he asked, simply.

Was that all he wanted?

– Why didn't you say?

You produced the roll of notes purloined from Jackie earlier in the morning, peeled one off and handed it to him. He inspected it, and seemed to find it satisfactory.

– Good man, he said, – good man.

He took your hand and shook it. You watched him amble off and disappear into one of the shops. You seemed to have survived your first encounter with the denizens of the city, gun or no gun. It was still bitterly cold though. The world outside was tempting, but it could wait until you had some warm, dry clothes.

You rubbed a hole in the condensation, and peered through the window of the shop identified as the launderette. It was all vaguely familiar. A woman was transferring a soggy bundle of clothes from one machine to another. She slammed the door, inserted a coin and turned a knob. The machine grumbled into life. A man in a track-suit sat opposite her, apparently oblivious to the world. You noticed wires coming out of his head. His eyes were closed, and the only clue to his sentience was a foot tapping on the tiled floor. The chances of being attacked seemed fairly limited, but you had learned from the television that once in the city, you might be jumped on from behind at any time. Danger lurked around every corner. The thing to do was to go in, take off Conway's wet clothes, put them in the machine, and change into the dry ones you had brought from the hospital. Thankfully, Dr Conway carried loose change in his trousers. Cautiously, you pushed open the door and entered. Neither of the other occupants looked up. You found an empty machine, and began to divest yourself of Conway's sodden clothes. The lab coat was first in, followed by jacket, shirt and vest. You rummaged in the bag for replacements. Then rummaged again. Again. A sick feeling rose from the pit of your stomach to your throat. You upended the bag. Three black, plastic oblongs clattered to the floor. The woman looked up from her magazine and scowled. What to do now? Your clothes were in the back of that madman's car, somewhere in London. Thankfully, the launderette was warm and dry. Trousers and pants followed the rest of your clothes into the dryer. You shut the door and waited for something to happen. In the machine next to yours, clothes were tumbling merrily as the barrel revolved. Yours, however, remained obstinately uncooperative. You produced a handful of coins. But which?

The man stared vacantly ahead. You decided to try the woman.

– Excuse me . . .

She lowered her magazine, and gasped. Her magazine slipped from her lap onto the floor. You thrust your coins into her face. She glanced at the coins, then back at you, then at the coins again, terrified.

– For the machine, you explained.

She pointed at one, and you inserted it into the slot. It fitted perfectly. Still no response, however. Her mouth flapped open and shut, but no sound emerged. You thumped the machine with your fist. She flinched.

– Why isn't it working? you demanded.

– Knob, she whispered.

You turned the knob. There was a clicking, and then, slowly at first but gradually picking up speed, the barrel began to revolve.

– I am not at home in the outside world, you explained.

She did not reply. Her eyes darted back and forth between your washing, your person, her washing and the door. You picked up her magazine, and handed it back to her. Nervously, she took it. It seemed incumbent upon one of you to speak, but she showed no inclination to do so.

– I left my clothes in the car of a psychopath, you explained.

She sat back down on the bench and disappeared behind her magazine. You too sat down to wait, amidst the rumbling of the machines and the tapping of the man's foot. A man emerged from a door at the rear of the launderette, his torso and head concealed behind a pile of neatly folded clothes. He walked through the shop, and deposited the clothes on a bench at the window, revealing a short stocky man in a string vest. What was revealed to *him* was a naked man in his launderette. His moustache bristled. Realising you were about to be addressed, you rose, and extended your hand in greeting. He stopped a foot away, and stared into your eyes.

– What the fuck – (here he prodded you in the chest) – what the FUCK – (another prod) – are you doing in my fucking launderette with no fucking clothes on? he demanded. – Eh?

You took a step backward.

– I'm using the machine, you explained.

– No, you're not.

You were not sure how to react to this flagrant disregard for the facts.

– Well, actually, I am.

– No, you're not.

The man seemed immune to rational argument.

– No (prod) you're (prod) fucking (prod) not (prod).

He was denying what was self-evidently true. You could only wish once again that you had been able to get your hands on a gun.

– I'm going to count to five, announced the man. – If you're still in this launderette by the time I get to five, I will rip your head off and bounce it down the high street. All right?

You looked around you for support, but the woman had retreated behind her magazine, and was attempting to make herself invisible, and the foot-tapper was entirely oblivious to your predicament.

– What about my clothes?

– One.

– I can hardly go back out there without my clothes.

– Two.

– I'll just dry my clothes, and then I'll . . .

– Three.

You realised you were failing to get your message across.

– At least let me put my trousers on, you pleaded.

– Four.

He wasn't joking either. He really meant it.

– All right, all right. I'm going, I'm going.

You forced open the door of the dryer, and began to rummage around for your shirt. It was still damp, though now slightly warmly damp.

– Four and a half.

You inserted an arm into one of the holes, and hopped around awkwardly trying to insert the other.

– Four and three-quarters . . .

– I really am . . .

But he was gone, back through the little door. When he emerged again, a few seconds later, he was carrying a long, menacing cylinder of wood, tapering from a thick end to a handle. You could not imagine the function of this implement, but it seemed likely that it involved the inculcation of terror as a prelude to the inflicting of pain.

– Nearly five, hissed the man.

– I'm putting my . . . OW.

He prodded you backwards towards the door. He really was serious.

– Please . . . you whimpered. – My trousers?

The alarming growl that filled the launderette, the way his teeth were clenched and his eyes glazed, and the thwack of the wood against his palm persuaded you not to make a point of principle over your trousers. You scrambled desperately behind your back for the door handle, found it, and stepped backward into the slush. The cold burned your skin, and your nipples solidified in agony. He raised his implement above his head, and his feint was enough to cause you to stumble backwards, and lose your footing.

– Five.

He closed the door between you, and stood there on the warm side, the side that contained your clothes, your money, everything you owned, baring his yellow teeth and swinging the weapon – thwack! – through the air into his open palm. You struggled to your feet and stared in. A ball of slush whizzed past your nose and skidded along the pavement. You turned in the direction from which it had been thrown. This was a mistake, for it ensured you caught the next one full in the face. Scooping the slush from your eye-socket, you saw through your stinging tears a group of children pointing and laughing, and scraping up the slush on the pavement. A fourth ball of slush exploded at your feet. A fifth whistled past your ear.

– Oi you! shouted the largest of them.

– What? you called back.

– Put some clothes on, the boy shouted back, and the group collapsed in giggles.

The passing crowds gave you a wide berth, hurrying past with frightened eyes, frowning and scowling, and wishing someone else would deal with it. The man in the launderette was grinning now. He shook his fist at you, a gesture whose exact meaning was unclear but whose gist could be guessed fairly easily. Whhhooff! Another ice-ball slammed into your chest. This one, though, had gravel in it. It stung. Your hand came away streaked with blood.

– Nudist! taunted the boys.

They were advancing towards you now. You glanced back and forth from the advancing boys to the still-revolving dryer, torn. Your instincts told you that you were hopelessly outnumbered, and on a foreign territory, and to run. Just run. But if you ran you would never see your clothes again. On the other hand, it didn't look much as if you were ever going to see your clothes again anyway, given the antipathy their custodian had developed towards you. Something hard glanced off your shoulder – not slush any more, but a clod of frozen earth.

– Piss off!

– Wanker!

– Nudist!

Stay or run? Stay or run? You ran. With a great adolescent whoop of triumph they gave chase. In and out of the lunch-time crowds you darted, sliding on the ice and stumbling through the slush. Horrified, the shoppers parted at the last moment to allow you through, their gasps and shrieks alerting those further up the high street of the approaching commotion, so that a passage was formed for your escape. Out into the road you stumbled, and a bus honked as you passed. Tearing down the road, you burst through a gate into an open space, tripped on a tyre and fell spread-eagled into the frozen mud-slush. You tried to rise, but your body rebelled. It had given up. You lay there, panting and steaming, waiting to be finished off.

But no blows came. They had abandoned their pursuit at the point where the guilt of persecuting the unfortunate overcame the pleasure of it. Your heart was pounding, your breath came in frantic gasps and every muscle in your body ached with exhaustion. Nervously, you lifted your head. A face loomed alarmingly above you, and instinctively you cowered back into the mud, covering your face with your hands in anticipation of boots. Still nothing. Just a man coughing. Again, you spread your fingertips, and peered through them. The face was friendly. Familiar, even.

– We meet again, he observed, extending a grubby hand.

Whether it was intended to help you up or to strike you down further you could not tell.

– Come on, mate, the man urged – up you come.

Having nothing to lose, you grasped his outstretched hand, and he heaved you squelching from the mud.

– Heave-ho.

A great yank, and you were on your feet once more. You looked around. The crowds were gone, and had been replaced by cars – not cars as you were familiar with, but cars in various stages of redundancy. Bones of cars – bumpers, fenders, tyres, doors, seats, wings. Each was collected into a pile of similar bits. Cars, disassembled into their constituents, and the constituents collected into piles. Here a mountain of tyres, there a mound of seats, there a stack of doors. Cars with their innards ripped out, their bodies crushed and piled one on top of another. Everywhere, twisted, rusted metal, ripped upholstery, hubcaps and rubber. A

great puddle of oil swilled across the courtyard, reflecting a grey
sky in a green-black rainbow.

– Where am I? you wondered aloud.

– Planet earth, replied the man.

You looked at him, puzzled.

– A cold and inhospitable planet, he went on, – inhabited by
creatures known as automobiles, and their subject races.

As the adrenaline receded, the sensation of terror once again
began to give away to that of cold.

– I'm freezing, you told your new acquaintance.

– Me too, he confided.

He tugged at a piece of string around his waist, and began to
divest himself of his trousers.

– Your need, he said, – is greater than mine.

He offered them to you. You hesitated.

– Go on, he said, – plenty more where they came from.

And it was patently true, for the removal of these trousers
had served merely to expose another, apparently identical pair
beneath. Like an artichoke, you recalled from some previous
existence.

– Go on, he urged.

He helped you fasten them with the string. Your feet still
squelched in the cold mud, but the trousers were sufficient to
protect you from the worst of a cruel wind that howled around
the scrap-yard.

– Come and warm yourself, he suggested.

He gestured towards a far corner, where a small fire sent
tongues of flame crackling into the gloom. You stood there,
unable to move. He took your elbow and led you gently over
the debris towards the reviving flames. As you approached
you became aware of figures concealed amongst the broken
vehicles. They stood, warming their hands and watching your
performance. It was not until you stood facing each other that
you realised who it was standing there.

– Tess! you spluttered.

The ten minutes you had spent with Tess Scoop were scorched
into your memory. They had been extrapolated during your
confinement in the hospital into an epic erotic encounter. She,

on the other hand, had very little memory of the encounter at all. She passed through her life in a blur of strong lager and amphetamines, having few incentives to seek to preserve the past, and every reason to run from it as fast as her drugs would carry her. Once a meeting slithered into the foul and fetid swamp where she kept her memories it was lost.

– Solomon, you reminded her – Solomon Grundy.

It meant nothing to her. She shook her head.

– That's your name is it?

– What's that then? asked your acquaintance, – Paki name or something is it?

– From the hospital, you persisted.

She took a step backwards, and looked you up and down. Recognition dawned in her eyes. You had managed to connect with her somehow.

– Bloody hell! she exclaimed, – what happened to you?

– Marriage, you explained.

You blushed furiously, and tried to maintain some dignity.

– I didn't recognise you. With that beard and everything. You look about twenty years older.

You put your fingers to your face, and were disconcerted to find that your beard had indeed returned, as vigorous and bushy as ever. It was irrepressible. The other man, the one who had not yet spoken, put his arm around Tess's shoulders and pulled her towards him. He regarded you down his nose, and curled his lip.

– What happened to your trousers? he asked.

– These are his, you said.

– Martin, the man introduced himself.

– Martin's.

– I know, said the other. – I can see that. What happened to yours?

You told your story, much as I am telling it now. The man sat and listened, inscrutable. When you reached the end he shook his head and clicked his tongue.

– Prat, he said.

You had no idea what this word meant, but it sounded vaguely sympathetic.

– It's not just the trousers, you said, – it's the money.

Instantly, Tess stopped laughing. The other man too looked up, and seemed to have acquired a new interest in your trousers.

– What money? he demanded.

– The money in the trousers.

– How much money?

– I don't know.

– A fat roll, said Martin. – It was a fat roll. I saw it.

– And it's in your trousers?

You nodded.

– In the launderette?

– Uh-huh.

– Let's go, said Tess.

– There is no way, you vowed, – I am going back to that place. Ever.

– I'll tell you what, said the man, – I'll go for you. I'll go and get your trousers for you.

– Would you?

He nodded.

– Well, that's awfully kind of you.

– Anything for a friend.

– See you later then, said Tess.

– You're coming too, he told her.

– Am I?

– Arentcha?

She shrugged.

– I suppose so.

They marched together towards the gate and disappeared into the road.

13.15

Chalkie White could, and did, sleep anywhere. He slept at his desk. He slept in the car at traffic lights. He slept in shop doorways when he was too drunk to drive home (in Chalkie's case 'too drunk to drive home' didn't mean 'slightly over the legal limit' it meant 'too drunk to find his car'). He slept standing up. He was just like a baby, though watching him now, unshaven, rumbling on the sofa like a distant tube train, it was hard to believe he had *ever* been a baby. But presumably he had had a mother once. Presumably she had loved him and kissed his cheek and changed his nappies. Chalkie's nappies. Tony Bowles retched. The retch became a yawn. He had been up all night, an experience which he was alarmed to find left him shattered the next day, and hardly able to keep his eyes open. The only available remedy – black coffee – was beginning to produce hallucinogenic side effects, as well as a cracking headache and a nagging terror that he was about to wet his trousers. The only consolation was that the rest of the council had even less stamina than himself. The Minister had been recalled to London to brief the Prime Minister. The Tizian ambassador had become increasingly melancholy and morbid, before descending into a stoned stupor. The rest of the Council had simply fallen asleep where they sat. This left Tony Bowles to hold the fort alone. Nothing had happened, now, for several hours.

He had used the time to begin the mental construction of the book he would write when it was all over. It was a bit thin. More a pamphlet than a book. It desperately needed a shot in the arm, a twist. Otherwise people lost interest. They began to skip pages. They put you down, and that was it. He sensed that the story of Solomon Grundy was losing interest in him, moving on to new plots, new characters. He was being left behind. This depressed and worried him on both spiritual and financial grounds. His reverie was shattered by the phone. Rendered jumpy by caffeine and irritation, he jumped. No one else stirred.

– What? he snapped into the receiver.
– Is that Sir John Parkes? asked the voice.
Interesting.
– Speaking, he improvised.
– It's about Solomon Grundy.
His heart skipped a beat.
– What about him? Who are you?
A pause.
– A friend.

– Where is he?

– I don't know.

– Is he safe?

– I don't know and I don't care.

Tony Bowles groaned.

– Well, what sort of a fucking friend are *you* then?

There was a long pause. He began to regret his rudeness. But it had been a long night.

– I want to speak to Sir John Parkes, the woman said.

– You are speaking to him, he assured her.

Another long pause.

– Are you sure you're him?

– No, hang on, let me check. Of course I'm sure I'm him. Who else could I be?

– I was with him, the voice said, – Solomon. We were going to London. Peckham. Until an hour ago. We had a row.

– Have you told anybody else?

– No, she said, I thought . . .

– You did the right thing.

– It doesn't feel like it, she said.

– Don't go away, he ordered, – I'll be there as soon as I can.

Tony Bowles was on the trail again. Stamina. That was what you needed. The ability to push yourself beyond the pain threshold. He called Pilsbury Station Taxis. The woman promised him one within the hour.

– An hour?

– Sorry, love, there's a rush on . . . it's that freak at the hospital.

– But . . .

– Every car we got's booked up three or four trips in advance. Now do you want this car or don't you?

– No.

– Well, get off the line then.

ABC Taxis told him the same story. The firm in Ramster, twenty miles away, were no more helpful. There seemed no alternative but to depart under the same propulsion as he had arrived. Not only did the prospect of re-entering Chalkie's ancient and unhygienic vehicle fill him with dread, however;

it also necessitated a slightly awkward theft. Chalkie's keys were in his jacket. Unfortunately, so was Chalkie. Chalkie was lying on his right side. Tony patted his left. Nothing. Bugger. But no. It was a miracle. With a grunt, Chalkie shuddered in his sleep, coughed up some phlegm and . . . yes, he was turning over. And there, on his hip, was a jagged bulge. Holding his breath, Tony inserted a hand into his colleague's trouser pocket. There they were. Slowly now. Concentrate. Yes. Inch by inch.

– Boo!

Tony Bowles stumbled backwards and tripped over the coffee table.

– Ssssshhhhh, hissed Chalkie, putting his finger to his lips.

Tony Bowles scanned the immediate vicinity but no weapon nasty enough came to hand.

– You would have driven off without me, wouldn't you? Chalkie accused.

– Only because it wasn't possible to drive off over you, Tony thought. But he fought to keep a grip on his temper.

– Look, he said – we're partners. There's no reason we have to be friends.

– Friends? said Chalkie. – We're not talking room on my horse for two here. We're talking don't try and rip off my fucking car while I'm taking forty winks. I mean, call me stupid. Call me out of touch. Call me idealistic.

– No one could ever accuse you of that.

– It's called taking without the owner's consent. Twocking. Twocker.

– Chalkie, Tony conciliated, – I don't have the time to argue the toss with you right now. Are you going to drive me or aren't you?

– Drive you where?

– Well, you don't think I'm going to tell you *that*, surely?

Chalkie appeared to be thinking. Tony watched in awe as the great brain moved slowly towards cogitation.

– All right, Chalkie capitulated. – But get this. We are friends no longer. From now on, our relationship is strictly professional. You scratch my back, and I'll scratch yours.

Tony was flabbergasted that Chalkie had ever imagined there was more to their relationship than that.

– Fine, he said.

Thankful to have found something upon which they could both agree, they shook hands on it. They now had two of the pieces of the puzzle – they knew more or less where you were, and they had a means of getting there. All that remained was to find someone who knew vaguely what you looked like.

14.30

– Here, try this, Martin offered – this'll warm you up.

From a pocket he produced a small bottle, and passed it to you. You unscrewed the top, and sniffed. Its odour was weak and vague. You took a gulp. Tasteless. You swallowed, and coughed. It burned the back of your throat and hit your stomach like a punch. You retched. After a few seconds, however, a warm eruption began to leak from your belly outwards into your organs.

– Cup of tea, Martin enlightened you.

You swayed slightly, and enjoyed the passage of the heat through your veins. It was true. It did warm you up. Martin slugged on the bottle and gazed into the fire. You felt yourself beginning to thaw. The fire crackled and spat, and transmitted minute quantities of heat to your frost-bitten extremities. It was enough, though, to get the circulation going again. Your experience since leaving the service station had persuaded you to take a less exacting view of life than hitherto. Everything was turning out to be rather relative. Comfort in particular, seemed to be entirely relative.

– There you are just an hour ago, Martin marvelled – peeling a twenty off a fat roll, and now here you come, an hour later, crawling into my yard on your hands and knees in your birthday suit. That's Einstein, see. What goes up must come down. It's all relativity.

– What about things that come down, though? you wondered aloud.

– Eh?

– Well, must they go up again?

Martin thought about it.

– No, he concluded, – not in my case anyway. Once things go down they tend to stay there, in my experience.

– Why's that then?

He shrugged.

– Inertia, he said. – The unbearable sluggishness of the universe. The unimaginable tedium of getting up in the morning again.

He passed you the bottle. You took it and held it to your lips, but only a few drops fell into your mouth. You tipped it upside down, and watched the drips drip into the slush.

– They've been gone an awfully long time, you pointed out. – Do you think they're all right? What if something's happened?

With every minute that passed, you were beginning to suspect the worst.

– They haven't forgotten us, Martin assured you.

– I'm going to go after them.

But Martin caught your arm.

– Patience, he counselled.

– Of all the things I am encouraged to be, you said, – patient is probably the one furthest from my nature.

– Patience is easy, said Martin. – Patience is an attitude. In my case, mind, it's more a question of not having any alternative. It's probably more a question of don't hold your breath.

– Have you got any more bottles?

– I'll show you.

He led you round the back of a heap of cars, and opened the boot of one. It was packed with empty bottles. He inserted the afternoon's contribution, and the bottles clinked pleasantly.

– You never know, said Martin, – when they might come in handy.

You couldn't really visualise a situation in which a hundred empty vodka bottles might come in handy.

– That, said Martin, – is because you are inexperienced in the ways of the world.

You were prepared to concede this possibility.

– Take a look at this.

He opened the adjacent boot to reveal half a dozen petrol cans. He picked one up, shook it and invited you to sniff. The smell was intoxicating, but made your eyes water.

– You know what's in these petrol cans?

You shook your head.

– Petrol, he revealed. – I siphon it off from these wrecks, see.

You watched as he tore a strip from an old rag, poured a half-inch of petrol into an empty bottle, and prodded the rag down after it. A quarter of the rag protruded from the lip of the bottle and the rest was concealed within.

– Wait here, he ordered, and was off.

The traffic rumbled, and the snow tumbled around, but a warm glow smouldered in the pit of your stomach and insulated you against the worst of the cold. For no reason at all, you began laughing. It was a good feeling, a release of tension. It was the first time you had laughed in a long time. You worried too much, that was your trouble. You approached life in a swarm of anxiety and suspicion, and what good did it do in the end? What was the point looking for certainties when there was nothing but one incalculable risk versus another? You looked for understanding in the hope that the world might then prove less bewildering, but it was only bewildering because you looked for understanding. It really was a question of attitude. It was no good chasing round after life: the thing to do was to sit tight, and let it wash over you. That would certainly be more comfortable, anyway.

Your new outlook filled you with an inner sense of peace. You were feeling stronger, revitalised, and ready to take on the world once more. There was only one slight worry: Tess. She and Leon seemed very thick. Perhaps they were married even. Marriage. The recollection occasioned a fresh outbreak of merriment. What a balls-up that had been. Though no permanent damage had been done, as far as you could tell. You had been very young, of course, and impressionable. And besides, you had only really done it as a sort of favour for Jackie. A thank you for doing all that driving. Not that she had been grateful. Silly bitch. Just cried. Thank heavens you were shot of her. Though it would be nice to have someone steady to lean against right now. A jumper to warm your hands under, that would be good. And some more of that vodka. And a piss.

– Oi! Martin called. – Don't piss there. I sleep there.

You giggled and sprayed.

– Come on.

He tugged you back towards the street.

– Round here.

The street was deserted. An ancient wooden fence, missing half its boards and plastered with torn posters, lined one side. The other was a long row of burned-out houses, overgrown front gardens littered with smashed glass, charred wood and builders' rubble. Most of the houses were open to the sky, and received the falling snow without protest.

– See that?

Martin indicated a skip overflowing with rubbish, fifty yards up the street. He glanced around, to check you were still alone. From one pocket he produced the bottle and rag assembly. From the other, after much fumbling, a box of matches. He ignited the rag, and let it burn for a few seconds. Suddenly, it was sailing through the air in a graceful arc from his out-stretched arm. As it hit the skip, it exploded into a burst of brilliant orange.

– Now do you see?

You tried desperately, but to no avail.

– Nope.

Martin shook his head in disbelief.

– I mean, what does it do, exactly?

– It sets fire to things, he said.

– Yes, but why?

He shrugged.

– Why not?

– What good does it do, setting fire to things?

– It passes the time. Come on, we better get out of here.

15.10

– Nearly two hundred quid, Tess's companion said. – A hundred each, he calculated. – Finders keepers, losers fuck off.

She thought about it.

– No, she said finally.

– Listen. You give me my half, you go play fairy godmothers with yours.

– It's not your half and my half, Leon. It's his.

He went to snatch the roll from her, but she had seen him coming.

– What's fucking wrong with you? he sneered, drilling his finger into his temple.

She didn't really know herself. Once you got your hands on something, you didn't let go of it till it was all used up. That was what she'd learned. Human beings had been made with two hands, one for holding on tight to their own stuff and the other for grabbing at other people's. But somehow, this felt different. Why this felt different, she didn't know. Part of it was simply curiosity. She wanted to know what you'd do. Part of it was the knowledge that she could always get it back off you, somehow or other. She could just ask to borrow it or something. You struck her as almost certainly the most gullible person she had ever met, and she had met a few gullible people in the remedial classes and children's homes by which she measured the passage of her life. No one was quite as gullible as the needy, and everyone was pretty needy these days, one way or the other. Part of it was an emotion she'd almost forgotten. Pity. She'd met people in a mess before. Everyone she met was in some kind of mess or another, usually several overlapping and interconnecting messes – but never anyone in quite such a mess as you were in. Without your clothes in this weather, you would die. You were half-dead already, shivering round the fire, your teeth chattering, your body blue with cold.

– You're fucking mad, said Leon.

But she had made up her mind.

You were overjoyed, and mildly astonished, to see them again. Martin had made it clear that your chances of retrieving your trousers were fairly minimal. If nobody else had nicked them in the meantime, Leon would. You had been cast down and outraged by this latest betrayal, until you put it in the context of the rest of the day, whereupon it began to seem vaguely inevitable. Martin pointed out that the loss of your trousers didn't make your situation any more hopeless than before, merely no less hopeless. This was clearly supposed to cheer you up, and you were trying to understand how Martin might have imagined it would have that effect when Tess and Leon appeared, with – oh joy! – your trousers. You ran to her, threw your arms around her and kissed her, but Leon grabbed your arm and twisted it behind your back.

– Just don't, he warned.

– Don't what?

– Just don't, right.

Leon's glare warned you not to pursue your interrogation. But, you were thankful to have your own clothes back, and prepared to endure a little more pain if that was the price demanded.

– Shoes, said Tess, handing them to you. – And dosh.

You had completely forgotten the money.

– You keep it, you said. – It's no use to me.

Leon groaned and began to hoof at the ground.

– No, she said. – It's yours. You have it.

– It's no use to me.

– Well, it's use to me, snatched Leon.

– He didn't offer it to you, Martin pointed out, – he offered it to her.

Leon's fist drew back.

– Money, Martin said, – it's more trouble than it's worth.

Leon spat. The spit sizzled on the snow.

– You know what I reckon we should do with it? asked Martin.

– Burn it, said Tess.

Martin stared at her, incredulous.

– Spend it! Fucking spend it, right now, before it causes any more trouble.

Two hours later the four of you stumbled out into the street, bloated and drunk. The roll of notes did not appear to have shrunk to any appreciable degree, but your spirits had risen considerably, and you had begun to revise your first impressions of the world outside. The food was certainly an improvement. The only dark and threatening cloud on the horizon was Leon, who seemed merely to be biding his time until an opportunity arose to . . . what exactly he intended was not at all clear, but you were in no hurry to find out. Quite why he hated you so, you had no idea. He just did. His mood seemed to operate in tandem with Tess's. The more she laughed, the more he scowled and bared his teeth. The more she smiled at you, the more he fumed. You were determined, however, that it should not spoil your afternoon. Life was too short, and every time you looked at her, you forgot him entirely. You had watched her shovel vegetable curry and pilau rice into her mouth for the past hour, and were completely infatuated. She was surely the loveliest creature that had ever walked the earth. The satisfaction of your visceral needs – warmth, then sustenance – had reminded you of another thirst, one slightly less tangible but no less real. You were reminded of Khan's artichoke, each leaf being removed merely to reveal another, one desire sated only to bring your attention to another. You recalled that at some climactic point, the final leaf was pulled away to reveal the heart, and all was made worthwhile. You must be close to that point now, surely. Your head was light and airy, and your whole body seemed to tingle with excitement.

Tess meanwhile was not ignorant of the effect she was having upon you, though she was relieved that you seemed to have gained a measure of self-control since your last encounter. It did, however, put her in rather an awkward position. She could see that the most likely outcome of this particular *ménage à trois* was that you, and quite possibly she too, would up end up bleeding from the gums in a shop doorway somewhere. Leon had had a reputation for random violence at the Larches, and since the Larches was by general consent the most randomly violent child-care institution in the South West, this was no mean feat. It was his way of showing that he cared. This wasn't to say that she saw any great future with you either. You were a liability, that much was self-evident. An endearing one, but a liability nonetheless. Her first responsibility was to herself. She couldn't think about taking on any dependants at the moment, not unless they were the kind that got you a flat and a cheque. And Leon was at least vaguely useful to her. Indispensable, for the moment. He was brutal, but that was more use to her than you were, or would ever be. She wasn't sure how she was going to play this one. She knew something would crop up though. It always did, one way or another. And in the meantime, there was your money to spend.

– What next? she asked.

– Drugs, said Leon.

– Votes for drugs, said Martin. The three of them raised their hands, so you did too.

– Unanimous, said Martin. – Carried unanimously.

Martin hailed a cab and you all bundled in, giggling. Martin sat in the front, with Tess between Leon and yourself in the back. Her thigh was pressed tight against yours, and her proximity was overwhelming. Life was good. Things were happening at last, real grown-up things. Your fingers sought hers, but she withdrew her hand, and shook her head. The cab drove through West London. The snow had disappeared from the roads now, though it still hung around on roofs and walls and parked cars. People, shops, houses, buses and cars flashed past in a drunken blur. Your stomach surged towards your mouth, and then dropped back again. The cab drew to a halt outside a dilapidated old building. You piled out.

– Nine pounds exactly, said the driver.

This was your department. You located the roll in a back pocket and peeled off a note. He handed you some change, which you waved away.

Martin was hammering at the door, and a window shot open above you. A head appeared, the hair green and the flesh adorned with metal studs, chains and rings.

– He's not here, said the head, enabling you to identify its gender as feminine.

– When's he coming back?

– Sooner or later. Probably.

– Can we wait?

The head withdrew briefly, then reappeared.

– Catch.

A key was lowered on a piece of string. Martin opened the door, and the four of you stumbled in. All was dark. The smell of catshit was overpowering. Two bicycles leant against the wall.

– Up here.

You fought to control your rebellious lunch against a further onslaught of nausea, and negotiated the hazards on the stairs. The wallpaper was damp and peeling, and the banisters missing completely in parts. You followed the others through into a large room with bare floorboards and no curtains. Several of the windows were boarded up. A fire flickered in the fireplace and chunks of smashed wood littered the surrounding area.

– Sit down, ordered another girl with no hair. – Make a chillum.

There was a mattress in one corner, with a sleeping bag and a pillow. A dozen books were propped up on a plank between two bricks. An upturned crate served as a table, under a bare light bulb. The only other article of furniture in the room was a grubby plastic sofa, upon which were lined up three characters – the owner of the head with green hair, a friend of hers with no hair and a third person, who was horizontal and apparently comatose.

– Where? you asked.

– Wherever you want.

You sat on the floor. Martin made a chillum, which did the rounds. It was the final straw.

– You've gone sort of pastel-green, observed Tess.

– I'm going to be sick, you blurted.

– Well don't be sick here, said the bald girl, tetchily, – it stinks enough as it is.

Two women manhandled you to the window and stuck your head out. Dutifully you ejaculated your curry over a shopping trolley rusting away sadly in the front garden, then remained there, hanging from the window, for what must have been several days. The cold air on your face was somehow comforting, like tears. You seemed to be dissolving into your surroundings now.

Gradually self-awareness returned and you became conscious of the city strung out beneath you. The house was on some sort of a hill, and the upstairs window commanded a panorama of trees, roofs and tower blocks. It really was spectacularly ugly, though also impressive in its ugliness. A monument to mediocrity and the second-rate, the half-finished and the waiting to be demolished. Each borough composed of streets, each street formed by houses, each house of bricks. One brick upon another, starting from bare earth and growing storey by storey until now, when you could gaze out upon it and think

– Why?

Just – Why?

Every house full of people. What did they all do, apart from get on each others' nerves? For the first time you understood the sheer volume of people crowding on to the surface of the planet. As you stared at the horizon, it began to dissolve and reform in front of your eyes. Plumes of smoke rose from tall chimneys and vapour trails bisected the sky. The snow was falling again. You became aware of a presence at your side, warm and friendly.

– All right? she asked.

You nodded, but once started found it difficult to stop.

– You don't look all right, she said. – Look at me.

She took your face in her hands, and made you look at her. Her face seemed to radiate an unearthly calm and beauty, suffusing the whole cityscape with promise and excitement.

– You're lovely, you said.

She giggled, but put her finger to her lips.

– Don't start that again, she warned.

– You're an angel.

– No I'm not, she said. – You're stoned.

Was that the word for the extraordinary sense of well-being that made you want to sing, to reach out and take her in your arms and . . .

– I want to kiss you, you warned her.

– Well don't, she said. – Not here.

– I want to sing.

– Oh shit.

– Only I don't know any songs.

– Well, that's a relief.

– What is this?

You swept your hand over the cityscape.

– It's London, she said, – Peckham.

– It's horrible, you said, – who built it?

– No one, she said. – Well, everyone. It just sort of . . . grows.
I don't know.

– Horrible, you repeated.

– I like it.

– Shut that fucking window, came a growl from behind your
back. – Fucking freezing in here.

The hair prickled on the back of your neck. The girl with
no hair had managed to rouse herself and place a blanket over
the comatose one, who had gone blue. Leon stood there, glaring,
holding a small handaxe and looking for something to split with
it. Finding a log, he balanced it on one end, steadied it with
one hand and cracked the axe down upon it. The log cleaved
and the two halves fell neatly apart. The performance seemed
to have been arranged for your benefit entirely, and you winced
in acknowledgement. Leon threw the two logs on the fire, over
which the girl with green hair was toasting another tin of
chillum mixture. The logs sent a shower of sparks scurrying
up the chimney. Suddenly a tremendous pounding erupted in
your skull, and the room began to pump rhythmically. Waves
of warm sound washed over you, infiltrating every nook and
cranny of your body and shaking your organs into jelly. The
bald girl seemed somehow to be responsible for this music: it
seemed to be coming out of her somehow. Martin was puffing
on the chillum, and he passed it to you. You inhaled twice as
much smoke as could comfortably be contained in two lungs and
coughed violently, propelling the glowing bung from the end of
the chillum off into some unknown corner of the room.

– Who brought this fuckwit? asked the bald girl, not quite
sotto voce.

But you did not hear, doubled up as you were on the back of
the sofa. A great wallop on the back expelled all the air from your
chest and most of the smoke with it, and your respiration began to
settle again. Tess offered you water, but the skin of grease across

its surface reduced its attractiveness. Leon was pacing around the room, kicking things menacingly. The music pounded in your head, your heart pounded in your chest and the blood pounded in your temples. You allowed yourself to be manipulated on to the sofa and a space was created for you between the armrest and the feet of the boy who had gone blue. This involved considerable manhandling of the blue boy, but with no apparent effect on his state of unconsciousness. You sat there clearing your throat and blinking.

– All right? Martin asked.

You turned, very slowly, to look at him, and burst out laughing. He looked as if his clothes had been inflated. His head peeked out from the top, several sizes too small. He grinned back at you. You liked him. He seemed to mean you no malice. The same could not be said for the bald girl, or for Leon, who crouched in the fireplace thwacking an axe into a chunk of wood, spraying little chips around the room. Tess was irresistible. Once you caught her eye, you could not stop looking at her. She scowled at you and stuck out her tongue, but still you could not remove your gaze. There was one particular strand of hair that hung down over her cheek. You longed to get up and brush it away, but when you made to rise the inertia of your body shocked you. You were wedged into the sofa, trapped. Tess got up and walked to the window, turning her back. No one spoke and when the music abruptly ceased the room was silent but for the late afternoon traffic in the street outside, the crackling of the fire and the chuck-chuck-chuck of Leon's axe. The atmosphere was suddenly tense, and the silence oppressive. Conversation seemed called for, but none of the others looked capable or interested in commencing one. You were also aware that you had somehow incurred the wrath of your hosts. The bald one sat chewing her nails. Green Hair stared into the fire. Martin had gone to sleep, and Tess's body language announced fairly unambiguously that she did not wish to be disturbed. Leon was disturbed enough already. You felt the urge to make amends for what had clearly been a faux pas with the chillum. You caught the bald girl's eye.

– You don't have much furniture, you observed.

She curled her top lip. The expression on her face was so

grotesque that you found it hard to know whether to cower in terror or to giggle.

– Who needs furniture? asked Green Hair over her shoulder.

– Fuck furniture, echoed the bald girl. – Fuck armchairs and sideboards and wardrobes. Fuck shelf units and bedsteads. Fuck hi-fi cabinets. Fuck chests of fucking drawers. Fuck tallboys, fuck . . .

– Fuck *what?* Leon interrupted.

– Nothing, blushed the bald girl.

– No, go on . . . what? Wall boys or something.

– Tallboys.

– What are they then?

– Never mind, she said. – It doesn't matter. You're better off without them. Without even knowing what they are.

– What are they?

– Possessions, explained Martin, wisely, opening one eye in order to wink at you.

– Property, confirmed the bald girl. – Things.

– What use are they in the end, asked Green Hair – things? Do they make you happy? Does furniture make you happy?

– It just makes you slightly less uncomfortable, you pointed out.

– What on earth use is furniture? thundered Green Hair.

You were relieved when Martin came to your aid.

– You can sell it and buy drugs, he said.

– Can you?

– It's too bloody heavy, Green Hair pointed out. – Credit cards, that's what you want. Portability.

– Videos, said Leon, unexpectedly.

Everyone turned to seek the source of this baffling non sequitur.

– Videos, he repeated, defensively.

– What about videos? demanded the bald girl.

– They're useful, Leon said. – Sometimes.

– Like, if you want to watch a video or something, Martin prompted.

Leon regarded him with a stare of intense and accumulating violence.

– So what? added Bald Girl.

You too were curious to discover the nature of the connection.

– They're useful, that's all, said Leon.

– Are they furniture? asked Green Hair. – Videos?

Leon thought about it.

– No, he conceded finally, crushed by her brutal logic.

Bald Girl raised her eyes skyward.

– Not like fucking wallboys obviously, he hissed in retaliation.

– Tallboys, Bald Girl corrected.

– Wallboys, tallboys, ballboys, whatever, sighed Green Hair.
– That's not the point.

– What is the point? you asked her, hopeful of illumination.

But you never found out, for at this point, the corpse shot suddenly and alarmingly to its feet, and sniffed the air.

– What's burning? it demanded. – Something's burning.

Everyone sniffed. It was true: there was indeed a nauseating odour of the combustion of something synthetic. The corpse strode over to the sleeping bag, over which hung a pall of thick white smoke. As he stared, a green flame suddenly leaped from it, and then another.

– My sleeping bag, he screamed. – My fucking sleeping bag.

He picked up a book and began to beat his sleeping bag manically. The white smoke filled the room, and collected in the back of your throat.

– It's on fire, observed Green Hair, alarmed, but apparently unable to rise from the floor to assist in the extinction of the conflagration.

– Put it out, suggested Bald Girl. – Someone.

Glancing round the room, your eyes fell upon a bucket of water. You had tipped the contents over the flames before you even realised you were doing so. It seemed the obvious thing to do. The way everyone was staring at you, however, suggested that they were aware of some counter arguments.

– Brilliant, sneered Bald Girl.

A fierce scraping from downstairs announced the arrival of presumably the person you were all waiting for (though quite why you were all waiting for him you had by now completely forgotten).

    – It looked like a bucket, you defended yourself.

    – It was a bucket, said Green Hair.

    – A bucket full of piss, giggled Martin.

    – And that was my bed, said the corpse, who appeared only slightly more alert in a vertical axis than he had been in the horizontal one. You heard, with a combination of relief and panic, footsteps coming up the stairs, a heavy tread, someone singing

    – Jack your body . . .

Move

And Groove

Hot lover

I love to watch you ow shit fuck

There was a terrible crunch of bone on masonry.

    – We've really gotta fix that, said Green Hair.

    – What about my bed? asked Corpse, forlornly.

    The five of you crowded around the bed, and scrutinised the sleeping bag. There was a ragged black hole in the middle, brittle around the edges like a burnt poppadum. The bag, and the mattress underneath, were sodden, and stank.

    – Looks like you've wet the bed, said Tess.

    – In a fairly major way, added Martin.

    The pair of them creased up. Even Leon was grinning. Bald Girl and Green Hair stared at them despairingly. The Corpse burst into tears and ran from the room, passing the new arrival in the doorway. Tess and Martin were temporarily stunned by his abrupt departure, then caught each other's eye and were off again. Even Bald Girl was now beginning to grin, though it was also possible that she was preparing to bite someone. The new arrival was dressed in hooded jacket and dirty jeans, and was bearded. The bald girl greeted him as John. John was rubbing his temple. He inspected his hand and frowned at the sight of blood. A long gash decorated his forehead.

    – I thought you said you was going to fix that nail, he accused Bald Girl.

    She blushed.

    – All right, Martin? the newcomer enquired.

– All right, Martin confirmed.

– Leon, he acknowledged.

– John.

– Who are you?

The question was addressed to Green Hair, who turned crimson.

– I'm Tiffany, she reminded him, – I live here.

– You do? Since when?

– Since you invited me to. About three weeks ago.

– Three weeks. Oh yeah. Yeah. Right. Sorry.

– Can you sort us out? asked Martin.

But John was pursuing a different line of thought entirely.

– Your hair, he was saying to Green Hair, – it used to be . . . different.

– Red, Green Hair reminded him.

– That's right. Red. Yeah. That's why I didn't recognise you, with the green hair. It makes you look . . .

He pursed his lips and tilted his head to one side, searching for the *mot juste*.

– Do you like it? she asked.

– It makes you look like a tomato, John pronounced.

Green Hair harrumphed indignantly.

– What's with Humphrey? asked John.

– He wet the bed, giggled Tess.

– *He* wet the bed, corrected Bald Girl, indicating yourself. John took you in for the first time.

– Who are you then?

– Solomon.

You held out your hand. He took it and shook it warmly.

– All right, Solomon?

– I think so.

– We'll soon fix that. Now then, gentlemen. Lady.

He rubbed his hands, and departed. Martin, Leon and Tess followed him. You were left with Bald Girl.

– Humphrey's gonna be really angry about his bed, she warned you.

– Why? you asked.

– He's really attached to it, she said, disapprovingly. – Things.

Possessions. Furniture. You see where it gets you. It's a problem for him, she diagnosed.

– Less of a problem now, you pointed out, making your exit.

A light round the edge of a door betrayed both the location of your colleagues and the fact that the dusk was beginning to thicken. Martin was making another chillum, and John had found a pair of scales and was fiddling with a bag of greyish powder and various tiny weights. Tess was idling through some CDs. This room, which presumably was John's, contained even less furniture than the last – a sleeping bag and a ghetto-briefcase, and a little pile of psychedelic CDs. You took a deep breath of the chillum, felt the thick black smoke coagulate in your lungs, managed to avoid coughing, and sent it on its way. Eventually, John achieved a satisfactory balance between the weights and the powder

– Money? he enquired.

– He's your man.

John stretched out an upturned palm and you transferred the roll of notes from your back pocket into it. He seemed suitably impressed, licking his finger and peeling off several notes, and then returning the roll to your safe keeping. Leon, meanwhile, had poured a cone of the powder onto a mirror and was chopping at it with a razor blade. He divided the powder into piles, a smaller and a larger. The former he divided into two, the larger into three. With an elegant movement of the blade, he drew the five little piles into five extended trails. It was an enchanting performance, during which no one spoke.

– Note, demanded Leon.

He rolled it into a tube, placed one end at the beginning of the thickest trail, the other up his nostril, and hoovered. When he had finished, he tapped the tube, mopping up the grains that dropped, together with the few he'd missed, on a dampened finger. He then cleared a space for John, and the process was repeated three times, each time the supplicant clearing a space in front of the mirror for the next. Before the mirror, each prostrated themselves on bended knee, and hoovered. The shortest and thinnest line was left for you. Getting down on all fours was far more demanding than you had anticipated. The original note had by now disappeared into someone's pocket, but there were plenty of others to hand. Rolling one into a tube took an age though – every time you had it where you wanted it, it sprang open again. The procedure required a great deal of concentration, which was not made easier by Leon's pacing about the room, muttering. Finally, Martin took charge. You inserted one end in your nostril, bent forward over the mirror and froze in horror. It was a full twenty-four hours since you had last seen yourself in a mirror – back at the hospital, as Jackie shaved you. *Then* you had been impressed by how handsome you were, how rugged and dynamic. The transformation you had undergone in the intervening period was horrifying. Your hairline, for a start, was beginning visibly to recede around the temples. You ran your fingers through your hair, and a clump came away in your hands. Your complexion had altered too – where you remembered yourself as a rude, vigorous pink, the mirror informed you that were now a rather undistinguished and putrid yellow-grey. Bags were collecting under your eyes, and crow's-feet forming at their corners. Your hair was lank and greasy. Above all though you were shocked to discover how tired you looked. You stared at your reflection and frowned. Your reflection frowned back at you, and you shared a moment of mutual sympathy together. You poked your tongue out at it. It poked its tongue back. You made yourself go cross-eyed.

– Come on, urged Leon, exasperated. – Come on, come on, come *on*.

He kicked the skirting board. Dust tumbled from the ceiling. You remembered suddenly why you were knelt there, with this tube up your nose. You swallowed, exhaled, and then hoovered. The powder burned into the back of your nostrils, and you dropped the tube in pain.

– Do you not want the rest? asked Martin.

Whilst he tidied up your portion, John collected the paraphernalia of weights, scales, bags and rubber bands, lifted a floorboard and replaced his enterprise beneath it. He spread a filthy rug over it. You were feeling better all the time.

– Where now? he asked, rubbing his hands.

– Wheatsheaf, said Martin.

– Wheatsheaf, echoed Leon.

Tess shrugged.

– Sounds good, she said.

They turned to you. Outside the window the street-lamps were burning and the dusk rapidly giving way to night. Having lost and found her once, you had no desire to be separated ever again from Tess. Wherever she went you would follow. Besides, you had nowhere else to go.

– Suits me.

The five of you negotiated the stairs.

– Mind the . . . there's a sort of . . . ow, warned John.

The path was frozen over, and you could see your breath in the glow from the street-lamps. John took his leave. He had business to attend to, he said. The other three set off at a brisk pace, whilst you slipped and slid and struggled to keep up. Their earlier taciturnity had given way to an inexplicable verbosity, and you could not escape the feeling that something extraordinary was about to happen. Your heart pounded within your ribcage, your palms sweated and your throat was dry. The hair stood up on the back of your neck. Quite what was about to happen you had no idea. Equally unclear was whether it was to be anticipated with excitement or with dread. You were increasingly confident, however, that whatever it was you could deal with it. You were beginning to suspect that the dangers that obsessed people in the modern world were hopelessly exaggerated. People allowed the bullies to walk all over them because they were too frightened to fight back, but there was no need to be frightened. You certainly weren't frightened. In fact you were only disappointed they weren't here right now, the bullies and the men with baseball bats, who preyed on the weak and the vulnerable and the easily intimidated. That man from the launderette most of all. If only you'd known then what you knew now. If only he was here now, then you'd show him. Now. Right now. Teach him a lesson. Tess suddenly stopped and turned towards you. You stopped too, entranced. She really was lovely, more lovely in the moonlight than ever before.

– Could you stop doing that?

– What? you asked.

– Grinding your teeth like that.

– Was I?

– You still are.

– Sorry.

– It makes me tense, she said. – Like I'm all coiled up.

Martin and Leon were disappearing into a doorway a hundred yards up the road. It was the first time since fate had reunited you with Tess that you had been alone together, and it might well prove to be the last. It was now or never. She turned to go, but you caught her sleeve.

– Tess . . .

– What? she asked, puzzled.

– Tess, ever since we first met, I've . . .

The words dried in your mouth. There they were, the feelings, preformed and packaged ready for communication in your heart, but as soon as they appeared in your mouth for conversion to words they evaporated.

– What? she repeated.

– I've thought about you. Endlessly. All the time.

She raised her eyes heavenwards and clicked her tongue.

– Leave it out, eh? she suggested.

She turned to go but you would not permit her to slip through your fingers so easily for a second time.

– Don't you see? Not once we've been thrown together but twice. We were meant to be.

– Solomon, you want to know something?

– What?

– You're all right, she said. – I like you.

You grinned from ear to ear. Your eyes closed, and your lips moved to meet hers.

– But you're fucking weirdy-woo.

Your bubble popped.

– Look out, she warned under her breath.

You followed the direction of her glance and were disconcerted to observe Leon standing under a street-light, arms folded, watching you watching him. Even at a distance of a hundred yards, the anger emanating from him raised the temperature several degrees. You waved, weakly. He did not wave back.

– Come on, she whispered, – we'd better go.

You stared at her in terror. The moment was slipping away. It was speak now or forever hold your peace.

– I love you, you said.

She shook her head in disbelief.

– 'I love you,' she mimicked. – That was what my dad used to say before . . . She trailed off, and began walking.

You ran to keep up.

– What? Before what?

– Never mind.

– But I do, you persisted, – I do love you. I can't help it.

She stopped.

– But what does it mean 'I love you', she asked.

– It means I think about you when I masturbate.

She sighed, and set off once more towards Leon.

– It's not the same thing at all, she said.

This was highly unexpected news.

– It isn't?

– No, she called back over her shoulder, – no it isn't.

– Oi, called Leon, – what are you two up to?

– Coming, she called to him.

Disconsolate, you followed ten paces behind. A few yards from the door, she turned to you.

– Solomon?

– What? you asked, hope and fear fighting for control of your expectations. Perhaps she had changed her mind?

– You're doing it again, she said.

– Eh?

– With your teeth.

– Sorry.

– It's driving me round the bend.

– Sorry.

But Leon pushed you over the threshold and into the crowd within.

Passing through the portal of the Wheatsheaf was the sort of transcendental experience granted to most mortals no more than once, if at all. It was the feeling of coming home, of finding a niche and thinking it familiar and lifting up the flap to find your name engraved upon it. You paused on the threshold, to savour the impressions thrust upon you. Despite the early hour, the saloon bar was packed, and steam rose from the heads and shoulders and condensed, dripping, on the ceiling. The floor was soaked with melting snow. A heavy odour of beer, cheap perfume and tobacco pervaded the room, mixing with a sweeter bouquet you recognised from the chillum. At last, you had found where the action was. The action had to be here: if not, why were so many others gathered in this place? And why did the air hang so thick with the promise of excitement? It was about to happen. Whatever it was. You could feel it in your bones and your muscles, but most of all in the dryness at the back of your throat.

– Scuse me, requested a woman in ersatz leopard-skin leggings, tottering past on high heels with three overflowing pint-glasses.

– This is where it's at, you said. – This is where it's happening. This is the place to be.

– It's just a fucking pub, said Leon.

Excited, you pushed forward into the wall of backs blocking the passage between yourself and Tess, who was now disappearing into an ante-chamber.

– Oi!

The shaven cranium of a face embedded with metal and overlaid in tattoos was thrust into yours.

– That's my fucking foot, it said.

– Well, get it out of the way then, you told him.

The skinhead stared at you, incredulous. Some instinct told him there was something out of the ordinary about the mouthy cunt standing on his foot.

– Sorry, mate, he said. – Here.

He moved aside to let you past. Leon followed in your wake. Leon's original intention had been simply to get you on your own and jump you. This plan, like armed robbery generally, combined business, pleasure and action in one neat package. But the scene he had just witnessed unnerved him. He did not like to enter fights where there was any doubt as to the eventual victor. There was, however, increasing urgency in the situation. The roll of notes was shrinking by the minute, and thrift demanded a stop be put to his profligate squandering of his money. He must wait his moment, he knew, but it must be soon.

You found Tess and Martin with their backs to a huge log-fire.

– A warm ass, said Martin. – It gives you a whole new perspective on things.

– You gonna get 'em in then? Leon enquired, though it was more a demand than an enquiry, and certainly not the kind one might answer in the negative.

– I'll come with you, offered Martin, steering you in the appropriate direction.

It was a tortuously slow journey – the fifteen or twenty yards from the wall to the bar, and Martin had plenty of time to say what he had to say on the way.

– Look, he said, – you will let me know if I'm out of order or anything, but I just thought you might like to know . . . for your own safety like . . .

– Know what?

– He's got a knife, said Martin.

– Who? Who's got a knife?

Martin stared at you, trying to decide if you were a hallucination or simply a halfwit.

– Leon, he said, – in his inside pocket.

22.40

– Now where?

– Left, your mother replied without hesitation.

With a screeching of brakes and a chorus of honking, Chalkie swung the car into the left-hand lane. Tony Bowles peered out at the road ahead through the gaps in his fingers.

– You indicate before, he reminded his driver, – not after. It's no use after.

– You what?

Chalkie's mouth was full of pasty.

– Down there, by that church, your mother directed.

Chalkie obeyed, less because he had any great confidence in the telepathic radar facility that your mother had suddenly developed than because he had no constructive alternative. In Pilsbury, if you wanted to find someone you just took up a stool at the bar of the Horseshoe. This gave you vantage of the war memorial. Everyone went past the war memorial sooner or later in the day: it was the hub of the town. Having been under the impression that London was just a bigger and uglier version of Pilsbury, he was becoming increasingly disconcerted by its ability to go on and on and on and on and on and on. He was by now thoroughly lost, and had increased his penny stake to the proverbial pound a long time ago.

– You could spend years driving around here, Chalkie pointed out. – Like looking for a contact lens in a bottle bank.

He ripped off another mouthful of pasty.

– What do we do then? Just drive around till something turns up?

– Basically yes, said Tony.

– OK.

Chalkie had no problems with this strategy. In so far as he had a philosophy of life, it would have consisted of pretty much that.

– Turn right here, interrupted your mother from the back seat.

Chalkie turned. Tony Bowles screamed. The bus honked and hissed. Chalkie span the wheel. The Cavalier clipped and mounted the kerb and bounced down again. As if in a slow-motion nightmare, Tony saw the terror on the faces of twenty-six adults with special needs as their bus removed Chalkie's wing mirror.

– Bloody nutters, hissed Chalkie, speeding away from the scene.

– It was a roundabout, Tony reminded him.

– Was it? Bloody stupid place to have a roundabout.

– Right-hand lane now, ordered your mother.

Sceptically, Chalkie obeyed.

– Mrs Grundy, began Tony, – can I ask you a question?

– I'm taking you to my boy, she said.

– And you know where he is?

– No, she admitted, – I'm following my maternal instincts. Left here.

Chalkie veered left.

– Your maternal instincts?

– I can't explain, she said, – you wouldn't understand. Only a mother would understand.

– I wouldn't understand then, Tony conceded.

– Where now? asked Chalkie.

– Straight on, said your mother.

– There's a wall in the way, Chalkie informed her.

– Straight on, said your mother. – Trust me.

Chalkie and Tony caught each other's eye, and found a rare moment of consensus.

– It's not that we don't trust you, said Tony.

– It's just that there's a wall in the way, Chalkie finished.

– He's out there somewhere, she said, – I know it. I feel it.

– The only question is where? Chalkie agreed.

Tony scanned Chalkie's face for evidence of ironic intent, but found none.

– I get this feeling, said your mother, – in my womb. It's like I have a homing pigeon in my womb.

– I definitely wouldn't understand, then, Tony acknowledged.

– Where are we? she asked.

– We're on the first storey of a multi-storey car park, Chalkie informed her.

– He's near, she said. – Turn the engine off.

Chalkie glanced at Tony. Tony shrugged. Chalkie turned the engine off. Together they listened. They could near nothing above the metronomic thudding of jungle music, the revving of cars, the whoops and screams and the tinkling of smashing glass that announced the proximity of a fairly wild party.

– I can smell him, your mother said.

They sniffed the car park.

– I can smell Kentucky Fried Chicken, said Chalkie.

– He's near, said your mother again. – Very near.

– All right, Mystic Meg, we get the message.

Tony was beginning to feel that his whole life had been transformed over the past twenty-four hours into a rather second-rate episode of 'Scooby Doo'. Wearily, he dismounted. The car park was empty and echoey. Chalkie helped your mother from the car. Tony remembered it was only forty-eight hours since she had given birth. She should be back at the hospital, convalescing. They should all be back at the hospital, convalescing. When this was all over he would go back to bed and convalesce for the rest of his life.

22.55

From above the hubbub came the ringing of a tiny bell, and the voice of authority.
   – Last orders at the bar, it intoned, – last orders at the bar.
   – What does that mean? you asked the man next to you.
Martin steered you away from yet another potential confrontation. Your visitation was turning out to be something of a mixed blessing. You appeared from nowhere bearing gifts, but you turned out to be just another of the walking wounded. Like everybody else only more so. Even by the standards of Martin's social circle you were a liability. But there was no question that he owed you a duty of care, at least to see you got back to wherever it was you'd come from without further mishap.
   – Last orders at the bar, came the voice again.
   – It means no more drink, explained Martin.
   – We've drunk it all?
   – Not exactly, no.
   – So why stop then? Why stop before it's finished?
   – It's the law, said Martin.
   – So what happens now?
   – They throw us out.
This piece of news sobered you up for a moment.
   – Into the street?
Martin confirmed your fears.

– Where are you headed for? he asked.

You shrugged.

– Where do you sleep?

Your life up to this point had contained two nights. The first had been spent at the hospital, the second at a motel attached to a service station somewhere. This latter was a place you would not at that point have been sorry to see again. It would be warm. But that was out of the question. You had no idea how to find it again, only that it was far enough away to prevent you walking. None of you had a vehicle.

– Wherever, you told him, – wherever I end up.

– You could . . .

Martin's imminent offer of a bed back at the yard was scuppered by the sight of Leon approaching. Martin decided against it. It would all end in tears, he knew, this particular *ménage à trois*.

– What? you asked, hopeful of a solution to the predicament.

– Nothing, he lied.

– What about everybody else? Where are they going?

– Home to bed, Martin enlightened you. – Back to their warm beds and their husbands and wives.

You recalled, with a pang of remorse, your own wife. That had been this morning. It seemed a lifetime ago.

– I'm married, you informed Martin, – or I was, once.

– Congratulations.

Leon was pushing through the crowd, dragging a reluctant Tess behind him. She was making faces at him behind his back.

– Are we stopping for another? he asked, – or are we off?

You really had no desire to move from this place. Life stretched before you. You were not sure how much more of it you could take. Two days you'd ploughed through so far. If what Conway had told you was to be believed there were another twenty-odd thousand to cope with.

– Off where? asked Martin.

– Wherever, shrugged Leon.

It was at this point that Bald Girl and Green Hair walked past, absorbed in animated conversation.

– I told him, Bald Girl was saying, – everyone has their limits and that's mine.

– Not for twenty quid, Green Hair supported her.

Leon grabbed her as she passed.

– Where's everyone going? he demanded.

– Party, she said. – Coming?

You could hear the party from several blocks away. The whole street seemed to be throbbing to its pulses. Cries and screams and the occasional smashing of glass emerged from a general hubbub of conversation that floated along on top of a thumping rhythm track, all set to flashing lights. The noise, faint at first, gathered slowly as you approached until, as you turned the corner into Angina Street, it exploded in your face. The exact location of the party was betrayed by the motley collection of vehicles blocking the pavement and road, and from the splinter groups stood outside, handing round cans and spliffs, laughing and fighting. Other revellers were sat on the wall lost in solitary meditation, and one was doubled up over the hedge vomiting into next door's flowerbeds. Competing musics emerged from the vehicles and all merged into the general cacophony. As you approached, you caught the bitter odour of wood smoke. The house was daubed in fluorescent hieroglyphics you were unqualified to decipher. The downstairs windows still preserved their protective armour of corrugated iron but the great steel bolts that had once secured the door had been removed and thrown aside and the door swung open in invitation. The rhythm that pounded the street was hypnotic. There was a sudden crash from an upper storey and glass rained down on the garden below. This was it. This was the place. This was the party at the end of the world.

– Looks OK, said Martin.

– Let's go, said Leon.

You stepped over a near-naked body collapsed in the gateway and made your way towards what was left of the front door. A figure in black rags emerged from the shadows demanding money, but Leon head-butted him and he fell backwards clutching his nose, and collapsed to the floor whimpering. You followed the others inside. All was a crush. The chillum smell was overpowering. You had the sensation of descending into a

pool of arms and heads and aggressive haircuts. Determined not
to let Tess out of your sight you took a deep breath and plunged
in. She surfaced again on the stairs, heading upwards through
little knots of people, stepping carefully over the comatose and
the coupling. Martin and Leon vanished on different currents
into the throng. You found yourself entangled in the various
human obstacles placed in your path. Someone passed you a
chillum, and you were torn. It seemed rude to decline.

When you next remembered to look for her, she was gone.
Clambering over the casualties and using your elbows and knees
to prise apart the reluctant, you attained the landing. Here the
crush was even more intense. Your temples throbbed, and a cold
sweat broke across your brow. Five doors led off the landing.
You barged your way into the first. The room was packed with
heads, all at the level of your waist, sprawled against cushions
along the walls and in the corners. People sat cross-legged in an
arrangement of inter-connecting circles. The scene was gothically
illuminated by a dozen candles flickering at various strategic
points in the room, and animated by a buzz of interweaving
and intersecting conversations, punctuated by sucking noises and
occasional gasps for breath. But none of the heads belonged to
Tess. You turned. Your path was blocked by Green Hair.

– You again, she observed.

She did not appear overjoyed to be reacquainted. As you
pushed past, you were amused to find your legs collapsing
underneath you.

– Whoops! you giggled, stumbling forward, and taking advantage of Green Hair's breasts to steady yourself.

– Get off, she hissed.

The next room was packed with dancers. Round and round
they span, arms flailing, crashing madly into the walls and each
other, sprawling across the floor and picking themselves up to
join the fray once more. The floor was covered in sweat and
beer slops. The noise was deafening. Martin's face appeared
from the crowd.

– My man!

An arm shot out from the melee, dragging you into the throng.
You were whirled round and round, buffeted from one body to

another, bounced off walls and floors and ceilings until horizontal and vertical became one and the same. Doom chukka doom chukka doom doom chukka doom doom doom chukka boomed the room, resonating through every bone in your body. Faces smiled at you in the blur and arms reached out to steady you when you stumbled and to pick you up when you fell. It was the most outlandish, marvellous, wildest ride you had ever experienced.

Half an hour later, you made your way back out on to the landing, which had been swelled by further arrivals into an advanced state of heavingness. A terrible thirst came upon you and you grabbed the nearest can to hand.

– Oi! barked its owner.

You drained it, belched, grinned and returned it for disposal. You were beginning to develop an appetite for this gassy yellow beverage. The next room was darker, and more subdued. A small, sad group was huddled around a candle, over which one of them was heating a spoon. The awe with which they focused on the spoon suggested that something dramatic was about to happen in it. You left them to it, and continued your search. You finally found her on the stairs. Her eyes were raw and puffy, as if she had been crying. She held out her arms, and slowly revolved them to illustrate the designs cut into them. The images were in various stages of scarification – some virtually healed up, some still raw and pink. The most recent were still bleeding, and clearly a product of the last half-hour. She sucked her arm to staunch the flow.

– Do you like it?

– No, you said, – it's repulsive.

She shrugged.

– I like it, she said. – Can you read what it says?

You were forced to admit that this particular skill was outside your current repertoire.

– I never had much of an education, you excused yourself.

– I did, she said, – years and years of it.

– What does it say? you asked.

– Bunt.

– Bunt?

– Bunt, she confirmed. – I did it on mushrooms. I was sort of tidying it up when the bus went over a pothole or something and I gouged out a great chunk of my arm. See?

She showed you the crater.

– I went to casualty, and they put three stitches in. When they took them out, it said Kunt. So I changed it to Bunt

– Doesn't it hurt? you wanted to know.

She stared at you, pityingly.

– Of course it hurts, she said, – that's the whole point.

– But why? Why hurt yourself?

– It saves everyone else the trouble, I guess, she said.

23.54

– Watch out!

Tony stepped smartly backwards to avoid the vomit that swooped noiselessly down from the first-floor window, but it still hit the pavement with sufficient force to spatter his shoes and the bottom of his trousers.

– Bad luck, Chalkie grinned.

– You're sure he's in here? Tony doubted your mother.

– If he isn't in there, I'll . . .

She trailed off. They had already wandered round Peckham for an hour, without even a sniff of you. If you proved not to be in there none of the three had the remotest idea what they would do. They were rather relying on it.

– Ladies first, invited Chalkie.

Both men stood aside. Your mother pushed past a man urinating in the porch and elbowed her way in. Tony Bowles hesitated. A sixth sense told him he was unlikely to find many of the other revellers attired in suit and tie, or that he could hope to remain inconspicuous in such garb.

– They won't bite, Chalkie reassured him. – I'd have thought you'd feel at home in a place like this. The night life of the capital.

– Not my people at all, Tony disillusioned his colleague. – More your kind of people I would have thought.

The baggy army fatigues; the ancient trench coats; the ripped leggings; the knee-high boots fastened with baler twine; the ripped T-shirts and hooded sweatshirts – Chalkie could pass himself off as some sort of elder statesman of style amongst these people.

– My kind of people wash, Chalkie claimed.

Tony doubted this.

– Blimey!

Tony followed the line of Chalkie's gaze to an upstairs window, in which a large spotty bottom was being bounced in the moonlight. From the distance came the unmistakable wail of sirens. The bottom retreated and was replaced by a head.

– Oi! it barked, – mind out below.

From above their heads came a tremendous smashing of glass and splintering of wood and a huge metal object descended like a thunderbolt from the sky and embedded itself in the front lawn, accompanied by flying glass and shards of wood. The music seemed suddenly several notches louder. There was a great drunken cheer from inside, jeers and whoops and clapping.

– What the bloody hell was that? gasped Tony.

– I think it was the fireplace, said Chalkie.

They ventured out into the garden to inspect it. It was the bath: the old metal kind, on four little lion's paws. There was a body in it, naked and oblivious. The sirens were approaching rapidly. Tony had covered this situation at college. If there was a riot, the lecturer had advised, one should position oneself behind one set of combatants or the other. It didn't matter much which side you found yourself on – what mattered was not to get caught in the middle.

– C'mon, Chalkie, he said, – we're safer in than out.

They shunted their way into the house and dragged the door shut behind them.

– Hey! said a girl with green hair, – you can't do that. There's no restrictions. It's an open door.

She focused on Tony's suit.

– Who the fuck are you anyway?

– I'm a gate crasher, said Tony.

– You can't be a gate crasher, she said. – There's no gate.

– There is now, Chalkie pointed out.

There was a polite ring of the doorbell.

– Don't answer it, Tony advised her.

She shook her head sadly.

– You two have a real attitude problem, she said.

The bell rang again.

– Really, I wouldn't, Chalkie reiterated.

The girl put her eye to the letter flap, and withdrew quickly. She had gone pale and was trembling.

– It's the law, she said, – with sledgehammers.

The bell rang again, more insistent.

– Open up, ordered the law.

The girl turned to the other revellers.

– Ssshhhhhh, she shhhhhssed them.

No one took the slightest notice.

They found your mother downstairs, staring into a corner and sniffing the air.

– He was here, she informed them, – not long ago. The scent is still fresh.

It was looking less and less likely.

– Trust me, she demanded.

Tony Bowles groaned. The words 'trust me' filled him with apprehension. People exhorted you to trust them only when they were unable to provide any convincing reason for you doing so. Emerging clearly from the row came the barking of a particularly savage-sounding dog.

– Do you think it's on our side? asked Chalkie.

– I'm a reporter, Tony reminded him, – I don't take sides.

– This is an illegal gathering, someone shouted through the door. – You have five minutes to disperse.

– This is a party, someone shouted back. – You have thirty seconds to get your kit off.

This witty retort produced a small cheer, followed by a scuffle.

– Go home, exhorted the voice, – go home.

– He's on the stairs, said your mother.

– Don't tell me, groaned Tony. – You can smell him.

– No, she said, – I can see him.

Chalkie was almost near enough to touch you. He made a heroic effort to grab your trouser-leg, but found himself struggling against an irresistible human tide. There seemed to be more people crammed into this tiny space now than there had been when they had arrived, and more arriving all the time. You disappeared upstairs.

– Go home! urged the voice. – This house is condemned. This house is unsafe.

– You know, Chalkie, said Tony, just before they were swept apart, – I have a gut feeling this is all going to end badly.

Took Ill on Thursday

00.01

Leon watched the city from an upstairs window. Self-satisfied, he gazed out over the city, picking his nose. The room buzzed with people sat cross-legged in little circles, smoking and talking. You were picking your way carefully through them, trying to avoid crushing ankles and hands as you passed. But the bodies were packed too tightly together, and the part of your brain that dealt with manoeuvring in tight spaces was not performing very satisfactorily by this stage. A chorus of 'ow's and 'watch it's followed in your wake, and thus the element of surprise – the one suit in which you held a few high cards – was sacrificed. Nonetheless, you imagined yourself looking pretty fierce, and were disconcerted to find Leon's face register not so much terror as relish. It suddenly occurred to you that you had confused the subject and object of the verb. You were not terrifying so much as terrified. On one level, this was a simple grammatical error. On another, the revelation put an entirely different gloss on the situation. You had no idea what to do next. The ends were not in question. You must punish him. You realised now that it might have been prudent to have given some thought to the means at your disposal as well as the ends. The glint in Leon's eye, the intimidating way he was cracking his knuckles, suggested it was probably too late now. You would have to improvise. This seemed to be what life in the world outside demanded above all else – constant improvisation. It was very draining.

Across a dozen unknowing, unseeing, uncaring heads you glared at each other, clenching and unclenching your fists. In your (by no means thorough) mental preparation for this encounter, you had bared your teeth and snarled, at which point he turned tail and ran. You now began to wonder if he hadn't been looking forward to this encounter all evening. He might even have engineered it, somehow. A few heads looked up to ascertain the source of the tension with which the air was suddenly humming. The more perceptive and alert began to shuffle their bottoms out of the way.

– Solomon!

It was Tess. Bugger. Having been on the point of a re-evaluation of valour in the light of discretion, you were now pretty much obliged to go through with this. You had promised to rid her kingdom of this pestilence. Hadn't you? You couldn't really remember what you'd said, or how you came to be in this room. You were aware of nothing beyond the pounding of your heart and the clamminess of your palms. The room seemed suddenly to have dropped several notches in volume, and risen several degrees in anticipation. Although inexperienced in the ways of men, you understood that whatever it was you were meant to be doing, you were already doing it now, and couldn't stop doing it until it was done. All eyes were upon you.

– Leave it, Solomon, Tess urged. – It's not worth it.

– I can handle this, you tried to convince yourself, and anyone else who was listening.

– Handle what? asked Leon, amused.

– No, you can't, Tess reminded you.

– Handle what? Leon persisted.

She was quite right. You couldn't handle it at all. You were very small and fragile. You cast around for – a what? a weapon? a trapdoor? a friend? but the spectators gathered in the bedroom were no more than curious to see who won and who lost, without having any desire to influence the outcome one way or the other. You suspected they had a pretty good idea who was going to come out on top in this particular head-to-head anyway. Leon's hand reached into his inside pocket.

– I've come to sort you out, you replied, failing to convince even yourself by now.

– I don't believe this, groaned Tess.

– Have you started yet? asked Leon.

– Yeah, come on then, urged another voice.

– Why does it always have to end in violence? complained a fourth observer (it was Green Hair).

– It's not *clever*, you know, pointed out her friend (Bald Girl).

Leon wheeled on her.

– I know, he said. – It's fucking *effective* though.

If anyone had a witty rejoinder to this observation, they kept it to themselves. Still you stared at each other. The onus was on you. What should you do? Two instincts presented themselves for consideration. The first was to turn around and run. That, or to burst into tears, grab him round the knees and beg him not to hit you too hard.

– BBBBOOOOOMMMM.

The house rocked on its foundations, and the pumping beat was swelled by the ripping and splintering of wood as the door frame buckled under the impact of the sledgehammers of authority.

– This is an illegal gathering, came salvation from an unlikely source. – You have five minutes to leave the premises.

Instantly, the room was in uproar. The entire room sprang to its collective feet and crowded round the windows trying to locate and abuse the source of the disturbance.

– It's the law, the more perceptive and sober amongst them explained to the others.

From downstairs came a crash and a crack, scuffles and protests and heavy boots on the stairs.

– They're coming up!

– Prepare to repel porkers!

You fixed Leon with your most menacing stare, and found words in your mouth.

– We'll continue this later, you warned him.

But he grabbed your arm.

– What's wrong with now? he growled.

You saw the steel blade in his hand. A sick feeling bubbled in the pit of your stomach.

– Go home! urged a man with a megaphone. – Go home!

Then there was a new smell on the air suddenly, a familiar smell, a terrible smell.

– Evacuate the building! screamed the man with the megaphone. – Evacuate the building!

The room was filling with smoke, but you could see nothing. Someone was standing on your toes. You pushed her in the back.

– I can't go anywhere, she pointed out.

It was Tess. Suddenly, a window was blown out and a gust of wind fanned the flames into a roar. The landing was ablaze, the fire casting grotesque shadows on the walls and ceilings.

– There's no way out, you said.

– Give us a bunk up, she ordered.

You cupped your hands and she put a foot into them.

– Hold tight, she warned.

She had one foot on a wardrobe, and the other on your shoulder. Your eyes and throat were stinging with the smoke and you struggled to keep your balance. Terror was mounting all around you.

– What are you . . . oof.

She swung her other leg on to your shoulder.

– Keep still, she ordered. – Hold on to my legs.

A sudden lurch as her knees locked threatened to overbalance the pair of you. A shower of dust fell around your shoulders.

– Let go, let go, let go, she was shouting now.

She kicked you in the face, and you released her ankles. You looked up to see her legs disappearing into a hole in the ceiling. After a minute, her head appeared in the opening. She reached down her hand.

– Come on, Solomon.

You raked your foot down the back of the calf of the man in front of you. He screamed, and bent at the knees. The split-second thus obtained was enough to enable you to swing yourself up on to the wardrobe, from where Tess pulled you up and through the little trapdoor into the loft. Now all was dark again.

– Where are you? you asked.

– Here.

You reached out an exploratory hand and felt for her in the darkness. You found something soft and warm.

– Is that you?

– Is what me?

You withdrew your hand immediately. She lit a match. It was a dead bird. You sniffed your finger and retched. The match burned down. She lit another. She was even more beautiful in the matchlight, which threw strange shadows over her features. You stood up, and cracked your head on a beam. From the trapdoor came the sounds of pandemonium beneath. In the dark it was impossible to know what was going on, except what could be inferred by the amount of swearing and shouting. The loft too was now filling with smoke. She lit another match. It revealed nothing but a battered old sofa weeping springs and stuffing, two rolls of crumbling carpet, several dead birds and the skeleton of an unidentifiable mammal. Water dripped through the slates in one corner. You wobbled your way together along the central beam, where the roof was high enough to walk almost upright, until you stood beneath a filthy skylight. She rubbed a hole in the grime with her arm, leaving a thin smudge of blood. Through the glass you could see the moon, smooth and white. From below came the sound of smashing glass and screams, from outside the wails of sirens and screeching of tyres. The snow was falling again, tumbling from the apparently inexhaustible and infinite heavens.

– Come on, then, she urged.

– Tess . . .

– Don't start, she warned. – Just help us get this open.

But it would not budge.

– It's nailed, you reported.

– Shit, she hissed, – shit shit shit shit.

The loft was clogging up with choking smoke. You felt your lungs fill with the poisonous vapours.

– It's the smoke that kills you, she said, – not the flames, the smoke.

With a strength born of desperation, you put your shoulder to the skylight. Suddenly, it was open. You gasped lungfuls of the cold London night. Tess was already through and scampering up the roof. You took rather longer, but finally managed to squeeze yourself through the opening. Casting your eyes briefly down, you shivered. It was a very long way. On the pavement below little figures were scurrying around with stretchers, and vehicles had been abandoned at random angles up and down the streets. Men in yellow helmets uncoiled a long tube. Flames shot from the front door. Someone had placed a ladder against the window of the room you had just vacated. You saw Leon halfway down it, holding his thigh and cursing. A group milled around at the bottom, dazed and disorientated. You recognised Bald Girl and Green Hair, particularly distinctive from an aerial view. The other inhabitants of the street had come out to watch. They stood in their porches in their slippers and dressing gowns, their T-shirts and knickers, enjoying the final razing to the ground of a building that had caused them a great deal of aggravation over the past nine months. Setting fire to the crusties' party was the only venture in which the Nazis and the Muslims of Angina Street ever found common cause. They hung around in extended families, pointing and laughing, and enjoying the excuse to stay up for another hour. Several people had camcorders.

Beyond Angina Street, however, in the next block, the neighbouring districts, the surrounding boroughs, all was tranquil. Great tower blocks loomed on the skyline. Each contained a thousand, no, two, three, four thousand people. And so it went on for ever, to the edge of the world. There was no end to it. You saw, suddenly, the extent of the city. It induced in you an overwhelming existential vertigo. Clouds scudded across the moon. A man was wandering around on the ground below, directing operations through a megaphone.

– You up there! he called, – you on the roof . . .

– Bugger, Tess cursed.

– Don't move, advised the voice. – Stay where you are.

– You must be joking, she sighed. – Come on, Solomon.

She set off, crawling up the incline on hands and knees and you attempted to follow. The slates were icy and none too secure, but already she had reached the top. She perched on the apex of

the roof, silhouetted against the moon, hugging the chimney. She
seemed a long way away.

– Don't look down, she warned.

You looked down. This was a mistake. You shut your eyes
and swallowed. A gust of wind caught you and a loose slate gave.
You felt yourself sliding agonisingly downwards and scrabbled
desperately for a handhold, but she had your wrist and dragged
you to safety. The slate tipped over the edge of the precipice,
and was lost from view. Up there on the top of the world the
moon was close enough to touch.

– You saved my life, you gasped.

– Yeah, she said. – Well, be more careful with it.

– Stay where you are! Stay where you are! screamed the
voice with the megaphone, furious at your failure to follow its
instructions.

– I'm not going down that ladder, Tess said, – I'm not going
back with them. Never.

You surveyed the city beneath you. The roof was noticeably
hotter now.

– There doesn't seem to be any other option, you pointed out,
– unless you have the power of flight.

It would not have surprised you, but she did not. Where the
roof gave way to nothingness, the tip of a ladder appeared.

– Are you coming with me? she asked, – or are you staying
with them?

– With you of course.

– Well, come on then.

She groped her way along the ridge of the roof, one leg on
either side, to the end of the house. Now there really was nowhere
else to go. Down below, you saw the passage that separated the
two houses, thrown into grotesque flickering relief by the flames.
It was a long fall, onto spiked metal railings, overflowing dustbins
and mountains of filled bin-liners. Suddenly, at the top of the
ladder, there was a head in a helmet.

– Don't move, it ordered.

She was now standing holding the TV aerial, and wobbling.
Suddenly, she sprung away from the roof. For an agonising
moment she seemed to hang in mid-air. Oh, it was an agonising

moment. The tension was unbearable. Would she make it to the other side, and safety, or would she fall to a grisly death on the railings below? Your heart stopped, and the crowd in the street below held its breath. Then she was down on the other side, and scrabbling for a handhold on the frozen tiles. She scampered back up to the top.

– Yeeeeesssssss! she yelled, punching the air with her fist.

– Come on, mate, the fireman urged, – you'll break your neck.

– Come on, Solomon, she yelled, ecstatic, – it's easy.

The fireman held out his hand.

– No heroics, eh?

– Jump, Solomon, she yelled, – come on.

You looked at her, then at him, then at the chasm between you and her, the three-storey drop that separated you.

– Don't be a hero, advised the fireman, – it's not worth it, mate.

– Come on.

– Solomon! A huge authoritative voice boomed upwards on the night from the street below. It was your mother. She had somehow got her hands on the megaphone.

– This is your mother, she informed you, unnecessarily. – Come down from there immediately, she ordered.

Her voice instilled in you a feeling composed of equal parts anger, humiliation and abject terror.

– Come on, Solomon, urged Tess, from the neighbouring roof.

– Right now, warned your mother, – or there'll be trouble. Real trouble. I mean it.

A tongue of fire shot upwards into the night from the chimney. The slates were becoming unpleasantly hot now.

– Come on, mate, pleaded the fireman.

– Come on, Solomon, screamed Tess.

– Solomon Grundy! bawled your mother, – get down from that roof at once!

A cloud of smoke drifted across your vision. You looked down, but all was lost in swirling currents of black smoke. You were paralysed. Last night you would have jumped without hesitation, with joy and with pride, into the void. But the experiences of the last twenty-four hours had dented your confidence in the beneficence of the future. The future, you were realising, had other things on its mind beside your own welfare. You longed to sink into crisp white sheets, to be brought what you needed when you asked for it. The modern world was warm, it was safe, it was comfortable and not life-threatening. All it asked in return was that you put up with the cretins who ran it. No, it was impossible. Your head was beaten to a soggy pulp by your heart. You coiled, waiting for the smoke to clear, ready to spring.

But when the smoke fell away she was gone.

– Come on, mate, said the fireman, – you're too old for this kind of lark.

He stretched out his hand, beckoning. In an instant, a great fog was lifted from your mind, and you beheld, as if for the first time, the true precariousness of your position. Panic grabbed you by the windpipe, inserting icy fingers into your groin and chest, and you clung to the chimney, quaking. What had got into you, to crawl out across the roof like that, to the very edge of the world? Gulping, you peered down into the street, but the figures scurrying beneath you induced another attack of dizziness.

The fireman folded you at the waist like a penknife and slung you over his shoulder.

00.36

– Siddown, instructed the voice in the darkness – and shuddup.

Thankfully, his instructions and your inclinations more or less coincided. Eventually, your heartbeat slowed, your breathing shallowed out and your eyes adapted to the gloom. You were in some sort of dark, windowless room. Periodically, doors at the rear were thrown open and the yellow light that penetrated revealed briefly the heads and shoulders of several others. Most were wearing gnome hats. All stared mutely ahead. You attempted to infer your location from the sounds that reached you from outside, but all was a hopeless collage of sirens and shouting, of tinkling glass and collapsing masonry. Then the room shot suddenly forward, throwing you down onto the floor. Once again, you were grabbed by the collar and yanked back up.

– I said siddown, the voice reminded you, – and shuddup.

– I'm going to be sick, announced one of your fellow passengers.

The van screeched to a sudden halt, the doors were thrown open and an hirsute man stumbled past. The hirsute man was pushed out into the night, followed by two of the men in gnome hats. From outside came the sound of retching. Eventually the three re-embarked, accompanied by a sickly appley smell. Someone rapped briskly on the side of the van, and you were on your way. After a while, the vehicle came to a halt that seemed less temporary than the previous ones. The engine was cut and the door thrown open. Out into the glare of headlights you staggered. Shielding your eyes, you were able to ascertain that you were in some sort of car park, surrounded by vehicles of the same design as the one in which you had arrived. Others stumbled, or were dragged, from the van behind you, cursing and moaning. A man in a gnome hat frog-marched you all up some stone steps, and in through a door in the corner of a wall. The others followed. Heavy keys crunched in massive locks.

– Don't even think about it, warned your captor.

You found yourself at a desk, on the other side of which a man in shirt-sleeves was typing into a machine. They had brought you to a Travelodge, though this seemed a very downmarket version. The light was wobbling in front of your eyes. Either that, or it was your head that was throbbing. Possibly the whole world was throbbing. You were losing the capacity to distinguish. The man spent a long time finishing whatever he was doing, before, with melodramatic finality, pressing a button. Now, you waited whilst a dozen pieces of paper emerged slowly and significantly from another machine. The man collected, shuffled and read them. He then deposited them in the bin.

– Name? he sighed.

You were pushed forward.

– Name? repeated the man, wearily.

You realised it was you to whom the question was addressed.
– Grundy, you informed him.
– Grundy what?
– Solomon Grundy.
– Spell it, he ordered.
But you were unable to do so. He fixed you with a hard ironic stare.
– Date of birth?
– You what?
– When were you born?
– On Monday, you remembered from somewhere.
Behind you, someone giggled. The man glared at you, and wrote something uncomplimentary on his form.
– Turn out your pockets, he ordered.
A surprising variety of objects was revealed by this operation, and laid upon the desk – some loose change, half a packet of mints, a bunch of keys, a leaky red biro, a little wallet . . . The man in the shirt-sleeves flicked through the wallet.
– Who's this then?
He was showing you a photograph. The face, when it came into focus, was vaguely familiar, from somewhere, a long time ago. It was all very blurred.
– He looks familiar, you admitted. – Do I know him?
– Dr Anthony J. Conway, the policeman read from the security pass. – Do you?
The face was familiar, the name was familiar, from some-where.
– I don't know, you admitted.
– Well, do you or don't you? Yes or no?
You found it impossible to answer sincerely using either of the alternatives offered. It seemed safest to say nothing.
– So how come you've got his Barclaycard? the man wanted to know.
He was flapping the little wallet in your face. You remembered now from where the face and the name were familiar. You recalled, with a shudder, Conway's nakedness, his eyes glazed and unresponsive as you hoiked him up on the bed. You knew every blotch and pimple of Dr Anthony J. Conway. It seemed

a reasonable assumption that rendering Dr Anthony J. Conway unconscious and robbing him of his clothes was not the sort of exploit the authorities were likely to applaud.

– I don't remember, you lied.

The man in the shirt-sleeves relieved you of your belt and shoelaces, but allowed you to make a phone call. You could not, however, think of anyone you wanted to ring, at least not anybody that was likely to answer. Your head was rapidly silting up. You found yourself obliged to lean upon the desk to support yourself.

– Name? the man demanded again.

This was bizarre. You had the distinct impression that you had just been through all this rigmarole. Then you realised your interview was over, and the man's attention had moved on to the woman behind you.

– Mother Theresa, she said.

The rest of the exchange was inaudible. You were led away, down a dim corridor without windows, to a pokey little room. The man in the gnome hat left, locking the door behind him. After a few seconds, a tiny hatch in the door was pulled back, and two eyes appeared.

– I'm still here, you reassured him.

The grille snapped shut.

The room had another occupant, who snored loudly on a concrete bench on the opposite wall, and was seemingly oblivious to your recent arrival. The walls were covered in the same hieroglyphics as the rest of the world, though these particular specimens were apparently scratched into its surface with nails and teeth. Some were daubed in dried blood and faeces. The illumination had been set at a level too bright to permit sleep and too dark to permit anything else. There was an oppressive and distressing smell, and a brief investigation revealed, in a little compartment at the back of the room, a fetid potty, overflowing with red-brown sludge. There was no other furniture. It was hardly luxurious. Still, all was relative. You thought back to the roof from which you had descended and shuddered. You seemed to have landed, if not exactly on your feet, then at least on your knees. It was warm, it was dry. It would do. You had grown less choosy by now, and more thankful for small mercies. It was a survival thing. One need, however, could not be overlooked; the smoke had brought upon you a terrible thirst. You hammered at the door. No response. You tried again. Finally the hatch shot back, and the eyes appeared, angry.

– What?

– What about the little tray with the kettle and the tea bags?

The hatch snapped shut, and footsteps receded down the corridor. You seemed to have failed to communicate your needs. Again, you battered at the door.

– Come back! you hollered. – Come back!

Your protestations had no effect beyond disturbing the other occupant of the room. He pulled the duvet around him and turned over, or would have done had he been in the bed in which he habitually slept. As it was, his manoeuvre only had the effect of causing him to fall off the bench onto the cold stone floor. He lay there foetally, his arms around his head, groaning. You watched him with distaste. It was one thing to share a room with a mother, or a wife: to share it with a stranger was a new and unsettling experience.

– Turn the light off, the man pleaded.

You searched the wall for a switch.

– There's no switch, you informed him.

He groaned.

– No switch, and no bed, and no tray with tea bags and little individual portions of milk. No shower. Not even any bog roll.

The man emerged, blinking, from the depths and focused upon his cellmate.

– What's going on? he wanted to know.

– Your guess is as good as mine, you confessed. – We seem to have been allocated a double room without bog roll in the Travelodge from hell.

He coughed, looked around him in sudden terror and finally remembered where he was.

– It's not a Travelodge, he said, – it's a cell.

Your head felt as if it had been cleft by an axe, your ribcage was tender and bruised, your vision was blurred, and the man

was quibbling over words. Your conversation was suddenly interrupted by rapid footfalls in the corridor outside. You strained
desperately to catch a hissed conversation beyond the door. The
hatch was pulled back. First one, then another, then a third and
finally a fourth pair of eyes peered in. All seemed vaguely familiar.
The key turned in the lock and the door swung open. She was
standing in the doorway, in tears.

– Solomon! she cried.

– Mum!

As you embraced, you were shocked by how much she had
shrunk since you had last seen her. How frail she seemed now.
Her hair had turned grey. She was in floods of tears.

– My baby, my baby, she was sobbing.

– There, there, Mum, you soothed, – it's all right now. It's
all gone now.

You became aware of three other men accompanying her –
the man who had locked you up and two others – and felt
suddenly self-conscious. Wasn't *she* supposed to be saying this
kind of thing to you? Somehow your roles seemed to have been
reversed. Tony Bowles was hardly any less embarrassed. Chalkie
White, meanwhile had a genetic immunity to embarrassment. He
was fiddling with some dials, as a prelude to the capture of the
moment for prosperity.

He grinned. Tony blushed. You shook hands. They seemed
very familiar. But everything was beginning to seem familiar
these days.

– What about me then? asked your cellmate. – Two days I've
been in here.

– Yes, what about him? you asked.

It seemed uncharitable to leave him behind.

– I don't know anything about your friend, said the man. –
That, I'll have to check.

It was a further half-hour before the clearance was authorised,
or the authorisation cleared, or whatever was required for the
authorities to relinquish their hold upon your friend. Then there
was the paperwork to complete in triplicate, a task at which
the men with gnome hats were revealed as none too proficient.
Eventually, however, the five of you found yourselves on the

front steps of the police station. You were surprised to find the
world still dark. You imagined yourself to have been confined
for years. Your mother said it was maybe an hour.

– Smile! ordered Chalkie.

– Pphhhhffff went the flash bulb. Red and purple blotches
swam in front of your eyes.

– Where now? asked your friend, thrilled to have found some
people who would put his life in order for him.

– I'm starving, said Chalkie.

– Solomon? Solomon? Are you all right, love?

You had gone a distressing green colour. Your knees buckled
beneath you, but your mother caught you and lowered you gently
onto the steps, and placed your head between your knees. You
were conscious of being the subject of a hissed conversation above
your head. A voice whispered in your ear.

– How are you feeling?

You took stock. Every bone and muscle in your body had been
reduced to jelly. Your head throbbed, and your forehead was
alternately hot and cold. Your skin was a patchwork of blisters,
bruises and goosebumps.

– Not too good, you summarised.

– Can you walk?

You tried to stand, but your knees would not lock. Once
again, the adults discussed their options. You drifted in and
out of consciousness, and were unable to follow the argument, conscious only that the word 'hospital' cropped up with
alarming regularity. It was around that point that you passed out.

11.13

You awoke, Lear-like and many months later, to birdsong. The
bed in which you found yourself was wide and comfortable,
though slightly damp where you had lain. Ethereal curtains
fluttered in the breeze at an open window, and for half an

hour you too fluttered in and out of consciousness, wondering whether perhaps your number had been called. Eventually, you understood from the muted rumble of traffic that you were not in heaven. At least, if you were in heaven, it was a very urban heaven. Since the image conjured up in your mind by the word was one of lambs gambolling by crystal streams, rather than of winos puking in the doorways of 7–Elevens, the balance of probabilities suggested you had still a few more dances on graves to complete before you were allowed to bow out. That you were still in the land of the living was confirmed by the presence of Chalkie and Tony, snoring in armchairs arranged around the end of the bed like guard-dogs. No heaven with any pretensions to exclusivity could operate a door policy allowing ingress to Chalkie White.

Pushing yourself up on to your elbows, you blinked the crusts of sleep from your eyes. Your mouth was dry and your bones weary. Someone had removed Conway's filthy clothes and dressed you in a delightfully soft suit of lightweight cotton, decorated in a floral pattern. The bed upon which you lay was huge and magnificent, with a tasselled canopy and covers so heavy you were scarcely able to lift them. The walls were panelled in oak of a bitter chocolate brown, set off by furnishings of emerald green. Apart from the two armchairs in which snored your guardian angels, there was an elegant, low glass coffee table, a huge leather sofa and a sideboard, covered in a lace doily. Whoever lived here clearly had a higher regard for furniture, and a considerably bigger budget, than Bald Girl and Green Hair.

Two doors led off into unidentified ante-chambers. Seized by curiosity, and discomforted by a bloated bladder, you raised yourself, threw off the covers and padded across the thick carpet to the first. It was, fortunately, an ensuite bathroom. A tug on the light switch caused an extractor fan to whirr into life. The noise grated down your consciousness like a spade down a blackboard, but once set in motion the thing could not apparently be stopped. Above the sink was a mirror, which you consulted for evidence of further physical disintegration. Your fears were amply confirmed. Your eyes had puffed up and your face assumed a wan grey hue. You pinched the wrinkled and mottled skin on the back of your hand. The lower half of your face was concealed beneath a thick bushy beard in desperate need of a trim. But most worrying of all, the excitements of the night before seemed to have caused your hair to fall out. You ran your fingers through it, and a clump came away in your hand. You stared at it in horror. All the colour had drained from it, leaving it wispy grey and lifeless. Your hairline seemed to be receding as you watched. At some point during the trials and tribulations of the past twenty-four hours, you had left behind at least three teeth, and the grimace that smiled back at you in the mirror appeared slightly demented. You looked frightful. You gulped several glasses of water, peed a bucketful and made your way back into the main room. Chalkie had been awoken by the noise, and was pulling on his filthy trousers.

– Morning! he greeted, unnecessarily cheerful. – Coffee?

But you were more concerned to ascertain your location.

– Hotel Metropole, Chalkie enlightened you. – Care for some breakfast?

You declined. Even the offer of food made you feel bilious. The axe embedded in your cranium now seemed to be glowing fluorescent pink and orange and pulsating. Chalkie called up room service, and ordered two breakfasts. He had a theory, based upon his own appetites, that people only ever turned down food, drink or sex because they thought it was polite. Politeness he regarded as a fairly benign form of hypocrisy.

– You'll want it when it's here, he warned.

You doubted it.

– You've got to eat, he reminded you. – Keep your strength up.

He made a further call and added some dried toast to the order.

– Just in case, he explained.

Tony Bowles stirred in his chair, and groaned, but did not awaken.

– How did I get here? you asked.

– I carried you, said Chalkie.

– But why here?

– Because it's the best, Chalkie explained, – and for you, nothing but the best will do.

This wasn't very helpful either. Who was this man anyway?

– Peter White, he introduced himself, offering his hand, – of the Pilsbury *Evening Sentinel*. But everyone calls me Chalkie.

– Why?

Chalkie shrugged. You lowered yourself gently into a chair. Flotsam from the shipwreck of last night was beginning to wash up on the beach of your short-term memory.

– Where's my mother? you asked.

– Next door, Chalkie replied.

You sat down at the end of the bed, and tried to bring the world back into the focus, to no avail. The events of the past few days tumbled through your mind in an apparently random procession of images and emotions. Still uncertain where you were, you crossed to the window and threw open the curtains. Tony Bowles moaned deliriously and covered his eyes with his forearm. A slow drizzle was falling and the skies were grey and overcast. Buses, cars and taxis splashed through the melting slush, and people hurried past with umbrellas in the street below.

– Kensington, Chalkie answered your unarticulated question, opening the door to a polite knock.

You were sure you knew them from somewhere, these two. Definitely. It was most perplexing. Why was there such a limited cast of characters in your life? There seemed to be millions of possibilities from which to choose, and yet somehow it was always the same people who cropped up, over and over again. The provocative odours of bacon, of mushrooms and scrambled eggs and black pudding, of fresh toast and coffee percolated out on the balcony. A cold white sweat broke out upon your forehead and your stomach rose towards your throat. Staggering to the bathroom, you deposited what remained of your curry into the mimosa-scented lavatory pan and keeled over on the bath-mat.

12.22

You came round to find Tony Bowles easing you out of your pyjamas, whilst Chalkie looked on, halfway through his second breakfast. The bathroom was filling with steam.

– Careful with my man there, urged Chalkie, jabbing a forkful of black pudding in your general direction to indicate his referent. Tony Bowles was evidently finding your deshabillement extremely distasteful.

– Did anyone ever tell you? he asked, – that you stink? Where have you *been*?

– Hanging out with some highly disreputable company, by all accounts, Chalkie reminded you.

At the thought of Tess a great heaviness descended upon your heart. You felt yourself shrink like a woodlouse to a tiny, armoured ball of shame and regret.

– How do you feel? asked Tony.

– Awful, you told him.

– What happened to your teeth? asked Chalkie.

You shrugged.

– I don't know.

– No great loss, he consoled you, – they're bastards, teeth.

He projected his top denture an inch forward out of his mouth, then sucked it back in.

– Who needs 'em? he asked.

Tony helped you out of your pyjamas and onto your feet.

– A nice hot bath, he prescribed, – that's all you need. You'll be as right as rain.

You were less confident that the damage inflicted by the past twenty-four hours could be quite so quickly and effortlessly repaired. It seemed more likely that something irreplaceable had been lost for ever. Three teeth for a start. Tony helped you into the bath.

– Now you have a good long soak, he advised, – we'll be in the next room, if you want anything.

You smiled weakly up at him, for you sensed he meant you

no harm. Whether he did or not made very little difference anyway. You were pretty much at his mercy. He departed and left you steaming in thought. Once again, things seemed to have worked out somehow. There really did seem to be someone up there watching out for you. It was a good job, too, for you were obviously incapable of looking after yourself. This new Travelodge was certainly a notch up on the previous one anyway. You inspected the bottles on the bath shelf. Each contained a distillation of colour – gorgeous, viscous deep strawberry reds and damson blues with rich fruity smells to match. You poured the contents of one bottle after another into the water, and sloshed the red and blue concentrates around until the bath was full of bubbles. You had by now sufficient understanding of the world outside to understand that such luxury was unlikely to come without strings attached, but you had nowhere else to go. You might as well enjoy it while it lasted. Perhaps you had made the sensible choice after all up there on the roof. It had been a very long way down. And in the end, nothing was gained by heroics: it was just self-indulgence really. Life was hazardous enough, and short enough, already. It didn't need any encouragement.

Tony's head appeared round the door.

– Sorry to disturb you, he disturbed you, – but there's been a development.

– A what?

He thought for a second.

– You'd better get dressed, he said at last.

Reluctantly you drained the water from the bath and went through into the next room. Your mother had surfaced. She seemed much younger than you remembered her, and she was looking vaguely sheepish.

– Hello, love, she said.

– Hi, mum.

– Hi, Simon, said the man from the cell.

– Solomon, you reminded him.

He mimed shooting himself in the head.

– Solomon. Of course. Sorry.

You acknowledged him with a masculine nod. You were rather less pleased to see your mother this morning than you had been last night. Your friend thrust a newspaper in your face.

– You're a celebrity, he said.

The front page was given over entirely to your face. The other papers all carried the same picture. It was not a very flattering likeness. It was not even, to judge by what you had just seen in the mirror, much of a likeness at all.

– Do I really look like that? you were worried.

– You did last night, your friend confirmed.

– The camera does not lie, Chalkie lied.

Tossing the papers on the floor, you collapsed in the space on the sofa thus vacated. The four of them looked at you, waiting for someone else to begin.

– There's something you ought to know, began Tony at last.

You were beginning to suspect that there were an awful lot of things you ought to know.

– The thing is . . .

– The thing is, Chalkie interrupted, – that you're a celebrity.

He seemed to be expecting some kind of response.

– Is that good or bad? you asked.

– It's . . . well, it's swings and roundabouts, you know? Tony explained.

– No.

You had spent your childhood in an institution, not a playground. You were beginning to become suspicious.

– On the down side, Tony said, – you have to . . . well, there are various things that come with the territory.

– Opening supermarkets, Chalkie illustrated. – That sort of thing.

– Going on game shows, your friend added. – That sort of thing.

– You have to be prepared, Tony warned you, – for a certain amount of intrusion into your private life. Can you handle that?

The modern world seemed to have offered an ideal schooling for such inconveniences. You felt as if you had spent most of your life in print already.

– On the up side, Chalkie continued, – you'll find yourself phenomenally wealthy, and a magnet for gorgeous women.

You stared at him, uncomprehending.

– Hideous women, then. Hideous men. Cattle. Whatever lights your candle.

– And the best thing, your friend concluded, – is that none of us will have to work again. Ever.

This struck you as a serious drawback. If you recalled correctly Dr Conway's reflections on the theme, work was a major component of most people's strategies to fill up the time between birth and death.

– So what do I do all day? you asked, – if I can't work?

– You'll think of something, your mother assured you.

– Like what, though?

– Listen, counselled Chalkie, – if you're worried about running out of totty, don't be. The world is full of totty. Believe me. No matter how insatiable your appetites, supply will always exceed demand.

You stared at him, bewildered. Tony Bowles decided to aim a little higher.

– You could improve your mind, he pointed out. – Read. Go for long walks. Think things over. Meditate. Write poetry. Compose symphonies.

– Raise a family, suggested your mother

– Travel, suggested Tony.

– Paint the spare room, suggested your friend.

– Dig the garden.

– Learn French.

– There's no end of ways to pass the time, Chalkie assured you. – Anyway, it's not a job interview. You *are* a celebrity. Some are born celebrities, he aphorised. – Some achieve celebrity status and some are stuck with it, whether they like it or not.

– Take a look out of the window, your friend suggested.

Puzzled, you obeyed. Where an hour ago there had been nothing but a street, now a tremendous crowd was assembled, extending as far as the eye could see in all directions. People of all ages were there, of all races, creeds and star-signs. There were turbans and tams and men with ringlets and women in purdah, men in skirts and women in trousers. Some carried banners, others cameras. You stared at them in horror.

– This is worse than the hospital, you groaned. – Don't I get any privacy at all?

– No, Chalkie said.

Your heart sank.

– It's the price of celebrity, your friend explained.

– But what do they want, all these people?

You gazed down upon the ocean of faces in the street below. Wherever you looked there were faces, faces in which all you could read was a grim determination not to lose their place in the queue.

– I know that man! you gasped.

It was the man from the launderette.

– You really do make a bee-line for the low-lifes, observed Tony, relieved to find himself separated from the man by several storeys.

Chalkie walked over and put his arms around your shoulders.

– Tell me what you see, he commanded.

You looked. Perhaps there was something important you were missing.

– I don't understand, you confessed. – What is it they want?

– It's not what they want, Chalkie put you right, – so much as what they need.

– And what do they need?

– Euthanasia. It's the only way.

You were not convinced.

– What am I going to do? you asked him.

– You're going to speak to them.

– What am I going to say?

– I don't know. You're the celebrity. Only get dressed first, eh? he suggested.

As well as the papers and his various breakfasts, Chalkie had had the foresight to commandeer most of the other services offered by the hotel: barber, dentist, manicurist, beauty therapist and tailor, as well as another young woman in a short skirt concerning whose function he waved away all enquiries. He put them all on the *Sentinel*'s credit card, and retired with the young woman in the short skirt.

– Back in a minute, he promised.

A minute was pushing it, thought Tony, even for Chalkie. But he bit his tongue. A host of self-important functionaries flitted in and out of the room carrying clipboards and tiny microphones, speaking into portable telephones and barking instructions at each other. The barber having cleared a path through the undergrowth, the beauty therapist began to touch up your blemishes. Since each blemish was inevitably a reminder of its origin, and since these origins were not for the most part events it gave you any pleasure to recall, you found the process very soothing. Being a celebrity certainly had its compensations. A thick foundation, a little blusher on the cheeks, a dab of lip gloss, and you were transformed. Whilst the manicurist cut and polished your nails, the tailor and his assistants passed tape measures around your girth and encircled your arms and legs. The dentist scrubbed and polished your teeth, fitting temporary plastic replacements for the ones you'd lost. Finally, the tailor returned with a selection of apparel, the trying on of which provided an excellent excuse to pass a very pleasant half-hour in front of the mirror, admiring your new self. The Solomon Grundy unearthed by the ministrations of the functionaries and floozies was a revelation. You'd always guessed that underneath it all you were pretty gorgeous: even you, however, were impressed by quite *how* gorgeous you turned out to be. You really were, it had to be said, a sexy old bugger. Suave, chic and debonair. Well nigh irresistible. You marvelled at the transformation your appearance had undergone since you had last come across your face, staring vacantly up at yourself behind a line of speed. The difference that could be wrought by human ingenuity in the inessential superficialities of life was extraordinary – touching up the bruises, tucking the imperfections away out of sight, restoring former glories and concealing last night's heartbreak. It was a shame no equivalent technology had been invented for the soul.

– All right? grinned Chalkie, who had reappeared from his discussions with the woman in the short skirt in an exceptionally good mood. Your mother and friend were allowed, somewhat reluctantly, to remain, and even permitted to finish off the remains of the breakfasts. The rest of the entourage Chalkie dismissed.

– What do you think, Mrs Grundy? asked Chalkie.

– He looks lovely, she said.

A tear welled in her eye, whether of grief or of pride you could not decipher.

– Lovely, she repeated.

– Very smart, confirmed your friend.

Proof of the skill of the hotel staff was that even Chalkie White had been rendered presentable. Spruced up with a shave, a haircut and a new suit, he performed an extraordinary manoeuvre that was apparently intended to resemble a pirouette.

– What do you think then, Smokey?

Chalkie's shirt-tails were protruding through his flies. Tony wondered whether to point this out to him, and decided . . . no.

A microphone had been set up for you on the balcony. Chalkie ushered you through the double doors. The crowd had swelled even further. It seemed as if every human being on the face of the planet had assembled in Kensington to hear what you had to say. A great cheer greeted your appearance. Tony was saying something into a telephone but his words were lost in the maelstrom of cheering and chanting and screaming that rose from the multitudes below. Horns were honked and drums beaten. Someone had a klaxon that played 'Colonel Bogey'.

– In this thing here? you asked and instantly jumped back, startled by the volume of your own voice. The microphone took your query and amplified it a thousand-fold, until it was audible across the entire planet.

– Some news that might interest you, Tony shouted in your ear, – that girl of yours . . .

At the mention of Tess, your heart stopped. The tumult around you seemed suddenly to melt away. You clutched his sleeve.

– Is she all right?

– Transport police picked her up this morning. They're taking her back to Millham House.

– Millham House? Where's that?

But Chalkie had taken your arm and was steering you towards the microphone. Your mother had wandered out on to the balcony behind you and stood there, grinning vacantly. Your friend even managed a little wave to the crowd below.

– Go on, mate, he urged, – say something.

You stepped forward to the mike. All noise ceased abruptly, as if a fuse had blown. The silence was somehow more unsettling than the noise, and you became even more conscious of the thousands of expectant faces upturned towards yours, waiting for your words of enlightenment.

– Look, you said.

It was intended as a whisper but it emerged as a tremendous roar, bouncing back at you from the buildings opposite and around about, re-echoing and rebounding in complex syncopation until it was hard to remember this appalling cacophony was the repercussion of your own tiny voice.

A woman shouted, – What's the answer?

And this demand was taken up by other voices, until it became almost a chant. You stepped towards the microphone and instantly the chant was quelled.

– What's the question? you asked.

The crowd was stunned and hushed. Someone shouted back.

– What shall we do?

This was a more straightforward question.

– Go home, you told them.

If you had known what they wanted, or even what they needed, you would have given it to them. But you had no more idea than they did.

– Go home, you repeated, flapping your arms uselessly. Then no more words came. You stood, paralysed, mouthing nothing in particular, like a fish. Someone was tapping you on the shoulder. It was your friend.

– Can I . . . ? he gestured toward the microphone.

Amazed, you stood back and gave him the floor. He tapped the mike with his finger and it crackled and crunched around the city. Again the crowd was hushed, expectant.

– Go home and be nicer to your children, he told them.

Someone shouted back, – Then what?

He paused.

– Mow the lawn? he suggested.

There was an audible groan.

– Listen, he ordered. – I'm going to tell you a story.

The crowd fidgeted in preparation. Your friend allowed them to settle before beginning.

– It's a true story, he said. – All stories are true stories. A few days ago, I was at my lowest ebb. I was a physical and emotional wreck.

– Aaaaaahhhhhh sang the crowd.

– A physical and emotional wreck, he continued, unperturbed. – Life had no meaning for me any more. Everything I ever cared about had disappeared. I thought about ending it all. Then you know what I did?

– Tell us, someone shouted.

– I went out and got drunk. And you know what?

– Tell us.

– When I woke up these gentleman had sorted the whole thing out for me.

The mood of the crowd was changing now, turning ugly. A half-full can of lager whizzed past your ear and smashed in an explosion of froth against the wall above your head. Your friend moved away from the microphone, ashen faced.

– I don't know, he was saying, – what is it they want?

– They want their heads seeing to, diagnosed Chalkie.

Suddenly, your mother wheeled upon him. There was real hatred in her eyes.

– All right, Mr Clever Clogs, she hissed, – if you're the one with all the answers, why don't *you* speak to them?

Chalkie was no less startled by her outburst than you were. He stared at her, and a grin spread round his lips.

– All right, he said. – All right I will.

He pushed you aside, stepped in front of the microphone and hushed the crowd.

– You want to know what to do? he asked.

– Yes! they bellowed back.

– Get a proper job, he said. – Get a fucking life.

The crowd erupted. You could feel their hostility crackling in the air around you. A rock smashed the window behind you.

– Come on, said Tony, – we'd better get back inside.

Chalkie burped ostentatiously, swept aside some shards of glass and collapsed on the sofa. Your friend shut the window, and the murderous rumble was muted, though still audible. Chalkie lit his pipe. Tony shook his head incredulously.

– What is this? he said. – What are we doing here?

– Well, if you don't know, said your mother, – I'm sure nobody else does.

– I'll tell you what we're doing here, said Chalkie, – I'll tell you. You see that picture there?

He picked up a random newspaper and brandished it at the four of you.

– Guess how much I got for that, he challenged.

But nobody was in the mood.

– Come on, demanded Chalkie, – guess.

– Fifty quid, your friend guessed eventually, without much conviction.

– More, said Chalkie.

– Fifty billion quid, guessed Tony.

– Less.

– We give up, your mother declined to guess.

– Come on. A proper guess.

– We give up, all right.

– A proper guess.

Tony Bowles leapt to his feet and grabbed his colleague by the scruff of the neck.

– Chalkie, we fucking give up, all right?

The two men stared into each other's eyes. Tony released him.

– Quarter of a million, said Chalkie. – Jealous?

Tony Bowles shook his head in disbelief.

– You keep plugging away, explained Chalkie, filling his pipe, – and one day you strike lucky. Patience, Smokey, that's what it takes. That's what you'll never understand. Patience. That's what makes a photographer. Someday your chance will come, and . . .

– You better take the lens cap off, Tony interrupted.

Chalkie sighed, and re-lit his pipe.

– If you're so clever, Smokey, he puffed, – and I'm so thick,

then how come it's me sitting on a small fortune, and you and
the Original Dysfunctional Family there sitting on sweet fanny
adams? Eh? Can you tell me?

– I can't, admitted Tony Bowles. – It worries me. But I
can't.

– Exactly. The trouble with you people, Smokey, is that . . .

There was no way Tony Bowles was going to sit and listen to
a lecture from Chalkie White that started 'the trouble with you
people'.

– Who the fuck are my people, Chalkie? Who?

– Cleverdicks, said Chalkie. – The trouble with you people is
you think you know it all. Me, I don't know much about much,
but I know that much.

– You reveal an unexpected breadth of experience.

– Do me a favour, will you, Smokey? Just fuck off, eh?

Tony Bowles had had enough.

– I've had enough of this, he announced, – I'm going back to
Pilsbury.

– Fine, hissed Chalkie through gritted teeth, – fine. You
do that.

– You coming?

You looked up at him, uncomprehending.

– I'll take you home, he explained.

Now Chalkie rose from his seat, a look of panic upon his
face.

– You can't do that, he said.

– You coming? Tony asked again.

– Can I?

You were unsure.

– No, said Chalkie.

– Yes, said Tony, simultaneously.

You were caught in the glare of indecision. You had no
reason to trust him, but there was no one else to trust either.
Certainly not your mother. She meant well, presumably. At
least, so everyone said, though the sheer fact that it needed
to be repeated so often indicated it was far from self-evident.
But what good were intentions? She sat on the sofa with your
friend, grinning nervously like a cow. The pair of them. What a

complete scissors and sellotape job they had made of their own lives, and now they had the nerve to try to run yours. As if a man could have no higher ambition in life than to wind up like his parents. They were the ones who needed rescuing. That was why she had come looking for you, you realised. She didn't know what to do without you.

– Last chance, warned Tony.

13.08

The two of you descended to the basement in silence. Tony found Chalkie's old Cavalier.

– Don't suppose he'll have much use for this any more, Tony supposed.

You went to climb in the passenger seat.

– If I were you, he advised, – I'd get in the boot.

You stared at him, uncertain.

– Suit yourself. You'll be safer in there. I'll let you out at the M25, he promised.

He was about to slam the boot, when you stopped him.

– Can I ask you a question?

– Sure, he shrugged, – why not?

– Do you ever feel like . . .

But it was not so easy to put it into words.

– Like what? he prompted.

– Like you're just going through the motions. Like your life is speeding up. Just getting faster and faster. And you can't be bothered with it any more?

Tony nodded.

– All the time.

– When I was young everything seemed to take for ever. Now whole hours pass and I've been thinking about something else entirely. But it's not really getting any faster, is it? It's just an illusion.

Tony thought about it.

– You know what I think? he said at last.

You shook your head.

– I think there's no such thing as illusions, he said.

You fixed him in the eye.

– I'm going to die, aren't I? you asked.

– Sooner or later, he said, and slammed the boot.

It was an hour before the police were able to clear your passage. (That's police brutality for you, Tony reflected, – never there when you need it.) Eventually however, a channel was opened up through the multitudes and circulation restored to the capital. Tony drove towards Pilsbury. Locked in the boot, you worried about your mother. She reminded you somehow of yourself, but an earlier self; one you had rapidly discarded as you realised its limitations and inadequacies. A point had been reached at which you had sailed past her somehow. The roles had been reversed. You were the grown-up now. At some point, briefly, you had confronted each other as equals, and found each other slightly disturbing. How could you not? There was too much of each other in each of you. You laboured under the delusion that you were unique, singular, but when you stared into other people's faces that fiction became impossible to maintain, until there was no option but to blink, and break the link. Locked in the boot, you fell into a reverie, and dreamt you were no more than a rearrangement of tiny fragments of everything else, and everything else in its turn was a rearrangement of tiny fragments of everything else, including you, so that ultimately everything was made from little bits of everything else. But if everything was just a rearrangement of everything else, then there wasn't anything at all, ultimately. What was there then? There were just stories, stories that crossed and recrossed and uncrossed each other, running in parallel grooves for a short while before they branched off again. It didn't really bear thinking about.

True to his word, Tony stopped at the first services beyond the interchange to let you out. Finding you sound asleep and frightened to penetrate a slumber so deep, he did not disturb you.

– Poor sod, he thought, – what a life.

It occurred to him that your sorrows and sufferings ought to put his own small-town frustrations into some sort of perspective.

But they didn't, obviously. He climbed back into the car and drove towards the setting sun.

18.45

– Wakey wakey.

Tony Bowles was shaking you gently. Behind him, the sun was setting orange and the dusk thickening purple against a skyline speared by inky poplars. A flock of crows cawed down by the river. You struggled to an upright position, blinking.

– End of the line, he explained.

You were in the car park of a sprawling single-storey building half-hidden behind a conifer hedge, in the corner of a piece of wasteland. You had clearly arrived by means of a road that snaked across the wasteland without sidebranches or other distractions, and ended abruptly where you stood. This road was hung like a necklace by street-lamps. The car park was all but empty at this time of night, and the building seemed to float upon it like an illuminated island. Its windows were tall and thin and its whole aspect indescribably gloomy. A screen of poplars hid the river, beyond which a city was preparing, without much enthusiasm, for another Thursday night. On either side, the wasteland simply disappeared into the dusk. Wherever you were, it was clearly on the way to nowhere else.

– Where are we? you asked, accepting his steadying arm as you clambered out.

– Pilsbury, he said.

You took another look. You felt you ought to recognise it. It was your home town after all. But you didn't.

– Where in Pilsbury?

– Millham House, said Tony. – I thought . . .

– Millham House?

– Yeah.

Tony shrugged.

– I live just down the road, he said.

You stared at each other.

– Good luck, he said at last.

– Thanks.

A pause.

– See you then.

– Yeah, he said, – yeah, maybe.

He climbed back in the car and fired the ignition, but made no attempt to leave.

– Go on then, he urged from the car.

You approached the door, and tried the bell. There was no reply. You hammered on the door.

– Hello?

The metallic voice came from a grille. It was far from welcoming.

– Go on, urged Tony from the car.

– Is anybody there? demanded the voice.

You took a deep breath.

– I've come to see Tess, you said.

Tony dipped the handbrake and sped off. You were on your own.

– Hold on, the voice instructed.

Several minutes passed. The last few seams of light dissolved into the gloom. From inside the building came voices raised in argument.

– Get off.

– Oooffff.

– I warned you . . .

Finally, you heard the rattling of keys in the lock on the other side of the door. It swung open to reveal a thin, tired woman with a black eye and an enormous bunch of keys.

– We had to have the bell disconnected, she said. – People kept ringing it.

– I want to see Tess, you said.

She was taken aback, and glanced at her watch. Then she stared at you, curious, pursing her lips.

– Don't I know you from somewhere? she asked. – Are you her grandfather? It's a bit late for visits.

– But I have to see her.

– I can't let you in without an appointment. Sorry.

– Please?

She shook her head. You made a feeble attempt to barge past her and through the doorway, but she was too well trained and saw you coming.

– You'll have to go through the channels, she said.

Dismayed by the ease with which she had repelled your attack, you slumped down on the doorstep and cradled your head in your hands. The woman was unable to close the door. She stood there for a few minutes, sighing.

– Look, she said eventually, – I don't make the rules. If it's that important, I'll ask her. What did you say your name was?

You told her.

– Solomon, she repeated.

You nodded. She frowned. You were ever so familiar somehow. But she couldn't place you.

– You'll have to wait outside, though, she said.

For ten minutes you waited. A thin drizzle condensed out of the grey evening chill. The argument went on, on and on, on and on and on.

– Get off.

– Oooffff.

– I warned you . . .

– Aaaaargggghhh.

– Oooffff.

– Get off.

– I warned you . . .

– Get off.

– Bastard.

– I warned you . . .

– Get off.

– Aaaaaaaaaarrrggh.

– I warned you.

– Oooffff.

Just as you were beginning to suspect you had dreamed your encounter, you heard once again the rattling of keys in the lock.

– Ten minutes, she said.

You entered the door and passed through a metal detector

into a corridor. Here you were obliged to wait while your guide located the appropriate key. A man appeared from an office and searched you lethargically.

– It's very kind of you, you said.

He glowered at you. On discovering your sincerity, however, he grunted in acknowledgement and unlocked another door. Another man appeared, and showed you into a room. The walls were covered in childish pictures. It resembled the place you had first met, at the hospital.

– Wait here, the man ordered.

You waited.

– How long have you known Tess? the woman asked.

– We were at school together.

She gave you a strange look. You realised you had better try and head off her enquiries before they proceeded any further.

– How about you?

– Sorry?

– How long have *you* known her?

– Tess? About six months personally. A lot longer by reputation. I'm her social worker.

– Lucky you.

She snorted incredulously, then frowned again.

– If you don't mind me asking, she said, – well, just how exactly are you related, you two?

– We're not, you said.

– Just friends.

– More like lovers.

Her jaw dropped. The door flew open, and Tess appeared.

– Solomon! she shrieked, and before either of her custodians could stop her, she had planted a big kiss on the top of your shiny bald head. You glowed with pleasure. The man guided her into the chair opposite. You grinned at her. She grinned back. She was looking better than ever. You thanked the two staff.

– You can leave us, Tess said.

But the woman shook her head.

– No.

– Aaaaaaawwww Janice.

– No, the woman insisted. – Sorry.

Tess realised she wasn't going to get anywhere. She stuck out her tongue and blew a raspberry, then turned her attention back to you.

– What happened to you? she asked. – You bricked it.

You blushed. It was true.

– Then what?

You filled her in with the story of your adventures over the past twenty-four hours, as much as you could remember. It didn't take very long. She didn't seem to be listening anyway, her attention flitting around the walls and out through the windows.

– What about you?

You were obliged to repeat the question several times. Finally, Janice nudged Tess back into the here and now.

– Me? said Tess. – Not much. Bunked the tubes and went round and round on the Circle line all morning. Fell asleep. Got woken up by the inspectors, dint I?

You took her hand across the table.

– Come away with me, you said.

She giggled. A worried look passed across Janice's face.

– Where? Tess wanted to know.

– Wherever you want.

She thought about it.

– Can Janice come?

You had not expected this.

– What about it, Janice? Tess asked her social worker.

Janice laughed and shook her head.

– Sorry, she said, – I'm booked up to next Christmas.

– But . . .

– I'm afraid Tess is not free to go with you, even if she wanted to, Janice explained, – she's subject to a Secure Accommodation Order.

– A what?

– A lock-up, Tess translated, – I'm locked up in here. Until I learn to behave. She pulled a face.

– We feel that by her behaviour Tess puts both herself and others at risk, explained the social worker.

– At risk of what?

– At risk of having a party, said Tess.

– At risk of serious harm, said the social worker.

– Oh.

– You go though, said Tess.

– Go where?

– Wherever you're going. Send us a postcard. I've never had a postcard, she said.

– What about when you get out? you asked.

Tess pursed her lips.

– I'm not getting out, she said.

– Tess will be staying here until we feel she is no longer at risk, said the woman.

– And how long will that be?

– Well, that's rather up to Tess.

– It is? asked Tess.

– You know it is, Janice told her.

– Can I stay for ever and ever?

– No.

– Can I leave now then?

– No.

– So how's it up to me then?

– You know what I mean, said the woman.

A man appeared in the doorway with a huge bunch of keys.

– Ten minutes, he said.

– You know something? asked Tess.

You didn't.

– You're the first person I've ever had visit me who didn't get paid for it.

You understood that the interview was about to be terminated. A terrible panic seized you by the throat and robbed you of the ability to communicate.

– Tess . . . I . . .

– You can come back tomorrow, suggested the social worker.

– Yeah, come back tomorrow, said Tess.

– But . . . there might not *be* a tomorrow, you said.

Tess laughed.

– Don't be stupid, she said. – There's always a tomorrow.

She kissed you on the forehead as she passed, and was escorted back to her room.

Janice showed you out. The argument was still continuing.

– Shall I call you a taxi? she asked.

But you had nowhere special to go, and were not in the mood for any company but your own.

– Where are you going? she enquired.

You shrugged.

– I don't know. Back into town I suppose.

– I'll give you a lift, she offered.

Again you declined.

– I'll walk, thanks.

– Do you know the way?

You didn't.

– Go down to the river, she suggested, – and follow the footpath.

– Thanks.

– See you tomorrow then.

You stared at her, uncomprehending.

– Between six and seven.

– Oh. Right. Yeah, maybe.

She closed the door. You wandered down to the river, and gazed for an hour at the reflection of the pink full moon in the black waters, thinking it over. You had managed to end up somehow back where you started, only now you had more yesterdays than tomorrows. There didn't really seem anywhere else to go.

Then a rustle in the bushes caused you to swing round. A man stood before you.

– I've been looking for you, he said.

It was Frank Parker.

Worse on Friday

03.14

In your bed, you slept ´the sleep of the overwhelmed and overcome. The cool, conditioned air of the hospital entered your nostrils and meandered through the myriad tiny vessels and chambers that formed your life-support system, but only your chest rose and fell, rose and fell, marking the passage of time. The world without your body was beyond your knowledge. All you knew was inside you – your stomach gurgling, your heart thumping, your bladder filling, your bowels opening. River gases bubbled in your interior and forced their way out in farts and belches, sludge was funnelled along your digestive system, your fingers clenched and unclenched, blood trickled through your veins. You swallowed. You had been terrified for a while back there, as you went down for the last time, and felt your lungs filling up with water, your clothes dragging you down, down, the terrible weight upon your chest. But now all was calm again.

You were aware of nothing beyond the appalling inertia, the terrible weight of your body. You could not lift your arms, and your head felt as if some mischievous sprite had poured quick-setting concrete in through your ears. At the same time, you knew that you could spring to your feet and walk away and leave this shell of a body behind you, and be free of it for ever, its aches and stubbed toes and migraines. It seemed such an obvious solution that you wondered why it had never occurred to you before. Your body and mind were becoming disentangled. For many hours you hovered between life and death – it loves me, it loves me not – before deciding that you did not wish to die just yet. A week was a tangle of threads that started nowhere and finished nowhere else, and in between tangled themselves up in a million other threads. There were still too many loose ends to be tied up, and some people you wanted to see again, people who owed you explanations: your father, for example. Then you would be ready.

10.20

Sir John Parkes circulated irritably amongst those who had unwittingly entrusted him with their lives, shaking his head and sighing. First the Solomon Grundy business, and now Cameron had keeled over and left him with a ward full of bodies; it had not been a good week. Sir John's surroundings did little to dispel his suspicion that things were falling apart, and he was the centre who was failing to hold it all together. The patients in Hawkins' ward reminded him of nothing so much as tubes of toothpaste. You could usually squeeze another few nights out of them, if you were determined enough. Medical science had solved the 'how' part of the problem a long time ago. They are waiting now for someone to come up with a convincing answer to the 'why' bit. One of the things Sir John Parkes had learned during a long and illustrious career was that when God decided to make your life miserable, he usually decided to make it fairly short as well. In his youth, this observation had spurred him to a brief flirtation with socialism. As he neared his own retirement it seemed more a tantalising glimpse of some hidden order to the world, and one that demanded great moral courage before it could be tampered with. God was not just, but neither was He without mercy. If he dealt you a bum hand, he at least let you make your excuses and leave the table. Most things in life were worth trying once but not all of these were worth doing

twice, and very few were worth doing day after Promethean day
in excruciating, synaesthetic agony and incontinence pants.

It was not so much the surgeon's knife that was in demand
this morning, anyway, as his biro. Most of Hawkins' patients
were worth more as scrap than as going concerns. They were
ripe for asset-stripping. Nothing was wasted. It was the kind of
thing that none of Sir John's generation would ever have imagined
possible back in the 50s, like satellite telly, and test-tube babies,
and mashed potatoes out of a packet; things that seemed to offer
such marvellous possibilities, and yet invariably turned out to be
rather unpleasant. Recycling the patients was, thankfully, not one
of Hawkins' responsibilities: Sir John was at least spared that.
Instead, it was his task, technology having ensured that the
parts were salvageable, to decide to what extent this description
could be applied to the wholes. Someone had to sign the death
certificate before the junior doctors could strip them down. This
was a task guaranteed to infuriate Sir John. He had never known
what to put on death certificates. What was the cause of death?
Life was the cause of death. Heart failure was just a symptom.

Sir John abandoned number B31245 – known as 'Bernard
Parkin' to his friends, and more recently to his neighbours as
'Mister Stinky' – to the recyclers, and moved on to the next bed.
No identification. Male, white European, mid sixties. Dragged
out of the river last night and not regained consciousness.
Suspected suicide. Sir John sighed. No one had the energy for
a fight any more. They reached the age of about four, found the
world less tractable than they had bargained for and abandoned
the effort. Still, it was hard not to feel some sympathy for them.
The human race was running out of steam, gridlocked by sheer
weight of numbers. No one could make any sense of it. One could
not trust science, or religion, or art, or politics. What could one
trust but one's own boredom threshold?

The swing doors propelled the nurse back into the ward. Sir
John's heart sank.

– I've got a message from your wife, she said. – From the
switchboard.

Sir John visualised Nora striding furiously up Digby Beacon,
a reluctant Caesar whimpering at her heels, her head-scarf

fluttering in the wind. But if lives were in your hands, you could
hardly say you had better things to do. That you'd promised to
play tennis with your wife. After all, other men spent their entire
lives waiting for the chance to do something more useful than
putting up a shelf.

– You shouldn't have married a surgeon, he would tell her,
wearily.

– We live and learn, she would reply, in that way she had.

Stupid cow.

– Sorry? enquired the nurse.

He had given voice to his thoughts. One day it would get him
into serious trouble. Senility was creeping up on him.

– Did you say something? asked the nurse.

– Dreadful, said Sir John, trying to sound sincere, – terrible.

This was usually a fairly safe comment in a hospital. Better
an excess of solemnity than an excess of levity.

– What is? she enquired.

He thought quickly.

– This . . . he gesticulated vaguely . . . all this.

– Yes, she said. – It certainly puts it all in perspective.

Put it into perspective. Stupid woman. It depended entirely
upon whose perspective you put it into. From the perspective
of this anonymous white male it was no doubt a trifling incon-
venience to miss a tennis match. From his wife's perspective,
this man's entire life and death were cause for nothing but
considerable irritation. He, Sir John, merely had the impossible
task of trying to reconcile the two. But there was no point taking
his irritation out on the nurse. It was just the sort of thing people
said in the presence of death. It was all you could say really. You
were just glad it had picked on someone else again.

The exchange did little to improve his humour. He cast a
professional eye over you, and was not impressed. Your cheeks
bristled with stubble, your hair was lank, grey and greasy. Your
skin was like bark. Presumably they had estimated your age by
slicing through your torso and counting the rings. You perfumed
the ward with a piquant bouquet of rats' piss, industrial sludge
and stagnant mud that Sir John recognised as originating from
the River Pill. The recyclers would clean you up, anyway. Who

could imagine what they might find under there? The description 'white European' was more an educated guess – there being after all eighty white Europeans in Pilsbury to every 'other' – than a statement of fact. In a fit of pique, Sir John inserted question marks into your notes. 'Male? White? European? Mid sixties?' Facts seemed much closer to his own experience of the world when followed by a question mark. They were pretty far-fetched, after all, most of them. A question mark reminded one how unknown, how unknowable, it all was.

It had been Sir John's habit, in his bachelor days, to plan his week's TV viewing on a Sunday afternoon. Planning, he had believed then, was the answer to the problem of time-management, and time-management was a serious headache for a junior doctor with several girlfriends and his socialist eyes on a Tory marginal. Programmes he felt he really ought to watch he marked with a star. Programmes he merely wanted to watch he marked with a question mark. This practice, however, subtly altered the intonation of the programme titles. His personal favourite soon became 'This is your life?', for which he extended the principle by adding italics '*This* is your life?' The celebrities who were subjected to the red book treatment remained oblivious to the change in perspective effected by this modification of typescript and punctuation. Sir John, however, found that where once the programme had made him feel small and useless, it now made him feel superior. It was a small, egalitarian gesture.

Sir John did not seek to belittle and undermine, for the sake of it. It was easy to mock – it was the instinctive reaction of any thinking being to the modern world – but great harm could be caused by thoughtless mockery. His intention was merely to instil a little humility into the enterprise. Nowadays he had no time for the telly at all, but the habit had stayed with him. It made him no more popular with friends and colleagues than it had done with the electorate of East Shirley. Bank managers snubbed him at formal suppers when he took to signing off his letters 'Yours sincerely?'. A lonely great aunt thought him impertinent when a card asking 'Merry Christmas?' dropped through the letterbox during the festive season, and cut him from her will. He was fighting a losing battle, he knew. His colleagues (the psychiatric, the teaching, the social work professions – you seemed to become a professional simply by professing something these days) were all doing their damnedest to raise people's self-esteem. It was their basic credo; everybody suffered from low self-esteem. No one was ever diagnosed as having excessively high self-esteem. For Sir John, on the other hand, self-esteem was roughly analogous to blood pressure. The self-esteem of most of the men and women he came across was far too high for their own good, or anybody else's, already. The job of the professors was not so much to promote the uncontrolled expansion of self-esteem as to forcibly ram it back into the Pandora's box from which it should never have been liberated, and then sit upon the lid. It was like cheerfulness – it was all right as far as it went, but all too often it just didn't know when to stop.

Grumbling, he moved on to the next bed. Your eyes fluttered open. The room in which you found yourself was immediately familiar. Quite what it was about the room that made it so familiar, you could not say. It was there, at the back of your mind, on the tip of your tongue, but just out of reach. It wasn't that it looked familiar. What it looked like you could not say, your perspective being entirely restricted to a broad area of the ceiling above you. This view offered no means of orientation beyond a plastic strip light, whose protective cover had become over the years a mass grave for winged insects. Beyond, and to either side of this sepulchral illumination, the world melted into a blur. Had you been able to raise or turn your head, you would have been disconcerted to find Sir John and Jackie at the foot of the bed. But you were neither able to nor willing to, and wherever the impediment lay it booted the idea of movement beyond the bounds of serious consideration.

That man's voice, now trailing away, was certainly familiar from somewhere, and emerged from a background of sounds no less familiar – creaking wheels, swishing curtains, clangings and bangings, slammings of doors, coughs and grunts, the sounds of people permanently on their way to somewhere else. The noises made by people making it clear to all concerned that there are a hundred and one other things they could and should be doing. You guessed from this gentle cacophony that you were back in the modern world. But this familiarity wasn't the kind that was familiar because it was everywhere; it was the kind that was familiar because it was only here, and because it wasn't like anywhere else. It was something vague, in the atmosphere, but you knew you had been here before.

It was the smell.

You smelled of the river mostly. You had swallowed, before they had dragged you out, several gallons of the River Pill. Small radioactive deposits remained encrusted behind your toe and fingernails. The blood your weary heart was feebly pumping around your body was three quarters Pill, of which at least one third was hazardous industrial waste and sewage. You could feel the toxic sediments of the carrier-bag factory clogging up your lymphatic system, your circulation growing ever more sluggish and foul. But it wasn't that smell: it was a smell behind that, underneath that. It was a smell of hospitals, but it wasn't a chemical smell. It was the smell the chemicals were supposed to drive away. It was something much stronger, more vivid. Whatever it was, it was bypassing your consciousness altogether and making straight for your endocrine system, from whence it sent its chemical needles pulsing forth into your organs and soft tissues.

It was half an hour before you were able, finally, to dissect and articulate it. It was the smell of the fear of death. It hung suspended in the room like a fine mist, infecting everyone upon whose lips it laid its cold kiss. It was what had kept you alive, and what kept you alive still.

15.52

Bitten by her conscience, Jackie O'Dowd had stopped to call the hospital and communicate such information as she had regarding your whereabouts to the relevant authorities. Then she had driven back to Pilsbury. She stopped again, to buy new wiper-blades, before discovering that it wasn't the snow that blurred her vision. What now? she wondered. The thought of going back filled her with horror. How could she face her life? The washing up furry and congealing in the sink, the stale messages on the ansafone, the cold stew in the fridge. Over the past few days she had met, married and now separated from Mr Right-Fuck-up. She had seen it coming in slow motion, watched it unfold in horrified fascination and had still been powerless to influence the outcome one way or the other. She worried that the wind had changed, and her appalling luck now been formalised into some kind of character trait.

What now, though? Kick over the traces? Change her name, dye her hair, burn her clothes? Join a nunnery? She could be one of those devotees with saffron robes and jasmine and tambourines who danced barefoot up and down Oxford Street. She could throw herself into the Thames. But it would make no difference, in the end. Eventually she would go back. Back to what she knew. Everybody did, in the end. There was nowhere else to go in the end, apart from back. They would laugh at her, and tease her, and comments would be whispered behind concealing hands, but there wasn't anything they could do, surely? It was a free country, after all. People could screw up their lives, if that was what they wanted to do. There was no law against it. Eventually, like Ozymandias, it would all be forgotten.

She had driven twice around Pilsbury's gyratory system, galvanised by vacillation, until she noticed that her next shift began in twenty minutes. What the hell, she had thought, it had to be faced sometime. Sooner or later – that was the only question. She had driven to the hospital, and reported for duty. Her colleagues had smiled, called greetings, did not seem at all surprised to see her. At first, every friendly 'morning gorgeous', every casual 'how's tricks?' had made her more paranoid than ever. But after half an hour she understood. No one knew. The authorities had kept it from them, for some obscure management reason. She changed, and went to find Sister Nuttall, but Sister Nuttall had been suspended pending an enquiry, and Carmen had been temporarily promoted to her job.

– Hi! said Carmen, showing off her badge. – It's an ill wind, eh?

Jackie searched her comment for innuendo, but found none. Carmen didn't know either. How could they all be so dim? she wondered, before realising that for a nurse to leave the hospital at the end of her shift was not in itself grounds for suspicion. And who was going to tell them? Sister Nuttall was suspended, Doctor Conway had lost all memory of who he was and where he worked, let alone of what had happened on Tuesday night. (– Apparently, Carmen confided, – he runs around naked, beating his chest and yodelling.) The security guard had been dismissed. The hospital was pursuing the search for scapegoats with far greater enthusiasm than it was pursuing the search for explanations. Perhaps she was safe after all. The only person who could blow her cover had more to lose by doing so than she herself.

In the evening, unable to sleep, she went for a long walk on the Beacon, where she found a dead lamb, and decided she had had enough of Maternity. She had lost her appetite for it. She had always wanted to hit them, those women who came to the ward entirely ignorant of the paternity of their offspring. (– You tell me when it was, darling, they would cackle, – and I'll tell you who it was.) They were so careless of the future, as if when one future proved disappointing they could move on to another. What was wrong with these women, she wondered, that they could not make a commitment that outlasted a contraceptive? Now she found herself hoist by her own petard. Her own marriage, after all, had lasted barely an hour. Even for a mad decade of a mad century, that must be some kind of record. Twelve hours of insanity. That was all she could plead – insanity. A moment of madness. An aberration. A one-off. Completely out of character. A never to be repeated, once in a lifetime how–could–this–happen–to–me? cock–up. Just like all the others. What could you do, except try and put them all behind you? Maternity was where she had met you, and everything in Maternity reminded her of you. She needed a clean break. She requested a transfer. The hospital was keen to oblige. There was always a shortage in Geriatrics. She jumped at the chance. It was about as far away from all the things that reminded her of you as she was likely to get. Now she took your temperature, and plumped up your pillows, but her mind was in another realm entirely. For a brief moment, you had been the possibility there might be more to the world than met the eye. As long as you had kept moving she had managed to sustain the illusion. It was only when you had stopped that things got sticky. She wiped a tear from her eye and went in search of a fresh hankie.

Neither, for your part, were you remotely aware of the recent proximity of your wife. You were slowly remembering from where the smell was familiar. You *had* been here before, once, a long lifetime ago. Monstrous trousered legs chased you through those swing doors, and you dived under this bed, and lay there shivering and terrified until they went away. Perhaps not this bed exactly, perhaps one just like it. Perhaps this very one. That was right at the beginning, before it all got properly started, a sort of preparation for the real life, which had been to come, and had now been and gone. Not quite though. Still, the embers glowed in the darkness. Still, the need to make sense of it all, that kept you going long after anyone else would have given up and gone home.

Summoning all your strength, you raised yourself up on to your elbows. The scene was much as you remembered it. A row of beds against each wall, each bed containing nothing but a head. You became aware for the first time of an ambient voice in the air around you. You had not noticed it before, but it had always been there. Its source was a television set perched on a little shelf in the corner of the ward. You brought it into focus. A man with a black eye was alerting the world to the imminence of the Apocalypse. He too seemed familiar. You struggled to place him, and realised eventually that he was your grandfather, and that the old man could not tolerate the idea of the world continuing without him. You saw another familiar figure, Dr Humphries, leaving the hospital the back way, in disgrace. He had his coat over his face, but you recognised the awkward loneliness of his gait. Then more faces: your mother, Chalkie. The only face you did not see was your own. Pictures of everything, everyone, except you. They had no image of you: nothing beyond the impressions you had made in other people's minds as you passed, nothing to prove you *had* passed but the one photograph, snapped by

Chalkie just before you went missing. You were playing on the floor of that room, on that corridor, in that wing – not really playing, just staring ahead. On the window-ledge behind you, you recognised the little night-shirt your father had dressed you in, casually discarded. How long ago was all this, really? Was it a week, or a lifetime?

Then more men in white coats, in a white land; scientists in the Arctic Circle. They had uncovered evidence that the world was falling apart even faster than had hitherto been feared, said the voice. The scientists now gave the world thirty years, tops. You wondered what this had to do with anything, before it occurred to you that there might be other news, news for other people, as well as your own news. England were 157 runs for eight and the pound was down two pfennings, said the woman on the screen.

– It's all lies and nonsense, said the man in the next bed, without lifting his head.

– What is? you asked.

– The news.

– Oh, you said, – I thought you meant the modern world.

– That as well, he said.

He hoisted himself up on his elbows.

– Paul, he introduced himself.

He offered his hand, but the gap between your beds was too great.

– Solomon, you replied.

He stared at you in amazement, then shook his head.

– My son's name, he explained. – Not my choice, mind. My wife's.

– What's wrong with it? you asked.

– Well, it's a bit, you know . . .

– What?

The man struggled for a synonym, but in vain.

– Stupid, that's all, he confessed. – It's a bit of a stupid name.

– What would you have called him then?

– I don't know. Something a bit less stupid. Simon or something. Mind you, he said, – given the way things have turned out . . .

He trailed off, lost in reminiscence.

– How did things turn out? you asked, irritated.

– Badly.

– But how?

– I haven't a clue, he admitted. – We lost touch.

– Well, how do you know it turned out badly then?

– I don't, he confessed. – I just assume it did. Things do.

Unprompted, he launched into a narration of the events leading to his current hospitalisation. The purpose of his narrative, however, seemed less the communication of information from one party to another than an attempt on his part to make some sense of it all. It was a narrative without much cohesion. He had walked out on his family. The subsequent events he could not accurately piece together. He remembered vaguely some of the places he'd been along the way. There was a pub involved, or several pubs perhaps, or perhaps the same pub from various angles (including, it seemed, the horizontal). At this point, he began reminiscing about his family, and became unbearably sentimental. He had thought he could teach his child to walk, he said, to catch him when he fell, to rock him to sleep, to pass on the fruits of his own experience so that his son need never make the same mistakes. But his son had not needed him, or even wanted him. He wondered if they'd even noticed him gone. They had forgotten him. No one was really interested in fathers until they started beating people up.

– What about you? he asked, finally.

You told him as much as you knew, and he appeared to listen, though you were not entirely convinced. Several times his eyes glazed over, and he seemed about to either fall out of the bed or regurgitate, or possibly both simultaneously. But he nodded at appropriate moments. When you had finished, he pursed his lips and seemed about to say something. Then he apparently thought better of it. You stared at each other, embarrassed.

– You *are* my son, then, he said.

You both suspected that such a revelation ought to prompt a spontaneous overflowing of powerful masculine emotions. As it turned out, you had very little to say to each other.

– The last thing you did to me, your father recalled, – was bite me.

He showed you the scar clamped by your milk teeth in his flesh. The wound was not so impressive as the depth of the tiny teeth-marks.

– Did I do that? you asked, incredulous.

You must have really meant it, at the time.

He nodded.

– 'Fraid so.

What he had done to provoke such fury you could not recall. But you were unrepentant.

– I'm sure you deserved it, you said.

He conceded the point.

– Just because you deserve it doesn't make it hurt less, though, he pointed out. – Quite the reverse.

– I hardly remember you, you told him, – I must have been very young when you left. It seems like another life.

– Tuesday morning, your father specified.

– A long time ago, you confirmed.

Again, you stared at each other, embarrassed by your word-lessness.

– I saw you on the TV, your father said.

– I didn't see you.

– I was never a celebrity, your father pointed out. – You were the celebrity. I was just supposed to hold the celebrity. And burp the celebrity. And wipe the celebrity's bottom. Nobody takes any notice of fathers, not until they start slapping people around. Then they move your family to a bigger flat, and take out an injunction to stop you seeing them.

– You chose me, you reminded him. – I never chose you.

Your father blushed, staring at his feet and picking a crust of dried vomit off his pyjama trouser turn up.

– I didn't exactly choose you, he admitted.

– You were coerced?

You were sceptical.

– Of course not. Look, I don't know how to say this to you . . . but . . . you were never planned as such. Now that's not to say you weren't wanted, and loved very much, when you did come, only . . . well you were a bit of an accident, really. Just one of those things.

– One of what things?

Your existence had always struck you as rather singular: you resented the insinuation that it was just an exemplar of a broader category of phenomena. Your father seemed to be searching for words.

– Explain, you insisted.

– It was on a houseboat, he said at last. – On the Norfolk Broads.

– Who are they?

– It's a place, he said, – not a person. Haven't we been through all this before?

– Not me, you reminded him, – I wasn't there yet.

– You were quite a turn up for the books, he said, – quite a surprise.

Again, his eyes glazed over, and he chuckled to himself in such a way as to make you fear for his sanity.

– It was our last attempt to patch things up, he explained, – your mother and me. We'd not been getting on. She thought I'd been sleeping with one of her friends.

– Had you? you asked.

– I was working up to it. That isn't the point though, really. The point was we'd reached a journey's end, your mother and me. Even then. We made a last attempt to sort it out, to salvage something from nearly four years, and we ended up with you. We thought you were a sign.

– A sign of what? you asked, incredulous.

– A sign we should stick together.

– I'm not a sign, you say, – I'm . . . I'm me.

– Stupid I know, he acknowledged. – People don't happen for any reason. People *are* the reason. We live and learn, eh?

You talked to your father until the nurses came to tell you to shut up, and gave you pills, and turned out the lights. You talked some more, until he fell asleep, then you lay there in the darkness, your mind liberated by the chemicals, trying to make sense of it all. You remembered a conversation with Jackie, as you sped down the motorway.

– Why are you doing this for me? you had asked her.

– I don't know, she admitted. – It seemed like a good idea, and then . . . She trailed off.

– Then what? you prompted.

– It all happened so fast, she explained. – Things happen like that. You'll see. You make a plan, and then a thousand and one things get in the way, and before you know it you're doing something else entirely, and you wonder how you ended up where you were.

– What sort of things? you asked.

– I don't know, she shrugged, – chance things.

You had not come across this little word before.

– What sort of things are those then?

– Chance is . . . chance is luck, she repeated, unconvincingly, wishing she'd never mentioned it. – I mean, really, you want to know why I'm here with you? There's no reason. It might have been Sandra on duty last night. Or Kirsty. I could be at home with a cup of cocoa and a good novel, and we'd never have met. Maybe I would have read about you in the paper in the morning. It's just chance. It doesn't . . .

She had stopped, conscious of a certain ambivalence having crept into her voice concerning the relative merits of the hypothetical as opposed to the actual course of events. She took one hand from the wheel, found yours and squeezed it.

– All I meant was that a hundred and one things might have happened and we wouldn't be here now together. We'd be somewhere else. Separate. We'd never have met, never even known of each other's existence. But none of those other things happened. That's what chance is. Some things just happen for no reason. No reason that I can see anyway.

– I can't believe that, you had decided finally. – That some things happen for no reason.

She laughed, and whistled through her teeth.

– You'd better believe it, she advised you.

– It just seems so unlikely, you went on, – I could believe that everything has a cause and I could believe that nothing has a cause, but I can't believe that some things have a cause and others don't.

– Which then? she had asked.

You were no nearer an answer now than you were then. No wiser, just older. And still quite alone. In the end, there was no way round it: you were on your own. It was no great hardship to be on your own if you enjoyed your own conversation, if your thoughts enchanted and stimulated you. But not when they horrified you. When you had no desire whatsoever to pursue the appalling alleyways full of lurking bogeymen down which your thoughts led you. When you staggered home drunk after a night with friends, fumbled with the key in the lock, staggered over the threshold, found the light, there you were, waiting for yourself on the sofa. And then you wanted to turn round and pretend that you hadn't noticed yourself sitting there and run straight back to the pub and never go home. But you had to go home sometime. The thing to do was to go home so drunk that you just fell asleep on the sofa, with the TV glowing and the front door wide open on to the street. But that sort of thing frightened friends away in the end. Presumably that was why people tended to end up in families. Families were unbearable of course but they were better than the alternatives. Better than being alone and better than being in a gang. Somehow, because families combined the crappy bits of both – the boredom of solitary life, the frustrations and aggravations of the social, they reminded you how grim the alternatives were.

There was a dissatisfaction in mud, a feeling that mud was not enough, a yearning for individuality, from which life was born. But there was a dissatisfaction in life, that life was not enough, a yearning for meaning. From this yearning, men and women were brought forth, kicking and screaming. That was why people were here: because, otherwise, it didn't make any sense, because people made sense of it all, and only people could do that. But there was a dissatisfaction in sense, too. You looked at the mud, and you looked at the sense, and all you could think of was 'how did I get from here to here?' You made sense of it, but you knew all the time that it was you making the sense. The sense didn't make itself – you had to make it. It required constant improvisation, and it was all very unsatisfactory.

Dissatisfaction, then, was what made people people. It was

their distinguishing feature, their hallmark even. What bred this dissatisfaction? What was it about humans? It was because they stood on two legs. When they stood on two legs, they lost interest in the scavenged bone at their feet and became aware of the gazelle grazing yonder. They began to ask themselves what life might be like over there. The grass certainly looked greener. They became aware for the first time of horizons, and began to imagine, against all the accumulated experience of the millennia, that it must be better over there than it was over here. They were dissatisfied with walking, and so they invented the helicopter. They were dissatisfied with decrepitude and so they invented medicine. They were dissatisfied with sex, and so they invented pornography. Now the skies were full of helicopters, the hospitals of the recycled, the news-stands glistened with tits and bums of all colours, shapes and sizes, and still they weren't satisfied. Things individually might be getting better – gene therapy, space travel, interactive pornography – but things generally were not getting any better. There was the paradox: that the more things individually got better, the more aware people became that things generally were as bad as they had ever been. They began to feel that perhaps the constant search for satisfaction was at the very root of their dissatisfaction. After several billion years of evolution, and several hundred years of empirical science, they reached the enlightened stage of dissatisfaction with their own dissatisfaction – a sort of meta-dissatisfaction. The only way to achieve satisfaction, in the end, was to stop trying.

You seemed to have come, somehow, to some sort of resolution.

Died on Saturday

11.43

Father Tew's life had not been dedicated, as were most men's, to the accumulation of chattels and pensions. Everything he owned – flat, car, furniture – he owed to the beneficence of the Health Authority. Neither was it easy to conceive of a means by which the skills of a hospital chaplain could be transferred to a commercial setting. Having thought through the issues, and following consultation with his ecclesiastical superiors, he had whittled his options down to two: the monk's life, or the hermit's. Father Tew was in no great hurry to return to the protective bosom of the cloister. A decade previously, he had entered a small retreat in an attempt to escape from the bewildering obsessions of the modern world. Shortly after his arrival it had become popular with a pop star who owned a mansion nearby, as a cheap drying-out clinic. Following a gushing feature in a colour supplement, the retreat expanded out of control and Father Tew somehow ended up running the Gifte Shoppe, dispensing monastic bath salts and John Taverner CDs and complaining that this was precisely the kind of thing he had entered the monastery to escape. The hermit's life thus struck him now as a sort of Hobson's choice. He would live in a cave, with nothing but a candle and his bible, and eat whatever the Lord saw fit to provide. He was rather looking forward to it.

Research into the avenues open to the prospective anchorite

in the last few years of the last century, however, had dispelled
his illusions. Not only were most of the eligible sites in the
region privately owned (mainly by the Ministry of Defence)
but those in the public domain invariably proved to have severe
drawbacks. The most promising sites naturally turned out to
be already occupied, in many cases by men whom extended
isolation from the conventions of social intercourse had rendered
aggressive when disturbed, and extremely pungent. Those sites
as did remain unoccupied predictably comprised very much the
scrapings of the spiritual barrel – they overlooked motorway
service stations, or were used as unoffical target practice by
the army, or were situated within earshot of secure mental
hospitals. His aspirations had gone into terminal tailspin with
the news that, even were he to locate a suitable site, he would
not be permitted to live there without planning permission,
a septic tank, adequate parking and a host of other arbitrary
impediments to the spiritual life. Surely, he had thought, there
must be somewhere left on the surface of the planet where a man
can go and be left alone. Further research revealed that, of course,
there were such places, and indeed several of them were owned
by the Church. Demand, however, was high and since turnover
was fairly sluggish they were heavily oversubscribed. The lady
he had spoken to had suggested he fill in an application form,
and go on the waiting list.

When the form arrived in the post the following morning, he
had skimmed through it and pinned it to his notice-board, with
the firm intention of filling it in one day. This had been six
months ago, and (following the general principle that any form
not completed within ten minutes of receipt is unlikely to be
completed at all) he still hadn't got round to it. Now, over the
past few days, the matter had taken on an added urgency. Quite
why his position at the hospital was any less tenable this weekend
than it had been last, he was not entirely sure. The decision had
arrived from the ether during the labyrinthine proceedings of
the fortnightly Ethics Committee, which it had been his turn
to attend. A seat on the Ethics Committee came *ex officio*, and
he was more or less obliged to attend and make the occasional
protest vote for the sake of his conscience and the reputation

of his order. Representatives were elected from all the major specialisms, and religion was treated as a medical specialism for the purposes of ethics, albeit an administratively awkward and slightly tiresome one (for the purposes of accounting, on the other hand, the priesthood was listed as a consultancy, because there wasn't a code for a priest within the complex taxonomies of the hospital accountants, whilst consultants occupied an entire sub-order within the primates). The Ethics Committee was chaired by Dame Barbara Hershkovitz. Both Father Tew and the Imam had hoped that the appointment of the latter would involve a doubling of the religious representation on the Ethics Committee, but neither had been particularly surprised to learn that they were expected to occupy their *ex officio* seat on a rota, in a similar arrangement as had been devised for the office. They were told this reflected the need to keep the numbers odd, so as to avoid too many ethical stalemates. The Ethics Committee regarded ethics as a sort of intellectual red-tape, devised to provide people who would otherwise be unemployable with the opportunity to interfere gratuitously with the smooth running of their organisation. They seemed to be under the impression that their hands were constantly tied by this red-tape, although as far as Father Tew could see they had more or less carte blanche to make whatever life and death decisions they felt were necessary as the circumstances arose, completely *a priori*. Their guiding principle seemed to be 'where there's a way there's a will'.

The debate had been scheduled to consider issues of confidentiality, but the meanderings of its discourse led Father Tew to the discovery that some of the junior doctors had been interpreting their patients' terror at the prospect of death as *prima facie* evidence of mental instability. These patients were then offered the services of a psychotherapist. The doctors explained that they were only trying to be helpful. Knowing how busy he was, they had merely been trying to spread his workload a little more evenly. The sincerity of this explanation was problematised, however, by the smirk that occupied their faces as they offered it, and the insolent giggling that Father Tew had learned to associate with those who don't really see what all the fuss is about.

– Why don't we put it to a vote? someone suggested.

– Put what to a vote? asked Dame Barbara.

– I don't know. Whatever we're arguing about.

– What *are* we arguing about? someone else asked.

All eyes turned toward Father Tew. He opened his mouth to explain, and then suddenly lost all interest in so doing.

– It doesn't matter, he said. – It really doesn't matter at all. You carry on. Don't mind me.

– I thought not, said Dame Barbara, before proceeding to the next agenda item.

In a less bureaucratic age, he might simply have walked straight out of the hospital and not stopped walking until he found himself sufficiently distant from the modern world to live out the rest of his days unmolested. Nowadays, he was obliged to serve a period of notice, as per his contractual obligations. Ordinarily, the administration didn't much care, but the Solomon Grundy business had put them all under a spotlight, and they were highly sensitive to any implicit criticism (though not, of course, to explicit criticism, which they rejected vehemently without reading). Father Tew might have called their bluff, but he sensed that the outside world, like the Ethics Committee, would fail to see the point. He had not found much evidence of any tendency in the outside world to regard the question of how a man should live as anything other than a technical one, one more or less equivalent to the question of what sort of car he should drive or what brand of fondue set he should purchase. He was beginning to wonder now if the fault might be his, rather than theirs. No one else seemed to have this problem.

Father Tew was one of those types (called conscientious by their friends and pedantic by their line-managers) for whom the completion of a form is intensely painful, as a result of the endless compromises with truth obliged by the demands of space. He also had what he was coming to recognise as a pathological inability to choose when offered only two equally facile alternatives. Given two boxes, 'yes' and 'no', and asked to tick one only, he invariably found himself placing his tick midway between the two, or adding a third box 'yes and no' and ticking that. Whilst these alterations gave his replies a little more integrity, he was aware that they also gave the impression he was illiterate, and unable to follow even the simplest instructions. After several false starts, he had resolved to compose his answers on a separate sheet of paper before copying them out on the form. The section dealing with the normal biographical stuff – where he was born, and when, and what sort of account he could give of his life in the period between then and now – was fairly straightforward. The tough part was to articulate why he in particular would make a suitable candidate for the occupancy of a hermitage, in preference to someone else no doubt equally deserving. They gave you eight lines. An awkward space. Hardly enough to get started. Although he sighed in exasperation at the knock, he was thus nonetheless rather glad of the excuse to break his concentration.

– Come, he called.

The door was pushed open. Having expected a woman with a mop and bucket, he was surprised and a little disconcerted to find Miss O'Dowd.

– Oh, he said, – I thought . . .

He could not diplomatically finish his sentence. He had thought – hoped, to be frank – she was out of his life by now. His ignorance of her transfer was partly a consequence of a determined effort on her part to keep the fact from him. Several times already she had ducked around the corner as he approached, and invented irrelevant errands so as to avoid being in the places he was likely to be in at the times he was likely to be there. It was doubtful, however, whether he would have taken much notice of her even had she taken to walking on water. His mind had been focused upon matters more immediately to hand. Now they stared at each other, embarrassed.

– Come in, he offered. – Sit down.

But she did not. Instead, she thrust something towards him, saying simply, – Look.

He inspected it, turning it over in his hands.

– It's a ring, he identified it. – With initials on the back . . .

He stopped. They were his own initials. It was his own ring. He remembered where he had last seen it, too, though he did not understand how it had come to be returned to him.

    – I don't understand, he confessed.

    – He's downstairs, she said.

This was the last piece of news Father Tew wished to hear. He tried to keep the disappointment from his face.

    – Only . . . she said, – only . . . he's so . . .

She seemed to be afraid of the word, whatever it was.

    – He's so what?

    – He's so old, she whispered, – like . . . like an old man.

    – You'd better come in, he suggested.

This time she did. He fetched two cups of hybrid coffee-type beverage from the machine, and she told him the story. She had been changing your sheets, she said, when she noticed the ring. It looked valuable. Then she realised it was just a cheap imitation. She remembered seeing one just like it somewhere before, she couldn't remember where. Where? It had bugged her all morning. When she remembered where she'd last seen it, she dropped what she was doing and panicked. She'd come straight to see the man who had married them, there being no one else she could tell, no one else who would believe her. She burst into tears, and the priest encircled her with a comforting arm.

    – There, there, he said, – there there.

Eventually she recovered sufficiently to drink some coffee-type beverage. Father Tew noticed, with some irritation, that the shoulder of his jacket was damp.

    – What are we going to do? she asked.

    – I don't know, he confessed. – What would you like to do?

    – I don't know. Only . . . he's my husband, isn't he? No matter what . . .

    – Well, in a manner of speaking. Your marriage is rather individual, the priest observed. – Rather unique.

    – More so than anyone else's? she asked.

Father Tew thought about it.

    – No, he said. – No more than anyone else's, I suppose.

She stared at him, obviously expecting some decisive action.

    – I suppose we'd better go take a look, he conceded.

12.10

From a vantage point somewhere near the ceiling, you watched the nurses' vain attempts at your resuscitation. The procedures were accompanied by much commotion, to little purpose. You wanted to tell them not to bother, that you were happy to go, and that there was little they could do about it. You understood, however, that communication with the inhabitants of the material world was no longer possible. You were in the spirit world now. There seemed little harm in letting them try, anyway. It livened up the afternoon, and afternoons in geriatric wards were unlikely to be spoilt by an excess of excitement. There was nothing to do but watch. One woman had both hands on your breast bone. She thrust suddenly downwards, and your body crumpled into the bedsheets. The swing doors were thrown open, and two others entered, dragging a machine. They connected two sink plungers to your chest with wiggly leads, and flicked a switch. Simultaneously, you saw your body arch upward in spasm, and felt a pleasant tingle in your extremities. It tickled, and you laughed.

After a while, you grew weary of their efforts, and cast your eyes around the rest of ward. Fifteen pairs of eyes stared vacantly upwards, but they did not see you. Their skin was stretched tight and yellow over the bones of their faces, and all colour had drained from their lips and cheeks. You wondered if you yourself looked any better, but the crowd around your bed made it impossible to see. The door opened once again to admit another nurse, and a man in a different sort of uniform altogether. Unbelievable! It was your wife! And the strange priest from the service station! What on earth where *they* doing here? Your wife gave a little scream, and her hand flew to her mouth. Without waiting, she ran towards the little cubicle that had been curtained off. Inside, the attendants had abandoned their efforts to revive a body that had long ago lost any interest in life, and were beginning the process of levering your floppy body off the bed and on to a trolley. Jackie flew at them,

tearing their arms away. Surprised, they dropped you back on
the bed.

– Leave him alone, she screamed, – leave him alone.

She fell on your body, and hugged it to her chest, sobbing.
The attendants stood awkwardly, unsure of how to proceed. The
uneasy silence was broken only by the sound of her sobs. Father
Tew arrived.

– It's all right, he reassured them. – She's the next of kin.

– His daughter? one of them queried.

– His wife.

The swing doors burst open, and in came the Sister. She
strode purposefully towards the curtained off cubicle, and stuck
her head inside.

– He dead yet? she wanted to know.

One of the nurses nodded.

– Well, what are we waiting for then?

She clapped her hands briskly

– Chop, chop. No time to lose.

Then she caught sight of the priest, and sighed. She came
into the cubicle, and closed the curtains behind her.

– Is there a problem? she asked.

– This lady, said Father Tew, – is the wife of the deceased.

The Sister stared at him, puzzled.

– What is this? she asked, – some sort of joke?

– Far from it, said Father Tew.

The Sister pursed her lips, and appeared to be wrestling with
a decision.

– I have my instructions, she said, – as follows. This man has
no living relatives. The hospital has a team of surgeons standing
by, and a similar team is standing by in Edinburgh. Anneka Rice
is expected any moment . . .

– I don't want him cut up, Jackie wailed. – I want him buried,
like a proper person.

– I'm afraid, said the Sister, – that time is of the essence in
these situations.

Father Tew stood his ground. You were intrigued to see how
it would all turn out.

The Sister was losing her patience.

– If you don't leave immediately, she said, – I shall . . .

– Are you threatening me? asked the priest.

– Of course I'm threatening you, she said. – What do you think I'm doing? Now get out of the way.

– No! said Jackie, and spread herself over your body.

The attendants looked sheepish.

– Put that man on that trolley now! ordered the Sister.

– Leave him alone! screamed your wife.

The Sister was furious.

– If that body is not in theatre in five minutes, she warned the attendants, – I will see to it that you never work in this hospital again.

And she strode off.

– Come on, love, urged one of the men.

For a minute they stood, awkward in the presence of grief. They began to try and extricate her arms. She was having none of it.

– Leave him alone, she warned them.

Then one of the men took your feet, and motioned to the others to do the same. Jackie bit his finger. Two of them held her back, while the others took your body, and placed it on the trolley. They began to wheel you away. But Jackie leaped suddenly forward, and fell upon you. The trolley skidded and overturned, and your body rolled on to the smooth tiles.

You had seen enough. You found yourself floating in light, borne on its currents, naked and warm. The last remaining aches and pains of existence fell away from your body as sleep falls away upon waking, and you floated out of the window into a warm spring afternoon. Around the hospital grounds, the rhododendrons were in bloom, and pigeons cooed in the trees. Little cars circulated in the car parks in search of spaces, and invalids in wheelchairs were being pushed around the grounds by their lovers and children. It was Saturday, and the neighbouring superstore was doing a brisk business. Now you were higher still, and all of Pilsbury was spread before you like a picnic, and the motorway beyond. You followed the grey ribbon of the River Pill out of town towards the Millham Unit, from where an argument floated up to you on the breeze.

– Get off.

– I warned you.

– Oooffff.

Then you rose above the clouds, and all was lost in their soft fluffy whiteness. Still you ascended. Was it a lifetime that was lasting a moment, or a moment that was lasting a lifetime? Suddenly, you found yourself in a warm, shallow pool, in the shade of an oak tree, and surrounded by ripe corn. Two small children were watching you. They seemed at home in this world, in a way in which you were not. A butterfly landed on your arm. It tickled. You laughed. They laughed too. One was as golden as the ripe corn, the other as brown as the bark of the tree. They took you by the hand. And here you are."

He shuts the file and smiles. He seems to be expecting some kind of response.

– It's not very . . . flattering, I oblige. – Not the kind of thing you'd want the servants to read.

– It's entirely confidential, he assures me. – Just you and me and the Boss. Anyway, it's not supposed to be flattering. It's supposed to be fair. Warts and all, as they say.

– It depends on how you look at it, I suggest.

He smiles, and shakes his head,

– Crap, he says.

I find this vaguely shocking. I don't expect a being of his calibre to say 'crap'. Not that I've ever really given it much thought – it's just another of those unexamined prejudices that pass for folk-wisdom where I've just come from. But I'm surprised nonetheless. People are continually surprising, thankfully. Even angels. This conversation is rather getting the better of me. It's unpleasantly hot.

– You're hardly likely to get an unbiased response out of *me*, I point out.

– Why not?

– Well, I'm something of an interested party, I remind him.

Again, he grins. I get the impression he knows something I don't, and he's enjoying letting me work it out for myself.

– If you had one word, he says, – to sum up your life, what would it be? Good or bad? Pass or fail?

I think about it.

– Too short, I say at last.

– Everybody says that, he says. – Anyway, that wasn't one of the choices, 'too short'. Apart from 'too short'.

– Well, it was, I protest.

– Shorter than some, longer than others, he says. – Longer than a mayfly, shorter than a tortoise. Longer than a dandelion, shorter than an oak tree.

I don't really understand these comparisons. He chuckles, and puts his hand on my arm.

– You see the problem, he says.

I don't.

– Sum up a life in a word, he says. – A good life or a bad life? Do you pass, or do you fail? Tick one box only. It's hopeless.

– But there's a lot hinging on this.

– No, no, no, he says. – It's not like that at all any more. There's none of that sheep and goats stuff any more. This is New Heaven. Welcome to New Heaven, he says. – We thought we'd try something new for the Millennium.

This is fairly momentous news, I feel. People ought to know this, back on earth.

– You can't do that, I tell him. – You can't just move the goalposts without telling anyone . . .

– Course we can, he says. – We do it all the time. I tell you, I used to work in local government, and that was an ocean of tranquillity compared to here. Constant reorganisation. God's still working his purpose out. Even after all these years. He's never satisfied.

This is a lot of information to take in at once.

– Hang on, hang on. Let me get this straight. This is Heaven, right?

I look around. It certainly seems pleasant enough.

He nods. – This is *New* Heaven, he confirms. – Like New Labour. The same only different.

– And *you* must be Saint Peter.

He shakes his head.

– Saint Peter got reshuffled.

– So who are you?

– I'm Saint Wayne.

We shake hands. I remember something else, from when I was christened.

– What happened to limbo?

– That's where you've just come from.

– I thought that was my life.

– A lot of people think that, he says. – It's an easy mistake to make. But no, that was limbo. We've done away with life.

I'm appalled.

– It was audience research. It was what people wanted. People weren't using their lives any more. Just sat in front of their tellies, most of them. Read the papers. Mowed the lawn. We thought, if that's all you're going to do with your life you might as well be in limbo. Might bring life back later, of course, if that's what people want. It's constant reorganisation here, always trying to improve things. But for the moment, we've replaced it with limbo. And then you come straight here. It cuts out all that sheep and goats crap.

It certainly has a compelling neatness about it. I can't help but feel, though, that there's something missing. Then I remember.

– So what happened to Hell? I ask.

He grins.

– That's the clever bit, he says. – It isn't anywhere. You carry it round with you. Your own personal, customised one. It's the memory of all the things you didn't do when you had the chance.

Buried on Sunday

11.24

Sunday morning. I've been here in New Heaven a whole twenty-four hours now, which means I'll still be here for an eternity. It's hard to get your head around that sort of thing. It feels like I've been here an eternity already, but I suppose it's all relative. I walk around thinking about my life down there, working out all the things I'd do different if I had my time again. Everything, I think sometimes. Then I think, nothing. Then I wonder what difference it would have made in the long run. If I'd have done things differently, then so would everybody else, presumably. It doesn't really bear thinking about.

Sunday morning in the material world means my funeral, apparently. I was pleased to have this last rite of passage to go through. The rules of New Heaven are fairly minimal. We're welcome to observe the material world for entertainment, so long as we don't try to interfere. I wanted to see all those people again, for one last time. The old-timers say the desire to keep in touch with the material world soon passes, but I didn't get much of a chance to get to know all these people while I was alive. There was never any time. Maybe I can get to know them better now the pressure's off a bit. You can get to know people better when they don't know you're watching them. People change when they know you're watching them. They put on an act. You feel you're getting closer to the real person when they don't know they're being watched. I've been watching people for a day or so now, and I've discovered that I prefer them when they know they're being watched. (The irony being, of course, that people *are* being watched the whole time, only they don't seem to count themselves. And by Saint Wayne and his Big Red Book, but I don't expect you to believe *that*. It's pretty implausible, I know.)

If it had been up to my wife, this funeral would have been a quiet affair, just her and the priest, and maybe someone from the social services. It's a nice job for a social worker, making up the numbers at a funeral. Fairly undemanding stuff – all you have to do really is not fart, giggle or pass out for an hour or so – and you get a nice mileage allowance and double time for Sundays, and you're still home in time for a slice of mad cow and a roast potato. But Father Tew wouldn't have that; it was his Christian duty, he said, to inform my parents. My brief passage across the face of the planet had already involved him in sins of commission, he said, and there was no way he was going to let me involve him in sins of omission as well. Jackie argued with him, but he was obstinate.

Of course the first thing my mother did was inform her agent, and the first thing Chalkie did was get *Wotcha!* on the phone and negotiate a five-figure sum. This was exactly the kind of thing Jackie had known would happen, but Father Tew said he was clearing his conscience. He said it like clearing your conscience was the same as clearing your desk, which I suppose for a priest it probably is. Part of the *Wotcha!* deal was that Chalkie find someone with some cleavage for the pictures, and he thought straight away of Tess, of course, but the social services said sorry, she was in Millham House and she wasn't coming out until they could be sure she wasn't going to show them up any more. But Chalkie persisted, and they didn't hold out very long. They said she could come on two conditions: firstly, that she wanted to come, and secondly that she was accompanied, and of course she wanted to come, and of course it was Janice who accompanied her. Another part of the *Wotcha!* deal, and one over which Chalkie fought a determined but ultimately fruitless campaign, was that the piece should be written by Tony Bowles. *Wotcha!* thought this was important. In the end they reached a deal. Tony would write the piece, and Chalkie would take the pictures, and neither of them would speak to each other either during or after the event, or act in such a way as to give the impression that they were in any way associated with the other. After that, they would never speak, or even refer, to each other ever again.

The other people who found out, of course, were the people who worked in the hospital. Dr Conway came, under medication and with a nurse, and yodelled quietly to himself throughout the service, and Dr Khan, and Sir John and Dame Barbara, and Percy Bowles. No one from the Cabinet though. The new Minister said she'd only been in the job a few days, and she didn't want to be associated with funerals, and she certainly didn't want anything to do with *mine*, since I was the person who'd cost her predecessor the post. As far as she was concerned, she said, she'd just prefer everyone forgot all about it, which is a fairly fortunate preference, since that's just exactly what everybody will do. People don't like it when their stories start to leak over from one week to the next. They like to start each new Monday morning with something new to talk about. Then by the weekend they've said and written everything they could possibly say or write about it, and about everything everybody else has said and written about it, and they need something new. People talk so much and write so much and read so much these days that within a very short space of time they forget what it is they're talking and reading and writing about, and they need to start again with something new.

Practically the whole hospital wanted to come, of course, and bring their boyfriends and girlfriends and children and dogs and station wagons, but my wife put her foot down at the escalating numbers and Sir John put his foot down at the escalating costs, and in the end attendance was restricted to people who could claim some sort of right to be there, on the grounds of having been involved with my life somehow. There was a little huddle of midwives from Maternity, who'd played a facilitating role in my birth, and a little group of nurses from the Geriatric ward, who'd played a facilitating role in my death. Even Frank Parker and Sister Nuttall showed up, less to pay their last respects I would guess than to make sure I was well and truly dead and buried. I was tempted to intervene, then, to say, 'That's him. That's the one who pushed me in.' But I didn't. I can't really hold it against him. He came along at about the right time, really. There was nowhere to go from there. I mean, you can't go on for ever, can you? It has to stop somewhere. And I had a good innings, all things considered. He did me a favour really.

Even with the tighter entrance criteria a whole host of people had to be turned down, people who'd made my bed and washed my sheets and so forth. You don't realise quite how many people's lives you *do* touch, even just in a week. You leave ripples everywhere you go that you don't even know about. Then of course there's the metaripples that you set up in other people's lives, that ripple off into other people's lives, and so on. There's no way of telling where it will all end up. I guess that's why good intentions are about as good as you're likely to get in this world. People say the road to hell is paved with good intentions, but the road to hell isn't paved with anything, because it's not a place you have to travel to get to.

So there they all are, all come to see me off. Practically everybody I've ever known. Even my father has been wheeled out of the ward for the occasion, though he says it's all lies and nonsense. It's like my whole shitty, wonderful life is laid out before me, and I feel like if I took a photograph it would be a photograph of a lifetime rather than of a churchyard. Half these people, of course, I don't recognise. They know me, or they claim to know me, but I don't remember *them*. Father Tew is giving the address. He's off to Madagascar tomorrow. The European Central Council for the Co-ordination and Registration of Hermits (motto: Et in Arcadia, ego) had a last-minute cancellation, and his form landed on their desk at the right moment. So this is his kind of swansong.

– From ashes are we born, and unto ashes do we return, he reminds everybody, as if they needed reminding.

The trouble is you spend half your life not really believing it, and by the time you realise it is true after all, you've already dug yourself into such a hole that you spend the rest of your life digging furiously in an attempt to get yourself out of it, and of course you never do, because ending up in a hole in the ground is the human condition, and of course the more you dig the deeper you get. This occurred to me this morning, smoking a cigar and watching the men digging my own hole. Now, they're lowering me into it, or at least lowering the casket that contains the body

I once briefly occupied into it. People are throwing little handfuls of dirt after me. That's how you end up getting buried – it's not that someone comes up and dumps a truckload of stuff on you all at once, it's everybody you know contributing a little handful. I would have thought Jackie would have gone first, but she seems to have disappeared somewhere. So it's my mother that starts it all off, and they all file past, dropping a handful.

Chalkie says, – Smile! and then remembers where he is, and laughs

– Hur hur hur and pouffff! goes the flash. People are outraged, of course, but Chalkie doesn't care, or probably doesn't even notice. He's missing whatever part of whatever chromosome contains the gene for self-consciousness. Tony Bowles is scribbling in his pad, but when I look over his shoulder I find it's just a doodle, a little Bo Diddley nursery rhyme:

> Solomon Grundy
> Born on a Monday
> Christened on Tuesday
> Married on Wednesday
> Took Ill on Thursday
> Worse on Friday
> Died on Saturday
> Buried on Sunday

He's obviously not getting paid by the word. Even so, it's a bit bald. People don't just want to know what happened, they want to know *why* it happened, and why it happened like it did, and not some other way that was how they thought it was going to happen. They want someone to make sense of it for them. So that's OK as notes, I guess, a kind of skeleton of the story, and then people have to put their own flesh on those bones. Make of it what they will.

Here comes my wife again, emerging from behind a bush.

– I just woke up this morning feeling awful, she tells Carmen.

Carmen stares at her, horrified.

– You're not . . .

– I think I am, says Jackie.

My stone sinks to the bottom of the pond, and all that's left are my ripples.